PRAISE FOR *SOCIAL CRIMES*

"The most entertaining look at a small but powerful section of American society since Dominick Dunne's engaging *The Two Mrs. Carrolls*. Were Truman Capote alive, he would probably try to take credit for it...And if Glenn Close is shopping around for a good movie, she can start by purchasing the film rights to this novel."

—*Bay Area Reporter*

"Beyond an elaborate plot featuring a swindle involving Marie Antoinette, SOCIAL CRIMES doubles as a primer on decorating and entertaining, upscale dos and don'ts gleaned from the gilded set Ms. Hitchcock knows so well."

—*New York Times*

"This novel's got everything—passion, betrayal, money, obsession, murder. It's the book Patricia Highsmith and Edith Wharton might have written together."

—Jim Lehrer, *Washingtonian*

"A revenge to die for; a brilliantly wicked tale set in the glittering world of New York high society and the dark world of obsession."

—Linda Fairstein

"Great reading."

—*Beverly Hills* magazine

more...

S0-AAE-155

"A quintessential beach book…How does Hitchcock's amusing saga differ from the scads of books involving money, murder, and high society? There's the economy and wit of her prose, and then there's Jo's awareness of how silly the upper crust is…Come summer, SOCIAL CRIMES is likely to show up in tote bags and on cabana tables from Boca and Bridgehampton to Beverly Hills."

—*Publishers Weekly*

"Foie gras, champagne, a famous pearl necklace, and socialites at each other's throats. Great fun."

—Christopher Buckley

"If you combined the dark imagination of Patricia Highsmith with the social savvy of Truman Capote, the result might be SOCIAL CRIMES."

—Susan Cheever

"Riveting…Hitchcock draws upon her intimate knowledge of the upper echelon to expose the dark secrets of a rarefied society."

—Liz Smith, *New York Post*

"Delicious…shatteringly effective."

—*W* magazine

"Has all the perfect page-turners: mystery, double-crossing, aristocracy, and murder…Drippingly good beach reading."

—DailyCandy.com

"There is enough real-life inspiration for the fictional characters to keep cocktail parties from Martha's Vineyard to the Hamptons abuzz all summer."

—*Avenue*

"Ruth Rendell meets Dominick Dunne...strongly recommended."

—*Library Journal*

"Hitchcock sets out to bring New York's high society low, in a witty little book that taxes only the rich."

—*New York Daily News*

"[A] rags-to-riches story [that] generates undeniable charm and will leave readers rooting for a magical Cinderella ending."

—*Booklist*

"Thrums with wicked wit and an insider's view of court life in the Manhattan and Southampton of the twenty-first century. Hitchcock has seen it and lived it and shares it all. She has a keen eye and a perfect ear."

—Marie Brenner,
author of *Great Dames*

ATTENTION: CORPORATIONS AND ORGANIZATIONS
Most WARNER books are available at quantity discounts
with bulk purchase for educational, business, or sales
promotional use. For information, please call or write:

Special Markets Department, Warner Books, Inc.,
135 W. 50th Street, New York, NY 10020-1393
Telephone: 1-800-222-6747 Fax: 1-800-477-5925

Social Crimes

Jane Stanton Hitchcock

WARNER BOOKS

NEW YORK   BOSTON

If you purchase this book without a cover you should be aware that this book may have been stolen property and reported as "unsold and destroyed" to the publisher. In such case neither the author nor the publisher has received any payment for this "stripped book."

Copyright © 2003 by Jane Stanton Hitchcock
All rights reserved. No part of this book may be reproduced in any form or by any electronic or mechanical means, including information storage and retrieval systems, without permission in writing from the publisher, except by a reviewer who may quote brief passages in a review.

This Warner Books edition is published by arrangement with Hyperion / Miramax Books.

Warner Books

Time Warner Book Group
1271 Avenue of the Americas, New York, NY 10020
Visit our Web site at www.twbookmark.com

Printed in the United States of America

First Warner Books Printing: August 2005

10 9 8 7 6 5 4 3 2 1

For Jim

Society it may be, but convivial it is not.

—Edmond and Jules de Goncourt,
The Woman of the Eighteenth Century

I

MURDER was never my goal in life. I'm a very sentimental person at heart. I cry in old movies. I love animals and children. I'm a pushover for a beggar in the street. So if anyone had told me five years ago that I could have willfully and with malice aforethought killed a fellow human being, I would have said they were crazy. But life has surprises in store for all of us, not the least of which is the gradual discovery of who we really are and what we are capable of. However, allow me to dwell for a moment on the last evening of what I think of as my innocence.

It was a perfect Southampton night, warm, clear, starlit, with a gentle breeze blowing in from the ocean. I was standing at the head of a small reception line, greeting guests at a birthday party being held in my honor. I can see my friends and acquaintances now in my mind's eye, filing past me, bristling with jewels, faces aglow with the hollow confidence that only money can bring.

I was deep in the world oxymoronically known as "New York Society," where the fish are bigger and the water is colder, or the fish are colder and the water is bigger, depending on your point of view. It was a world I felt entirely at home in. I was Mrs. Lucius Slater—Jo, to my friends—wife of one of the richest and most prominent businessmen in New York.

People described me then as a "socialite," a label I loathe. It cast me in a lurid and ridiculous light, implying a life of privileged frivolity where everyone flits around from one party to the next wearing calculated clothes and expensive smiles. I would have preferred "social leader," since distractions like the gala that night were only part of a more substantial milieu in which I played a significant role: a world of money and power in general, and, more specifically, the governance of the great institutions of New York.

I understood better than anyone that Dick Bromire, my host, was slightly using me to polish up his tarnishing reputation. A gregarious real estate magnate and a figure of note in the cozy older social circles of New York, Dick was facing indictment for income tax evasion—a charge he vehemently denied.

Standing in line next to Dick, I watched him out of the corner of my eye. A beefy man of sixty-five with a moon face and a jaunty manner, he was clad in a white dinner jacket, greeting the arriving guests with a handshake and a slightly automatic grin.

"Good to see ya, good to see ya, thanks for coming, thanks for coming," he said over and over without pausing to chitchat. Being at the center of the scandal *du jour,* he may have been afraid of inviting any probing comments.

His gruffness was, as usual, softened by the charm of Trish, his much younger wife, a sporty blonde from Florida who looked as if she had a mean backhand but whose real idea of an athletic afternoon was cleaning out her closets. She stood next to her husband, showing off her bare, well-toned midriff in a striking outfit of gold lamé harem pants and a short matching top. Her heavy emerald and diamond earrings, custom-made by Raj, a reclusive Indian jeweler whose unmarked shop in Paris was Mecca for the gem-loving rich, reminded me of military decorations from some defunct Mittel-european monarchy.

My husband, Lucius, and I had known the Bromires for years. Lucius and Dick were old golfing buddies. Lucius had helped Dick get into the National years ago. Trish was a member of my summer reading group—an extension of the late Clara Wilman's New York reading group—the "Billionaire Reading Group," as it was facetiously referred to by envious outsiders because all the women in it had rich husbands and because between our discussions of Proust, Trollope, and Flaubert, the stock tips were reputed to fly faster than a covey of quail.

The Bromires had always been extremely kind to us, but it was when Lucius had his heart attack three months prior to my birthday party that night that they really came through. Dick put his helicopter at our disposal to transport Lucius from Southampton to New York. Dick and Trish had both kept me company—along with my best friends Betty Waterman and June Kahn—in the depressing fluorescent hallways of New York Hospital during my long vigil when I thought Lucius might die.

"I may not remember, but I never forget" is my motto,

and I felt very badly for Dick now that he was the target of a criminal investigation. I was letting him celebrate me (even though several of my friends had warned me to "steer clear," as they put it) because I liked him, pure and simple.

Since I have no children of my own, my friends are like my family. I stick by them even when it's inconvenient to do so. This is something I learned as a girl growing up in Oklahoma. "United we stand, divided we're screwed," is what my father always said. We may have been unsophisticated back there in the panhandle, but God knows we were loyal.

Trish Bromire visibly preened at the appearance of Miranda Somers, whose presence at a party signified to our little set that we were in the right place. Miranda Somers, a canny beauty of indeterminate age, is society's cheerleader. She writes a column for *Nous* magazine under the pen name "Daisy." *Nous* is society's scrapbook, dedicated to fashion, celebrity, and making social life appear fun, even on those frequent occasions when it's more tedious than jury duty. Miranda sprinkles stardust plus a soupçon of satire on the events she covers.

She was on the arm of Ethan Monk, a curator at the Municipal Museum, another one of my closest friends. The Monk, as he is referred to in the art world, is a blond, bespectacled, boyish-looking man whose wholesome midwestern looks are complemented by an appealing affability. Ethan is knowledgeable without being pedantic. He knows more about eighteenth-century French furniture than anyone in America, and he helped me shape the collection Lucius and I donated to the museum. I adore Ethan for many reasons, not the least of which is that he's never averse to a light spot of gossip here and there—though he refuses to make it the carrion feast it is for many of our friends.

Trish fawned a little too hard over Miranda and Ethan, neither of whom have much patience for obvious flattery. They soon moved on to me. Miranda air-kissed me in her famous Miranda way so neither party's hair or makeup is ever spoiled. "Honey, you're a real trouper," she said.

Next I saw my darling June Kahn waltzing toward me, looking like a middle-aged Sugar Plum Fairy. June's quest to appear ever youthful had taken a macabre turn in the form of a pink organza dress more suited to a third grader in a ballet recital than a petite, dark-haired woman of fifty. As she hugged me, she said, "You look fabulous. Isn't the tent divine? Just like a big glowing onion. Who's here? Who's coming? Oh, my tootsies ache already!"

June was at concert pitch that night, strung taut with the excitement of the party, her eyes stealthily on the move like a pair of heat-seeking missiles in pursuit of celebrities. Suddenly hitting a target—a well-known newswoman who was also a prominent New York hostess—they brightened and she was off. I found June's weakness for famous people endearing. She reminded me of a little girl in a poodle skirt straining to get her autograph book signed by an oblivious star.

Trailing behind his wife in line was Charlie Kahn, June's husband, a slim, aristocratic-looking, silver-haired man of sixty. He gave me a thin smile and a nervous squeeze of my right hand, which was the way he always greeted June's friends. Charlie reminded me of a timid dog who was wary of being petted.

"So where's the big man? Still alive, I trust?" he said.

"Alive and well, Charlie, dear," I replied. "Just not up to standing in the receiving line."

"It's like I always say: You can't take it with you, but if you have enough of it, you don't go!" he said, referring to Lucius's recent brush with death.

He laughed. I didn't.

Next to come through the line was Betty Waterman. She leaned in and whispered, "You can take the girl out of the harem but you can't take the harem out of the girl, what?" eyeing Trish Bromire's Arabian Nights getup. I thought this remark a bit pot and kettle-ish given her own choice of outfits. Betty, a robust redhead, was a standout that night in a banana yellow caftan heavily embroidered with a gold and blue bib.

"This outfit weighs a ton," she said, attempting to adjust the shoulders with both hands. "Gil says it makes me look like Tutankhamen."

Gil, her husband, was right on the mark. I helped her align the costume but it still looked funereal.

I knew the Watermans had some sort of French countess staying with them and that Betty had asked Trish Bromire if she could bring her to the party at the last minute. Dear Trish, who had privately complained to me that very afternoon about the inconvenience of having to rearrange the seating, was secretly pleased to accommodate a titled lady.

"So where's the Countess?"

"With Gil," Betty said. "We took separate cars because I want to leave early. I have a tennis game at the crack." She spread her arms out in a gesture of welcome and cried, "Hello, rat fuck!" as she walked toward the crowd.

The reception line dispersed. I strolled into the tent to

check on Lucius. He was easy to spot because he was the only man in a black tuxedo. The invitation had specifically said "white dinner jackets" for the men, "festive dress" for the women. But Lucius refused to wear white, proclaiming, "White is for waiters and corpses." Lucius always did as he pleased. I admired that about him. He was not as mindful of other people's opinions as I was.

I found my husband seated on one of ten small gold ballroom chairs at a table near the dance floor. He smiled and chatted as a steady stream of friends dropped by to pay him court and say hello. As I neared, I overheard a few awkward pleasantries concomitant upon the return of a man who had recently been snatched from the jaws of death: "Wonderful to see you in such good shape, fella!" "You look great, guy!" "I better watch myself on the golf course, kiddo, now that you're all recovered!"

All lies.

The truth is Lucius looked like hell, a shadow of his former robust self. The athletic and elegant older man I had married, who had kept his youthful looks and boyish vitality well beyond the normal span, was now frail and wan. Having lost more than thirty pounds, he looked like a scarecrow. His shoulders, elbows, and knee joints jutted out like hangers under the black fabric of his now very loose-fitting tuxedo. His face was gaunt and gray, the keen shine of his navy blue eyes dimmed by bouts of pain and fear. Lucius's brush with the Reaper had failed to humble him in any significant way, however. He still had the slightly sour, imperious air of a deposed monarch.

"Where the hell have you been?" he said.

"In the receiving line."

"All this time? Jesus."

Like many rich men, Lucius wanted a wife who constantly catered to him in a variety of ways: part nanny, part sexpot, part ornament. It was often a daunting task. Ignoring his irritated tone, I bent down and gave him a peck on the cheek.

"How are you holding up, my darling? Seeing lots of pals?"

"All the usual suspects. If you want to know the truth, I'm ready to go home."

"So am I. But we can't."

I noticed he was drinking champagne and I plucked the flute from his hand.

"Sweetheart, you know what the doctors said."

The doctors had warned us: "No sex and no booze," for the time being.

"I'll sit with you," I said, pulling up a chair close beside him. My first priority was always Lucius.

The minute I acquiesced to him, he softened his tone.

"No, Jo. You go circulate. It's your night. Enjoy it."

The fact is I didn't care much for big parties and I would have much preferred to sit and talk with my husband. As the guest of honor, however, I knew I had an obligation to my host and hostess.

"This too shall pass, my darling," I said.

I gave Lucius a knowing wink, strapped on my social toe shoes, and danced off into the crowd.

The candlelit tent was a sea of round dining tables dominated by tall glass vases overflowing with flowers and ribbons. An orchestra played the butter-smooth melodies of the High Debutante era. The lucite dance floor, embedded with seashells, was lit from beneath and for some unfathomable reason it seemed to float above the wooden floor like a futuristic magic carpet. It was the only modern touch in view. Pretty as it was, the party felt somehow lumbering and out of date, like a majestic old galleon. It had a heavy, Old Economy feel to it. And that's what I liked about it. It was mercifully familiar, anchored in a time that seemed now almost as remote as its spiritual forebear, the Gilded Age.

People had flown in from all over the world just for this occasion. Many of them weren't even staying the night. Their private planes and chauffeured cars were standing by waiting to take them back to wherever they came from as soon as the evening was over, or before if they were bored. Bobbing up and down among the crowd, I saw almost everyone I'd ever known. In some ways, it felt like drowning—or what drowning is reputed to feel like—in that my entire life was flashing before me.

The *amis mondains* were out in full force. I should mention here that I divided my circle of acquaintances into two basic groups: real friends and *amis mondains*. My real friends were the people I genuinely liked. *Amis mondains*—"worldly friends"—were the people I cultivated strictly for the sake of social life, not because I especially liked them or because they especially liked me, but because we were all players in the same game. Though we all competed with one another nonstop, it still made us feel secure to hang out together. Money and, most particularly, the way in which we liked to spend it—in pursuit of the unique, the rarefied, and the extraordinary in art, in luxury, and in life—was the connective tissue that bound us all together. We smiled and laughed and gossiped among ourselves at the various festivities we all went to, *but*—and in New York, nothing counts until the *but*—we rarely missed a chance to "dish" one another in private.

Friendly and charming as always, the *amis mondains* treated Dick and Trish Bromire as if nothing were amiss. Quite the contrary, they all gave Dick assurances of their support. Yet I knew that even as they ate his hors d'oeuvres and drank his champagne, they were speculating on the particulars of his impending downfall. I overheard snippets of conversation like, "Do you think he'll be indicted?" . . . "Did you see that ghastly article on him in the *Wall Street Journal*?" . . . "They say the Feds are really after him," and so on and so on. Some people were downright nasty about Dick, but their alibi for not missing this big, splashy party, of course, was that they had all come, not for him, but for me.

Dick was wounded game, in danger of losing his reputation and, worse—far worse—his entire fortune. I hated it that he was being stalked by gossipmongers in his very own house, but such is the way of social life in New York: Live by money, die by money.

I played my part, smiling and greeting everyone graciously, pretending to be oblivious to the provocative whispers circulating about our dear host. Many people told me how well I looked that evening. They may have just been being polite, of course, but I was pleased nonetheless. For the past few months I'd been under a great strain and, as everyone knows, stress always takes a toll on one's looks. Lucius was not an easy patient, to say the least. Organizing round-the-clock nurses was difficult enough. But when Lucius didn't like a particular nurse, he ordered her out of the house on the spot, which forced me to either find a replacement on a minute's notice or else sit with him for eight hours at a stretch myself. We managed to get through the worst of it. Lucius was feeling much better. Caspar, our chauffeur, had become his regular attendant. I was grateful Lucius was recovering, but I was still tired and anxious about his health, so it was nice to hear I didn't show it.

If I had to describe myself then, I should have said that I was an average height, attractive woman of a certain age, well preserved by my own dedication to discipline and enough money to take advantage of the latest beauty developments. I had a full, round face, a fair, even complexion, and a sprightly walk that gave me the air of a younger woman. Favoring a neat, stylish appearance over a softer, more flattering one, I wore my straight blond hair short, sculpted over my head like a helmet. My best feature, so everyone told me, was my inquisitive, teal-colored eyes. Though I was showing some signs of aging—a few wrinkles here and there, a loosening of the skin around the neck and jowls—I'd not yet dared a face-lift, fearing the startled alien look cosmetic surgery had thrust on several of my friends. I always chose plain but well-cut clothes. I was not a beauty, by any means, but there were days when I caught a glimpse of myself in the mirror and thought, "Well, it could be worse." If my mannerisms were a bit studied at large gatherings, it was because I've always felt self-conscious in crowds.

The night of my birthday, I was wearing a long white silk sheath to show off the possession I loved most in the world: a black pearl, ruby, and diamond necklace that had once belonged to Marie Antoinette. Lucius had given it to me as a present for our first anniversary.

I was wending my way through the crowd when I felt a tap on my shoulder. It was Tutankhamen Betty holding a large glass of scotch in her hand.

"Christ, Jo, it's bankbooks at dawn around here," she said. "I want you to know that I've been trapped in *three* separate conversations about private planes. How much can you say about jet decoration?"

We both paused to listen to a man standing near us who was loudly boasting about the billion dollars he had just raised for his hedge fund despite the flagging economy. Betty rolled her eyes heavenward and said under her breath to me: "Tell me there aren't people here who've made a pact with the devil."

"I would, too, if I knew where to get in touch with him."

"I've tried. His number is constantly busy."

Betty, who was on a roll, lifted her gaze to the enormous crystal chandelier sparkling above the center of the tent. She raised her voice and said: "*Satan, are you listening? If you want to round up all the souls in Southampton, all you have to do is land here in a G-5! And I'd rather fly with you than most of these assholes!*" Then she turned to me with a tipsy look in her eye. "I have an idea, Jo. Let's go say 'fuck you' to everyone we hate."

"I have a better idea. Let's go find your houseguest," I said, hoping to divert her attention away from the bonfire she was bent on lighting.

"I'm so fucking sick of the rich," she said as we walked through the crowd.

"You need to meet some new people."

"No new people! Not unless their names begin with X,

Y, or Z. No room in the old address book . . . Oh! There she is over there."

Betty pointed to the back of the tent where a pretty, pixie-faced, younger woman with short dark hair was seated by herself, sipping a glass of white wine, surveying the crowd from a distance. Her skin was very white and glowed with a kind of ethereal pallor. She was dressed in a long black skirt and a simple black top with a single strand of pearls around her neck. She looked vaguely disconsolate, as people often do when sitting alone at big gatherings.

"So what's her story now?" I said under my breath as we approached.

"I told you. Her husband, Michel, was a friend of Gil's. He died about a year ago. We ran into her at a party in New York and I—fool that I am—casually invited her out here. I mean, who expects anyone to take them up on an invitation like that? Fuck. And of course the English come and stay forever. Let's hope the French are different."

Betty introduced me to Countess Monique de Passy, who rose from her chair as deferentially as if I were the Queen Mother and shook my hand. Her grip was firm and forthright, not one of those tepid, tentative extensions you get from so many European women.

"Countess."

"*Monique,* please, Mrs. Slater."

"Call me Jo."

Having got that straight, we all sat down.

"It's an honor to meet you, Jo," Monique said with a very light French accent. "I've admired you for so long."

The Countess's sparkling brown eyes and open man-

ner were an engaging combination. She was not sycophantic but *sympathique,* as the French say. I sensed her
relief at having someone to talk to. Giving the unknown
newcomer a warm welcome is not something our little
group was known for—unless they were very, *very* rich.

"It's fascinating to meet an American who is so interested in Marie Antoinette," she said.

"In the Louis Sixteenth period," I corrected her.
"Marie Antoinette was a bit of a featherbrain, I'm afraid."

"She had great taste, though. That belonged to her,"
Betty said, pointing to my necklace, which I touched
without thinking.

Monique seemed impressed with the provenance.
"Really? That necklace belonged to Marie Antoinette?
Where did you get it, if I may ask?"

"My husband gave it to me for our first anniversary."

"Tell her the whole story," Betty said.

I was happy to comply.

"Actually, it's quite interesting," I said. "After she was
imprisoned, Marie Antoinette smuggled this to one of her
maids with instructions to go to England and sell it. The
maid was supposed to return to France with the money to
help the Queen and the royal family escape. She obeyed
two of the Queen's instructions. She went to London and
she sold it to a duke. But she never went back to France.
She stayed in England and set herself up in high style."

"Even then good help was hard to find," Betty said
with a laugh.

"It's all documented," I said. "Lucius bought the
necklace directly from the duke's family."

Monique was delighted. "My late husband would have
adored that story. He used to take me to the Conciergerie

where they list all the people who lost their heads on the guillotine. There are about six or seven de Passys on the register. It's a wonder there are any left."

A little fanfare from the orchestra signaled it was time for dinner.

"Speaking of the guillotine, you should see who I'm seated with. *Oy!*" Betty swiped her index finger across her throat as if it were a knife. The three of us rose to go to our respective tables. Monique shook my hand good-bye.

"It was lovely to meet you, Mrs. Slater—*Jo,* excuse me. I hope to see you again."

"Why don't you and Betty come over for lunch tomorrow?"

"Can't, sweetie," Betty said. "I've got the plumbers coming at one. All Gil cares about these days is the goddamn water pressure in the shower. But you go," she said to Monique.

The Countess demurred. "I don't want to impose."

"For Christ's sake, you've been bugging me to see Jo's house. Now's your chance," Betty said. Monique blushed. "You're her idol, Jo. She told me the first thing she did when she got to New York was to go to the Slater Gallery."

Betty often had the habit of talking about people in the third person as if they weren't standing right there. I felt sorry for the Countess, who continued to redden with embarrassment. I was very flattered. How nice to be someone's idol, I thought. I remembered the days when Clara Wilman had been *my* idol and how thrilled I'd been the first time I met her.

"Do come," I said, feeling the need to rescue the

young woman from Betty's barrage. "I'd love to show it to you if you're interested."

Monique smiled. "In that case, I accept with pleasure."

———∽∽———

THE dinner was long and predictable. No expense had been spared. For the first course, waiters passed around silver tubs from which we all scooped heaping portions of caviar onto silver dollar–size stacks of blinis. Next came salmon *en croûte,* then salad. Just before the birthday cake, I caught Dick Bromire flinging a glance at Ethan Monk, who was on my other side. I guessed what was about to happen.

"Please God, no toasts," I whispered to Ethan.

He patted my arm as he rose from his seat: *"Courage, ma chère."* He walked to the standing microphone on the dance floor in long strides, intent as a marsh bird hunting for food. A chorus of pinging crystal sent a hush over the room. I sat in my chair, very erect, with a frozen smile on my face as he began a witty, Ethanesque voyage down Memory Lane, starting with the early days of our friendship and concluding by describing the Slater Gallery, which Lucius and I had donated to the Municipal Museum in 1990.

He told the now-famous anecdote about how I'd recognized a great eighteenth-century portrait by David hanging in an obscure library in upstate New York. He talked about how my generosity had contributed to "the cultural heritage of America."

Here, he tooted his own horn a little. But he deserved to. Many agreed that the collection of eighteenth-century French furniture I had bought with Ethan's invaluable counsel rivaled even the glorious Wrightsman Rooms at the Metropolitan. I thought about how, just the other day, when I was on my way to a Muni board meeting, I'd stopped by the gallery and been so pleased and touched to see a group of inner-city schoolchildren standing in front of the replica of one of Marie Antoinette's private apartments asking all sorts of questions about the beautiful room they were looking at and the ill-fated queen who had lived there. I felt I'd had a hand in opening up a new world for them.

When Ethan sat down, I thought I was out of the woods. But no. I saw Lucius stumbling to his feet at the next table, then walking to the microphone in measured steps. I held my breath. Lucius toasting me in public was a first.

"Jo, now don't you give me that look!" he shouted so loud into the mike feedback ricocheted throughout the tent. Everybody laughed. "As most of you here know, the only kind of toast my wife can abide is served with butter and jam. But there comes a time in a man's life when he has to stand up and show everyone who's boss . . . So, Boss," he said, looking directly at me, "tonight, at the risk of being redundant, I'm gonna tell all your pals something they already know: what a remarkable woman you are. And for once, you're just going to have to shut up and listen. Okay?"

Though I shook my head no, the truth is I was secretly pleased.

As my frail husband talked about my life and how I came to be Mrs. Slater, telling that old lie about how he'd fallen for me at a dinner party given by Betty and Gil Waterman, I glanced around the room. I wondered how many people still referred to me behind my back as "the salesgirl." To this day, the only person in the world who knew the truth about how Lucius and I really met was Lucius's lawyer, Nate Nathaniel.

Lucius finished by saying, "I'm grateful to you, Jo, for getting me through these godawful last few months and for being a great wife and a great woman. Here's looking at you, kid!" The round of applause that followed was meant more for him than for me. Feeble as he was, he was a survivor. People admired that. I walked over to him, and gave him a big kiss. The room went wild.

Once we sat down again, Dick Bromire stood up and signaled the orchestra. They played a few fanfare bars of the "Marseillaise." At that point, I caught sight of the Countess, who was staring at me. She smiled and nodded a silent tribute. She looked so pretty, yet so forlorn.

Two waiters wheeled a huge cake out onto the dance floor—a miniature replica of Le Petit Trianon covered in vanilla frosting.

Everybody sang "Happy Birthday" to me, after which Dick Bromire gave the final toast of the evening. He went on about my "legendary style," "extraordinary taste," and "stupendous generosity," concluding his kind remarks by raising his glass of champagne to me and addressing me directly:

"Jo, you're a great benefactress in all ways. I, personally, am tremendously grateful to you for your generosity to me and to Trish. In being our guest of honor tonight and in letting us celebrate your birthday, you proclaim to the world what you think of us. And let me say this . . . If we're good enough for you, dear lady—the standard by which all elegance is measured—then we are quite simply . . . good enough! *To the one and only, Jo Slater!*"

The next thing I knew, everyone was on their feet applauding me. I was so touched and pleased, I didn't even realize I was crying. I wished my parents had lived to see me that night, being the toast of the cream of New York. My dad would've gotten a real kick out of it, but my mom would have been solemnly proud. I thought to myself, still with continuing amazement, Kiddo, you're a galaxy away from that poor little hick in the sticks you used to be. How did you ever get here?

2

THE old saying that some people are "born in the wrong cradle" applies to me. Early on I knew I wasn't destined to spend the rest of my life in Oklahoma City, where I was born and raised. Still, my steady progression from student to restaurant hostess to salesgirl to collector and philanthropist and, finally, to one of the grandes dames of New York is a pretty remarkable story, even if I do say so myself. I've been thinking about it a lot lately, in the wake of all that's happened to me. Sometimes you need to go backward in order to go forward. You need to understand where you've been in order to make any sense of where you are.

I was born Jolie Ann Meers, only child of Myrna and Dyson Meers of Oklahoma City, Oklahoma. I have to give credit to my parents, who tried their best to raise me as a God-fearing, responsible citizen. This is not an easy task under any circumstances, but it was particularly taxing in our family, where several of our closest relatives were at least "two cards short of a full deck," as my father used to say.

Uncle Laddie, my mother's brother, a funeral director, wasn't crazy in the conventional sense. But he came within a hairsbreadth of being indicted for murder. The police suspected that he had pushed my crepe-hanging Aunt Tillie out the window of a hotel in Tulsa on New Year's Eve, 1964. Uncle Laddie claimed she jumped and produced a suicide note that was subsequently examined by several handwriting experts with inconclusive results. We all thought he did it—and with good reason. Aunt Tillie was a font of gloom who hated life and those who enjoyed it. My mother declared that she was the perfect companion for a funeral director. My father said, "Apparently not."

Then there was my cousin Derek, my father's sister's son, who never finished high school and somehow became a millionaire. He used to give cars to perfect strangers, just like "the King," as he referred to Elvis, who had the same birthday as Derek. When Derek got out of jail, he was still rich, which made it hard for my parents to insist that crime didn't pay.

My mother, Myrna, was a salesperson at Balliet's, an upscale women's department store in Oklahoma City. She was also an excellent seamstress and did alterations on the side to make extra money. As a teenager, she had been the runner-up in the Oklahoma State Beauty Pageant. She was still a very attractive woman, and I don't think she quite understood how her looks had failed to purchase her a better situation in life.

My father, a chiropractor, had a chronic roving eye. It

seemed he liked aligning women's bodies in more ways than one. Mother suffered his infidelities silently, sublimating her grief in glossy decorating magazines. Sometimes, she would sit me down beside her and we would thumb through the pages, pointing out the rooms and objects we liked best. Surprisingly, my mother had more than a provincial's sense of style—though where she learned it, I'll never know. The more I see, the more I think that style is like relative or perfect pitch. Some have it, some don't. Mother was fairly sophisticated in her tastes. Relative pitch, not perfect.

One day, when I was fourteen, she took me to an appointment she had with one of her clients, Mrs. Fortes, an oil-rich lady with a huge house. While Mother was fitting clothes on Mrs. Fortes in the bedroom, I went off exploring. I remember picking up an exotic china figurine from one of the side tables in the cavernous living room. I was examining his colorful turban when a voice across the room yelled, "Put that down!" I was so startled, I nearly dropped the little man. The voice belonged to a peeved maid who strode across the room and grabbed the figure away from me.

"Don't you know you're not supposed to touch things in other people's houses?" she said, setting it back gingerly on the table.

She yanked me by the hand and sat me down on the sofa, spreading a big picture book that was on the coffee table across my lap.

"There now. You just sit here and look at this 'til your mother finishes. Understand?"

There are certain moments in life that you remember so clearly—not because they're particularly memorable at the time, but because when you look back on them you see your destiny crystallizing. Thumbing through the pages of that book was just such a moment. It was filled with pictures of an extraordinary house, a spectacularly beautiful place. I thought that maybe God lived there. Or if He didn't, He should.

When it was time for Mother and me to go, I closed the book and noticed the title emblazoned on the cover in big gold letters. It was called, simply, *Versailles*.

On the way home in the car, I asked my mother what *Vur-sails*—as I pronounced it then—was. Typical mother, we immediately stopped at the library and she checked out a young reader's book for me on the history of that great palace. That night, she started reading it to me. The kings, queens, and nobles of the French court invaded my imagination like an army of archangels. After that, I devoured everything I could get my hands on on the subject. I became fascinated with the story of Marie Antoinette.

The year I graduated from college my father had a stroke. He was partially paralyzed on his right side and couldn't walk or talk. He sat in a wheelchair at home, seemingly quite alert despite his condition, watching television all day. He still had a twinkle in his eye. It's odd to say, but having my father at home like that, completely dependent upon my mother, seemed to make her happier than she'd ever been—maybe because he was now hers at long last, and hers alone. She fussed over him day and night.

Naturally, my father's chiropractic office closed. His medical bills wiped out our savings. We got into a real financial crunch. Though I was scheduled to go to graduate school at the University of Tulsa on a scholarship, there was no way my mother could make ends meet by herself. For the time being, I abandoned my hopes of an M.A. in French history and took a job as a hostess at Burnham's, a steak house located near the Penn Plaza. The hours were decent, the tips were great, and it wasn't a bad job meeting and greeting the upscale crowd who dined there.

In a town like Oklahoma City, which is full of fast-food restaurants, Burnham's was considered a fancy joint. It was decorated with wood paneling, ersatz Remington sculptures of cowboys, and reproduction C. M. Russell paintings of migrating Indians in the old west. The clientele consisted mainly of businessmen and out-of-towners.

I'd been working at Burnham's for about eight months when, on April Fool's Day, 1974, a regular customer named John Shanks called to say he would be late and I was to take good care of his guest, a Mr. Lucius Slater, when he arrived. A little before eight, a silver-haired man with deep-set navy blue eyes and an elegant bearing walked up to the hostess station. He was one of those people who fills a room with his presence, a man of substance. He approached me and said, "Good evening. I'm meeting Mr. Shanks for dinner," in a husky, cultured voice.

I figured he was from back east. Though he carried himself well, there was a certain diffidence about him that I found instantly likable. He had none of the swagger of his absent host.

"Mr. Slater?" I said. He nodded with a hint of surprise. "Mr. Shanks just called to say he was running late. Would you like to have a drink at the bar or would you prefer to be seated?"

"I'll go to the table, thank you."

I picked up a menu and showed him to Mr. Shanks's regular table in a quiet corner of the restaurant directly under a painting of two Indians on horseback in the snow. He sat down on the red leather banquette. I handed him the menu and asked if I could get him a drink. He folded his hands in a little cathedral and thought for a moment.

"I think I'm in the mood for a kir royale."

I had no idea what that was. "I beg your pardon?"

He smiled. "Champagne with a little crème de cassis?"

I'd never heard of it.

"I don't think we have that, sir."

"All right. Then just a glass of plain champagne, please."

"I think you have to order a whole bottle, sir. We don't serve champagne by the glass."

"Fine. I'll order a bottle. Will you help me drink it?" He flashed me a quick smile but lowered his eyes. I sensed the question had just slipped out, that it wasn't calculated.

I replied, "I wish I could." My response wasn't calculated, either. To this day I don't know how I had the nerve to say it. I'd never flirted with a customer before.

He looked up at me again. "Why can't you?"

I felt myself blushing to my toes. "Oh, I just . . . can't."

"Tell you what. I'll order a bottle anyway and maybe you'll change your mind. Maybe?"

"Maybe."

He stared at me with those wonderful wise eyes of his. I could tell he liked me. And I liked him, even though he was obviously much older than I was and, indeed, much older than anyone I'd ever dated. I figured he was probably close to fifty or fifty-five, which was nearly my dad's age. Probably that was part of the initial attraction. I don't think I'd really come to grips with how frightened I was of losing my dad to another stroke at that point. Maybe falling in love with Lucius was a way of holding on to my father.

Years later, when Lucius and I reminisced about our first meeting, he maintained he knew he was going to marry me that very night. I could never have predicted it then, and as my mother always warned me, the course of true love never does run smooth. Lucius came to Oklahoma City more and more often on business. He always dined at Burnham's. One night he dined there all alone and asked me out. On our first date he told me he was in the process of separating from his wife, to whom he had been married for twenty-one years. According to him, the divorce was amicable, and the only reason he and his wife had stayed together was on account of their son, Lucius Slater Jr., who was eighteen years old (only about five years younger than I) and about to enter his freshman year at college. I was satisfied he was telling me the truth. We began seeing each other regularly, and before long, we fell madly in love.

Lucius assured me his divorce was proceeding as planned and he begged me to move to New York. Though I longed to go with him, I didn't relish carrying on with a married man. It went against my moral grain. I didn't fancy joining the ranks of "other women," like the ones who had made my mother so unhappy all those years before my father got sick.

I quickly learned, however, that when Lucius Slater wanted something, he wouldn't stop until he got it. He made it very clear he wanted me. I wanted him just as badly. For starters, we were physically crazy about each other. The chemistry between us was so intense that when he took me to Paris to show me the city of my dreams, we spent the first two days in bed and I saw nothing but four walls and a ceiling. But sex wasn't the only thing that bound us together. We seemed to have the same rhythms, likes, and dislikes. Paris was where we really got to know each other.

For a naïve young woman from Oklahoma City, the City of Light was a revelation. I was bowled over by its luminous beauty. Lucius knew his way around and he spoke French. But I knew a lot of things that he didn't. For me, it was kind of like visiting a huge historical theme park where I finally got to see all the places I had read about and studied. When he took me out to Versailles, for example, he was amazed at how much I knew about it. I managed to get by on my college French and found I had a real affinity for the language. I was speaking with a credible accent by the time we left.

On our last night together, we had dinner in one of Lucius's favorite little bistros. He took my hand across the table and said: "I've got it all worked out . . . You move to New York. I'll get you an apartment. The minute I'm divorced, we'll be married." He reached into his pocket and slipped a diamond ring on my finger.

"What about my mom and dad? I can't just leave them."

"I'll see to it that your parents are very well provided for. I'd planned to do that anyway—even if you decide not to come to New York. That is, if you'll allow me to."

I thought he was the sexiest, kindest, most wonderful man I had ever known. I nodded like an obedient little girl. There was no point in protesting. I wanted him. And I wanted another life.

After a tearful good-bye to my parents, I moved to New York to be with Lucius. My father was almost completely out of it at this point, and my mother was too tired and too concerned about my father to press me about where I was getting the money. She was grateful for the help I was giving her. I'm sure she knew I had a "sugar daddy," as she called rich men, but she didn't ask any questions. She just wished me luck and told me I deserved everything good in the world.

Lucius set me up in a nice little apartment in a modern building on Third Avenue and Sixty-fourth Street. I got a job working at Tiffany's in the silver department. On the application, I wrote Josephine Meers instead of Jolie Ann. I liked people to call me Jo, however, because it was what Lucius always called me, plus it sounded so much more sophisticated, like Josephine.

New York was as intoxicating to me as Paris, but in a completely different way. I went to the opera, the ballet, the symphony, the theater. I visited all the museums—the Metropolitan, the Modern, the Frick, the Museum of Natural History, the Municipal Museum.

But the thing I loved best about the city was the antiques shops and the auction houses where I could actually touch and examine some of the greatest furniture and paintings ever created. I was astonished to learn that one could actually buy pieces made by the great *ébénistes,* such as Jacob and Riesener, and that there were people in New York who had collections rivaling any museum in the world.

Lucius told me about a few very expensive antiques shops and art galleries that were tucked away in private houses with no sign on the door indicating they were there. It began to dawn on me that New York was a city where many of the things one wanted to see, like many of the people one wanted to know, were hidden from view.

The settlement agreement was all drawn up when Ruth, Lucius's wife, was diagnosed with pancreatic cancer. I felt ten times more guilty about her than Lucius, who had been openly scornful of his wife: "Ruth's idea of stimulating dinner conversation is assisted suicide versus managed health care." That was the one thing I really didn't like about Lucius—the disrespect he had for Ruth.

I, on the other hand, obsessed over the idea that I had somehow caused her illness. I pictured Ruth as a worthy, if dull woman, certainly undeserving of such a terrible blow. But Lucius swore to me she didn't have a clue about us. I told Lucius that I wouldn't see him until her fate had been decided. I even urged him to try to get back together with her. He assured me she didn't want a reconciliation.

The progress of Ruth Slater's grave condition gave me a good idea of how desperate women in New York were to snag a rich man. Though I refused to see Lucius, he called me every day with fresh tales of how several of Ruth's friends, both married and single, had made passes at him already, veiling their real purpose in supposed concern for Ruth. They wept with her at her bedside, only to wink at Lucius behind her back. He caught one of her very best friends having a confidential chat with her doctor, trying to ascertain how long she had to live. Two months after she was diagnosed, Ruth died. Lucius was on the open market.

A widower is the Holy Grail of eligibles. His fortune is still intact, and men who have liked being married once tend to want to be married again. It is the state of married bliss, as much as the deceased, for which the widower presumably mourns. No decent interval had passed before Lucius was attacked by a swarm of hopeful females anxious to be the next Mrs. Slater. But he kept his word to me.

Now Lucius had to figure out a way to introduce me into his life without ever letting on we'd been lovers for the past year. It was at this juncture that I learned how very crafty my future husband was. He worked out an ingenious plan.

He arranged for me to be invited to a dinner party at Betty and Gil Waterman's house. Then he announced that we had met there for the first time.

"Betty introduced us. She seated us next to each other and I was madly in love by dessert," was his line. And naturally, no one believed him. Clever New Yorkers knew better: They knew that Lucius Slater had really met me while I was working behind the counter at Tiffany's. There was this urban legend of how Lucius went in to buy a silver pen and how I recognized him from a picture I'd cut out from *Fortune* magazine on America's leading businessmen. Apparently, I had then slipped him my phone number and subsequently snared him with certain celebrated sexual skills. All his friends referred to me as "the salesgirl" behind my back.

Lucius made me promise one thing: "If anyone ever asks you if you worked at Tiffany's, you have to deny it," he told me.

"Why?"

"Because it's true. And because it's so easy to find out you worked there."

I was still perplexed.

Lucius explained: "It's simple. If we give the gossips something really good to gossip about, they won't look beyond their noses. You deny you were a salesgirl. They'll find out you were. They'll think they've discovered the deep dark truth about you and be so bitchy about that, they won't bother to dig any deeper. Take my word for it: The lie within the lie always works in this town."

Lucius was right. His strategy was on the mark. No one suspected we'd been lovers before Ruth died and that he'd brought me to New York as his mistress. We were married in a small ceremony at the Fifth Avenue apartment of his great friends June and Charlie Kahn. The only other people present were his son, Little Lucius, Betty and Gil Waterman, and Nate Nathaniel, Lucius's lawyer and friend.

My father was too ill to attend. Though Lucius offered to fly my mother to New York in a private plane, she declined, saying she didn't want to leave my dad. However, I sensed there was a deeper reason. She didn't really approve of Lucius or of me for having married him. She had an idea of the real story and I remember her telling me then, "Watch your step, Jolie Ann. What they'll do to one, they'll do to another."

The fact that people made fun of my humble background irked me at first. But—and as I said, in New York nothing counts until the *but*—I learned that I was far from an anomaly. Very few people in so-called New York Society were to the manner born. In fact, it was chock-full of former salesgirls, secretaries and stewardesses and ex-hookers who, like myself, had married rich men. Caesar's wives, I called us, because our husbands' power made us above contempt (if not suspicion)—at least to our faces.

The great sorrow of my life was that Lucius and I never had a child. I had wanted one, but he didn't. I thought it had to do with the fact that his only child had been such a disappointment to him. Whenever I brought up the subject of having a baby, Lucius would grow hostile and distant, saying he didn't want another enormous responsibility. "You have a duty to your flesh and blood no matter what," he said. "When you get to be my age, you'll realize you can't just have a child without dedicating your life to it. And I don't want to dedicate my life to another kid."

I resigned myself to the sacrifice, consoling myself with the rather absurd and erroneous notion that the lack of a child would somehow keep our marriage ever young and vital.

Even though I was coasting into middle age—not the easiest time for a woman—I have to say I loved my life and considered myself extraordinarily lucky. Though I tried never to take anything for granted, after twenty years of marriage, I naturally assumed I was on a set course, that whatever happened to Lucius and me in terms of health and the usual ups and downs of everyday life, we were a team: I would always take care of him, and he would always take care of me. I thought I was in the right cradle at last.

Given all that, it's still hard for me to believe that I, Jo Slater, supposed great connoisseur of furniture, failed to detect the deep and ancient rot beneath the veneer in my very own house.

3

OUR house in Southampton was a mammoth brown-shingled "summer cottage," as they were once called, located on five acres of land on First Neck Lane, about an eighth of a mile from the ocean and the Beach Club. Built at the turn of the century for a prosperous New York lawyer named Thaddeus McClelland, the huge beetle-shaped house had a long, wide porch enhanced by a row of massive white cylindrical columns. The four-story interior boasted large entertaining rooms and comfortable quarters, plus a rabbit warren of servants' rooms and a huge kitchen and butler's pantry. Lucius and I had purchased it from a busted bond trader years ago, mainly for the grounds, which were spacious, lush, and green, planted with stately old shade trees that towered above the lawn. It was originally called "Three Fountains" but Lucius renamed it "Beer Hall," mainly to tweak the sensibilities of some of our stuffier friends. He found Southampton a little pretentious sometimes.

The morning after my birthday party, the phone started ringing at eight o'clock. For me, big parties were generally much more fun the next day when I rehashed the details with pals. Everyone who called pronounced the evening a great success—even Betty—which in New York, oddly enough, has nothing to do with whether or not it was fun. It was simply the place to be, which is what counts.

After breakfast, I wrote a thank-you note to Trish Bromire and had it hand-delivered immediately, along with a basket of flowers from the garden. (I had already sent her an antique gold box to thank her before the evening. Giving and receiving pretty presents is something our little group loves to do.) Early on in my New York life, I'd changed my handwriting from the loopy script I'd learned in public school to a breezy boarding school print that resembled Clara Wilman's. Lucius told me handwriting was like an accent; it gave your background away. He was conscious of such things in others, but oblivious to them in himself. His own handwriting was atrocious.

Since his heart attack, Lucius and I had occupied separate bedrooms. I insisted he take over the former master bedroom because it was so cheerful with its crisp blue and white decor and elongated bay windows overlooking the garden. On a clear day a ribbon of ocean was visible in the distance. Lucius usually stayed in bed until ten or so, having breakfast and reading the papers, but this morning he was not in his room. I found him downstairs in the library, seated behind the desk, on the phone. He peered at me over the tops of his spectacles and motioned me to come in and sit down.

"So how's the birthday girl?" he said, hanging up the phone.

"Everyone loved the party."

"The hell with everybody. Did *you* love it?"

"I did. I really did. I especially loved your toast. Why are you up so early?"

"Is it early? By the way, Nate's Fedexing some stuff out to me this morning. I need to sign it and send it back today."

Nate was Nathaniel P. Nathaniel, Lucius's lawyer. It was he who had drawn up the harsh prenuptial agreement in which I waived all my rights to Lucius's estate should we divorce or should Lucius die. He bet Lucius I wouldn't sign it. But, of course, I did. I wasn't interested in Lucius's money—I didn't even know he had a fortune in the beginning. But Nate didn't trust me. I think he was surprised when I put up no protest whatsoever. I wanted Lucius to know in no uncertain terms that I had not married him for his money. Having lost face, Nate told Lucius in confidence to watch out for me nonetheless.

"I know her type," he had said. "She'll try to change it in a few years. Mark my words."

Naturally, Lucius repeated this remark to me. I vowed to myself then and there that I would never, ever try to change that agreement. I was bound and determined to prove Nathaniel P. Nathaniel, Esq. wrong. There were even times when I prayed Lucius would lose all his money just so I could show everyone that I had once, did now, and would forever love my husband for himself, and himself alone.

To be fair to Nate, however, I have to say that his position was understandable. From his point of view, I was nothing but a poor nobody from Oklahoma who'd finagled herself into becoming the mistress of an enormously rich, married man. The fact that I was nearly thirty years younger than Lucius didn't help any more than the fact that Nate had been like a second son to Ruth, who adored him.

Lucius, on the other hand, really understood how much I loved him. He told me not to worry because he had made a will that divided his fortune equally between myself and his only son. This will overrode the prenuptial agreement. Like many rich men, Lucius considered divorce, not death, a real possibility. I was very touched, but frankly, money was the last thing on my mind in those days.

Over the years, Nate and I called a truce. We both understood that since neither one of us was going away, we'd have to tolerate each other for the sake of the man we both loved.

"What are you up to today, sweetheart?" I asked.

"Playing golf with Gil."

"I invited their houseguest over for lunch. Did you meet her last night? She's attractive."

"A frog, right?"

"A frog countess. Join us, why don't you? A little new blood for you."

"I doubt I'll be back in time. I'll try and join you for dessert."

Lucius was always pushing me to reel in glittery fish for his amusement. As he so often jokingly said: "Ask not for whom my wife trolls: She trolls for me."

—⁓—

IT was glorious weather. A high canopy of tree leaves glinting with sunlight cast a delicate web of shadows over the garden. I took a long swim. The refreshing water melted away the vestiges of a slight hangover.

Monique arrived at the house promptly at twelve-thirty. She looked older in the daylight—mid-thirties, rather than late twenties as I'd originally pegged her. Dressed in shorts and a T-shirt, she reminded me of a dark version of myself in my younger days when I was more toned and looked less like an overripe peach. We had the same basic conformation: broad shoulders, medium-size breasts, svelte midriff, and long, shapely legs. Monique's attributes were still buoyant with youth, however, while mine were sagging into middle age despite a trainer, a masseuse, and ten glasses of water a day.

I asked the Countess if she wanted to take a swim before lunch, but she said she preferred to have a tour, if that wasn't too inconvenient. I adored showing visitors around so I was quick to oblige.

Monique wanted to know every detail of the renovation of the main house and the landscaping—who had helped me, how I had decided on this, that, and the other thing. I found out we both loved to garden. She was eager to know about all aspects of my household—everything from my linens, china, glasses, and silverware, to what candles I burned, what flowers I preferred, and what my breakfast trays looked like, how I organized my staff.

As we strolled around peering into all the nooks and crannies, she hung on my words with rapt attention, seemingly fascinated by everything I said. In others, I might have found this behavior somewhat cloying, but the light way Monique had of giving a compliment made her sound sincere rather than sycophantic. I felt flattered, not fawned over.

"Tell me again how you know the Watermans?" I asked her as we strolled toward the far end of the property.

"My husband owned a small art gallery in Paris," she replied. "He was a friend of Gil's."

Whenever she spoke of her husband, she got a faraway air about her that made me think his death had hit her very hard and that she was by no means over it, but she was putting up a brave front.

"Betty was so sweet to invite me out here," she continued. "It's such a beautiful place—so green and luscious right up to the sea. It reminds me a bit of the south of France."

We crossed the emerald lawn and walked down an intricate terrain of terraces and brightly colored flower beds leading to a little woods, through a leafy bower, at the end of which was a cottage covered in sweet-smelling honeysuckle and wisteria, inspired by Le Hameau, Marie Antoinette's famous rustic retreat.

"The guest house," I announced.

Monique clapped her hands in delight when she saw it. "*C'est une merveille!*" she exclaimed.

I unlocked the door and we went inside. I pulled up the shades and opened the windows to air the place out.

"We usually have guests in and out all summer," I explained. "But this year, Lucius has been too ill."

Taking a careful look around at the cheerful hunting toiles, the latticework on the walls, and the finely made wicker furniture, Monique commented on what she called the "studied quaintness" of the little house. She immediately recognized the porcelain milk pails flanking the mantelpiece as copies of the ones Marie Antoinette had made for her play "dairy."

As we were walking back to the main house, the Countess turned to me and said, "I am not disappointed. They are right. You do have the greatest taste of anyone, Jo. You do."

"I wish I could take all the credit myself. I had help from a brilliant landscape designer—Pearson Potts. The secret is not so much knowing how to do it yourself—it's knowing whom to *choose*, as my dear friend Clara Wilman used to say. But I am a little house proud, I admit. Particularly of the guest house, which I did design myself. The Hadley Museum includes us on their garden tour every summer, which is very nice."

"Betty tells me you have the most beautiful apartment in New York as well."

"Betty's a pal. Lucius insisted on a very grand style in the city. You know, lots of gilded furniture and silk curtains woven by the nuns at Beauvais, which took two years to make—that sort of thing. I like it, but to be honest, this house is much more my taste."

"Betty said he's been quite ill, your husband?"

"Heart attack. We're not supposed to say that but everybody knows."

"My husband died of a heart attack. It was very sudden." Monique stopped walking. She buried her head in her hand.

I touched her lightly on the arm.

"I'm still not used to it," she said. Looking up, she

wiped a tear from the corner of her eye and made an effort to smile. "Forgive me."

"Please don't apologize. I'm so sorry for your loss."

—◦—

MONIQUE and I sat out on the terrace and had one of those magical lunches where the atmosphere, the food, the wine, and the conversation all merge into a sublime conviviality. Though we chatted about my birthday party and touched on a variety of innocuous subjects— gardening, eighteenth-century furniture, clothes, face-lifts, books, travel, food, and so on—what we were really doing was exploring the possibility of becoming friends.

It was evident that Monique knew a lot about me— superficially, at any rate—and that she regarded me as a kind of role model. She reminded me of a young apprentice of beauty who had come to learn from someone she considered a mistress of the art. I, who had once felt exactly the same way myself about the late, great Clara Wilman, one of the most beloved grandes dames of New York society, recognized the signs of heroine worship and was touched the roles were now reversed.

Clara had taught me nearly everything I knew about style and about the ins and outs of New York. People considered her my mentor, which is important in society because the person who takes you into a group—any group—will define your friends for some period of time, if not forever. Clara considered me her protégée, as she often told me. She was much older than I and she always emphasized the importance, particularly as one got older, of making new, young friends.

"Having youth around you will keep you young," Clara always said.

My problem was that most young people weren't particularly interested in the things I'm interested in. I'd never really been able to find anyone who could share my intense fascination with Marie Antoinette and her period. Ethan came close, but Ethan had a complicated and secret private life that he was reluctant to share with the world, even me. I longed for a companion of the soul to replace Clara. Though Monique wasn't that much younger than I—only about ten years or so—her energy, enthusiasm, anxiousness to please, and, above all, curiosity about all the things that I loved were a tonic to me. The roles had switched. I was Clara. She was me.

Not all of our talk was on an elevated plane, either. We gossiped quite a bit. Monique went out of her way to be kind about Dick Bromire, which impressed me because many of his friends were predicting his doom. Several of my morning confidantes had mentioned that great as the party was, it looked like the swan song of a crook.

—⁓—

MONIQUE and I were still sitting out on the terrace talking when Lucius appeared in a long terrycloth robe, headed for the pool. He was trailed by Caspar, his chauffeur and attendant, a squat fireplug of a man, with a large head and a wide, creased face. Upon seeing us, Lucius quickly closed his robe to hide the scar from his heart operation. Though his skin was as loose as an elephant's and his gait lumbering, Lucius was a man who dwarfed his surroundings with an aura of majesty.

"How'd you make out, sweetheart?" I cried.

"I birdied the ninth. Gil's mad as a hornet."

"Come say hi to my new best friend, Countess de Passy."

Lucius ambled over to the table and shook hands with Monique.

"We met last night," she said. "But very briefly."

"Join us," I said. "Would you like something to drink?"

"I'm dying for a cup of coffee." Then quickly raising his hand before I could protest, he added, "I know, I know! No caffeine." He turned to Monique and said, "She watches me like a hawk."

I asked Caspar to bring us a fresh pitcher of herbal iced tea.

"So, what have you two ladies been up to all afternoon?" Lucius inquired.

"Your wife gave me a tour of your marvelous property," Monique said. "Then we had the most delicious lunch—lobster soufflé and a wonderful white wine."

"So I see," he laughed, nodding toward the empty bottle.

Lucius leaned back in his chair, crossed his hands behind his head, and turned his face up to the cloudless blue sky.

"What a day, huh? Gorgeous. It was so beautiful out on the golf course. The only good thing about having been sick is that you really appreciate everything so much more . . . So Gil says you have a Monet you want to sell?" he said. "I collect a few Impressionists. Maybe I should take a look at it."

"My painting is definitely not for you," Monique said.

"No? How come?"

"It has Monet's signature on it. But I'm afraid he was having a bad day. Monet with a migraine, I call it."

As we all laughed, Lucius pinned her with his gaze. I knew that look of his. He was intrigued by her. I was happy she amused him.

"Well, if anyone can flog it for you, Gil can," he said. "He's the consummate salesman. He once talked me into a Pissarro on Prozac."

"And a suicidal Seurat," I reminded him.

We all laughed again.

"So how long are you out here for, Countess?" Lucius asked, loosening up considerably.

"Please call me Monique. As long as Betty and Gil will put up with me. I wanted to rent something but everything is so expensive. Worse than Saint Tropez, where we used to go."

"Well, if you get stuck, we've got a decent little guest house," Lucius said, winking at me.

"That house is a *dream*," Monique said.

"So come and live in a dream," I said.

"No, no . . . I could not impose." She gave me the sort of vaguely incredulous, awestruck look I gave Clara the first time she had invited me to her celebrated house in Virginia. Clara was my idol, and her friendship seemed slightly unreal to me in the beginning. I wanted to be around her but I was a little frightened of her as well— afraid I would do or say the wrong thing and put her off. I was sure Monique was reacting to me in much the same way.

"It's no imposition," I assured her. "We'd love to have you stay for a few days if you want to come."

"You play backgammon?" Lucius inquired.

Monique suddenly beamed. "I adore backgammon," she said. "I'll have you know I once won twenty francs from a Saudi sheik in Biarritz . . . I was fifteen."

"Well, that settles that," I said. "Lucius has been trying to teach me backgammon since the day we were married. I'll never get the hang of it. It always looks to me like a game you make up as you go along."

Lucius forgot about his swim and immediately challenged Monique to a game. I knew he would. I went to get the backgammon set in the library, leaving Lucius and Monique laughing and chatting together on the terrace. She seemed more relaxed with Lucius than she did with me. I suspected I intimidated her a bit.

Monique and Lucius played backgammon until five o'clock, which gave me some precious time to myself. I sat back on a lawn chair, reading de Maupassant for my reading group, lulled by the sound of the rolling dice and the murmurings of the players.

—⁊⁊⁊—

MONIQUE came over for lunch two more times that week. Each of her visits was a pleasure for me. We laughed a lot, talked a lot. And, I confess, having this cultivated, attractive younger woman around hanging on my every word was very flattering.

After our third lunch together, a very endearing thing happened—a small thing, but significant in the way that small things often are. Just before getting up, Monique, who had always casually thrown her napkin down on the table after meals, carefully folded it up and placed it beside her plate, just as I always did. Either way was correct, of course. But she had watched me and adopted my style.

The next morning, Monique called me, ostensibly to say good-bye. I was surprised. She said that Betty told her rather unceremoniously that she needed her guest room back. I was tempted to ask Monique to come and stay with us. I knew she'd be wonderful company for me. But there was Lucius to consider as well.

Lucius had become even more difficult of late, ever since my birthday party, in fact. He was a man who literally couldn't bear to be alone, not even for five minutes, growing bored and restless when there was no one around to entertain him. It was striking how little in the way of inner resources he had to keep himself occupied. Though very bright, he wasn't a great reader, which is one way I found of passing pleasurable hunks of time. He loathed television. He had no hobbies. What he needed to distract him was live company.

Our marriage was childless, and Lucius was estranged from his only son. Country life, therefore, was not a family affair. It was purely social. We depended on friends to take up the slack. If no one was around, Lucius grew sullen and angry, hunting me to ground with arrows of sarcasm, tormenting me with shackling silences. I dreaded those moods of his. In past summers, I always made sure there was a constant stream of houseguests to deflect his depression. But this summer I couldn't plan anything on account of his health.

I told Monique to hang on for a moment while I consulted with Lucius. I ran downstairs to the gym in the basement to ask him if it was all right with him if she came and stayed with us for a few days. He was working out and didn't seem to care one way or the other.

"Whatever you want," he puffed, continuing to lift two

ten-pound dumbbells up and down under Caspar's supervision.

I ran back upstairs and invited Monique to come over
and spend a few days with us. She was overjoyed.

That very afternoon, Monique moved into our guest
cottage. We invited her for a week. She stayed the
summer.

4

IN all fairness, I have to say that Betty warned me.

"You're crazy letting that gorgeous frog in your house," she said.

I laughed her off. "Why? Because of Lucius? *Please.* She wouldn't be interested, believe me."

"What about him? He might be interested."

"Not his style, trust me. Anyway, he can't have sex. He could die."

"Are you *kidding?* That's how they all dream of going."

I paid no attention to Betty. Lucius wasn't a philanderer. Several very attractive girlfriends of mine had come to stay over the years and there had never been a problem. Lucius wanted to be amused, not seduced.

Like most married couples, Lucius and I knew each other's bodies, rhythms, likes, and dislikes so well that over the years the act of making love had become a kind of genteel cruise we took together, after which we both felt refreshed. But Lucius wasn't interested in sex anymore. We hadn't made love in ages, even before his heart attack. He blamed his lack of libido on age. Being a good deal younger than he, I was often nostalgic for the passion of the old days, but I didn't dwell on it. My life was good in so many other ways. I had my health and plenty to keep me occupied. I accepted the fact that we had settled into a kind of cozy companionship fueled by deluxe diversions and an active social life.

The arrival of the Countess was an unexpected lift for both of us. Monique was the perfect guest. Lucius looked forward to their daily backgammon games when he could manage them. He was still weak and tired from his recent operation, so he rested a great deal and saw little of us during the day. The three of us usually got together for dinner and we had some very jolly meals. Most of the time, however, Monique palled around with me.

Nothing escaped the Countess. I could tell she was watching me closely from the moment she arrived. At first she was dismissive of the servants, barking at them to be careful with her luggage, not thanking them for their efforts, ordering them around. She treated Mrs. Mathilde, Caspar, and the others in an offhand, arrogant manner. It was disconcerting. Granted, sometimes people who aren't used to dealing with servants try to make themselves seem grander by treating the help rudely when, in fact, just the opposite is true. I felt the Countess should have known better. Still, when she saw the way in which I spoke to my staff, she quickly changed her tune and began greeting them all warmly—perhaps even growing a bit too chummy with Alain, the chef, who was

French and with whom she enjoyed conversing in her native tongue.

I didn't hold Monique's initial haughtiness against her, particularly when she went out of her way to make amends. She won over the staff in short order—all except Mrs. Mathilde, whom I sensed remained none too fond of the Countess. I caught the old housekeeper eyeing Monique warily—even contemptuously—on many occasions. I chalked this up to nothing more than the unfortunate first impression Monique had made on her. As usual, Mrs. Mathilde kept her feelings to herself. I, of course, never pressed her for an opinion of my guest.

The Countess seemed to be observing everything about me, down to the smallest detail: the way I dressed, how I talked, what I ate, the manner in which I entertained and organized my household, even the perfume I wore and the wine I drank. Sometimes she even sounded like me. The way she answered the telephone was exactly the way I did—a cool "Hello." Clara always told me that you should make every effort to avoid answering the phone yourself, but that if you were forced to, it was wise to sound a bit distant until you found out who it was.

Trivia that was second nature to me came as a revelation to Monique. I taught her all the little tricks that add up to a more civilized way of life. I kept meticulous records of all my dinner parties, for example, noting the food (always bearing in mind the preferences of my guests), the wines, the seating, the flowers, the music, what I wore. I made notes on what my guests particularly liked or disliked and who got along with whom, so that the next time they came to my house, I could make them even more comfortable.

Clara had taught me how important it was to make people feel special and appreciated. When she was invited to a dinner, she made sure flowers were delivered *before* the party, so they could be displayed at the hostess's discretion. If she sent a present *after* a dinner, it was usually a book. She always wrote her host or hostess a thank-you note the night she got home from a party before she went to bed so it could be hand-delivered the next morning. She never forgot a friend's birthday or their children's birthdays. She sent thoughtful presents, not merely expensive ones.

Another thing about Clara was that she never distinguished between who was "important" or "unimportant." There was no such thing as "the good china" or "the great wine" in Clara's house. All guests, no matter who they were—from the lowliest staff member at the Municipal Museum, where she was on the board, to the highest head of state—got the same treatment. She lived by Shaw's dictum that whether one has good manners or bad manners is irrelevant as long as one has the *same* manners for everyone.

"If you're rude to the waiter, you better be rude to me, too," she often said.

She had given me endless tips on how to make a house more cozy, like keeping a pot of apples simmering on the stove in late fall so a delicious, inviting aroma would permeate the atmosphere. Clara always issued and answered invitations herself, rarely relying on a secretary as a buffer. She believed that true grandness stemmed from being unpretentious. Although she maintained a large staff in all her houses, she loved privacy. Her servants were unobtrusive.

"My idea of luxury," she used to say, "is to come back into a room you've just left and have the pillows all fluffed up by unseen hands."

Clara's death at the age of eighty-five had left a gaping hole in my life. I knew that nothing could replace the tender camaraderie and intellectual compatibility she and I had shared. I missed her presiding eye, her sly wit, her supreme generosity, and most of all, her mischievous sense of humor. I told Monique all about Clara and how much she had meant to me. I described her funeral, five years earlier at St. John the Divine, which ranked as one of the great social occasions of New York. Dignitaries, financiers, and celebrities, as well as countless friends and admirers, came from all over the world to pay homage to this remarkable and generous woman who had been a fixture of the cultural and social life of New York.

—⁓—

SINCE Monique and I went everywhere together, it was inevitable that people started to talk. Just as there had been speculation about Clara and me once upon a time, there was speculation now that Monique and I were more than friends, shall we say. The fact is, though, that Monique and I were not lovers. We had what was called in the eighteenth century an *amitié amoureuse*, a "loving friendship," similar to ones Marie Antoinette had with a few attractive, younger noblewomen in her court. In the Queen's case, these relationships helped alleviate the pain of an unconsummated marriage. In my case, it was just pleasant to have a vital younger person around with whom I could laugh and talk and share confidences.

A new friendship always holds out the possibility of perfection—an alluring concept. Monique and I soon discovered we were kindred spirits. She was different from my other friends in that I felt I had more in common with her intellectually and emotionally. Oh, I loved Betty and June, but they weren't really interested in the same things I was. I was bound to them chiefly through long acquaintance. And Ethan, with whom I had a strong intellectual bond, wasn't around much in the summer. He tripped off to Patmos for six weeks in July and August to be with the monks.

In a world where most people repeated one another's secrets in strictest confidence over lunch, Monique de Passy was a tomb. I told her things I would never have dared tell Betty or June or even Ethan. She told me things, too. Day after day, our friendship deepened as we shared our most private thoughts with each other—everything from how we felt about sex to whom we secretly disliked despite our public postures. We often joked that if there were a tape recorder anywhere in the vicinity both our gooses would be foie gras.

Nancy, my social secretary of two years, had quit in the beginning of the summer to go on a trip around the world. I was surprised at her sudden departure, and, indeed, I wondered where on earth she was getting the money for such an adventure. It wasn't my business, however. Her decision was firm and there was nothing I could do except give her a bonus and wish her good luck. But she had left me in the lurch.

Monique very kindly offered to help me with my bills and correspondence until I found a replacement. I felt a little guilty about putting a guest to work. But she insisted, telling me it was a small way to pay me back for all the kindness I'd shown her.

I took her everywhere—to the club, to cocktail parties, to my reading group. She especially shone in that setting, I must say. Our guest leader, Lon Fatterly, an Englishman and former Oxford don who was compiling a book of absurd syllogisms while he spent the summer in Southampton as an itinerant houseguest, welcomed Monique as an addition. She was perceptive, intelligent, and apparently well read. During one meeting, we were discussing *Madame Bovary*. Monique held the group spellbound with an informed and rather moving discourse on the soul of Emma as compared to Flaubert's own vision of the artist. Even Betty, who, for some reason, now clearly loathed the Countess, was impressed with Monique's sharp analysis.

—⁓—

ONE day in mid-July on our regular early morning walk along the beach, Monique asked me an odd question. We were strolling down by the sun-spangled ocean, letting the waves lap over our feet, when she said: "Jo, has Betty ever said anything to you about me?"

This was a delicate subject because Betty was constantly telling me how much she disliked Monique.

"Why do you ask?"

"Because I know she hates me."

"I don't think she hates you," I said, lying.

"She does. And she has good reason to."

I stopped walking and gave her a searching look. "Oh? Why?"

"Please, Jo, if I tell you this, you must swear you will never, *ever* repeat it."

"Listen, we've already made a pact. Everything we say to each other is to the grave."

Monique hesitated, staring out at the horizon.

"The real reason I left Betty's house is not because she needed the guest room but because . . . well . . . Gil made a pass at me."

I was shocked. "You're *kidding*."

"No. It was extremely uncomfortable for me. You see, I was very fond of Betty. She had been so good to me. And I felt awful to be put in that position. I immediately pulled away, of course, and told him I wasn't interested. He didn't press at all, but—what is it you always say, Jo? Nothing counts until the but . . . Betty saw us."

"Oh my God. Poor you . . . poor Betty."

"She never said anything to you?"

"No. Nothing. I mean, well, it's true I don't think she's overly fond of you. But she never said anything specific . . . I must say I never would have imagined anything like that of Gil."

"From the look on her face when she walked in on us, I was certain that she thought it was me who had made a pass at him. Can you imagine?" Monique said with a grim chuckle. "I would never get involved with a married man. Ever. And Gil Waterman is certainly not my type. He's a bit oily, don't you think?"

I'd known Gil for years. I wouldn't have called him oily, but he was definitely a smooth, attractive-looking guy, who had the slick friendliness of a good salesman. Extraordinarily knowledgeable about art, he had the particular talent of being able to locate great paintings from obscure or difficult sources and broker them to very rich clients. He had never struck me as a philanderer. But I now recalled how recently Betty had been complaining about the number of business trips he was taking. Though Betty and Gil seemed happy together, years of observation had taught me that one can never really tell what's going on in other people's marriages, and that idle speculation on such matters was futile, if indeed one of the conversational staples of social life.

I honestly didn't know what to say. I loved Betty and felt sorry for her. And though I was fond of Gil and had trouble imagining him in such a brazen role—particularly as I thought of him as being much more interested in making deals than in making love—I knew Monique would never lie about something like that. Why, after all? It was not in her interest. We walked on in silence.

"You were brave to tell me," I said after a time, sensing her discomfort.

"I wanted you to know, Jo. I don't want to have any secrets from you."

I smiled at her. "I know."

We turned around and headed back toward home.

"How did you meet Lucius?" Monique inquired as we walked.

Our previous confidences made me reluctant to give her the usual party line. She wasn't keeping any secrets from me so I thought it was only fair that I not keep any secrets from her. Besides, it was an old secret now.

"Please never tell anyone what I'm about to tell you," I said. "Not that it matters much anymore, but no one in the world knows the truth about how we met—not even Betty or June."

Monique stopped walking and looked at me earnestly. "Jo, please don't tell me something you will regret my knowing. I would die if anything ever came between us."

Her response made me trust her all the more. That afternoon, I told Monique the whole story of how Lucius and I really met, explaining Lucius's theory of using "a lie within a lie" to cover up the truth.

"I felt so guilty when Ruth died," I said. "Even though I knew rationally it wasn't my fault."

"She didn't even know about you, did she?"

"I don't know. I think women know these things subconsciously. Don't you?"

"Oh yes," Monique agreed. "I would certainly have known if Michel had had an affair."

"Well, Lucius can't have an affair at the moment. He's too sick. Anyway, he never would. He's moody but faithful."

Monique nodded. "He is madly in love with you. One can see it."

—⁓—

Now there was virtually nothing Monique didn't know about me. I adored and trusted her and we both agreed that she had to find a way to stay in New York. Neither of us wanted her to go back to Paris where there were sad memories and a grim little apartment in the 12th arrondissement—the only thing she could afford after Michel's death. We discussed the various jobs she might apply for. I thought being a U.N. interpreter might be one option since she spoke English so well, but she was determined to be in the art world. She said Gil had offered to help her before the famous incident, but now, of course, she could never approach him. I went to Dick Bromire—

always a generous friend—and asked him if there were
anything he could do. He said he'd work on it, but he was
clearly too preoccupied with his own troubles to give it
his full attention. I knew the heads of all the big auction
houses, Chapel's, Christie's, and Sotheby's. I put in calls
to everyone, but it was summertime. People were on
vacation. Monique assured me there was no great rush.

—⁓—

THE Bromire scandal dragged on throughout the summer
with everyone speculating about whether or not Dick
would be indicted. The problem, as I understood it, had to
do with several counts of tax evasion. Dick had apparently been trading stocks in a foreign account and not
declaring the interest, plus he was accused of charging
personal goods to his real estate company. Lucius
explained it all to me once, but not having a head for
business, I really didn't understand the particulars. The
rather convoluted general consensus was that Dick was
too smart to get caught for whatever it was the government said he did, and that he probably shouldn't have
done it—whatever it was—even though businessmen
did far worse and got away with it every day. The antici-
patory glee that he could conceivably go to jail was carefully cloaked in deep concern.

"I'm so worried about poor Dick," said the *amis
mondains*. "What do you think will happen?"

Translation: "Have you heard anything horrible that I
haven't heard?"

Two articles appeared in the *Wall Street Journal* ana-
lyzing Dick's predicament and the effect it was having on
his company's stock. Although the stock price fluctuated

a bit, it didn't plummet as the pundits had predicted it would, and Dick and Trish were still giving the biggest parties in town. Trish was spotted buying an extravagant new bauble at Pearce's. She had the British ambassador to the U.N. and his wife to stay with her and gave them a gala dinner rivaling the one she gave for me. Some said Dick was about to go under, but he seemed to be floating quite happily on the surface for the time being, ignoring his critics and celebrating his friends, seemingly oblivious to the shots of speculation spiking the summer gossip punch.

—⚕—

AUGUST rolled around. Time was running out for Monique. So was her money—the little she had of it. I knew that one sure way for her to stay in America was to get married. She laughed when I suggested that idea. However, she did hint that she might like to at least start dating, and I immediately set about fixing her up with the various bachelors I knew around town.

I took her to the Beach Club, where we scoped out the various eligibles. If she found one of my candidates even vaguely palatable, I invited him to dine with us. The result made for some unintentionally hilarious evenings where she and I both reached the conclusion that heterosexual men in New York—no matter how unattractive, stupid, or poor—spoiled quicker than good caviar.

Things got so desperate I even thought of fixing her up with Nate Nathaniel. Nate was one of those perennial bachelors whom everyone assumes to be gay but is in reality a closet heterosexual. Men felt safe if he accompanied their wives to the opera or the ballet when he was, in fact, far more dangerous than your average gigolo. Some women found him irresistible. The Nathaniel school of charm eluded me, however. From the moment I clapped eyes on him all those years ago, I found his superciliousness a little tough to take—even before he goaded me into signing that ridiculous prenuptial agreement.

Nate came from a genteelly poor WASP family in Connecticut. He'd attended all the right schools: Choate, Princeton, Harvard Law School; he'd headed the Law Review and clerked one summer for a Supreme Court justice. Nate's mind was an agile and devious creature that coiled its way around problems rather than attacking them head on, thus enabling him to see all sides of an issue at once. Needless to say, he was an excellent lawyer.

Lucius took Nate under his wing early on, in part, I strongly believe, because Lucius, a totally self-made man, the only son of a day care nurse and a Queens pharmacist named Slattery (Lucius shortened the name when he went into business), wanted to *be* Nate on some level. Failing that, he wanted Nate as a son.

Lucius's own son, Lucius Slater Jr., or "Little Lucius," as he was called, was a bitter disappointment to his father. Lucius referred to the shy, awkward boy as "that oddball son of mine who's only interested in fish." (Little Lucius eventually became an oceanographer and moved to Miami.) It pained me that Lucius used our marriage as an excuse to further distance himself from his only child.

Lucius's marriage to Ruth had been serviceable but never happy, and for many years, he submerged the cares of an unsatisfactory personal life under the swell of great ambition. The more successful he became, however, the less content he felt. He blamed his own chronic dissatisfaction on his hapless son.

I rather liked Little Lucius, ungainly and withdrawn as he was, and I disliked the fact that Lucius treated him with such contempt. But what could I do? I tried my best to bring the two of them together, but Lucius made our family gatherings hell for everyone between his constant criticisms of Little Lucius and a hair-trigger temper that fired off irrationally whenever the young man was around. I finally gave up.

Nate Nathaniel, on the other hand, had a calming influence on Lucius. They got along extremely well. I believe Nate genuinely admired my husband for his brilliance and his drive in business. But it was Ruth whom Nate had really adored. Ruth Beersman, the daughter of a prosperous accountant in Great Neck, Long Island, met Lucius during their sophomore year at New York University. Her father put up the seed money for Lucius's first business venture. Ruth, so I gathered from those who knew her, was a genuine do-gooder who was not much fun. According to Betty, she dressed "like a North Korean" and was "as heavy as a cheese fondue." But Ruth had been like a second mother to Nate—or so Lucius led me to believe—and Nate had taken her death very hard.

Lucius's own relationship with Nate was complex. I believe Lucius gave Nate the illusion of power, while Nate gave Lucius the illusion of gentility. They were extremely protective of each other—henchmen of the heart, so to speak. I suspected there was some deep bond between them that even I could not fathom, much less break. In the twenty years I'd been married to Lucius, I never dared say one word against Nate Nathaniel.

Nate visited us every Labor Day, but it occurred to me that he and Monique might get along, so I decided to invite him a little earlier. I somehow had it in my mind that if he and Monique hooked up, it would be a way of drawing her closer into the family. Nate gladly accepted my invitation to come out the following weekend.

5

ON a hot Friday afternoon in August, Nate sailed into the living room like a clipper ship, all smiles and breezy remarks, exuding a thick aura of houseguest charm. Dressed in pressed white ducks, tattered loafers, and a pastel pink T-shirt, he carried a canvas duffel bag from which the handle of a tennis racket protruded like an ax. Nate could be quite engaging when he chose to be, albeit in a cutting, preppy way. I learned from my ongoing contact with him that it's possible to dislike someone and still find them good company. But I was always very careful what I said around Nate.

"Traffic was murder"—*meurh-dah,* as he pronounced it in the exaggerated mid-Atlantic accent he cultivated. "Where do you want me, Lady Jo?"

"Third floor, blue room. Mrs. Mathilde will take your bag up."

He made a long face. "No guest house?"

"It's occupied."

"Oh-ho! Important company, have we? Who's here? Some royal-in-waiting, no doubt?" This was a sly reference to an occasion three summers ago when I'd bumped him from the guest house in favor of Nicky Brubetskoi, a relative of Tsar Nicholas II.

Nate was in the middle of fixing himself a gin and tonic when Monique, out of breath and glistening with the sweat of exercise, pranced into the room in skimpy running shorts and a tank top. He took one long look at her leggy conformation and that, as they say, was that. He trailed around her for the rest of the weekend like an assiduous hound. Not that it did him much good. She wasn't interested. She constantly referred to him as "that iguana in the pink shirt."

Nate's essence was indeed reptilian, but on the surface he was an attractive-looking man. He had thick sandy hair, marsh-colored eyes, and an impish air common to aging boys. People liked him, but they were wary of him. His tendency to ace snide comments into a conversation put them off. Nevertheless, he was smart, rich, and amusing in a world sorely lacking in eligible men.

Monique's indifference and often downright rudeness to Nate failed to deter him. Throughout the weekend he tried to engage her attention, regaling her ad nauseam with anecdotes about his two appearances on *Court TV,* offering to take her to hear a case in the Supreme Court, inviting her to go swimming, play tennis, take a jog, anything to get her alone.

She finally took him up on his offer to play backgammon. She fixed the stakes: five dollars a point. She and Nate played a round-robin tournament with Lucius out by the pool. Monique was proficient at the game and lucky with the dice. A subtle toughness crept over her when she gambled. She was so good that Nate joked she could make a living at it. She won game after game. Lucius clenched his jaw and squirmed in his chair every time he lost. Nate's cool gambler imitation was unsuccessful. He didn't like losing any more than Lucius did.

When Monique finally beat both men, winning close to three hundred dollars, it seemed to heighten Nate's ardor. She got up and excused herself. Nate ran after her. I watched the two of them strolling across the lawn, laughing and talking. I was somewhat surprised she was acting so friendly toward him all of a sudden, given all the things she'd said about him to me behind his back.

"Do we think Nate has found true love?" I said casually to Lucius.

He glared at me. "What the hell are you talking about?"

"Nothing." I was surprised by the vehemence of his reaction. "He just seems quite taken with Monique, that's all. He's been following her around all weekend. Haven't you noticed?"

"Why don't you mind your own damn business, Jo?"

"What on earth's the matter with you?" I said, perplexed. "You love Nate and you like Monique. I should think you'd be delighted if they got together."

"Quit matchmaking."

"She needs to meet someone."

"Why?"

"So she can stay in New York."

"Why can't she stay in New York anyway?"

"I don't think she wants to live with us for the rest of

her life—although I wouldn't mind, I must say. It's wonderful having her here."

He looked at me rather oddly, I thought. "You really like her, don't you?"

"What a question. Of course I like her. Why? Don't you?"

"I guess," he said tentatively.

"I thought you really enjoyed her company. Even though I know you don't like getting fleeced at backgammon. How much do you owe her now?"

I knew he wasn't listening to me. He heaved a weary sigh and said: "Are you sorry we never had a child, Jo?"

Now I really was taken aback. "Where on earth did *that* come from?" I asked him.

"I don't know. I've been watching you two together. You'd have made a good mother."

I was utterly nonplussed. "Contrary to what you may think, I'm not really old enough to be her mother, thanks very much."

"I wish I'd been a better father to Little Lucius," he said.

"It's not too late." I edged myself down next to him on the lounge chair.

I'd never heard him like this. Usually when an introspective thought got loose in the room, Lucius swatted it like a fly.

I stroked his fine white hair and gazed into his troubled eyes, trying to fathom the cause of his mood.

He looked down, tilting his head away from my caress. "When you think of all the rotten things that can happen to kids in this world . . ."

"What's the matter, sweetheart?"

"Nothing . . . nothing's the matter." He sighed deeply. "I was just thinking, that's all . . . Do me a favor, will you? Quit butting your head into other people's business, Jo."

"What do you mean?"

"Quit matchmaking for starters."

"Oh, come *on*. Monique says she wants to meet someone and I just thought it was amusing the way Nate's been following her around, that's all. I mean, honestly. Aren't I allowed to make an observation?"

"Look, I'm tired. I need a nap," he said, rising with some effort.

I stood up and tried to help him to his feet. "I'll take you upstairs."

He stuck his hand out in front of him, palm toward me, so I backed off. "Quit fussing," he said.

"Fine. I just thought it would be nice to walk with you, that's all."

He stood up and pulled his shirt down over his shorts, smoothing out the wrinkles. "One day soon you and I need to sit down and have a serious talk," he said.

I cocked my head to one side. "What about?"

"I don't know. Values."

"What about them?"

"Just . . ." He started to say something, then stopped out of sheer frustration. "Nothing . . . Never mind."

I watched Lucius as he hobbled on up to the house. He was acting mighty strangely. I attributed his mood to fatigue and too much sun and didn't dwell on it until the following morning when Lucius summoned me to the library.

He was sitting on the couch, wearing a white polo

shirt, his thin white legs protruding from a pair of loose-fitting shorts like two sticks of kindling. His hands were folded across the top of the sleek gold-capped mahogany cane he sometimes used for support when he walked. Caspar stood in front of the window, gazing into space as usual, his arms folded across his muscular torso.

"Sit down," Lucius said to me as I entered. "We need to discuss something."

I sat down warily. Lucius handed me a letter. It was from Edmond Norbeau, the director of the Municipal Museum.

> *Dear Jo,*
>
> *Just a note to let you know that the marvelous Fragonard painting we viewed together some months ago has now become available for purchase, as you hoped. We have just completed negotiations with the owner. I thought you'd be delighted to know that your pledge of one million dollars has made this acquisition possible. As always, you are a generous friend.*
>
> *Please give my best to Lucius. I hear he's making a splendid recovery. Christine and I look forward to seeing you both when we return from our travels in September.*
>
> *With fondest regards,*
>
> *Edmond*

"What about it?" I asked, handing it back to him.

"Where are you getting the money to honor this pledge?"

"Where I always get it. From you," I said.

"Not this year. I really don't want to do it this year."

"Why not?"

"I just don't."

"Lucius, are you in some sort of financial difficulties?"

"Not at all. I just don't want to do it. We've given them enough."

I let out an involuntary guffaw. "But that's ridiculous! I have no money of my own."

"Then I suggest you call Edmond and tell him that before he goes ahead and gets the picture."

I was incredulous. "Sweetie, I'm sure it's too late. You read the letter."

"I'm sorry, Jo. It's not my problem," he said, putting the letter aside. He slid the glasses he had perched on the top of his forehead down near the tip of his nose, picked up the newspaper, and started reading.

I sat and stared at him, open-mouthed, for a long moment.

"Lucius, am I missing something here? Is this supposed to be our conversation about values?" I said, recalling our odd discussion out by the pool. "Because if it is, I think honoring a pledge is about the most basic value there is. It's a debt of honor."

He looked at me over the tops of his glasses.

"That's your business, Jo. This is your deal. It's always been your deal—"

"Oh now, that's not true and you know it!"

"Sure it is. You know what? I woke up this morning and said, fuck it. My priorities are all screwed up. Instead of supporting paintings, I'd like to support people for a change."

"You can do that if you want. I think that's great. But this is a long-standing pledge. I'm on the board. This year we have to honor it, that's all."

"No."

"What do you mean, *no?*"

"I want to give money to some of the unfashionable charities for a change. Okay? End of subject," he said, screening himself with the newspaper.

The charitable and institutional world in New York, like Caesar's Gaul, can be divided into three parts: fashionable, unfashionable, and indeterminate. The fashionable institutions are the grand old ones that deal with art, music, and culture, like the New York Public Library, the Metropolitan Museum, the Museum of Modern Art, the Metropolitan Opera, the New York City Ballet, Carnegie Hall, and, of course, the Municipal Museum. Unfashionable institutions, which are too numerous to mention, deal with human beings and their problems, like poverty, substance abuse, disease, and education. Indeterminate charities, which encompass all the rest, are all those dealing with animals, minor museums, and small dance and theater companies. Occasionally, an unfashionable charity will come into fashion if the right people become associated with it. Of late, this has been true of breast cancer, dogs, and AIDS. Lucius's reference to unfashionable charities was an allusion to Ruth, who was active in hospice care—a sphere, by the way, that Lucius sorely detested when I met him. He longed for the glitter and prominence of the fashionable world.

It was inconceivable to me that he was serious.

"Lucius," I said after a time, "next year your money can go to the moon, for all I care. But this year, we have to honor our pledge."

"Your pledge. You honor it," he said from behind the newspaper.

It was all I could do to remain calm. "If we don't honor the pledge, I'll have to resign from the board. And when word gets out, it'll be quite a scandal."

"I don't really care."

"Lucius, would you mind putting the paper down so we can talk about this rationally?" He lowered the newspaper slowly. "What don't you care about?" I continued. "The fact that it would be a scandal or that I would be personally humiliated?"

He was staring at me with a vacant, sullen expression. I had no idea what he was thinking. I went on, occasionally biting my lower lip to contain my rising anger.

"If I renege, it's just the same as if you did, you know. I pledge money every year. They all know it comes from you . . . Look, sweetie, what's this really about? Are you upset with me about something? Is there something going on here I don't know about?" I heard my voice cracking from the strain. Lucius turned his head and looked out the window.

"Lucius, look at me, for heaven's sake!" I was beginning to lose my temper now. "What's this all about?"

He turned sharply and pinned me with his gaze. "What's it about? What's it about?" he cried, sounding like a macaw. "It's about *things,* Jo, *things.* You care more for *things* than you do for me. Our life is stuffed to the gills with objects, paintings, furniture, pledges . . . *Things.* I'm so fucking sick of *things!*" He raked his hand through his hair and stared out the window again.

I really thought he'd gone mad. We both knew that our collection brought pleasure and knowledge to thousands of people every year. The Slater Gallery was a shared legacy and in many ways the child we never had. It was our contribution to posterity. And although Lucius liked to downplay it, affecting an offhand attitude about its immense monetary value and its historical significance in order to appear grand, he wasn't kidding me.

Through the Slater Gallery, Lucius proclaimed his worth and taste to the world without having to say a word. When he'd been married to Ruth no one had ever heard of him. Now he was a king, in no small part thanks to me. If I had used his money, he had used my eye. It was a very successful partnership. I couldn't, for the life of me, understand this outburst.

"God only knows what's gotten into you," I said, rising. "But if I have to hock everything in this house, we're going to honor that pledge."

"The hell with it. Never mind," he said dismissively.

"What does that mean? Are you going to honor it or not?"

He heaved a weary sigh. "Yes."

"Promise?"

He grunted and went back to his paper. I gave him a hug. "Don't scare me like that, sweetheart. Next year you can decide where the money goes."

Later on, when I thought about this encounter, I marveled at how Lucius had managed to manipulate me. He had made me grateful for something that was a given in our life.

6

LATER that week, June invited me over for tea. I was relieved to get out of the house. Lucius's erratic behavior was exhausting me. It was a damp day. We sat in the library, where June had lit a fire. The house was like a Madison Avenue antiques shop, cluttered with gilt furniture, overstuffed couches, and expensive bric-a-brac—to my mind, nothing like a beach house ought to be. Clara always said that the definition of real elegance is the appropriate made supremely comfortable. June's house was inappropriately grand even by Southampton standards. But she adored it.

"Betty and I had a long talk this morning," June began as she poured the herbal tea she swore by, which smelled like manure. She handed me a cup. "She made me promise not to say anything, *but* I really think I have to talk to you, Jo—as a friend."

I braced myself.

"Jo, dear, this may be kill the messenger, but I think you should know what's being said," she began.

"Okay."

Her face contorted with concern. This was obviously difficult for her.

"Jo . . . How well do you know Monique?"

Uh-oh, here it comes. Having suspected for some time that Betty and June were jealous of my close friendship with the Countess, I put down my cup and folded my arms across my chest defensively. "What do you mean?"

"Well, I don't know if you know this or not, but the reason Betty got rid of her is because she made a pass at Gil."

"Betty told you that, did she?"

"She did. She overheard Monique propositioning Gil."

June studied my face for a reaction. Far be it from me to betray a confidence, however. I just sat there, trying to look sphinxlike, saying nothing.

"I must say, you don't seem surprised," June said, probing.

"Well, I think it's a pretty awful story if it's true."

June narrowed her eyes. "Okay. What did she tell you. . . ? Come on. Monique obviously told you something. What did she say?"

"Nothing," I lied.

June put down her cup. "Jo! We've been friends for too long. I know when you're lying. Come on."

It was no use trying to escape from June. "Well, isn't it just possible that Betty may have misinterpreted the situation?"

June scowled and shook her head. "Oooh! She's such a manipulating so-and-so, that one! I'll bet she told you Gil made a pass at *her*." I was silent. "She did, didn't she? And that's because she knew you were going to hear the truth from one of us eventually so she covered her damn tracks!" June was seething.

"And Betty's never been known to exaggerate, I suppose."

June looked at me intently. "Jo, who are you going to believe? Betty and me or someone you've known for five minutes? Wake *up!* She's a viper. Don't you have *any idea* what's going on?"

"No. Enlighten me."

"Jo, you know I love you—"

"Please do not preface malice with affection. Just spit it out, June." I was pissed.

"Okay," she said curtly. "Monique and Lucius."

I bridled for an instant. "What about them?"

"Everyone knows they're having an affair."

I guffawed. "Well, it's the first *I've* heard of it."

"No doubt," June said primly picking up her cup. "Betty and I debated whether or not to tell you. But then I thought if it were Charlie, I'd want to know. My advice to you is to get her out of there A.S.A.P."

I shook my head in mild amusement. It was no fun being the target of slander, I grant you, but I knew it was all summer doldrums bullshit so I could afford to have a little fun with her.

"Actually, we're having a ménage à trois, June. That's what's really going on."

June sighed in exasperation. "You think this is funny, Jo. It's not. You better watch out."

I turned serious. "Look, June, for one thing, they don't have the chance. Trust me. They're never alone together.

Caspar's always with Lucius. I'm usually with Monique. This is a silly malicious rumor concocted by a lot of bored gossips who are obviously depressed that Dick Bromire hasn't been indicted yet so they can have something really juicy to talk about."

June sipped her tea with a self-righteous air. "Fine. Have it your way, Jo. But don't say I didn't warn you."

"And June, the truth is that Monique is much more *my* friend. She and Lucius barely speak to one another."

This time June put down her cup so hard it rattled. "Jo! That's it! Don't you know that one of the best ways to tell when two people are having an affair is when they stop speaking to each other in public?"

I was exasperated. "June, they are *not* having an affair. You wanna get down to brass tacks? Listen to me: Lucius isn't *capable*. Get it? And even if he were, he wouldn't risk it. He could die."

"Very well," she said. "Sorry I mentioned it."

"Me, too, believe me."

Not one to ever let a subject drop, she added under her breath—just loud enough so I'd hear it: " 'There are none so blind as those who will not see.' "

Her persistence made me furious. "Remember back a couple of months ago when everyone thought Monique and I were having an affair?" I reminded her. "People were calling us lesbitrinas or some such charming epithet, I believe?"

June shrugged off the suggestion. "Well, that was utterly ridiculous. And I told everyone so."

"Right. Fine. So is this!"

June raised her eyebrows and pursed her lips, looking at me with a pious obstinacy that further fueled my wrath.

"Monique is a wonderful person and a very, very good friend to me," I went on sternly. "She's been extremely supportive of me all summer. You think it's easy living with an invalid? Lucius is sick and scared and he's in a foul mood most of the time, threatening me with God knows what. Where the hell have you and Betty been?"

"Now that's not fair!" she snapped. "We've both called you a million times. You put us off! You're always with *her*."

I pointed an accusatory finger at June. "And that's what this is *really* about, isn't it? You're jealous of my friendship with Monique. Well, I've got news for you. So is Lucius! You have no idea how he's been acting. The whole bunch of you are just jealous!"

June dismissed the accusation with a little wave of her hand.

"Rubbish," she said. "That woman is really bad news and she's definitely *not* your friend, Jo."

I stared hard at her. "What about you, June? You think telling me my husband's having an affair with another woman is a friendly act?"

"I'm very sorry I did it," she said. "I thought it was for your own good."

I rose from my chair, walked to the door, and turned back just as I was about to leave. "Remember the proverbial road to hell, June?"

I let my words hang in the air for a moment. Then I stalked out.

I got into my car and slammed the door hard. I caught a glimpse of myself in the rearview mirror. My face was flushed with anger. To my mind, June was a prying busybody, stirring up trouble for no reason.

There are two opposing schools of thought on whether you should tell a friend if you suspect her husband is having an affair. One is, you should; the other is, you shouldn't. I firmly believe in the latter simply because people are more married than you think. There are those who simply may not wish to know if they are being cheated on. Or there are those who actually *do* know they are being cheated on but don't wish to be publicly confronted with the fact. And, last but not least, there are those, like myself, who neither think nor know they are being cheated on, and who view the teller of such tales as a mischievous, misinformed gossip.

—⁓—

IT was close to five when I pulled into my driveway. All the regular cars were there, except Caspar's because it was his day off. I trotted up the front porch steps into the house. The front hall was silent save the heavy ticking of the grandfather clock on the landing. The dampness of the day cast a gray pall over the interior. There was a chill in the air.

I thumbed through the pile of mail that was stacked, as usual, on a silver tray on the round hall table. Mrs. Mathilde entered from the pantry carrying a large glass vase filled with colorful flowers. The old Jamaican housekeeper gave me a welcoming smile.

"Afternoon, Mrs. Slater."

"Hello, Mrs. Mathilde. Have you seen Countess de Passy?"

"No, ma'am." Her tone turned icy whenever I mentioned Monique. She set the vase down on the hall table and stepped back to admire the arrangement.

"Is Mr. Slater around?"

"I haven't seen him, ma'am."

I refused her offer to make me a cup of tea. I walked back outside over to the guest cottage in search of Monique. The little house was deserted. A lead-colored sky threatened rain. An eerie stillness gripped the atmosphere. Where is everyone, I wondered?

I snaked back around to the pool.

There was an odd sound, not quite the cry of a bird . . .

It came again—a little stab of a scream, lost in the air. Where was it coming from?

I listened closely, heard nothing more, and walked on until a succession of small sounds caught my attention. I tracked them to their source: the pool house, my little columned Palladian folly with a large patio and changing rooms on either side in back, one for men, one for women. Hand-painted porcelain plaques hung on the separate entrances, reading *Rois* and *Reines*, respectively.

I cupped my ear to the door of the *Rois* changing room where I heard rhythmic low grunts, like the beating of a tom-tom or an animal trapped inside. I opened the door cautiously, recalling the rabid raccoon that had been trapped inside there a few summers ago. It was very dim inside. My eyes took a couple of seconds to adjust to the light. Then I recognized Lucius standing naked with nothing but a towel around his waist.

"*Jo!*" he cried in a strangled whisper.

"Sorry, sweetheart, I didn't realize—"

I stopped short, realizing he was not alone. Someone else was in that tiny room. Behind him stood Monique, who was just closing her white terrycloth robe.

"What's going on?" I heard myself say. "Monique?" She looked away.

At that point, Lucius reached out to me and touched my hand. But at the moment of contact he sort of lurched back and grabbed his chest with both hands, his features suddenly twisting in pain like a corkscrew. He crumpled to the floor coughing and gasping for air. His towel fell away.

"*Can't breathe . . . Can't breathe . . .*" he cried, heaving and writhing on the cold blue tiles.

I swooped down and cradled him in my arms. He clutched at my clothing, clawing my blouse, pulling me in close and wheezing something between gasps that I couldn't understand but which sounded like, "Give me . . ." Fear and apology flickered in his eyes, which quickly grew teary from all the wheezing, bulging grotesquely out from their sockets. His face turned livid as he gasped more desperately for air.

I looked up and screamed at Monique. "*Get help! Call an ambulance!*"

I can still see her standing above me in her white robe, arms crossed, looking down at the two of us, emotionless, as if we were specimens in a jar. I suddenly realized she had no intention of helping me, so I leapt up from the floor, bolted out the door, and fled around the corner to the main pool house to call 911.

"*My husband's having a heart attack! We need an ambulance!*" I screamed into the phone.

I gave the operator the details. My whole body was shaking by the time I put down the phone. Assured that help was on the way, I ran back into the dressing room where I was greeted by an eerie quiet. Lucius lay sprawled out on the blue tile floor like a great white shark, eyes wide and glassy, mouth open, expression gone. I stopped abruptly when I saw him, then looked at Monique.

"Is he—?"

She shrugged.

I stared down at my husband for a long time, unwilling or unable to comprehend that he was dead.

I lay down beside him on the floor and rested my head against his. My tears mingled with his cold perspiration.

"Oh, Lucius, Lucius . . ." I sobbed softly. "Don't leave me. Please don't leave me . . ."

When I looked up, Monique was gone.

7

LUCIUS was taken to the Southampton hospital where he was pronounced dead on arrival. I was shattered by his death and couldn't accept the fact that the man I had loved and shared my life with for twenty years was suddenly gone. I felt his spirit all around me, my mind constantly drifting back over the time we'd spent together. During those blurry, wearying days, I mourned Lucius deeply, unable or unwilling to admit what I had seen. Mrs. Mathilde stopped crying long enough to inform me that Caspar had helped Monique clear all of her things out of the guest house just after the ambulance arrived. The Countess had left in a taxi. No one knew where she went.

In piecing together the fragments of that puzzling picture in the pool house I denied the obvious, despite my conversation with June. It was impossible for me to believe that I had been deceived by the two people I loved most in the world—especially Lucius. Trying to come to terms with the emptiness of my life without my husband was a terrible enough thing without imagining he had betrayed me. I kept telling myself there had to be a rational explanation as to why the two of them were in that little changing room together half naked.

The flurry of activity inevitably following any death took my mind off that unpleasant subject for a time. As word spread, a host of friends and *amis mondains* dropped by the house to condole with me. Ethan rang from Patmos to say he was cutting short his vacation and flying home to comfort me. Betty, June, and the Bromires took turns staying in the house, fielding the endless calls from all over the world. I found it vaguely surreal that all the same people who had come to celebrate my birthday two months before were now calling me to find out when Lucius's funeral was.

Over the next few days, with the help of June, Betty, Trish, and Trebor Bellini, who drove out from the city to do the flowers, I threw myself into the planning of Lucius's funeral. I expressly didn't want to make it a social event, but in New York, death takes on a life of its own. People were anxious to be involved, to show how close they were to me and to Lucius by participating in the service, or at least by getting a good seat in the church. I had to make sure no one was left out and that no one's feelings got hurt.

Lucius was not a spiritual man, in any sense of the word. A motley religious background—Jewish mother, Catholic father—had left him an avowed atheist. He had often told me he wanted to be buried with no fanfare whatsoever in one of the five plots he had purchased twenty years before in the Southampton Cemetery. But funerals are for the living, not for the dead. For my own peace of mind, and for the sake of his friends, I wanted to put my husband to rest with a dignified ceremony.

Little Lucius and his wife, Rebecca, traveled up from Florida. I had told Little Lucius on the phone that his father had died of a heart attack, period. I didn't go into details.

The couple arrived in a dusty rental car with two trail bikes strapped to the back and a surfboard tied on top. When they got out of the car, Little Lucius stepped forward to hug me. He'd never done that before, having always viewed me as an interloper, another obstacle between himself and the father who had never loved him. The change in his attitude made me teary. I sensed he was making an effort toward me because his father's death had lifted a heavy burden from his shoulders. At last he was his own man. Rebecca, too, was very friendly. I put them in the guest house vacated by Monique.

I hadn't seen Little Lucius since March when he came up to see his father in the hospital. He looked exactly the same as he always did: medium height with small shoulders and wide hips, almost like a woman's, brown hair like a brush, a wiry beard, and a generally rumpled appearance. I was not surprised to see him dressed in a colorful Hawaiian shirt and baggy pants. That was his uniform.

Sartorially challenged as he was, he was a commendable soul. The thirty-nine-year-old man had inherited his late mother's looks as well as her devotion to duty and civic-mindedness. He was a marine biologist who spent his free time teaching Miami schoolchildren about the importance of sea life to the environment.

Rebecca was tall and slim and angular, reminiscent of a Modigliani painting. Becky, as everyone called her, was also a worthy person. She worked as a guidance counselor, helping bright children from underprivileged families obtain college scholarships.

The three of us had dinner together the night before the funeral. Little Lucius spoke more that night than he had in the twenty years I'd known him. At the end of the meal, I broke down in tears and told him how much I missed his father. He replied: "I've missed him all my life."

—m—

ON the morning of September 9, the Sacred Hearts of Jesus and Mary Church in Southampton was filled almost to capacity. Two huge bouquets of white flowers flanked the altar. Once again, people had flown in from all over the world to pay their last respects to one of the uncrowned kings of New York. The aggregate net worth of the individuals there could have paid off the national debt.

Ethan arrived from Patmos, looking tan and fit. Rebecca showed up dressed in sandals, a turquoise shift covered with teensy dolls made of multicolored threads, and dangly silver earrings. Betty whispered to me: "What's with that outfit? She looks like a high school teacher on sabbatical in Cuernavaca." A little later on, Betty observed that Little Lucius, portly, pear-shaped, and as colorfully dressed as his wife, reminded her of "a piñata."

The service was short by any standards—only two eulogies, one given by Gil Waterman, the other by

Charlie Kahn. They both spoke briefly and surprisingly eloquently about the man who had been their good friend. Janina Jones, the great soprano, who just happened to be spending the weekend with some friends in Southampton, sang Verdi's "Pace, pace, Dio Mio," and Cole Porter's "Night and Day," which was Lucius's and my favorite song. Little Lucius was conspicuously dry-eyed throughout the proceedings.

I vaguely wondered why Monique hadn't shown up. As the choir sang, "In Paradiso" from Fauré's *Requiem,* my mind wandered. I kept thinking back to the pool house. What else could they have been doing, I wondered? Was there another explanation? He was practically naked. She had on a bathrobe. If she's innocent, why isn't she here?

As I sat there surrounded by my friends and *amis mondains,* a new sensation cut through my mind like a shark's fin appearing out of the depths of the ocean—a twinge of deep anger.

—◊◊◊—

LUCIUS was buried under a shade tree in one of the plots he had purchased in the Southampton Cemetery. As on the day he died, the sky was gray and overcast; a good storm was needed to clear the air. Afterward, the graveside mourners, who consisted of me, Little Lucius, Rebecca, the Watermans, the Kahns, the Bromires, and Ethan, went back to the house, where we were joined by all those who had been at the church. Lucius would have approved, I'm sure. He always liked a good party. I had Alain prepare a big buffet and all manner of tea sandwiches, particularly the tomato ones Lucius loved. But everyone was more interested in the booze. People drank champagne and talked and laughed and generally forgot that it was a somber occasion.

Monique's absence was lost on no one. I believe it was Betty who first broached the subject in her inimitably tactful way: "So where in hell's the dear Cuntess in your hour of need?" she said, wolfing down three tea sandwiches at once.

"She left," I said.

With an eye to protecting my own dignity as well as Lucius's, I didn't want people to know the real circumstances under which he had died. My story was simply that he had had a heart attack in the swimming pool changing room and that the ambulance arrived too late to revive him. Period.

Nobody believed me, of course, least of all Betty and June, who suspected something much more ghastly had happened by the reserved way I was acting toward them. In a situation like that, one longs to confide in one's friends, but I knew if I didn't keep my mouth shut tight it would be all over Southampton that Lucius had died *in flagrante* and there would be so many embellishments to the story that I would soon hear I had actually walked in on them going at it on the floor.

—∞—

SURE enough, less than a week later, June and Betty and I were having lunch at my house when June, genetically incapable of keeping gossip to herself, blurted out: "Jo, how come you didn't tell us you walked in on them going at it on the floor?"

"And just where did you hear *that*?" I said, nearly choking on my salad.

"It's all around town," Betty said, as she poured herself a third glass of white wine. "The old horn toad."

I knew they were guessing but I was too exhausted to keep up a front. Having gradually accustomed myself to the sordid truth, I no longer cared about protecting Lucius's dignity, or my own, for that matter. For the rest of lunch, I told June and Betty in hushed tones exactly what had happened, careful to stop talking whenever the servants came in to clear our places, though I suspected they knew everything.

"Look, I can't be absolutely sure of what was going on. I certainly didn't walk in on them going at it on the floor," I said. "But the more I think about it, the more I believe you girls were right. I mean, June, you told me that very afternoon they were having an affair under my nose and I simply couldn't conceive of it. Then, of course, I came back home and discovered them in the pool house. But the funny thing is, even then, I still didn't believe it, you know?"

June, obviously thrilled with her timing plus having the satisfaction of her worst gossip confirmed, refrained from saying, "I told you so."

"Well, you believe it now, don't you?" Betty said.

"I guess so. It's hard. Very hard."

"God, Jo, don't you wonder how long it had been going on, or when it started?" June asked.

I pushed away my plate, folded my napkin, and stood up from the table.

"*No*. It's time to move on. Let's go have coffee." I saw no point dwelling on the matter.

June and Betty followed me into the sunroom.

"I guess I should have known it was all too good to be true," I said, pouring the coffee.

"And too true to be good," Betty added.

———m———

TEN days after that, in late September, I was back in New York, sitting by the window in the library of my apartment overlooking Fifth Avenue, watching the midmorning traffic below, waiting for Nate Nathaniel to arrive. Nate, along with the National Trust Bank, was the executor of Lucius's will. Nate said he had something he needed to discuss with me concerning the estate.

I was dressed all in black to proclaim a bereavement that, in truth, was now sullied by anger. I'd had ample opportunity to reflect on the sordid circumstances of Lucius's death. The images of my husband's fatal last moments played over in my mind more like film clips than actual memories. Piecing them together and imagining what had gone on under my nose all summer and, indeed, just prior to my unexpected entrance into the changing room made me hark back again and again to June's famous last words to me at tea: "There are none so blind as those who will not see." My anger now was focused far more on Monique than Lucius. I felt she had led him down an evil path and that he, frightened by his brush with death, had been too weak or too vain to resist her wiles.

My apartment, on the fifteenth floor of one of the most sought-after co-op buildings in the city, afforded me a spectacular view of Fifth Avenue and of Central Park. I stared down at the trees, spread out like a mottled cloak stretching to the horizon. The days would be growing noticeably shorter soon. Summer was ending in more ways than one, I thought to myself, as I contemplated the mighty chapter of my own life that was coming to a close. Fall was my favorite time in New York. I always looked forward to the opening of the opera, the ballet, the concerts at Carnegie Hall, and all the festivities commencing the new season. I wondered how well I would cope with widowhood.

I was playing with the idea of taking a short trip to clear my head—to some out-of-the-way place I'd always wanted to go to, like Angkor Wat or Petra—when Mrs. Mathilde came in and announced the arrival of Mr. Nathaniel.

Nate followed close behind her carrying a briefcase. He was wearing a dark three-piece suit and an even darker expression. He put the briefcase down, glided across the room, took both my hands in his, and planted a kiss on my cheek. It was a warmer greeting than he had ever given me. He looked somberly into my eyes and said: "Jo, you're so brave. We need to talk."

His maudlin and overly solicitous manner irritated me. For one thing, now that Lucius was dead, we would soon be rid of each other. From everything I had intuited over the past twenty years, our parting of the ways would suit Nate as handily as it suited me. What use was there in keeping up the charade for a ghost, I wondered?

"Let's get this over with, shall we?" I said, motioning him to the pair of red velvet chairs flanking the fireplace. He sat down on one, I on the other. He propped his elbows on the armrests and folded his hands in an ersatz prayer position in front of him, touching the tip of his nose with his fingers. He stared down at the floor for a long moment, apparently lost in thought.

"Where to begin . . . Where to begin," he said.

I was just anxious to conclude our business as I had a lunch date with an old friend from Europe.

"Can you give me a rough idea of when things will be settled?" I said, ignoring his dramatic behavior. "I'm thinking of taking a trip. God knows I need a change of scene."

"Yes . . . Yes . . . I can understand that." He looked up suddenly and pinned me with his gaze. "Jo . . . How strong a person are you?"

The question startled me. "Given the last two weeks? Call me Atlas. Why?"

"Because you need to prepare yourself for a shock."

"*Another* one? Gee, thanks."

"This one may be worse."

"Don't tell me I've been disinherited," I said lightly.

Nate winced with surprise. I looked at him harder.

"Nate . . . Don't joke with me."

He continued staring at me, shaking his head slightly from side to side. I felt my insides slowly crumbling before I realized I couldn't catch my breath.

"What? No. Come *on*. You're not *serious*."

I saw his head bobbing up and down and from that point on, everything seemed to be happening in slow motion. I sat stunned. Nate rose from his chair, walked to the corner where he'd put his briefcase, picked it up, and returned to his seat. He rested the case on his knees, flicked open the locks with marked precision, lifted the cover, pulled out a pale blue folder, and handed it to me. On the front in black letters was typed: LAST WILL AND TESTAMENT OF LUCIUS SLATER. I took the folder from his hand and opened it. Inside was a typewritten, two-page will, with the signatures of Lucius and three witnesses at the bottom.

"This is it? This is the will? This is *not* the will, Nate. I've seen Lucius's will. It looks like a novel, for Christ's sake, it's so thick! Clearly, there's been a mistake," I said, fairly tossing the document back at him.

He made a nimble catch, then proffered it to me once more. I refused to touch it.

"No mistake, Jo," he said, continuing to hold it out. "Lucius typed the will out himself at home and went to Kevin Sullivan a couple of days before he died. Kevin's an excellent lawyer. I've used his office out there many times to notarize things. It's a short document but it's typed and properly witnessed and, unfortunately for you, absolutely legal. Don't think I haven't checked."

I finally took the folder back and opened it. But when I attempted to read what was written, the print blurred in front of my eyes. I couldn't concentrate. I felt light-headed. The whole world was turning a hazy silver color.

"I . . . I can't . . . just tell me what it says."

Nate stared at me with a deeply chagrined expression on his face.

"Basically, it divides the estate between his son, Lucius Slater, Jr., and . . ." he hesitated.

"Charity?" I said, thinking back to the conversation I had with Lucius about my pledge to the Muni and his wish to donate his money to other causes.

"No."

"Oh my God. Who? . . . Who, Nate, *who?*"

Nate exhaled fiercely. "Countess Monique de Passy," he said softly.

I was too dumbfounded to utter a sound. Nate shook his head slowly from side to side, saying over and over: "I'm so sorry, Jo. I'm so sorry. I don't know what to say. I'm just so sorry . . ."

I continued to stare at him, uncomprehending. What does this mean? How can this be?

The scene in the changing room suddenly burst into my mind more vividly than ever. She killed him. Monique killed him. She got him to change his will and then she killed him. The lovemaking was all a setup to make him die.

I rose from my chair, and the second I was on my feet I was seized by a terrible nauseating dizziness. My knees buckled. Everything went black. I fainted.

8

THE next morning, I was awakened by a sound of soft insistent knocking on my door. I opened my eyes. I was in bed in my nightgown. The curtains were drawn. My head felt like a ball of lead. I vaguely remembered that a doctor had come and given me a sedative. I must have slept all night. Mrs. Mathilde entered the room, bringing me breakfast on a tray as usual. She informed me in her lilting Caribbean accent that "Mr. Natan-E-Ell," as she pronounced his name, had just arrived. I didn't even bother to get dressed. I leapt up, threw on a robe, and raced downstairs.

Nate was strolling around the living room. It was a bright sunny morning, unfortunately. I was in no mood for light. I felt like a vampire eager to return to my coffin and close the lid. Even the gilt on the furniture hurt my eyes. I called to him and asked him to come into the darker "fumoire," as I jokingly referred to the smoking room. He followed me into the room that housed Lucius's cigars in a giant temperature-controlled humidor in the closet. Though the room hadn't been used all summer, it still held a faint aroma of cigar smoke. The brown hand-tooled Moroccan leather walls gave the space a nice cavelike atmosphere even in the daytime—which perfectly suited my mood. Nate and I made ourselves comfortable on two cushy leather chairs.

"How are you, Jo?" Nate said in a cloying tone of voice.

"Just great, Nate, and you?"

"Silly question. I'm sorry."

I picked obsessively at a worn patch of leather on the arm of the chair. Nate cleared his throat.

"I came here today to fill you in on a few things," he said. "First of all, the will stipulates that you have six months from Lucius's death to vacate these premises and the house in Southampton . . . "

"You don't think I have a case?"

"I don't."

I raked my hands through my hair. "Jesus, Nate . . . There must be *something* I can do. I was married to the man for twenty years, for Christ's sake! They can't just throw me out on the street, can they?"

"Well, in fact, they can. Because in the prenup, as you well know, you waived your right to elect against the estate."

"That was twenty years ago, Nate. *Twenty years.*"

"I know, Jo, but a contract is a contract."

"Yes, but you and I both know that Lucius promised to take care of me in his will. I mean, if I'd had any inkling something like this would happen—" My voice trailed off as I reflected on my own stupidity.

"What can I say, Jo? He broke his promise . . . Let me go on so you understand all the facts. Under the prenup, you're entitled to a million dollars."

"That's gone," I said with a dismissive little wave of my hand. "I've already pledged it to the Muni."

Nate leaned toward me. "Jo, you've given a fortune to that museum over the years. I'm sure they'll understand if you have to postpone your gift for the moment, or indeed, indefinitely."

"I can't renege on a pledge."

"But under the circumstances—"

I interrupted him. "It's not even a question, Nate. That museum is my life. I've pledged the money. Commitments have already been made . . . No . . . I can't go back on my word. I *won't* go back on my word."

"Well, that's your business," he said. "The will says nothing about jewelry, so you can keep that."

"At least I get to keep my necklace," I said with relief.

"Yes. You get to keep your necklace. Any work of art or piece of furniture worth over twenty thousand dollars belongs to the estate. We have to get the appraisers in. My coexecutor is the National Trust Bank, as you know. The estate is very large, Jo, the administration is very complex, and, frankly, it could take quite a while before the executors are in a position to satisfy your claim for the one million dollars you're entitled to under the prenup."

"When do I have to leave my apartment again?"

"Six months from September fourth, the day Lucius died."

"Why six months? Who says?"

"The will says."

"Even if it's not settled?"

"Jo, the clock started the day of his death. You have to clear out in March."

I got up and walked over to the window. "I'm going to fight this, Nate. I am. This is not right. If he'd left it to charity or to his son that's one thing, but . . ." I didn't even bother to finish the sentence. I was too exhausted. I stared down at the toy traffic on Fifth Avenue.

"I'm happy to give you the names of some excellent attorneys. But I know they're all going to tell you the same thing. You won't win. And you'll spend a fortune to lose."

I slumped against the windowsill, utterly defeated. "I never tried to change that prenuptial agreement on account of you, you know."

"I know . . . Jo, if it's any consolation to you, I'm appalled Lucius did this to you. I really am."

Barely hearing what he said, I went on talking in a monotone, mainly to myself.

"It was important to me that you both understood how much I loved him. I really did love him, you know. We were passionate about each other. I wanted to prove I didn't marry him for his money. I didn't marry him for his money. I really didn't. And so in the end it turns out I got just exactly what I'd bargained for. I didn't marry him for his money and he didn't leave it to me. But you know something, Nate? Now that he's cut me out of everything in favor of her, it feels different. I mean, it hurts. It's not just the money, it's the hurt . . . the betrayal."

I don't know precisely what prevented me from mentioning my suspicions about Monique to Nate at that time. Perhaps it was because I didn't fully trust him, or didn't fully trust myself. Who knows? But whatever the reason, I kept those dark thoughts to myself as I watched him prepare to leave.

"What can I say, Jo?" he said, standing at the door, briefcase in hand. "Except that I'm so, so sorry this happened to you of all people."

"Thank you, Nate. That makes two of us."

9

THERE was, of course, a hailstorm of publicity about the scandal. All the gossip columns were thrilled with the story since it proved how deeply dysfunctional the very rich were and once again reassured everyone that having money clearly isn't all it is cracked up to be.

Needless to say, *le tout New York* was on my side. I was assured both publicly and privately that Monique would be persona non grata wherever she went—even though she still hadn't surfaced. Given the circumstances, I honestly didn't expect it to be any other way. Even in these days of absurdly relaxed social standards, I was fairly confident that people would balk at the idea of having the scarlet Countess to dine, especially in light of the fact that I'd been so recently widowed. I decided to keep my hunch that she was a murderess to myself for the moment, sensing that such a wild accusation by me could backfire, both diluting my credibility and injuring my reputation.

On the will front, Nate referred me to a pit-bull lady lawyer by the name of Patricia McCluskey who had a summer house in Sagaponack. I called her up. She had a husky, cigarette-stained voice with a slight Brooklyn accent. She punctuated my abbreviated account of my predicament with "uh-huhs" and "yeahs," as if she were taking notes.

I was spending as much time as I could in Southampton, fearing everything was soon to be taken from me. McCluskey asked me if it would be convenient to meet her in the country. One Saturday afternoon in late October, I drove to her house near Bridge Lane. I brought all the documents Nate Nathaniel had left me.

McCluskey's house, a charming saltbox with weathered shingles and white trim, stood on a small patch of flat land that had once been part of a potato field. A few thin trees dotted the property. When I pulled into the square white gravel driveway, I saw a woman potting plants on the front porch. She looked up and waved, wiping her hands with a checked towel. She rose to greet me as I walked up the porch steps. "Patricia McCluskey," she said, shaking my hand.

She was shorter and frailer looking than I'd expected from her tough telephone voice. Wearing a flowered muumuu with a bandanna tied around her head, she looked more like a hausfrau than a slick attorney. But she had a hearty handshake and a sharp, shiny look in her eye.

"C'mon in," McCluskey said, ushering me into a light, airy living room with wooden floors, colorful area rugs, and serviceable modern furniture. A large pair of oil paintings depicting the local landscape hung on opposite walls. Opera music was playing on the stereo.

"*Don Giovanni,* one of my favorites," I said.

"I play it to remind myself what shits men are," McCluskey replied, turning down the volume.

She motioned me to sit down. She poured us two mugs of coffee from a stainless steel thermos.

"So now," she said, settling in, "let's see what's cooking."

I handed her the will and the prenuptial agreement. Her face hardened into full concentration as she examined the documents.

"Mind if I smoke?" I asked after a few minutes. I had taken up the habit again after years of abstinence.

"Blow it my way." Without looking up, she pushed a ceramic dish on the coffee table my way. I lit my cigarette and studied her as she read.

When she finished, she leaned back in her chair with a pensive expression, fashioning a little cathedral with her fingers.

"I'd have to study all this more closely, but for what it's worth, here's my initial reaction. The prenuptial agreement is well drafted. You were represented by competent counsel. There were no ambiguities and there was full disclosure. You voluntarily waived your rights of election against your husband's estate pursuant to statute, which, as you're well aware, means you get zip unless he makes you a beneficiary in his will."

"But he *did!* I *was* the principal beneficiary practically up until the day of his death when he changed it."

"People can change their wills, Mrs. Slater. And frequently do."

"But that's not fair! Look at that will, for God's sake. It's two pages long. Two miserable pages. His original will was thicker than *War and Peace.*"

"It's flimsy, but legal . . . Less is more in this case . . . Look, when you signed this agreement, you understood the extent of your husband's wealth and the rights you waived, did you not?"

"I guess."

"Then why did you sign it?"

"I wanted him to know I wasn't marrying him for his money."

"You got your wish."

"I trusted him."

"Why?"

"He promised he'd take care of me."

She looked at me in wonderment. "You're not a little girl, Mrs. Slater."

"Nate said it was standard practice."

"Ah, yes," she nodded, "Nate the Enforcer. We've done battle on many occasions . . . The fact is clauses like this one are written to protect the estate in case a man dies two weeks after marrying some bimbo. It's supposed to discourage murder."

"Or provoke it."

McCluskey laughed. "Be that as it may. You were represented by competent counsel. There was full disclosure of his assets. You knew your husband was very, very rich when you married him. You signed the agreement voluntarily. And I think a court would hold, under these circumstances, that an agreement is an agreement. A prenup is valid and binding, assuming there's full disclosure and representation by counsel if it's conscionable when the agreement is made and when it's sought to be enforced. Of course, you could make the argument that it's unconscionable now when it's being enforced. But you're still entitled to a million dollars, and most judges won't view that as a clothes allowance, I assure you. People have been left with far less . . . You have no children, right?"

"No. I wanted them but, well, I won't go into it. Lucius has a son from a previous marriage. They didn't get along. He got less than half the estate."

"Bottom line? As I just said, you can contest the prenup, Mrs. Slater, but in my opinion you won't win. Nate Nathaniel dots his I's twice. You'll get a million dollars but you could easily eat up most of that in legal fees. You don't know how a court will come out on any issue and you can certainly take a chance. But the law here is pretty settled and she's got a lot more money to fight you with. If I were you, I'd take the million dollars and move on with your life."

"The other problem is, I've already pledged a million dollars to the Municipal Museum. I have to pay it."

"Why?"

"It's a debt of honor."

She shrugged. "Honor seems fairly flexible these days."

"Not to me, Ms. McCluskey."

She gave a little nod of approval. "I applaud your integrity, but I'm afraid the courts don't take pledges into account."

—∞—

I consulted three other lawyers whose opinions were basically the same as McCluskey's—all except one, a known publicity hound with high-profile clients who told me he could definitely help me for a retainer fee of fifty thousand dollars. Under closer scrutiny, however, he refused to guarantee anything and, as I was leaving his office, asked me if he could issue a press release about our meeting. I said I would sue him if he dared.

—⁓—

MY last hope was Little Lucius. I just couldn't bear to see Monique wind up with everything. Lucius's only child was the logical choice to lead a suit against Monique. First, however, I had to find out where he stood.

Early one morning, I went to visit him in the Seward, a genteel, run-down hotel on upper Madison Avenue where he and Rebecca always stayed when they came to New York because it was comparatively cheap. Although I had invited him to stay with me, he refused. He never stayed with us in New York, even when his father was alive.

The hotel room, on a low floor overlooking Madison Avenue, was noisy and utterly without charm. White walls, graying with age, were a forlorn backdrop for the flimsy, faded chintz curtains framing two square windows with old-fashioned panes. The constant hum of street traffic was occasionally pierced by banshee sirens. Little Lucius was still in his bathrobe, lingering over coffee and the morning paper, when I arrived. He opened the door and informed me that Rebecca was out jogging in Central Park. He was uneasy and awkward from the start, offering me some coffee out of Rebecca's used cup.

I talked to him for a long time about the situation, begging him to take action against Monique. He was most unreceptive, stealing glances at the newspaper while I was making key points. I ignored his apathy and pressed on. It was inconceivable to me that Little Lucius was willing to let more than half his father's fortune pass into the hands of a scheming, gold-digging murderess.

"She planned the whole thing," I said in no uncertain terms. "She got your father to change his will, then she purposely aroused him knowing how weak his heart was. Even if you don't care about the money, don't you care about your father?"

Little Lucius, visibly ill at ease, broke the crust off a piece of toast on the plate in front of him. "I guess," he replied.

He popped the twig of crust into his mouth and washed it down with cold coffee, speaking as he chewed. "Frankly, though, Dad and I parted company long before he died. I mean, if he left her a lot of stuff, yunno, I guess that's how he wanted it."

"Don't you understand? She *knew* he was going to die."

Little Lucius cocked his head to one side, looking at me quizzically. "Yeah, well, sure . . . He had a weak heart."

"And she *knew* that."

My imploring gaze was met with blank indifference.

Finally, this poor, disheveled man rose to his feet, fumbling with his bathrobe. He walked to the door—an unsubtle hint. His familiar stutter, miraculously absent since his father's death, suddenly returned.

"Well, anyway, B-B-Becky and I have to get back to F-F-Florida. K-k-keep me p-p-po . . . Call me." He opened the door onto a dim mushroom-colored corridor.

I knew by the way he looked at me he wanted nothing more to do with the situation. The son's revenge on the tyrannical father who had been so tough on him all his life was simply not to give a damn whether he'd been killed or not. Lucius was dead. That was that. Too bad.

—∽∽∽—

I came to the wrenching decision that it would be fruitless and prohibitively costly for me to challenge the will. I now had ample time to reflect on the enormity of what had transpired. Had Lucius artfully hidden his real self from me under the rich fabric of our social life? Or was I somehow at fault? Had I simply ignored the signs of his discontent, thus paving the way for Monique to successfully seduce him?

I remembered my mother's words: "What they'll do to one, they'll do to another."

Lucius was capable of erotic obsession. I knew that only too well because I had once been a grand passion of his. The truth was that I had interrupted his marriage to Ruth in much the same way Monique had interrupted his marriage to me. Ruth, of course, had conveniently died, paving the way for me to marry him. Monique knew I would not be quite so obliging.

But why Monique? How had this little French hustler made him so gaga about her in two short months that he left her half his fortune?

Lucius was no fool. He was a canny, rich skinflint who shared his wealth only when it benefited him directly. Though he liked to be amused, he had a keen nose for sycophancy. Cautious and skeptical, he was contemptuous of those who tried to cash in on the perks of his position. This was the man who often told me: "A lot of people think money is catching—like a cold . . . I got news for them: I ain't contagious."

He was rarely generous unless he was sure his bounty would be rewarded in kind, but I simply refused to believe that the Countess's charms were worth more than two hundred million dollars.

So why her?

10

I went to pack up the Southampton house after the New Year. Driving out to the country with Mrs. Mathilde at my side, I felt terrible pangs of nostalgia, but the fact that it was mid-January took the edge off having to say good-bye to the property. When I pulled into the driveway I was almost relieved to find that the house, bathed in cold gray light, had a stark, unwelcoming appearance. The garden was barren except for the evergreens. Scattered over the dead, faded grass were patches of icy snow left over from a heavy storm the previous week. Even the charm of my precious guest cottage had withered under the spell of a harsh winter. Difficult as it was, I knew it would have been far more of an ordeal for me to quit the place during a season where the flowers were in bloom.

Aside from being a good organizer, Mrs. Mathilde was a sympathetic presence, the one person in the world I could trust. Her kindness and cheerful attitude made the packing up a great deal easier. Most of the things I took with me had little more than sentimental value. According to Nate, I was not supposed to remove anything from the house other than my clothes and personal effects. But I defied him or anyone else to deny me the flower drawings that hung in the library or my favorite Sèvres dessert plates, which had belonged to the Empress Eugénie. Together, Mrs. Mathilde and I wandered through years of memories, recalling the events that had taken place in that house as we sifted through what I now jokingly dubbed the "glorious rubble" of my past life. We even shared a few good laughs remembering some of the people I'd entertained and the funny things that had gone on. I thought, well, at least I'd had a wonderful time.

Everything had gone along smoothly under the circumstances until it came time for me to actually go into the guest cottage. Standing in front of that quaint little replica of "Le Hameau," its perfect proportions even more visible now that the wisteria and honeysuckle vines covering the façade were bare, my resolve suddenly failed. I couldn't bring myself to go in, particularly when I thought about who had lived there and what she had done to me and how she would soon be the mistress of all my domains. Mrs. Mathilde put her arm around me while I stood out in the icy cold and wept, the tears freezing on my face. Later on that evening, the old housekeeper brought me the two Sèvres milk pails from the cottage. I thanked her but told her to put them back. I didn't want them anymore.

Before I left for good, I walked down to the pool house and opened the door to the *Rois* changing room. I couldn't help myself. I needed to see it one last time. I opened the door and stared down at the cold blue tiles, recalling the events of that terrible afternoon.

Mrs. Mathilde was waiting for me in the car. We drove off toward the city. Neither of us said a word the whole way home.

—*m*—

SOUTHAMPTON was history. On to New York. June and Betty dropped in to lend me their support during that ghastly week in March, when I had to vacate my Fifth Avenue apartment so that Countess de Passy, the new owner, could take possession.

I took a break in the middle of packing. Just for the hell of it, I'd put on the Marie Antoinette necklace over my turtleneck sweater as a statement of defiance. My jewelry was pretty much the only thing of substantial value I had left. I regretted not accumulating more of it during my marriage like so many wives of other rich men did as an insurance policy against just the sort of thing that was now happening to me.

I was in a fuck-it-all mood as I opened a bottle of champagne in the living room. The cork popped out and a spurt of white foam trickled onto the Aubusson rug. I didn't even attempt to clean it up. It wasn't going to be mine for much longer. June had brought me a box of my favorite chocolate covered caramels from Fouquet's in Paris. We all sat around eating chocolate and drinking champagne.

The glaring March sunshine was cosmetically unforgiving on my friends. June's taut cheeks were studded with pale brown spots unconcealed by her makeup. Betty's neck resembled wrinkled linen. The sight of them sitting there on my yellow silk couch, in their tailored little suits with their matching shoes and bags, really depressed me—not just because Betty had ruined her outfit with a hideous gold bug pin perched on her right lapel, but because through them, I understood for the first time how much I, myself, had aged. They were undoubtedly thinking the same thing about me—how old I looked, how tired. I couldn't help thinking what a ghastly time it was for me to be starting life all over again, virtually from scratch.

Betty's and June's combined attempt to be upbeat didn't last long. There was no denying the horror of the situation. As I refilled our glasses, I said to them: "Can you believe he didn't see through her? Even assuming she was the greatest lay on earth, how could he have not seen through her? I mean, she obviously planned the whole thing . . . Well, of course, I didn't see through her so—" I stopped when I saw them exchanging surreptitious glances with each other. "Okay, what's up, you two?"

"Nothing," June replied much too quickly.

"Don't screw around with me, girls. If you know something—"

"I'm not telling you anything ever again," June said priggishly. "Remember what happened the last time."

"I'll tell her if you won't," Betty said.

"What? Tell me *what*?" I was in no mood to be trifled with.

"She didn't plan it. *He* did," Betty blurted out.

"Who?"

"Lucius."

My eyes narrowed with intense interest. "What are you saying?"

Betty cleared away the frog in her throat. "They say

that Lucius was having an affair with Monique long before you so obligingly befriended her. Long before she ever even came to Southampton."

They—the human jungle drums who spread gossip throughout the social tribes of New York—were legendary for their accuracy in hindsight.

"I don't believe it."

June chimed in: "You didn't believe it when I told you they were having an affair, either. And look how that turned out."

"Apparently, she met him in Paris a couple of years ago when you were on that Marie Antoinette trip to Austria," Betty said.

"We warned you not to leave him alone so much," June said.

It was Betty who delivered the coup de grâce. "And did you know she was living in New York?" she said.

"No, she wasn't. She was *visiting* New York. I know that to be a fact because we were trying to figure out a way for her to stay here. That was when I started fixing her up, hoping someone would marry her. I fixed her up with Nate."

Betty shook her head. "Uh-uh, sweetie. She was living here almost a year. Ever since her husband died."

"No," I said, refusing to believe it. "That simply can't be."

June's head was bobbing up and down like a marionette's in agreement with Betty.

"And guess *where* she was living?" Betty went on. "Actually, it's where she's *still* living until you clear out of this apartment."

"Where?"

"You'll love this," June said.

"In your old apartment building," Betty said. "How's that for a fucking coincidence?"

A firecracker hit the top of my skull. Suddenly everything made sense.

My mind raced to grasp the breadth of the concept— no, the *familiarity* of the concept! It was the same damn thing he'd done with me years ago—artfully hiding our true relationship from the world by creating a lie within a lie to hide the truth. Betty and June had no idea that I, too, had known Lucius for months before we supposedly met. They had no idea that he was the one who put me up in that very apartment building, a nice rental on East Sixty-fourth Street. But *I* knew it. I knew his whole M.O. because I'd *lived* it.

"So you see," Betty went on, "Lucius is the real culprit. Gil and I were just beards, although we didn't know it. Lucius planned the whole thing."

She also didn't know that they were the beards the last time, too—for me.

"How do you know all this?" I demanded.

"I found out where she was living because she sent me an invitation to a party, if you can believe it. How's that for nerve?" Betty said.

"And Isabelle Catrousse told Trish Bromire that everyone in Paris knew Lucius was having an affair with her ages ago," June said.

Isabelle Catrousse, an elegant Frenchwoman, was the well-connected mistress of a famous French financier. She traveled widely and was a font of international gossip, usually reliable.

My mouth was dry. I could barely speak. "What exactly did Isabelle say?"

June straightened herself up in her chair and spoke with the self-important confidentiality demanded in such circumstances.

"Well," she began in a breathy voice, "Isabelle told Trish that people had seen them together in Paris a year ago. No one thought too much of it at the time—you know how the French are about things like that, and Isabelle's no one to throw stones, let's face it."

"*Go on!*" I ordered her.

"But when he left her all the money it was *le scandale, n'est-ce pas?*"

I stalked around the room with my head in my hands, muttering, "I can't believe it, I just can't believe it," over and over again like a madwoman. Betty and June continued to fill me in on the details, but their voices faded to distant echoes in my ears. Gradually, I ran out of steam and sank down onto a chair. I had fallen into that void of panic always yawning just beneath the surface of my psyche. I stared into space.

"*Yo, Jo!*" Betty cried. "Snap out of it."

"Why did you let her stay with you?" I whispered hoarsely, trying to contain an incredulity fast bubbling into blind rage.

Betty grew defensive. "What did *I* know, for Chrissakes? Gil and Michel were old friends. Monique pulled all that helpless widow crap. Men fall for that shit, what can I tell you? Gil felt sorry for her. So did I, in the beginning. So did *you.*"

"Piranhas in distress," June said, neatly flicking a stray thread off her skirt.

"Look, Jo, I hate her, too," Betty said. "Hell, she made a pass at Gil."

"You knew that and you let her come to me?" I said.

"Excuse me, but let's be frank here. Who'd've thought she'd be interested in a sick old man?" Betty said defensively.

June sighed. "Let's face it, girls, no rich man is safe until he's dead."

"Not even then," I said.

—⟋⟍—

AFTER Betty and June left I hit the hard stuff. I poured myself a tumbler of scotch and wandered around the apartment thinking. Could this really be true? Had Lucius planned the whole thing or was this just one more rumor courtesy of New York's gossip loom, so famous for weaving gorgeous lies out of puny, colorless threads?

Much as I tried to deny it, I couldn't escape the clincher: She was living in my old apartment building. That was certainly no coincidence. I chuckled rather grimly when I thought back at how Monique had reminded me of myself. Little did I suspect then how *much* she was like me, including being my replacement. I remembered how Lucius had complained to me about Ruth and I wondered if he had complained the same way to Monique about me.

The truth is, I *had* neglected Lucius a little, particularly in our last few years together when we became increasingly tangled up in social life. We were like two actors who got dressed up every night and went out on stage. But in private, the magic cord that bound us together had turned into a fraying rope. We lost the cozy sense of conspiracy we once had. In an odd way, social life became a way for us to avoid each other. We gave our allegiance to other people over and above ourselves. If I'd purposely ignored signs we were drifting apart, it was because I figured—quite mistakenly as it turned out— we'd always drift back together again. What is marriage, after all, but constant drifting back and forth? I saw nothing unusual in our pattern. Yet I knew it was skewed. Through all of it, however, I loved him. And I thought love would carry the day.

The one bright side to Lucius's heart attack was that his sudden incapacitation brought us very close very quickly, like my father's stroke had done with my parents. Or so I thought.

Looking at the white marble staircase that spilled out onto the foyer like a wedding train, I tried to understand just what had happened to my life. The persona I'd created for myself suddenly seemed as fragile as a candle flame. As I trudged up those wide white steps, I remembered how often I had glided down them to receive my guests at dinner parties. Shades of my glory days crowded in on me like a parade of mummers, silent and sinister. It had taken me twenty years to create two magnificent houses and a great collection of eighteenth-century art and furniture. Now, in a matter of months, I was being shown the door. I felt, suddenly, very lonely and slightly ridiculous, the butt of a terrible joke.

I retreated to my bedroom. I was going to lie down but I was drawn instead to the secluded little stone balcony where I used to greet the sun unobserved on warm spring mornings. I opened the French doors. A blast of cold air hit me as I walked outside onto the narrow half-moon of stone. The light was fast fading to a wintry sunset. I looked down over the low balustrade, staring at the deserted back alleyway fifteen floors below. In a moment of pure self-pity, I thought how easy it would be to jump. One wrong move in that cramped little space and all my worries would be over.

I moved precariously close to the edge, peering further over the railing. The cavernous drop, hemmed in by the brick walls of neighboring buildings, yawned in front of me, beckoning me to fall into its jaws. At that moment it seemed clear to me that my current fate was an expression of some kind of divine retribution. Ruth was getting even from the grave.

Just then I heard a voice cry, "Jo!"

I was startled. I almost lost my balance and had to grab hold of the transom to keep from falling. A dark shape, silhouetted against the bright light of the hallway, stepped into the bedroom and flicked up the light switch on the wall. It was Monique.

"You . . ." I whispered.

It had been almost six months since we'd clapped eyes on each other—not since that fateful day in Southampton. I had trained myself over the years never to display unseemly behavior, particularly not to those whom I loathed. I straightened up and stood my ground.

"How are you, Jo?" she asked in a farcically melodramatic voice.

"As well as can be expected, thank you."

Her face darkened. She looked as if she were about to burst into tears. "Jo, you must believe me when I tell you how terrible I feel about what has happened."

"How kind of you," I said with a frosty smile.

"Would you sit down and let me talk to you for a moment?" She walked across the room and closed the terrace doors.

"Why?"

"I want to explain."

"What? How you and Lucius set me up? Spare me, please."

Monique sat down on the bed.

"Please, Jo, sit down."

I was tempted to simply walk out of the room, but a feeling of intense curiosity came over me. What was she up to? I wondered. I decided to oblige her. I sat down on the dressing table stool, which was a fair distance from the bed. We faced each other across the room, challengers on the playing field.

"Jo, I want you to know that it was all his idea, not mine."

"Oh? Was it his idea for you to kill him, too?" I inquired, articulating my suspicions for the first time.

Monique looked shocked. She crossed her hands over her breast as if I'd just delivered her a mortal wound.

"My God, Jo! What are you saying?"

"Spare me the theatrics. We both know what happened."

"You can't possibly believe that I . . . ? Oh please, Jo, you don't really think that I could have—?" She stopped short, and when I met her imploring gaze with a look of utter disdain, she burst into tears and sobbed into her hands.

What a performance. It was no use pressing her. I knew she'd never admit it. But I wanted her to know that I knew.

After a time, she looked up, sighed heavily, and said, "Lucius Slater deserved what he got."

"I won't argue with you there. But surely you don't think you deserved what *you* got, do you? Two hundred million dollars after a year's work?"

"Jo, I would give anything if we could be friends again. I worship you. *Please* don't hate me." She brushed the tears off her cheeks with her fingers. She looked like a little girl.

I addressed her in an even, measured voice, as devoid of emotion as I could manage. "Monique, let me be perfectly clear about something. I don't hate you. You simply don't exist for me anymore. If we should accidentally run into each other somewhere, I'll be civil. But that's it. From now on, we live in different worlds."

"But I want to be in your world, Jo. You are my mentor. You said so yourself."

There was something absurdly naïve about her. After all her scheming and treachery, she just didn't get it.

"We can't always have what we want in life."

"I know, but people in New York and Paris won't speak to me because of you," she said.

"You have to take that up with them," I replied.

"I don't expect Betty and June or your friend Ethan or Trish to talk to me yet. But I saw Roger Lowry at a party and he refused to shake my hand. He barely said hello."

A tinge of elation pierced my gloomy mood. It was gratifying to think New York was not rushing to embrace the woman who had usurped my life.

"Roger's an old friend."

"But you have so many friends, Jo. I mean, if Clara

Wilman had suddenly dropped you, what would you have done?"

I ignored this ridiculous question. "New York's a very big city, Monique. With two hundred million dollars, I doubt you'll have much trouble finding new friends of your own."

"But you know all the right people."

"Look, I've explained my position. So if you don't mind, I'd like you to leave now. This apartment is still mine until tomorrow."

"Jo . . ." She paused theatrically, looking at me with her big sad eyes. "I have a favor to ask you."

"A favor? And what might that be?" I was riveted to hear what she had in mind.

"I would like very much to go on the board of the Municipal Museum. And I know you could help me if you wanted to."

This time I was unable to stifle a contemptuous guffaw. I looked at her in utter and complete astonishment.

"I don't believe it," I said.

"You don't even have to propose me. Just don't block me."

I shook my head from side to side in grim amusement. Collecting my thoughts before speaking, I drew myself up to my full height on the stool and addressed her in a calm, measured voice.

"Monique, let me put this as delicately as I can: You have absolutely no connection with that institution whatsoever, so the only possible reason you could want to go on the board is in order to use it as a stepping stone to social power. And take heart, dear, you're not alone, believe me. There are many others who've tried it. Some have even succeeded with enough money. But that's another story . . . Your question to me is, will I block you from such an effort . . . ? Let me respond: If there's a choice between blowing up the Slater Gallery and seeing you go on that board, I, personally, will supply the dynamite. I will refuse to so much as enter the museum if you ever have anything to do with it. And I intend to make that perfectly clear to anyone who asks—or who doesn't ask. In short, I will do anything and everything in my power to see that you never, ever achieve that particular goal. Does that answer your question?"

"If you knew what I have been through, you wouldn't be so cruel, Jo," she said, her eyes welling once more with tears.

I finally lost my temper. Enough was enough.

"What *you've* been through?" I shouted. "How about what *I've* been through?! Twenty years of being the best wife I knew how and this is my reward! Chucked over for some little upstart? How dare you? How dare you? *How dare you?*"

Monique's lip quivered as I yelled at her. I refused to let up.

"I was his wife, for Christ's sake! His wife! His loyal and loving *wife!* And you . . . you . . . You were nothing but his, his—"

"I was going to have his child!" she cried, interrupting me with a grand air of vindication.

The word "child" hit me like blunt force trauma.

"What?"

"Yes. I was pregnant."

"Not with Lucius Slater's baby you weren't."

"Oh yes. It was his baby."

"Really? He couldn't make love. He was impotent."

"Not with me," Monique said with infuriating smugness.

"I don't believe you. So where's the baby?"

"I was so upset at what happened that I had a miscarriage. That's why I didn't come to the funeral."

I burst out laughing. "You expect me to believe that?"

"Believe what you want. It's the truth."

"Where exactly did you have this miscarriage?"

"In New York. In my apartment."

"The apartment Lucius set you up in."

"Yes."

"Did you see a doctor?"

"No. I just stayed alone and cried."

She was lying, of course. Still, this was a painful subject for me.

"Lucius never wanted another child. Why do you think I never had one?"

"He wanted one with me," she said.

I hated her more by the second.

"And just when did you tell him you were pregnant?"

"Two weeks before he . . ." She paused for effect.

"And he fell for it?"

"I know you don't believe me, Jo, but it's true. I swear it! He promised to take care of me. We loved each other so much . . . I'm sorry, Jo. I really had no idea what he was going to do. Oh, Jo, please forgive me," she said, her dark eyes glittering with tears.

Whether her story was true or not, there was nothing I could do about it now. I felt utterly defeated. "When did all this start?" I asked her.

"Two years ago, in Paris. We met at a party at Michel's

gallery. Lucius came by the next day and asked me out for lunch. I went."

"So you were married when you started having an affair with my husband."

Monique bit her lip. "I was very unhappy, Jo, and I am not proud of what happened. Michel and I were having a bad time. Lucius was very *sympathique*. He begged me to confide in him. And as you know, it's so much easier to tell your problems to a stranger. We fell in love. And after Michel died, he brought me to New York."

"He set you up in an apartment in New York?"

"Like he did with you," she said. I ignored the comparison. She went on. "He told me that you and he were not happy."

"He said we weren't happy?" I repeated, thinking that was exactly what he'd told me about himself and Ruth when I first met him.

"That's what he said . . . Then, after he had his heart attack, he wanted to be with me even more. I went to visit him in the hospital—"

"*What?* When? I was there almost every minute."

"I dressed up as a nurse. I waited until you left. And then I went in to sit with him. He said that he didn't want to wait any longer. He told me he wanted to divorce you and marry me before it was too late."

"Oh, come on," I said impatiently.

"You don't believe me, Jo, but it's true. He was going to ask you for a divorce this summer, but it was so difficult for him. He didn't want to hurt you. He thought that maybe he could persuade you to ask him."

"What? For a divorce?" I stared at her, uncomprehending. "Why on *earth* would I have done a thing like that?"

"I don't know. He told me you might, that's all."

All at once, Lucius's refusal to honor my pledge to the Muni became clear. Perhaps, in some twisted, obsessed way, Lucius thought that if he denied me the things I was accustomed to I'd get fed up and leave him. It was a ridiculous notion but I knew from my own experience that he had a dark, secretive side and that when he became obsessed with a woman or even a deal, for that matter, he began to think in strange ways. Nothing could stop him.

"Let me ask you something. How do the Watermans figure in all this?"

"Lucius got me invited to a big party in New York. Gil and Michel were old friends, you know. I went up to Betty and she very kindly invited me out to Southampton."

"What would you have done without Betty's convenient invitation—not to mention my own?"

"That was just a stroke of luck. Actually, we had a different plan."

"Which was?"

"Lucius said he had to have me near him in the summer. He had already booked a room for me in a motel near Southampton. He told me that he paid your old secretary to leave suddenly so I could come and take her place. He was going to tell you that I was from his office."

It was true that Nancy, my social secretary, had left abruptly. And, indeed, I'd wondered at the time where she'd gotten the money to go around the world. I didn't want to let Monique see how upset I was, however. I continued questioning her in a cool, businesslike manner.

"I see. So you planned to get into our house as my social secretary?"

She nodded. "In a way, that's what happened. Only you asked me there yourself."

I shook my head in amused despair, knowing I probably would have fallen for Lucius's ruse. He very well could have brought Monique into our house that way. Indeed, he had managed to bring her into the house without my suspecting a thing. I loathed him more and more by the second, and myself for being so naïve.

"I wanted to tell you the truth, Jo."

"Oh, I'm sure you did."

"No, *really*. I did. But Lucius promised me he would tell you himself before the end of the summer. He promised."

I got up and paced around the room, hardly able to think straight. Even though I believed Lucius Slater capable of anything at that point, there was still something about Monique's story that didn't ring true.

"You knew how dangerous it was for Lucius to become overstimulated, didn't you?"

"I don't know. He said the doctors were too cautious. He was thrilled when I told him we were going to have a child."

I felt physically ill. It was all I could do to maintain my composure.

"In the pool house, I told you to call an ambulance. You just stood there."

"Jo, I was in shock. Lucius was gasping. You were so upset. I'm sorry. I didn't know what I was doing. Forgive me. I know I reacted badly . . . Later on, I was certain that you would blame me for his death in some way. I blamed myself, even though I knew it wasn't my fault. Nothing was going on between us in the pool house that day, I promise. It was when you walked in on us that he became so upset."

"I see. So it's my fault."

"It's nobody's fault, Jo. It just *happened*. I loved him. I adored him. I was so distressed about everything that I had a miscarriage . . . *Yes* . . . I know that's what caused it. It's horrible. The worst thing you can imagine. I was so frightened and so sad. I felt so alone. I was desperate to have his child just so I could have a part of him with me always."

I stared at her without flinching. It must have been clear I didn't believe a word she'd said.

"You do have a part of him with you always," I said. "Two hundred million dollars."

She flinched. "Jo, I swear to you on my life that I didn't know anything about the will. I swear it!"

Then she did an astonishing thing. She got up, ran across the room, and knelt at my feet.

"Forgive me, Jo. Your friendship means everything to me."

The scene was awkward and embarrassing, like having some sort of demented captive begging for mercy in front of me. I got up and moved away as quickly as I could. Monique stared up at me from the floor with cow eyes. She failed to make a good impression.

"Well, this has certainly been an education," I said matter-of-factly. "And now, if you don't mind, I still have some time left in my apartment and I'd like to spend it alone."

"Can't we please be friends again, Jo?" she said, rising from the floor.

"No."

"Why not?"

"Why not . . . ? Monique, I'm not sure I believe you and I certainly don't trust you. You can't be friends with someone you don't trust. As I told you at the beginning of this conversation, I intend to lead my life as if you don't exist. You and I will simply go our separate ways in this city. And that's the end of it."

"All your friends will follow you."

"Why are you so interested in my friends?"

"I don't want to be thought of as a terrible person," she said.

"I can't help what people think of you, Monique."

We both knew this was not strictly true. I knew my opinion still counted for something in New York. Suddenly, her expression changed. A moment before she had been meek and imploring. Now a look of icy determination hardened her face. I'd never seen anything quite like it.

"So you refuse to help me?" she said in a low, almost threatening tone.

"I refuse to *know* you."

"And you will block me from getting on the board of the Municipal Museum?"

At last, the real agenda.

"What's the French equivalent for 'over my dead body'?" I inquired.

She looked me up and down, then raised her right fist to her face and tipped it toward me as if it were a fencing épée.

"*En garde, mon amie,*" she said, and walked out of the room.

———ш———

AFTER she left, I sat in the bedroom for a long, long time, thinking about the tale Monique had told me and about my late husband. I felt rather like one of those women I sometimes watched with grim fascination on TV—the hapless wives of bigamists, perverts, and serial killers who tearfully confess how utterly astonished they'd been to learn of their husbands' secret lives and depravity. Her tale of woe was a bit too operatic for my taste. I kept wishing I'd asked her more questions. There were too many gaps in the story. But I'd been so flummoxed by the initial revelation I wasn't thinking straight.

What makes this woman tick? I wondered. There was definitely something weird about her. What was this need to remain close to me after all that had happened? She'd won. She could go and make a hundred new lives with two hundred million dollars.

She had my houses. She had my money. Now she wanted my life. And the first rung was getting on the board of the Muni. In New York, money is worthless to the social climber who fails to make the right connections. I'd taught her that myself. The city was full of rich aspirants craving invitations from the so-called A-list. If I froze Monique out, she'd be just another woman in a couture suit looking for a lunch date, denied access to the true precincts of social power.

I was so lost in thought I didn't even realize that night had fallen and I was sitting in the dark. I switched on a light and got ready for bed. It took me a while to fall asleep. My mind was still racing.

Monique was a strange bird, I thought as I closed my eyes. I didn't relish having her for an enemy, but it struck me as marginally less dangerous than having her for a friend.

I I

I figured the one person who might be able to shed some light on Monique's behavior was Nate Nathaniel. I was none too fond of Nate, but there's something about having known a person for years—adversary or not—that bonds you to them when an interloper enters the picture. We had been comrades-at-arms as far as the will was concerned. Nate had bent over backward to be kind to me since Lucius died for the simple reason, I believe, that he loathed seeing half of Lucius's estate go to a complete stranger almost as much as I did.

I asked Nate to have lunch with me. We met at the Oyster Bar in the Plaza Hotel because it was near his midtown offices. Nate was sitting at the table when I arrived. He stood up as I neared, all polish and politesse, immaculately dressed in a three-piece pinstripe suit, his thick sandy hair neatly parted on the side, wearing his supernaturally youthful looks like a badge of honor.

We ordered lunch and chitchatted about nothing in particular until it arrived. I had a glass of white wine to loosen me up.

"Nate, you knew Lucius better than anyone. I have to ask you something: Did you know he wanted to marry Monique?"

The circumspect lawyer jabbed absently at the shaved ice of the oyster platter with his fork. It was clear he did know. I clenched my teeth.

"How long have you known?" I asked him. He was silent. "Look, I understand you're not supposed to violate attorney-client privilege, or whatever they call it. But under the circumstances . . . ? Come on, Nate, I need to know."

"How did you find out?"

"The prospective bride informed me herself."

Nate's head bobbed up and down. "I figured she might. She's very upset."

"*She's* upset?"

"Come on, Jo. She's been through hell." He narrowed his eyes. "Did she tell you everything?"

"You mean about the baby? Yes. She told me. I don't believe her for a minute."

"Oh, I think it's true."

"Why? She could have made the whole thing up. Who would know?"

"Without going into details, I have reason to believe it is, that's all."

I eyed him suspiciously. "How do you know so much about it?"

"I just do."

"Well, obviously, she must have given you the same sob story she gave me. But you believe her."

"I think I do, yes."

"Did you know that she's been here for nearly a year? And that Lucius put her up in the same apartment building where he put me up years ago?"

"I had no idea about all that until I came out for the weekend."

"He told you then?"

"Yes."

I felt my heart beat faster with anxiety. "What exactly did he say?"

"Jo, what's the point of all this?"

"The point is I want to *know*."

"What good will it do? It'll only hurt you."

"I want to know, Nate. Now what *exactly* did he say?"

Nate heaved a sigh. "He told me he was in love with her and that he was going to ask you for a divorce."

"And what did you say?"

"I told him he was nuts."

"Thank you, Nate," I said in no more than a whisper. I was on the verge of tears. It was all I could do to keep my composure. "Did you know he was planning to change his will?"

Nate dropped his fork and raised his hand like a traffic policeman. "*Absolutely not*," he said. "There was never a discussion of the will. I swear to you. He went to Sullivan on his own. I wasn't even there. You know that."

I let go an inadvertent sigh. "Did you know she was pregnant?"

"He told me that she suspected she was."

"You were so friendly with her that weekend. Why?"

"Well, I didn't know anything until the last day I was

there. I thought you'd invited me out to meet her. I had no idea anything was going on between them."

"Weren't you shocked when he told you?"

"To be honest . . . How shall I put this? Yes and no."

"Well, there's a lawyerly answer. What do you mean?"

Nate leveled me with a deep gaze. "He'd done it before, Jo."

I swallowed hard. I got his drift. "Have you been waiting twenty years to say that to me, Nate?"

He shook his head. "No, Jo . . . I just knew he was capable of it, that's all."

"So you weren't shocked?"

"Come on, Jo, of course I was. I'm saying his behavior didn't come out of the blue, that's all."

"There was a precedent: me."

"If you like."

"Well, maybe it'll shock you to hear this. I believe that Monique may have had a hand in Lucius's death."

Nate cocked his head to one side. "What do you mean?"

I leaned in toward him across the table and spoke softly.

"The doctors absolutely forbade Lucius to have sex. You knew it. I knew it. *She* knew it. In light of this will, it would make sense that she would seduce him, knowing what might happen, don't you agree?"

Nate leaned back and shook his head in mild amusement. "Sex as a deadly weapon? Difficult to prove. You didn't actually *see* them going at it, did you?"

"No . . . But they obviously were. They were having an affair."

"Yes, but that day? That minute?"

"Look, Nate, when I walked in on them in the pool house, something was definitely going on."

"But you say he was alive when you walked in?"

"Yes, so what? The minute I opened the door he started gasping."

"Perhaps because you caught him."

"She put him in danger."

"If you thought that, why did you leave her alone with him?"

"He was having a heart attack, for God's sake! I had to call the ambulance, didn't I? She wouldn't do it."

"What can I say, Jo? It's unlikely she used sex to kill him."

"No? With a two-hundred-million-dollar motive? Why not?" I drained my glass of white wine.

"Jo, I hate to be crude, but it seems to me that the only smoking gun here, possibly, was Lucius's."

"Well, I think she did it. I think she seduced him, told him she was in love with him, made him believe she was pregnant, got him to change his will, and then killed him. Maybe not literally. But she knew damn well he could have another heart attack."

"Sounds pretty diabolical," Nate said.

"Exactly." I stared at him unblinking until he looked away.

"Jo, you're understandably upset. But I think you're complicating things."

"What's complicated? It's very simple: She murdered him for the money. Second oldest motive in the world."

"What's the first?" he inquired, slipping the last oyster into his mouth.

"Murdering for love."

"Interesting choice of words."

The waiter asked me if I was finished eating. I'd barely touched my shrimp salad. I nodded for him to take it away. He cleared our places. We ordered coffee but no dessert.

"Jo," Nate said, after a time. "You've made some very serious accusations here today. I hope you're not intending to share these thoughts with anyone but me."

"Believe me, I'd like to tell the whole world."

"Well, don't. Or you could find yourself in a big, fat, juicy lawsuit for slander."

"She wants to go on the board of the Muni, Nate. *And* she wants me to help her. Imagine? She thinks she can just take over my existence. Well, she's got another thing coming."

"You don't have to have anything to do with her. Just be careful what you say. I don't want to see you have any more problems."

"You know what she said to me when I saw her? *'En garde.'* Like we're now in a duel. You should have seen her face. It was scary."

"Don't obsess, Jo. She's not worth it."

"She won't succeed here, Nate. Not if I have anything to do with it. I happen to believe that in spite of everything my opinion still counts for a lot. Don't you think?"

I was trying to bolster myself up. But the truth was, I felt insecure. Nate must have sensed this because he reached across the table and patted my hand reassuringly.

"Your opinion means everything in this town. You're still Jo Slater."

I felt curiously relieved when he said this. It was the first time I had ever really liked Nate. His kindness touched me deeply. I thought I'd probably been mistaken about him all these years. It was Lucius I should have been wary of, not Nate.

———ᴿ———

I knew that after I honored my pledge to the Municipal Museum, I would be effectively broke. I had a few drawings and some jewelry I could sell to tide me over for a time, but these things were hardly enough to sustain me. I had to find a job. Starting all over again at my age was terrifying. Still, other women had done it. Besides, I had no choice.

I accepted June Kahn's kind offer to move in with her temporarily until I could find a decent place to rent. New York was insanely expensive. A rental the size of the powder room in my old apartment was offered to me for three thousand dollars a month.

June and Charlie Kahn lived in a sprawling duplex in the second most fashionable building on Fifth Avenue. The apartment, whose grand, boxy entertaining rooms overlooked Central Park, was fussily decorated with gaudy French furniture and nineteenth-century oil paintings of Paris street scenes where well-dressed ladies carrying parasols coped with small dogs. The orange moiré silk living room was, to my mind, a subdefinition of hell.

"Here we are, sweetie, all nice and tucked away from the rest of the house," June said, showing me into a spacious guest room at the end of a long corridor in the back of the apartment—a room so relentlessly white and lacy it looked like a giant doily.

"I'm sorry there's so much luggage," I said as I helped a beleaguered-looking young Irishwoman carry my suitcases. "I feel like one of the Joads." June looked at me blankly. *"The Grapes of Wrath?"* I reminded her. "The group read it year before last."

"Oh yes, *that* book, lord . . . Sweetie, you're welcome to stay as long as you like. You know, until you find someplace else."

I caught June rolling her eyes at the maid who placed the last of the suitcases on a luggage rack at the end of the bed. No matter how close friends are, moving in on them is always an imposition.

When June left, I lay down on the canopied queen-size bed and stared up at the ceiling, where a group of frisky cherubs painted in the circle of the canopy's crown stared down at me with oversized eyes and angelic smiles. June and her cherubs. Still, she was a good soul to put me up and I was grateful.

12

Not long after I'd settled in with June, Roger Lowry, the president of the Municipal Museum, called me up and asked me to join him for lunch. I saw this as a fortuitous coincidence because I'd been thinking of sounding Roger out about a job. I was toying with several ideas, one of which was starting a consulting business that would basically advise people how to form a museum-quality collection.

Lowry, a tall, silver-haired man with a crinkly face and an affable manner, was an old friend, much indebted to me professionally. It was I who had plucked him out of an obscure foundation and recommended him for his current plum position. My faith in Roger had been amply justified. He'd been a great success, raising vast amounts of money, persuading important collectors to bequeath their paintings to the museum, initiating exchange programs with other top museums around the world, beefing up conservation efforts, expanding the gift shop. He and his vivacious, determined wife, Lil, were much-sought-after fixtures on the New York social scene.

We ate in the Municipal's private dining room, where white-jacketed waiters hovered watchfully and the tinkling of silver on china broke the general hush. Being somewhat of a social cryptographer, as it were, I didn't take long to decipher the decorous conversation we were having over green salads and grilled fish.

Lowry thanked me profusely for my million-dollar pledge, five hundred thousand dollars of which I had already given. He had the good grace not to mention the other five that was still owing, though we both knew one of the purposes of the lunch was to find out exactly when or indeed *if* those monies would be paid. I was well aware that Lowry, along with practically everyone else in New York—and the whole Northern Hemisphere, it seemed—knew the details of my current situation.

Under the guise of reassuring me that my position at the Muni was "absolutely golden," as he put it, Lowry, using nothing but praise and flattery, adroitly watered the seeds of doubt already flowering in my own mind about my ability to serve the institution I loved. I could hear the rumblings. I imagined there were those who felt my coveted seat on the board should eventually be given to someone more equipped to handle the financial obligations required of such an honor. By never saying anything explicit and, indeed, by reinforcing the museum's as well as his own great debt to me—"The Slater Gallery is incomparable, Jo"—Lowry, without meaning to, I'm sure, confirmed to me that my resignation had undoubtedly been discussed at length. I was prepared, of course.

I'd been around long enough to know this was an unfortunate inevitability. The point was if I could weather the storm, that's all.

As Lowry's slick patter segued into the fresh fruit cup dessert, talking about the "new money" out there and how exciting it was to see "these young rich kids" taking an interest in art, I thought of all the CEO's who'd give their golden parachutes to take my place on the board of that prestigious institution. There was no limit to the number of social climbers desperate to see their names chiseled onto commemorative marble plaques or carved into the mahogany lintels of new galleries. The Muni was a grand old New York institution, and people were willing to pay mightily to be associated with it.

As he escorted me out of the dining room, I said, "Look, Roger, I don't feel it's necessary, at least not at this time, for me to resign from the board—"

He blanched at the suggestion. "My God, Jo, I never meant to imply—"

I cut him off with a gentle pat on his arm and a wan smile. "Roger, dear, we've known each other too long. You have to think about the museum, I know that. Just because I've been reelected for the past fifteen years doesn't mean, well, that I'll automatically be reelected again. I think that's what you're really telling me, isn't it?"

He looked at me squarely. "Jo, you know you'll always have my full support. I wouldn't be here if it weren't for you. I never meant to imply anything."

"I have a good eye, Roger . . . And a good ear."

On my way out, I spotted Ethan Monk walking pensively in long strides, head down, as was his wont.

"Ethan!" My voice echoed through the marble corridor.

The Monk stopped abruptly and looked around. "Jo?" he said tentatively, focusing his myopic gaze.

"I just had lunch with Roger," I said, approaching him. "Ethan, tell me honestly: Do you think I should resign from the board?"

Ethan looked at me quizzically. "Roger didn't suggest that, did he?"

"He didn't have to. I get the drift . . . I probably should resign. It's not as if I can put my money where my taste is anymore."

"Come with me," Ethan said sternly.

Ethan grabbed my hand and led me through the Roman antiquities rooms to the Armor Hall and down a flight of stairs to the Slater Gallery, where one of the finest collections of eighteenth-century French furniture in the world was on display. He stopped in front of the first room, Le Petit Salon, a reconstruction of one of Marie Antoinette's private apartments in Versailles. There, the lovely writing desk made for the Queen by Jacob, the great *ébéniste,* shone richly against a backdrop of hand-painted floral silk. Most of the pieces in the gallery had been in Lucius's and my own personal collection until we donated them to the Muni. The rest I'd bought from private collections in France and at auction in order to complete the various rooms.

The gem of the collection was the famous "Sèvres Commode," made by Riesener. This exquisite chest of drawers was inlaid with individual Sèvres porcelain plaques, each one a different flower. The story of how I found the chest was famous: I'd spotted it in a thrift shop on the lower east side of New York, of all places—quite near, coincidentally, the now defunct antiques store where Gerald van der Kemp had found the Queen's bedspread in the early 1950s. The plaques had been painted over and the maître's signature was obscured by dirt. Still, I recognized it for the treasure it was and bought it. I had it restored to a glory no one dreamed possible. Later on, Ethan helped me authenticate the piece, a record of which was found in the Queen's household inventory for Le Petit Trianon.

As we strolled past the gallery's majestic interiors, I recalled the genesis of various purchases. The privilege of collecting often sent me on a great treasure hunt with all the mystery, intrigue, frustration, and (with luck) satisfaction attendant on such an adventure. Each example of furniture, each painting, each piece of porcelain was a witness to history with its own little story. Those objects had survived revolutions, world wars, ignorance, and, in my case, an insane adventuress. Thank God, at least these things are in the museum where Monique can't get her hands on them, I thought. Let's hear it for the inanimate object.

"Just remember who's responsible for all this, Jo," Ethan said as we stopped to survey the Queen's private library. "No one's going to forget what you've done for this institution—hell—for this *city*."

But—a New York *but*—I'd lived in New York long enough to know the silken ropes. Out of money, out of mind.

"Then why do I feel like Marie Antoinette without the guillotine?" I said with a grim chuckle.

—∿—

I soon discovered that it was one thing to be best friends with someone and quite another to live with them. June, an eleemosynary workhorse, dedicated to committee meetings and organizing benefits for her pet causes, was far more controlling at home than I'd ever imagined. Her attention to detail was precisely why she was good at getting things done.

Living with her, however, was a nightmare. At first June accommodated me in every way she could, treating me as an honored guest. But as the days wore on and I settled in, the amenities she first offered were gradually taken away, mainly because although June and Charlie presented a very grand façade to the outside world, they lived on a veritable shoestring in private. June thought nothing of spending thousands of dollars on clothes, but when it came time to pay for help, she was a skinflint.

Colleen, the Irish maid who had helped me with my bags, was the only servant the Kahns employed on a full-time basis, except for the cook. When they had a party, which was quite often, they hired a small battalion of waiters and waitresses who were familiar faces to all of us who frequented the Kahns' house. I, like everyone in New York, just assumed this little army worked for them. They didn't. Colleen cleaned the entire apartment herself and she did the laundry. Having even a single guest to stay for any extended period of time, therefore, basically increased the poor woman's workload by one third.

June dropped a polite hint that it might be "a tad easier for the staff"—as she referred to the hapless maid—if I joined her and Charlie at *6:45 sharp* at the small round table in front of the window in the dining room where the Kahns ritually had their breakfast every morning.

I began to dread the sight of June wearing that fuzzy pink bathrobe, her face glistening with cold cream, her hair in pincurls, fretting about "the zillion things" she had to do that day. I was frankly amazed she let Charlie see her like that—June, who was usually so meticulous about her appearance in public—"band-box" pretty, as my mother used to say. Then again, Charlie was oblivious to human contact at that or, now that I think of it, pretty much any hour. Always nattily dressed in his navy cashmere slippers and matching cashmere bathrobe over striped pajamas buttoned up to the neck, the rail-thin man sat in resolute silence at the breakfast table, sipping his coffee at rhythmic intervals, studying the obituaries of *The New York Times,* which he referred to as "mini novels."

"Death invigorates him," June once whispered to me.

Other things began to drive me crazy as well: the way June fussed over every little thing, making sure every object in the house was angled correctly, dust-free, polished bright. Her fetish about punctuality seemed to grow exponentially with each passing day. Though a stickler for detail myself, I nonetheless felt that June carried control into the realm of obsession. She even had the nerve to go into my room to tidy it up when I wasn't there, further emphasizing the fact that we were no longer on an equal footing.

On the morning I announced I was leaving, June feigned sadness, but the relief in her voice was palpable.

"Naturally, I can't stop you. But where will you go?" she said with mock concern.

"To Betty's," I said. "It's time you and Charlie had a break."

I packed my bags—so many bags—tipped Colleen several hundred dollars to try to make up in part for the salary I knew June wasn't paying her, and went off to stay with the Watermans.

Betty said, referring to the Kahns: "I don't know how you stood it so long with those two. They're both so god-damn anal. We spent a week with them in Lyford Cay one year and I was ready to throw myself to the sharks."

Gil and Betty Waterman lived in an elegant limestone townhouse on a pretty tree-lined block on East Seventy-third Street. Their house was right across the street from another elegant limestone townhouse where Gil had his art gallery. A small brass plaque to the right of the door read simply: 32. Gil saw clients only through referrals. He wasn't interested in street trade.

Their house was crammed with great art from Rembrandt to Rothko that everyone knew was for sale at the right price. My favorite was the Matisse collage sweeping over one entire wall of the dining room like wallpaper.

"I'm putting you upstairs with the family," Betty told me.

I followed her up four flights of stairs to a top-floor bedroom across the hall from her daughter, Missy.

Missy Waterman was a twenty-five-year-old teenager with long hair, a long face, and a frisky gait. She reminded me of an Afghan hound. She was sunny at times, sullen at others, and wholly preoccupied with her-self. My pleas to her to turn down the music or close her door when she was talking on the phone at three in the morning were met with profuse apologies then immedi-ate recurrence. Nothing I ever said to her seemed to make an impact. She worked downtown as a video artist. She showed me some of her work: an hour-long tape of a woman sitting on a toilet reading the *National Enquirer* was one of her efforts. Missy was basically a sweet young woman, but just like the fruits of her chosen profession, a little of Missy went a long way.

Life with the Watermans was oddly much less of a strain than life with the Kahns, even though the Waterman household was louder and more chaotic. Gil Waterman, a young-looking fifty-four-year-old, was extremely fond of opera, which he played at full volume whenever he was home. I liked the opera, too, but I thought if I had to listen to Aïda dying at fifty decibels one more day in a row, I'd kill myself.

Betty was an amateur potter. She had a studio with a skylight on the top floor where she made plates that had "FUCK YOU" written on the underside of them so if people turned them over to see where they were from, they would get the message. She also drank quite a bit and was always exhorting me to join her. The sun often went over the yardarm for Betty as early as eleven in the morning, which was another drawback to living there because talking to her when she was in this condition was like playing tennis against a backboard. Rather than try, I drank too.

I knew I had to get cracking, though, and in fairly short order, I went out in search of my own apartment. Some of the real estate agents who took me around were women who, like myself, had fallen on hard financial times fairly late in life. It looked like a rather lucrative occupation if you had the temperament for it. I didn't. The people who were good at it were savvy and tough in a way I wasn't. They were interesting to talk to because they often got wind of what was really up in New York before anyone else did.

"When they ask you to come and appraise their apartment for quote unquote 'insurance purposes,' you can bet there's trouble in the marriage," one of them told me.

It was through a real estate agent that I learned Monique had put my old apartment on the market for eighteen million dollars.

"I hear she's moving to Paris," the woman told me.

I felt an intense sense of relief, not only because I had a vague dread of the Countess, but because I knew that the only reason she would be selling the apartment was because she had effectively been frozen out of the world she so coveted. People were loyal, after all. Money was not always the golden key.

I couldn't find anything decent to rent or to buy, nothing I could afford, at any rate. But then, I had a bit of luck. A friend of Betty's who owned a small apartment on Park Avenue and Seventy-seventh Street was moving to Bangkok for a year. The building's stuffy board refused to let her sublet the apartment. She needed someone trustworthy to basically house-sit until she got back. I moved in.

The apartment was beige and bland. I rearranged the furniture and bought some pillows and throws to make it look less like a hotel room. It was heavenly to be alone; I now set about seriously planning the rest of my life.

13

My former existence was fading faster than a dream. Reentry into Real Life, as I now thought of it, was a stark adjustment. I quickly realized how dependent I'd become on wealth and the freedom and distractions it afforded. My earning potential and, indeed, the very desire to make my own living had atrophied in the warm climate of wealth. Little did I know I'd been living in a spa. But I certainly knew it now that I was back out in the cold. No longer a lady of leisure, I desperately needed a job.

I knew a lot about eighteenth-century art and furniture, but I was primarily self-taught with comparatively little in the way of a formal education. Except college. Even though I'd consulted with some of the greatest scholars over the years, I, myself, had no academic credentials. That meant I couldn't get a job as a teacher or a curator, which I would have enjoyed.

I tossed around a few ideas with friends: becoming a

consultant to an auction house; setting up a small antiques shop; teaching people how to form museum-quality collections; writing a book on the great *ébénistes*. But the general consensus among those who knew me best was that I would make a great interior decorator.

I must say the thought had often occurred to me, even when I didn't need the money. I loved hunting for art and furniture and marvelous fabrics. I loved auctions. My idea of a sublime day was to roam around the flea markets and antiques shops of any city I happened to be in.

"Who's more qualified than you?" Betty said. "You've got the greatest taste in the world."

And indeed, Henri St. Martin, the late, great French decorator, from whom I'd learned so much when we had worked together on my various abodes, had always told me: *"Vous êtes douée"*—I was "a natural." I'd studied at the master's knee and I had a flair for creating an elegant atmosphere. I knew a lot of marvelous, quirky fabric houses and antiques shops. It would be difficult to sell me a fake. And I had a resale number that I'd often used to save money, even in the days when money wasn't a consideration. I saw no point in needless waste.

JUNE got the ball rolling very generously, commissioning me to "spruce up her ratty old dining room," as she put it. She and Betty gave me a big luncheon to launch my new career. They took over Pug's, a fashionable bistro on Lexington Avenue in the seventies, and rallied the troops behind me.

I saw no signs of my popularity waning. I'd obviously

kept my cachet. Even the *amis mondains* came out to honor me, which was amazing considering downturns in fortune as severe as my own usually sent them scattering fast. Over the years, I'd made a little study of the people who used celebrated or rich friends to enhance themselves. There was a whole group of them. Everyone knew who they were. They courted rising stars with a vengeance, but when the chips were down, their silence was audible.

At lunch, everyone went out of their way to tell me how much they admired me for "getting on with my life." I thought if I heard that particular phrase one more time I was going to scream. I felt rather like the latest fashionable cause people had taken up—either because they genuinely liked me, or because they were sorry for me, or simply because they feared a similar misfortune might hit them one day and they were hedging their bets.

Monique's name was not mentioned once—not within my hearing distance, at any rate. After having endured endless stories about Monique being snubbed wherever she went (I often heard three or four versions of the same tale, embellished by enthusiasm with each telling), I finally made it crystal clear she didn't exist for me. I didn't want to hear her name.

Afterward, Betty told me that no one had seen or spoken to "the Cuntess," as Betty always referred to her, in months.

"She probably got fed up and went back to hell," Betty said.

I was relieved not to have to think about her anymore.

—⁓—

Jo Slater, Inc. officially opened in June of 1997. The hectic pace of my new job invigorated me. I scurried around to auction previews, fabric houses, and little out-of-the-way antiques shops around town, hunting for bric-a-brac and bargains. If there was a jewel in the junk, I found it. My first job went smoothly. June was delighted with her new dining room. Word spread. Soon I had a few clients. I hired an assistant, Melissa, an eager young woman who had just graduated from design school. The two of us worked out of my apartment to save money. I tried to keep the place organized, but soon it was overflowing with swatches and sketches.

It was hard work but I was having fun. I was written up in *Nous* and *House Décor*. Business was good. I didn't want to kid myself, however. I knew I was the flavor of the month and that there was a lot of competition out there. I figured that when the novelty of my situation wore off and people learned I was working out of a borrowed apartment, decorating in order to make ends meet, not merely as a ladylike hobby, my luster would dim a bit. That was to be expected. But I was determined to make a success of Jo Slater, Inc. I wanted people to come to me because of my talent, not because of my name. I invested my heart and soul in every single detail of every single job.

— ·m· —

THEN I got my big break. Trish Bromire called me up one afternoon and told me about some friends of theirs from Cincinnati called Neil and Agatha Dent. The Dents were one of those attractive, socially mobile couples who, having made a fortune, grow bored with whatever city they're in and move to New York seeking to expand their horizons. I'd watched many such types come and go over the years. Some had stayed and become fixtures of the community; others had left, either because they were never accepted in the way they envisioned, or went broke, or got involved in a scandal, or simply grew sick and tired of the whole scene and decided home wasn't so provincial after all.

Neil and Agatha were an uncommonly tall and handsome couple, both in their mid-fifties. Though they were a tad too earnest and careful to be really good fun, they were a pleasant pair, easy to be around. Neil was a venture capitalist who had made scads of money in the telecommunications field and sold out way before it went belly-up. He had a blunt Rotarian sense of humor. He liked bathroom jokes that were often quite funny.

Agatha was more refined though a bit overanxious to do everything "right." It was clear to me from the start that she had gleaned the little she knew about New York social life primarily from the pages of *Nous* magazine, which she pronounced "Noose," until Trish corrected her. And like most out-of-towners, she invariably got it wrong at first. (It's always difficult to convince people who move to New York that many of the people they really want to know are ones they've never heard of.)

Agatha, far more than Neil, was desperate to know the "top people," as she called them. And she did know something about social climbing. Having jumped the first hurdle—namely, buying a great apartment in a very fashionable building on Park Avenue—she now had to choose the right decorator.

The Dents' original choice had been Dieter Lucino, a

scrappy, talented architect-designer from California, who had built his reputation creating sweepingly grand interiors for new money who wanted to look like old royalty. Agatha told Trish Bromire she wanted Lucino because she had read the profile on him in *Nous*. I knew the piece she was referring to:

> *Lucino gives estimates for estimates and drops clients faster than he drops names if they so much as question a bill. His motto is, "if you have to ask, you can't afford me." He prides himself on being a snob and won't take on just any client, even if they are rich.*

I knew this made him doubly attractive to those whose self-importance relied heavily on the exclusion of others. The article went on to say:

> *Social climbers hoping to make an immediate splash in New York hire Lucino to decorate their houses, figuring that if their own drawing power is not sufficient, Lucino's is. How right they are. Everyone wants to see the master's work and speculate on how much it all cost.*

What the article didn't mention was that Lucino's services included the redesign of his clients' lives as well as their houses. There were people who depended on him so much they insisted he select the Christmas and birthday presents they gave. One woman I knew consulted him on every single accessory that came into her house, including the shade of her toilet paper. Another insisted he go to the couture collections with her in Paris to pick out her clothes to complement the rooms he had decorated. I myself had used him on several occasions. I admired his work. He was an aggressive little genius— the Napoleon of decorators.

Agatha Dent was all set to use Lucino when her tough and suspicious husband flatly refused to sign a contract that included a fairly standard "arbitration" clause. Lucino refused to work without one, so the deal fell through. It was at this point that Trish Bromire introduced the couple to me.

The four of us had lunch. Trish promoted me shamelessly all through the meal, telling the Dents what great taste I had and how socially impeccable I was.

"Dieter's taste is grand grand, but Jo's is cozy grand—much chicer," she said. "And besides, Jo's the real thing."

Agatha Dent's deferential air toward me made me think she had some idea who I was. Trish may have filled her in on the full details, but as a devout reader of *Nous,* Agatha would surely have followed my story. In hindsight, I believe Mrs. Dent cared less about my talents as a decorator and more about my suitability as a launching pad for her social career in New York.

"You were a great friend of Clara Wilman's," she said with awe in her voice, thus confirming my suspicions. Clara's name still evoked the Old Guard—as opposed to the Gold Card—magic of New York society. Clara, unlike me and most others who were now socially prominent, had been the real thing in every way, not just a piece of self-invention.

By the end of that lunch, the job was mine.

14

THE Dents, attractive, not too boring, and rich, rich, rich, were ideal new blood for a jaded city. Soon they were on everybody's guest list—a circumstance somewhat attributable to me. Agatha Dent was entranced with New York. Everyone she met was her new best friend. Whenever we went out shopping together, she regaled me with tales of dinner parties, rather like Marco Polo coming back from the court of Kublai Khan full of awe and wonderment. She did have the annoying habit, however, of constantly asking me if I knew people I'd actually introduced her to. But I forgave her. She was experiencing that first, heady taste of the high life in New York. I knew from experience how intoxicating it could be.

The next few months were a happy time for me, one of the best periods of my life. I had a feeling of real accomplishment. The Dent apartment was architecturally challenging with its vast entertaining rooms devoid of decorative detail. Agatha, who was very unsure of her own taste, relied heavily on my suggestions, which meant I could pretty much do as I pleased. I told her I thought the apartment should be sumptuous and understated, not grand in the expected sense. I showed her pictures of Versailles and Le Petit Trianon and explained the difference.

"Versailles was rather vulgar and not very cozy," I told her. "So Marie Antoinette preferred the Petit Trianon, created by Gabriel for Madame de Pompadour. It was the essence of elegance and chic and the only place aside from Le Hameau where the Queen could be herself. '*Là, je suis moi,*' she said. We're going to make your apartment the Trianon."

Agatha seemed to go along with the idea. She certainly nodded a lot.

I was gliding along smoothly, concentrating on my new job, trying to find office space I could afford, looking around for a permanent apartment, focusing on what was ahead rather than dwelling on what was past. In short, I felt my life was on a nice new track when, early one mild November morning, Betty called me up and spoke the five most feared words in New York: "Have you seen Page Six?"

I immediately opened up my *New York Post* to that infamous page of gossip and reeled back at the sight of the hideous quarter-page picture of myself walking along Madison Avenue, slack-jawed, wearing dark glasses, weighted down by a shopping bag of samples. The caption underneath read: "Jo Slater: The Unmerry Widow."

Jo Slater, socialite widow turned social decorator, is about to find herself embroiled in a lawsuit with the city's latest upwardly mobile billionaire couple. Neil Dent, a venture capitalist from Cincinnati, and his wife, Agatha, hired Slater to decorate their twenty-two-million-dollar duplex apartment on Park Avenue. Now the couple are claiming that the elegant Mrs. Slater has grossly overcharged them for shoddy craftsmanship and failed to deliver work on time.

In an exclusive interview with the POST, *Mrs. Dent said: "Jo Slater's a fraud. She got where she is by using other people's know-how. She thought that just because we were from out of town she could pull the wool over our eyes. Well, she can't. We're not hicks."*

Mrs. Dent also had this to say about the stylish socialite widow: "She's supposed to be so fancy. She's not. She's from Oklahoma—a girl from the sticks, just like me."

Mrs. Slater has been a major philanthropic and social force in New York for years. A former salesperson at Tiffany & Co., she snatched Lucius Slater, the prominent investment banker, from the sorrows of widowerhood in 1976. Throughout his life, Mr. Slater maintained he met the former Jolie Ann Meers at a dinner party, denying the persistent rumors they were acquaintances of long standing at the time of his first wife's death.

The couple gifted the Municipal Museum with the Slater Gallery in 1990, re-creations of eighteenth-century French royal apartments composed largely of furniture and paintings from their own private collection.

When Mrs. Slater was cut out of her husband's will in favor of French aristocrat Monique de Passy, she immediately parlayed her sterling reputation and legendary style into a lucrative decorating business, using her social connections to attract wealthy clients. Mrs. Slater could not be reached for comment.

I sat in bed in a kind of stupor, trying to figure out which was worse: the threat of a lawsuit or the implica-

tion that I had been Lucius's mistress before Ruth died.
The phone rang. It was Betty again.

"Well?" she said.

"I'm in shock."

"What's all this about you and Lucius being 'acquaintances of long standing' at the time of Ruth's death?
Where'd they get that crap?"

"Oh, Betty . . ." It was too early in the morning to lie.

"Jesus Christ, Jo. That's not true, is it?"

"I'd rather not go into it."

"Well, you know, I'd rather that you *did* go into it
because I'm the dupe in this. Lest you forget, *I'm* the one
you guys used to supposedly introduce you. Remember?"
She was irate.

"It was Lucius's idea."

"I'm aware of that, thank you. He called me and asked
if I'd invite you to my dinner party. And he asked me to
pretend I was a friend of yours so people wouldn't find
out you were a salesgirl he'd just met. I never gave a shit
about your being a salesgirl, Jo, but I do care if you
tricked me. *Were* you carrying on with Lucius when he
was married to Ruth?"

"Why rake up ancient history?"

"Why? Ruth was a friend of mine. I mean, I didn't particularly like her, but she was a *friend.*"

"I know. I'm sorry."

"So *were* you two having an affair before she died?
Yes or no?"

"They were getting a divorce."

"Because of *you.*"

"No! Not because of me. Way before he met me."

There was a long silence.

"Betty?"

"I'm pissed," she said. "I don't know who the hell you are anymore."

She hung up. Then June called. The jungle drums were beating.

"Jo, have you seen Page Six?"

"Yes."

"Oh." I heard her disappointment at not being the messenger of doom. She recovered fast. "Well, I just want you to know I'm so, so sorry. It's disgraceful."

"Thanks."

A friendly voice. What a relief.

"Is it true that you and Lucius had been having an affair for years before Ruth died?"

"Did you just talk to Betty?"

"No."

"Then who?" I knew she'd been talking to someone.

"I can't say."

"*Who*, June?"

"Don't tell her I told you . . . Trish Bromire."

"Trish Bromire wasn't even around then. She was Miss Tallahassee, or something."

"They're saying Lucius killed Ruth so he could marry you."

"*What?*" I nearly dropped the phone I was so angry.

"Well, not literally. But apparently he didn't do everything he could to save her life . . . Hello? Jo? Are you there?"

"I'm here."

"Did you hear what I just said?"

"Vaguely. It's absolute nonsense. All this comes as a result of this damn article? I can't believe it."

"Don't blame me. I'm just repeating what I heard. So *did* you know him before?" June asked.

I sighed in exasperation. "What does it matter now? He's *dead*."

"I know, but you're not. That whole thing about how you cut Lucius's picture out of *Fortune* and then gave him a blow job in the men's room at Tiffany's—that isn't true?"

I sank down into my pillows in disgust. While I'd always been well aware people scoffed at me behind my back for being a salesgirl, this was the first inkling I got of just how lurid the story had actually been. There was such a thing as too much information, and this was it. I was hurt that June, a supposedly dear friend of mind, had been so coarse and blunt.

"Does anyone care that I'm about to be sued?" I said angrily.

"I was just curious, that's all," June said in her snippiest voice.

While I realized certain of my friends would only be interested in getting the real story of how Lucius and I really met, I had far more important matters to attend to. This publicity was wildly damaging to me and to my business, even if it wasn't true.

I got June off the phone and immediately phoned up Agatha Dent. She didn't take my call. A bad sign. I asked to speak to Mr. Dent. He was at the office, the maid informed me. I called him there. He wasn't in—or at least he wasn't in to me. I asked to speak to Shawna, his private secretary, with whom I'd dealt on numerous occasions regarding bills and scheduling for the apartment.

"Shawna, hi, it's Jo Slater," I said, trying to sound as

composed as possible. "Listen, I've just had a bit of a shock. I opened Page Six in the *Post* and I see that the Dents are suing me . . . ?" The forced laugh I mustered met with a menacing silence on the other end of the line.

"I know it's absurd," I continued, "but please tell Mr. Dent I'm anxious to speak with him as soon as possible, will you? We need to get this sorted out before any real damage is done."

Shawna, an import from Cincinnati whom I'd never met, had one of those earnest singsong midwestern twangs, meant, I imagined, to inspire confidence in investors.

"Mrs. Slater, Mr. Dent asked me to inform you if you called that you will be hearing from his lawyer sometime today or tomorrow."

"His lawyer? About what, may I ask?"

"I am not at liberty to discuss that with you, Mrs. Slater. But, as I said, I do believe you will be hearing from Mr. Dent's lawyer sometime today or tomorrow." She had the irritating habit of always repeating herself verbatim.

"Do you know where I can get in touch with Mr. Dent *now*?" I asked her.

"No. Sorry. I sure don't."

"Do you know who Mr. Dent's lawyer *is*? I'll call him myself."

"No, I sure don't."

"Well, do you know when Mr. Dent will be available?"

"No, I sure don't."

"You're sure you sure don't?" I said. I just couldn't help myself.

"Beg pardon, ma'am?"

"Never mind. Thank you."

I hung up the phone. I was shaking. The doorbell rang. Darling Ethan Monk had sent me two dozen white roses with a note:

> *"Every newspaper, from the first line to the last, is nothing but a tissue of horror . . . I am unable to comprehend how a man of honor could take a newspaper into his hands without a shudder of disgust."*
>
> —*Baudelaire*

I'm here if you need me, Ethan.

Now there, at last, was a real friend.

I got up and made myself a cup of coffee. As soon as I could think straight, the light began to dawn. There had never been any rumors about Lucius and me at the time of Ruth's death—or at any other time, for that matter. Only two people in the world knew the truth about how Lucius and I had met. One was Nate Nathaniel, who had kept his mouth shut for twenty years. The other was Monique.

Suddenly, there wasn't a scintilla of doubt in my mind who was behind this whole thing.

I immediately called Nate. He wasn't home. I tried his office. He picked up the phone himself.

"Nate?"

He didn't even bother with hello. "Jesus, Jo, I just saw Page Six. What the hell's going on?"

"Monique. She did this to me. I know she fed them the story. She's the only other one aside from you who knows the truth about me and Lucius."

"Who told her?"

"I did, I confess. But she knew it already. Lucius told her. Didn't I tell you she was out to get me?"

"Are you really being sued?"

"Who knows? I called Neil's office and his secretary told me to expect a call from his lawyer."

"Have you got an arbitration clause?"

"No."

"Oy."

An arbitration clause in a contract afforded some protection in case of a dispute. It stipulated that a board composed of qualified decorators (my peers) would determine whether or not I had properly done my job. And while such panels were obviously meant to be fair and impartial—what decorator had not faced the wrath of a disgruntled client?—such a jury was bound to lean to my side. Dieter Lucino had refused to work for Dent without that clause, which was why he had lost the job. Neil Dent was dead set against it.

"Why should I sign something where the jury's gonna be on your side?" Dent told me at the time.

But I was hungry so I went ahead without one. My mistake.

—⁓—

IN my wildest dreams, I couldn't imagine what the Dents could possibly have had against me. I thought the work I had done for them was really quite exquisite—subtle, elegant, and altogether *bien,* as the French say. True, we were running a little behind schedule and a little over budget, but nothing serious—nothing I hadn't warned them about when I took the job. I told them they'd have to be a little "flexible" on a project of this size. They had seemed to understand perfectly at the time.

That afternoon, the Dents' lawyer, a surly-sounding

man named Whitney Colter, called to inform me he was faxing over copies of two separate letters: one terminating my services immediately, and another listing the charges against me. My fax machine belched them both out at three o'clock. The first was short and unsweet, an unceremonious dumping. The second letter was a litany of complaints against me that included things like not completing work "in a timely fashion," "grossly" overcharging for "certain items of decoration and furniture," and substituting "inferior" materials for the "costly" ones specified on the invoices.

At best the letter accused me of incompetence; at worst, it accused me of fraud. Either way it was an outrage. I harked back to something Lucius always said: "If you really want to get even with someone, don't kill them, sue them."

I knew two things for certain: One was that my reputation was, if not totally ruined, severely damaged; and two, that Monique de Passy was somehow behind the entire debacle—not simply the egregious newspaper article.

I had no choice but to fight back. Financially, however, I was in no position to defend myself against a lawsuit, no less countersue for defamation of character.

—⁂—

WHEN all my efforts to contact either Agatha or Neil Dent failed, I called Trish Bromire and asked for her help. Trish was not only the person who had introduced the Dents to me, she had been instrumental in getting me the job. I felt terrible for her sake as well as my own, but I needed her to intervene.

Trish invited me over to her apartment, a penthouse on Park Avenue with wraparound terraces and sweeping views of the city. The simplicity of the decor, with its white and beige color scheme and sleek modern furniture, showed off the very fine contemporary art and sculpture collection Gil Waterman had helped the Bromires assemble over the years.

Trish and I sat on one of four elongated white wool sofas in the living room. A whimsical Calder mobile dangled high above our heads. Trish looked drawn and pale. She was understandably upset.

"Jo, I can't get in the middle of this thing, I really can't," she began. "Dick and I have enough problems of our own at the moment." She was referring, of course, to the endless tax investigation that was always rumored to be concluding, but then somehow dragged on and on.

"Trish, I'm mortified to have to put you in this position. But Agatha won't talk to me. It's just so irrational. I thought she might have spoken to you."

"Look, the truth is we don't know them all that well," Trish confessed. "Dick's done business with Neil, and we've had dinner with them several times. But Agatha's not that good a friend of mine . . . I'm sorry, Jo. I honestly thought I was doing you a favor. I just never imagined—" She threw her hands up in frustration. "Jesus Christ, I wish I'd never gotten involved! Dick is right. I should learn to mind my own business."

"No good deed," I said, not even bothering to finish the old saw.

"Goes unpunished, I know," she chimed in.

"Seriously, Trish, I have no idea why they're so upset.

The apartment's coming along beautifully. You should see it."

"The only thing I can tell you is that Dick says that Neil's a very tough guy who's very insecure."

"A lethal combination."

"Right. *And* he's litigious. Particularly if he thinks he's been taken advantage of."

"*Taken advantage of—!*" I cried. "My God, you know me, Trish! I would never take advantage of *anyone*. Just the opposite. If you want to know the truth, they're slow payers, so I've even gone ahead and ordered things using my own money!"

"Was that smart?"

"Apparently not. But I wanted to get the job done. They approved everything I ordered. Look, they want a grand apartment. Grand apartments in New York cost money."

"I know, but they're from Cincinnati."

"Trish, listen to me. I don't think this is all about money. I think someone got to them. Influenced them. And what's more, I think I know who that someone is."

Trish cocked her head to one side. "Who?"

"Monique."

Trish's eyes widened. "Monique? Nobody sees her. Nobody *dares* on account of you."

"I know, I know . . . Don't ask me how, but I would bet you a million dollars that Agatha Dent and Monique de Passy have somehow gotten to know each other. For one thing, how did the newspapers get that story? *I* didn't even know I was being sued."

"Agatha or Neil could have told them, couldn't they?"

"Trust me, tough they may be, savvy they are not . . .

Somebody leaked that story, and then Page Six called Agatha . . . No, I believe there's a far more nefarious hand at work here."

Trish looked at me sympathetically. "I keep score every day," she said.

"What do you mean?"

"Some days the good guys are winning, some days the bad guys are winning. It's a bad guy day."

I couldn't have agreed with her more.

15

IF Lucius's death was an earthquake, this event was a terrible aftershock. My decorating business was something that I had created all on my own. I was proud of it, proud of the fact that I had not succumbed to maudlin self-pity after Lucius died and instead picked myself up and gotten on with my life. Now my new livelihood—and indeed, my whole reputation—was in jeopardy.

On the financial front, I had made personal commitments to several of my suppliers regarding the Dent job. It's the custom of decorators to send the client an invoice for a work order that the client then pays before work is commenced so the decorator will not be out of pocket. In order to save time, however, I went ahead and ordered some of the custom-made upholstery and curtains without waiting for the Dents to send me their money. The job was so big, I felt it was a reasonable risk. Because I'd commissioned these pieces, I owed about seventy-five thousand dollars to various fabric houses and workrooms. That amount, plus the five hundred thousand I still owed to the Muni, plus the lawyer's fees I was going to have to shell out to defend myself against these cockamamie accusations meant that I was facing an even deeper monetary crisis.

The worst aspect of the whole Dent debacle, however, was the way it distanced me from my very closest pals. Betty was furious at me because of what she felt was a personal betrayal, harking back years. We finally had a long, serious talk one afternoon where I told her the whole story of my relationship with Lucius, starting with our meeting at Burnham's. I explained why he'd felt it necessary to cover up the truth about us, not just to avoid besmirching Ruth's memory, but also for his son's sake. Betty turned out to be a good enough friend to forgive me for having kept the truth from her all these years. True friendship always has to be bigger than the sum of its parts. We got back on a more or less even keel, but the seas were rough for a time.

June was another story. I was the one who was miffed at her. Having had time to reflect on our conversation the morning the infamous article appeared on Page Six, I didn't appreciate her blurting out—however innocently—that the way I had snared Lucius was through a "blow job in the men's room at Tiffany's." I couldn't help looking at June with a slightly jaundiced eye after that. Even though we eventually kissed and made up, I had to wonder if she really wished me well.

Ethan had behaved beautifully. I was grateful to him for all his support *until* a scant ten days later when he called me up to tell me he'd been seated next to Agatha

Dent at a dinner party. I was on edge already and when I heard this it was all I could do not to hit the ceiling.

"*Et tu, Ethan?*" I said softly and hung up the phone.

He called me back immediately and pleaded with me to meet him for a drink at the Carlyle that evening around six. I arrived first, wearing a black suit and dark sunglasses to hide my puffy eyes. I sank down on one of the plushy couches in the little drinks area and ordered a double vodka, warning the waiter to be on guard for a second round quite quickly. Ethan arrived a short time later looking like a disheveled professor, as usual. He sat down and said: "Sorry I'm late. God, Jo, you're so thin."

"Right. I'm thin and not at all rich," I said, belting back the dregs of the vodka.

Ethan smiled. He ordered a Campari and soda from the waiter. I just handed the man my empty glass. He got the point.

"Ethan, I can't believe you sat next to Agatha Dent. That woman and her crazy husband have ruined my life. Do you have any idea what I'm going through?"

"It was a seated dinner," he said, as if that explained everything.

"You should have switched the place cards."

"*Moi?* Switch a place card? What would dear old Ward say?"

The reference was to Ward McAllister, a nineteenth-century fussbudget who was the first arbiter of New York Society who subscribed to the code of manners that says there is absolutely no excuse for switching place cards or for failing to show up at a dinner one has accepted— including death. "In case you die," McAllister advised his social flock, "you must send your executor in your place." His name was a private joke between Ethan and myself.

"Look, I didn't inform you of this to hurt your feelings," Ethan went on. "I have a little gossip for you—not that you're interested."

I sat back and folded my arms across my chest. "What?" I said petulantly.

"First of all, did you know that Dieter Lucino is redoing the Dent apartment?"

"I'd heard that, yes. I was told that it looks like Cleopatra goes to the Third Reich. So?"

"Your pal Agatha and I spent half the dinner discussing real marble versus faux marble. Agatha prefers real."

"You're telling *me?*" I sighed. "As Princess Arnofi once said, 'It'll take her a lifetime to understand wicker.'"

"But here's the deal," Ethan went on. "Apparently, a certain person went around their apartment when you were decorating it and told her your work was tacky."

"Tacky—?"

"Wait . . . And apparently, this person put a bee in dear Agatha's bonnet, telling her it wasn't nearly grand enough for all the money they'd shelled out, and that when people saw it, she, Agatha, would be a laughing-stock in New York."

I suddenly twigged. As I opened my mouth, Ethan cut in, "You guessed it. 'The Countess,' as Mrs. Dent insists on referring to her. Dear Agatha's obsessed with titles. Her dream in life is for Mr. Dent to be appointed ambassador to England."

"God save the Queen. Didn't I tell you Monique was behind this whole thing?"

"I fear you're right. And here's the capper," he continued. "Guess who's a heavy investor in two of Neil Dent's deals?"

That was the last straw. But I was beyond outrage. I just shook my head in despair. "I should have known. It's all about money. What else is new?"

Our drinks arrived. I chugged mine down quickly for anesthetizing purposes and handed the empty glass back to the waiter before he could escape.

"Fill'er up," I said.

Ethan looked at me askance. "You taking drinking lessons from Betty?"

I ignored the remark. "Here's what I bet happened. Monique found out I was decorating their apartment. In fact, I recall there was a little blurb about it in *Nous* at the time. So she makes an appointment with Neil Dent and puts a big chunk of dough into his company. Then she somehow gets friendly with Agatha—which wouldn't be difficult since Agatha's about as discriminating as a puppy. I'm sure Agatha swooned when she found out Monique was a countess. She worships the 'noblety,' as she calls it. She subscribes to *Royalty* magazine and *Hola* by the way," I said, forgetting all about Ethan's own incongruous penchant for those particular publications.

"Please. I adore all those happy royal faces. Such a relief from real life," he said.

"Monique deliberately sabotaged me," I mused. "Can't you just picture Monique taking Agatha around the apartment trashing my work? 'Oh look at ziss, Agassa . . . Ziss is not grand eenough for a great Tsarina such as yourself . . .'" I said in a mock French accent. "Christ, the Dents' idea of grandeur is a footman behind every chair."

"They ain't the only ones," Ethan said. "Agatha has a ways to go before she understands Le Hameau. She still wants Versailles."

"Maybe she should just forget the paintings and frame the checks . . . " I sank back in the chair, suddenly feeling the effects of the vodka.

"Anyway, I thought you'd be interested. Jo, are you there?"

I was in despair. "Ethan, do you realize Monique's ruined me? For the second time."

"She hasn't ruined you."

"No? I have two jobs I'm working on. When they're over, that's it. I haven't gotten a single new client since this whole thing happened."

Ethan shifted uncomfortably in his seat.

"I thought she was leaving New York," he said.

"Apparently not."

Sitting there with Ethan, I felt a change come over me. Monique's image was somehow trapped in my mind's eye. I tried to shake it off, but even when Ethan steered the conversation onto the more pleasant topic of the paintings coming up in the Old Master sale at Chapel's, I couldn't stop thinking about her. I recognized the seed of obsession planting itself in my brain. I tried to prevent it from taking root, for my own sake even more than Monique's. But long after Ethan and I had said good-bye to each other, long after I had turned out the lights and gone to bed, I lay awake in the darkness seeing Monique's face.

—⚭—

REPUTATION is everything in business—particularly in the decorating business because it literally hits people where they live. Word of mouth is crucial. A dissatisfied client can sully the most eminent and well-established firm, no less a fledgling one like mine. If prominent clients spread the word they've been cheated or taken advantage of by a decorator, that decorator is cooked.

After talking to the Dents' lawyer, it was clear to me that they just wanted out of their contract. For some reason, Neil Dent felt the most expeditious way to terminate my services was to go on the offensive and threaten to sue me. I informed the lawyer that under the circumstances I'd happily bow out of the job, but that I did have outstanding commitments to several workrooms. The lawyer informed me that the Dents had no intention of paying me another cent and that, in effect, I would just have to lump it or face them in court. Rather than hire a lawyer and amass a pile of legal fees, I agreed to let them off the hook. The episode, however, had damaged both my finances and, far worse than that, my good name.

If that weren't enough, there was a mysterious barrage of bad press about me.

Unlike many of my friends, I'd never actively sought publicity. On the contrary, I cherished my privacy and strongly believed in the elegance of silence. Having been known primarily to the readers of *Nous,* that nice, cozy, social periodical with a limited readership, I was horrified when the whole scandal involving Lucius's will had made my life fodder for the tabloids. This latest fiasco set the media hounds on my trail again. There was a snide piece on me in Eve Mindy's column in the *Daily News.* Mindy implied I was no more than a dilettante using my connections to shepherd aspiring climbers in gaining a foothold in what Mindy described as "The Golden Circle of New York's Social Elite."

To compound this insult, the press were suddenly, mysteriously fascinated with Monique—or "The Countess de Passy," as she was always referred to in print. Mindy depicted her as an alluring young foreigner who had somehow managed to snag the heart and fortune of one of the city's richest men.

Another particularly egregious puff piece appeared in *Madison Magazine,* a monthly giveaway distributed in the lobbies of all the upmarket New York apartment buildings. Accompanied by a wistful picture of Monique standing on Bethesda Terrace in Central Park, looking out at the "Angel of the Waters" fountain, it read:

> *Countess de Passy, who declines all requests for interviews, spends her time going for long walks in Central Park, communing with nature, and frequenting museums. If she is aware of the rumors swirling around about her, she keeps silent, as if she were guarding some deep secret of her own. Although she is uninterested in playing the social game, she contributes heavily to charity and enjoys giving small dinners in her magnificent duplex overlooking Fifth Avenue.*

I had to hand it to Monique. She wisely kept her mouth shut, refusing to fall into the famous trap of telling her side of the story.

Shortly after that piece appeared, I found out from June that Monique had hired a press agent. June discovered this little tidbit because the same firm she used to publicize her benefits also handled private clients, though they were very secretive about the fact. Gerry Harcourt, June's public relations pal in the firm, told June in strictest confidence that Monique was now a client.

Gerry, an attractive, straight-shooting divorcée, wasn't at all enamored of the Countess, who affected an imperious air with the firm's employees—including Gerry.

"She's a real C. U. Next Tuesday," Gerry told June.

What concerned me deeply was the fact that I'd confided so many secrets to Monique that summer when we were such great friends. I feared that some of those confidences—such as who I disliked in the social world and certain tales I knew about members of our little set—would, like my real relationship with Lucius in the beginning, eventually find their way into print. And some of them did. Eve Mindy reported that I had a long-standing dislike of Bootsie Baines, a prominent *amie mondaine,* known for having a sour, arrogant attitude and a sweet, long-suffering husband. When I ran into Bootsie at June's *Medea* benefit for Children in Crisis, she cut me dead.

Then something else happened—one of those little things that seem fairly inconsequential at the time, but which, in hindsight, are harbingers of doom. Betty called me, asking if I wanted her to swing by and pick me up for Marcy Lorenz's annual Christmas season luncheon the following week, to which she obviously assumed I'd been invited. When I told her I didn't know anything about it, she got all embarrassed and hung up. Five minutes later, Marcy called and said there'd been a ghastly mistake.

"Some of the invitations went astray, Jo, and I've just been too busy to call everyone and reconfirm," Marcy said nervously. "But of course you're invited!"

Seeing through that old ploy, I thanked her and declined, saying I was attending a funeral that day.

Not only was I now being invited places only because

my loyal friends were insisting I still be included, I sensed a real sea change in people's attitudes toward me. Don't get me wrong, I was still going to a lot of parties where everyone was very polite to my face. However, the effusiveness with which I had formerly been greeted by one and all was replaced by—how shall I describe it?—a kind of flippant camaraderie, the hurried, empty attention people give when they feel obliged to say hello for form's sake but don't wish to linger on for a conversation.

The security of feeling that I automatically belonged started to evaporate. I felt the piranhas moving in on me fast, taking their first nips. All the people who had been secretly jealous of me now had their chance to whittle me down to size. I loathed being the main dish at the gossips' banquet in New York, where Schadenfreude is a culinary art form. There I was, nonetheless, tender and juicy as a choice prime rib. And there was nothing I could do about it.

I was a fashionable loser. Publicly feeling sorry for Jo Slater was the newest spectator sport.

16

IT had been nearly a year and a half since Lucius's death and three months since the famous Dent debacle. My decorating business was effectively over. I was finishing up the last job when my dear friend Eugenie Pourtant phoned from Paris, insisting I come stay with her.

"Jo," she said, "I have found someone you must meet."

When I asked Eugenie who it was, she refused to tell me. "Just come," she urged me, refusing to take no for an answer.

I was in need of a break from New York anyway, so I took her up on her offer, figuring I could do some shopping for the client as well as see a few old friends.

I suspected the person she wanted me to meet had some connection with Monique. Eons ago, when Monique and I'd been friends, I casually asked Eugenie if she knew the Countess. She didn't. Then, when the whole thing happened with Lucius and the will, Eugenie called me again and promised to find out everything she could about Monique.

"It's too late," I told her. I had other things on my mind.

Eugenie, like a terrier with a bone, wasn't one to let things drop.

—∿—

I flew to Paris in economy class on a nonrefundable round-trip ticket. I mention this only because it was the first time in years I'd flown anything but first class, if you don't count private jets. Quite frankly, it wasn't as bad as I thought it was going to be. I had very nice seat companions, an affable young couple from Hartford who were taking their first trip to Europe. I told them I envied them seeing Paris for the first time and gave them tips on several out-of-the-way places to visit.

I arrived at Charles de Gaulle on a rainy February morning. I took a taxi to Eugenie's house on the Rue du Bac on the Left Bank. The damp Parisian winter chilled me to the bone and I looked forward to Eugenie's apartment, which was always warm and welcoming.

The taxi driver was unexpectedly obliging. He helped me carry my luggage into the hidden courtyard where a square of ancient cobblestones led to the slightly run-down eighteenth-century *hotel particulier* where Eugenie occupied the top two floors. Eugenie's Algerian maid, Feli, came downstairs to help me with my bags. The short, pockmarked young woman showed me up to the small guest room on the top floor and informed me in shattered, almost unintelligible French that her mistress would be back in a short time. The apartment had Old World grandeur but few modern comforts. The bathrooms were small, the living quarters cramped. But the entertaining rooms were glorious, decorated in what I thought of as "bohemian chic."

After freshening up from the long flight, I wandered downstairs. The main salon, overlooking a barren back garden, had high ceilings and pale gray boiserie. The decor was an eclectic mixture of fine family heirlooms and exotic junk Eugenie had picked up on her travels. The combination of paisley shawls thrown over well-worn velvet couches, peacock feathers stuck behind ancestral portraits, and cheap bric-a-brac elevated by its proximity to fine antiques attested to the artistic, offbeat sensibility of the occupant. As always, the apartment had a rich musky aroma from the perfumed paper rings Eugenie burned on her lamp bulbs.

I was dozing on a bottle green velvet divan when Eugenie burst into the room, crying, "*Jo, ma chère! Je suis ravie de te voir!*"

I, too, was delighted to see my old friend. Though we'd spoken on the phone many times, we hadn't seen each other in person since well before Lucius's death. I reflected on how much my life had changed since our last meeting.

Though Eugenie still moved with the graceful agility of a ballerina, she looked older. She'd had what the French call a *coup de vieux*—a sudden aging that is particularly noticeable in women who have looked much younger than their years for a long time. Her features, prominent to begin with, now jutted out on her face like crags on a cliff, coarsening the bold, chiseled beauty that had once captivated men and women alike. Her body was still lithe and, as always, she was chicly dressed in an original way where nothing matched but everything went together. She was wearing a striking gold necklace that I recognized as one of her own design.

Feli came in carrying a brass tray with two steaming toddy glasses and a plate of miniature croissants. The sweet concoction of hot tea mixed with strawberry preserves warmed my insides and revived me a little. Never one to beat about the bush, Eugenie got straight to the point.

"My darling Jo, you look beautiful but exhausted. Tell me how you are."

"Lousy," I confessed.

"Are you still decorating?"

"I'd like to be. But my business is ruined. I have one client left."

"But *why?* Just because of those awful people? Clients get upset all the time. It's not so tragic."

"I know, but when you're just starting out . . . The perception is that I cheated a pair of decent, rich out-of-towners."

"Jo, anyone who knows you knows that you couldn't cheat anyone."

"Let's just say that Mrs. Dent is a woman who will never comprehend the subtlety of hand-painted silk. She wants gold brocade. And her husband is a psychopath. I found out that lawsuits are his avocation."

"And all this because of Monique de Passy?"

"Hey, she's a Countess. They're from Cincinnati. What can I tell you?" I spooned up the preserves from the bottom of my glass. "The knives are out for me anyway," I said, savoring their sweet, warm taste. "One thing you never really realize when you're so insulated is how envious people are."

"Envy makes the world go 'round, darling," she said. "It's a marvelous spectator sport. Cheap and you can do it anywhere!" Eugenie rubbed her hands together as if she were about to dig into a feast. "Now Jo, I have found out a great deal about your *Countess*," she said with a derogatory inflection. "She is a very dangerous person."

I couldn't help laughing. "You're telling *me?* Are we old and good enough friends so that if I tell you something, I can trust you not to repeat it?"

"*Ça va sans dire, Jo.* I'm not June Kahn," Eugenie said with a little chuckle. Everyone who knew June knew she was about as discreet as the Internet.

"You know how everyone thinks that Monique was Lucius's mistress and that's why he left her a fortune? Well, according to her, he wanted to divorce me and marry her so she could have his child."

Eugenie's jaw dropped slightly. She set her glass back down on the tray. "His *child? Mon Dieu!* How old was he? Seventy?"

"Exactly. She told me she was pregnant and that she had a miscarriage after he died."

"You believed her?"

I shrugged. "Who knows? Would I have believed Lucius capable of what he did to me? Nate Nathaniel confirmed it. Nate was his great confidant, as you know. It's so hard to tell."

Eugenie looked at me with a compassion tinged with irritation. "Jo, I have seen you in the library of the Louvre, poring over ancient inventories to confirm the authenticity of an inkwell. I have traveled with you to the far corners of Europe to check out the provenance of a painting. Why are you so willing to accept the word of a confidence woman? How do we really know he wanted to marry her and that she was pregnant? Because *she* says so? Please."

"She obviously convinced *him*."

"A gorgeous young woman can convince an old man of *anything*."

"I know, but what does it really matter now? The point is he left her the money."

"Bastard. Why didn't you fight the will?"

"I talked to five lawyers. They all told me I'd lose. I probably would've contested it if I'd had the money. But I just couldn't afford to lose."

"Are you sure that's the only reason?"

I looked at her quizzically. "What do you mean?"

"The last time you were here you told me you felt guilty being so fortunate in life when other people had nothing, you remember?"

"You think subconsciously I believe I got what I deserved?" I said.

"We all suffer from that a bit, no? We have nice comfortable lives so we must pay for them in some way."

"Maybe."

"You are not in a Kafka novel, my darling. You are not guilty of anything except having been a good wife to that shit of a man."

"He always promised he'd take care of me. That was my mistake—wanting, needing, to be taken care of. That's why I loved my decorating business so much, because it was mine. No one else's. No one gave it to me. And now she's taken that away, too."

Eugenie sipped her tea. "There is someone who wants very much to meet you," she said.

"Who?"

"Anne-Marie de Passy. Her brother, Michel, was married to Monique."

"The one who died."

"You will love this old woman. She's fascinating. And the stories she tells about her sister-in-law—my dear!" Eugenie rolled her eyes.

"They can't be any worse than mine."

"That is exactly why you two will adore one another. Nothing bonds people more quickly than a common hatred."

At this moment, I was tempted to confide in Eugenie, telling her all my suspicions about Monique's involvement in Lucius's death. But I decided it was wiser not to mention it.

"Where did you meet this woman?" I inquired.

"Michel de Passy owned an art gallery here, you know. Friends of mine knew him. I didn't know he had a sister until recently, however. She's quite a recluse. But I found her and I went to see her. She would like to meet you."

I was eager to meet Anne-Marie de Passy, thinking what a lift it would be to sit down and have a discussion with someone else who knew Monique's treachery firsthand. I had an inkling I was entering further into that dangerous realm of obsession where one is attracted to the thing one most despises, and where, if one isn't careful, one can become both the hurricane and the house it destroys. The truth is, I didn't care. All I wanted to do was talk about Monique, to hate her out loud.

—⟿—

EUGENIE refused to accompany me to the meeting she arranged with old Mademoiselle de Passy. "She will tell you more if you see her alone," Eugenie said.

Anne-Marie de Passy lived in a tiny apartment on the Rue du Cherche-Midi, opposite Monsieur Poilâne's Boulangerie, one of the oldest bakeries in Paris, famous for its crispy apple tarts and tasty baguettes baked in pre-Revolutionary ovens. She occupied cramped quarters in the back of a seedy, ancient house. The small living room had no light and smelled of cats. Indeed, several scraggly looking felines drifted around in corners like gray dust-balls as she poured me tea into two exquisite porcelain cups whose pattern I recognized. Finely painted nymphs and satyrs danced around a luminous indigo ground. I asked her if they were copies of the famous service that Hetlinger, the head of the Sèvres factory, had designed for Marie Antoinette in 1782.

"They are not copies," she said tersely.

I was impressed. Only the Queen of England possessed a complete set of this quality. For me, it was like drinking from the Holy Grail.

Anne-Marie de Passy, however, was clearly not interested in the cups or anything else except her erstwhile sister-in-law. Monique had become the obsession of her life, as she was now threatening to become the obsession of mine. I quickly learned that she hated Monique with a passion so deep that when she talked about her for any length of time she began to tremble with an involuntary, deep-seated rage.

"You have come to talk to me about the woman who led my brother into hell," she began. "You must understand that Michel and I were extremely close. I brought him up when our mother died. I adored him, but he was a weak man, susceptible to two things: beauty and drugs. Monique supplied him both in abundant quantities."

The old spinster, who spoke a cultivated English with almost no French accent, sounded more like an upper-class Brit than a native Frenchwoman. She described Monique as a scheming predator who had married a much older man for his social position and all the family treasures she could steal, a picture that only reinforced my own jaundiced view of the Countess.

"How did your brother meet her?" I asked.

"God knows. But he hired her to work in his art gallery. I loathed her from the moment I set eyes on her. She fooled everyone but me. I knew her type. I understood instantly she was after Michel, not because she loved him, but because he was rich and well connected. I also knew that she would get him in the end because he was so weak and so terrified of getting old. She was very beautiful, very manipulative, and very evil."

"Oh, I know. She fooled me," I said. "Did she ever talk to you about her own family background?"

"What background?" she scoffed. "*Elle n'est pas née.*" I knew the French expression, which literally meant, "She isn't born." It was used to describe people who come from families of no particular distinction.

"How long were Monique and your brother married?"

"Three and a half years. Then he died," she said, visibly deflating. "He didn't really want to marry her, you know. But she tricked him. She told him she was pregnant and that she was going to have the child with or without him."

I blanched at this revelation. "That's exactly what she told *my* husband—that she was pregnant with his child."

De Passy gave a grim little chuckle. "I'm not surprised. She was not only a sexual predator but an emotional predator as well."

"Did she have the baby?"

"What baby?" she said with a dismissive wave of her hand. "She was never pregnant. It was all a story. I found out she couldn't have children, the merciful result of a botched abortion when she was twenty-one. God forbid there should be another one like her roaming the earth."

I was stunned. "How did you find all this out?"

"I hired a private detective, my dear. Naturally, I wanted to protect my darling brother's interests, as well as my own . . . She was called Monique Bourot, a little girl from Normandy. She was like Emma Bovary, only sadistic and adept at getting what she wanted. She was married twice before Michel, once to a musician when she was very young, and once to another rich older man."

"What happened to them?"

"She divorced the musician. But the rich older man died."

"How?"

"We were never quite sure. There was an official inquiry, but it was hushed up for some reason. The detective tried to find out more, but you know, in France, all these things are very difficult to learn."

"Did your brother know about all this?"

"Indeed he did. I showed him the report and begged him not to marry her. But she had an amazing hold on him, undoubtedly sexual in nature. These things always are. And, of course, it was compounded by the drugs.

Michel was quite literally possessed by her. After he read the report, he ordered me to leave his house. Can you imagine? Me, his own sister, who had been like a mother *and* a father to him. Me, whom he adored and who was trying to protect him. We didn't speak for nearly two and a half years—not until he started having trouble with her. *Then* he came back to me," she said proudly.

I could hardly believe my ears. Though the facts were different, the essence of the old woman's story was amazingly similar to my own.

"Do you still have that report?"

"No. I threw it away."

"What about the private detective? Is he still around? I wonder if I could talk to him."

"I have no idea. I don't care anymore."

"Do you remember the name of her second husband?"

"He was called Pierre Marcel and he owned quite a lot of property in Neuilly."

"Is that where she lived with him?"

"Yes. Rue Parmentier. But what's the point of dwelling on this? I found out everything it was possible to find out about her. And now, quite frankly, what does it matter? There is nothing to be done."

The frail woman leaned down and plucked a cigarette from a malachite and gold box on the coffee table. She offered me one. I declined. She pulled a reedy black holder from her pocket and slid the cigarette into it with her long bony fingers. The process took some time because she was arthritic. She lit the cigarette with a gold lighter and took several puffs, seemingly caught up in a web of memory.

I studied her face. She was a wizened older woman

with faint claims to an aristocratic pre-Revolutionary beauty. Her profile was pure ancien régime—a prominent nose angled upward, a haughty forehead, high cheekbones, sunken cheeks, and a thin strip of a mouth. Her pale blue eyes were clouded with cataracts and sadness. Her velvety white hair was swept up in a wispy, lopsided chignon fastened with tortoiseshell pins.

"Monique bled my brother dry financially, sexually, and emotionally. She used him and he refused to see it."

"How did she use him?"

"She spent all his money. She met the best people in Paris. She always wanted to be on the top."

"Of what?"

"*La bonne société.* High society, you call it."

"Your brother died of a heart attack, I understand."

"That is what they said, *but*—" she paused to exhale a long stream of smoke. "I am certain she had something to do with it. She took everything of value from him: his manhood, his self-respect, and I believe, ultimately, his life."

My stomach lurched. "Do you have any proof?"

"Just a moment," she said, stubbing out her cigarette in the ashtray.

She stood up with some effort and left the room, returning moments later with something in her hand. She sat down again.

"Michel was a drug addict. She knew it, but she did nothing to prevent him. On the contrary . . . I cannot prove that she gave him an overdose to kill him, but I am certain something like that happened," she said, handing me a vial containing packaged tablets.

It was a prescription in Monique's name for something called Rotinal.

"What's this?"

"It's a drug like Valium, only many, many times more potent and highly addictive. Illegal in America, I believe. A sex drug," she said in disgust. "Michel once told me it was like making love wrapped in a cloud. But my doctor told me that more than four will give you a seizure and put you under the ground."

I examined the vial. Monique's name was typed out on the label.

"It's in Monique's name."

"Exactly. She said she took them for anxiety, but she was too calculating to be anxious. I know she got them to give to my brother, to addict him, and worse. I told the police my suspicions, but they did nothing."

I tried to hand the vial back to her.

"No, no, please keep it," she said, refusing to take it from me. "I was going to get rid of it anyway. I don't dare have it around anymore."

The tone of defeat and melancholy in her voice told me she had perhaps been tempted to use the pills on herself.

"What makes you think Monique killed your brother?" I asked, tucking the vial away in my purse.

"Michel was planning to leave her and she would have been left with nothing," she said matter-of-factly. "One day my brother came to see me. He was very upset. He showed me a letter he had found. He discovered she was having an affair."

"Yes. With *my* husband."

"It could be. Michel told me he was an American."

"Did he tell you his name?"

She shook her head. "If he did, I don't remember it.

Michel was quite a narcissist when it came to women. He tolerated a great deal from them, but never infidelity. If they betrayed him, he left."

"You don't, by any chance, have that letter, do you?"

"Perhaps," she said, motioning to a far corner of the room. In the gloom I saw a pile of boxes and books and old photograph albums stacked up high against the wall. A cat jumped down from the heap. "All those things belonged to Michel. I salvaged them from his apartment. She must have thought they were worthless, which is why she left them behind. To me, however, they are precious because they are a record of my brother's life. It's all I have left of my family."

"If you ever do find that letter, I'd be very curious to see it."

"You are welcome to look for it yourself. I will never have the energy."

Eugenie had told her the vague outlines of my own story with Monique. She listened intently as I filled her in on all the details of my relationship with Monique, up to and including Monique's final revelation to me that she was pregnant with Lucius's child.

"You see? *Plus ça change,*" she said with a little laugh. "She tricked him too."

I suddenly felt ill. The twilight and potpourri atmosphere of the apartment enveloped me like a shroud. I had to escape from there, get some fresh air. I thanked the old woman for the tea and her time. Before I left, she handed me a photograph. It was of a much older man with a mustache standing alongside of Monique, who looked very girlish in a short white dress and a little white hat with a veil, holding a bouquet of lilies of the valley.

"My brother on his wedding day," she said bitterly.

When I looked closely, I saw the resemblance. Brother and sister both had the same Old World aristocratic looks, the same weary regal air, the last gasp of a proud heritage without consequence in today's world. The Count, with dark circles under his eyes that were beyond tired, offered the camera a crooked, cynical smile. As I tucked the photograph into my handbag, the old woman said: "My brother was all I had in the world."

She waved a sad little good-bye to me. I left Anne-Marie de Passy wishing in many ways I'd never gone to see her, fascinating as our visit had been. She was so sad and lonely. I had a vision of myself in reduced circumstances like that one day, in some phase of organized decay, living with cats. But worse than that, her conviction that Monique had killed her brother solidified my own view that she had somehow killed Lucius as well—or at a minimum purposely induced the fatal heart attack. Descending to the ground floor in an elevator as cramped as a coffin, I suddenly saw the obvious: Monique had killed Michel, just as his sister suspected, in order to trade up to Lucius, who was far richer and more powerful. Then she killed Lucius, just as I suspected. I resolved to find out what had happened to this predator's second husband.

17

I walked back to Eugenie's feeling agitated. A bright late afternoon sun glinted across the ever-bustling Boulevard Saint Germain. I stopped by the Café de Flore for a brandy. It was too cold to sit outside, but I did anyway. The winter streets were crowded with cars and passersby. The brandy warmed my insides but not my spirit. All I could think of was Monique and how evil she was.

Eugenie was waiting for me at the apartment anxious to know how the meeting had gone. She saw immediately how upset I was. She sat me down in the salon and poured me another brandy, which I was only too happy to drink. I was fast becoming a devotee of the Betty Waterman school of problem solving: "Just say when." I told Eugenie everything that the old woman had told me, including her suspicions that Monique had killed her brother. I showed her the photograph of Michel and Monique on their wedding day. Eugenie studied the picture for a long moment.

"She thinks Monique may have used these." I handed her the vial of Rotinal.

"Ah, Rotinal. I've heard it can do rather interesting things. Shall we try it this evening after dinner? Might be amusing," she said with an impish smile. "Don't worry, I'm joking." Eugenie handed me back the bottle and the photo. "So, do you think she killed Lucius?"

"The thought has crossed my mind," I said softly. "I really want to know what happened to her second husband."

"The rich old guy."

"Exactly."

"Do you think she could have killed him, too?" Eugenie said just like a wide-eyed kid.

"Who knows?"

Eugenie laughed. "So you believe Monique de Passy is a serial killer . . . A real Scheherazade of crime! You must find out."

"I intend to."

—⁓—

I rang up my dear old friend Bernard Longueville, who had once served as the French consul general in New York and who was now assistant to the president in the Elysée Palace. If anyone could help me, Bernard could.

Longueville, a gregarious and cultivated bachelor, had been a favorite of mine during his tenure in New York. His frank, open countenance, impeccable manners, and contrarian humor made him an ideal extra man. He was a constant fixture at our dinner parties. When Lucius was out of sorts or away on business, I often tapped Bernard to accompany me to the opera and other cultural events. We both shared a passion for Louis XVI furniture.

I met Bernard at the Ritz bar for lunch. In palmier days, I always stayed at the Ritz in a small suite on the top floor overlooking the rooftops of Paris. I preferred that suite to the far grander Chanel suite favored by Lucius because it was cozy, more intimate, less like a hotel. I'd always invite Bernard to lunch in the bar. It was a little ritual. We both enjoyed the Ritz version of a salade niçoise.

Bernard was punctual as usual. We gave each other a long embrace—the meaningful, knowing embrace of two old friends who have not seen each other in a while, one of whom has incurred much sadness since their last meeting. We sat down across from one another at a small corner table in the dark, wood-paneled bar. At first, we exchanged pleasantries, catching up on all the superficial New York and Parisian gossip. After Bernard ordered our salads and we both had a couple of glasses of wine to loosen up, he looked across the table at me and said, "Jo, my dear, you look wonderful, as always."

I looked back at him and replied without hesitation, "Bernard, how in God's name were you such a successful diplomat when you're such a rotten liar?"

Longueville shook his head and chuckled. "Ah, Jo, you know me too well. *Franchement,* I could not believe it when I heard what had happened. You know, I always thought Lucius was a rather strange man, but I never dreamed he would do something like that to you. You, of all people."

"No, me neither. But he did. And now I need your help," I said, coming straight to the point.

Bernard leaned forward and said with utmost sincerity, "Anything, Jo. How can I be of service to you?"

"This Frenchwoman, Monique de Passy, whom Lucius left the money to—she was married before. I need to find out about her second husband and particularly how he died. Apparently, there was an inquiry but it was hushed up for some reason."

I knew that Longueville would be tactful enough not to ask me why I needed the information.

"Do you know his family name and where he was from?"

"Pierre Marcel. He owned real estate in Neuilly. They lived on Rue Parmentier when they were married. That's all I know. Here's a picture of Monique with her third husband, Count de Passy." I handed him the wedding photo Anne-Marie de Passy had given me. He examined it.

"She's pretty."

"Pretty lethal."

Bernard's eyes flicked up at me. "*Évidemment . . .*" He turned the photo around where Monique's and Michel's names were written on the back. "Bourot . . . An ugly name. Uncommon," Longueville reflected. "Even so, Jo, I must be frank with you. It's not easy to check on records in France. Family records are the most difficult. Did you know that all birth and death certificates in this country are strictly private unless they are over one hundred years old?"

"No. Why?"

"France is not America, Jo. This law was made to prevent a recurrence of what happened in the '30s and '40s when the Nazis obtained records of people's heredity so they could uncover any Jewish ancestry. After the war, it was decided that all personal records should be sealed to the public. You can understand why."

"I see. But this is more of a police matter. Isn't that a bit different?"

"Still, it's a record of a death. It's a bit risky to try to go into these things—not to mention illegal."

"Forget it then. God knows I don't want you to get into any trouble on my account."

The diplomat laughed. "Heavens, no. I can get into enough trouble on my own account. Let me see what I can do. I might be able to 'flirt with the law' a little, as we say. May I keep this?"

"Of course."

He tucked the photograph into his breast pocket, raised his glass of wine to me, and said: "You know how fond I am of you, Jo. And 'the mind is always the dupe of the heart,' as La Rochefoucauld said."

AFTER lunch, just for the hell of it, I wandered over to the Conciergerie and walked around the old castle where Marie Antoinette had spent the last months of her life. Oddly enough, I'd never been to that dank place before, always preferring to visit Versailles, Le Petit Trianon, and Le Hameau, the venues of the Queen's happier days.

As tourists around me came and went, I stood staring into the claustrophobic cell where the Queen was imprisoned until her death. Seated at a small wooden table, dressed in peasant clothes, was a life-size gray-haired mannequin of the Queen. As she was depicted there, alone in stifling quarters, old before her time, one could not help but feel sorry for this rather silly woman whose tragic fate awoke a dormant regal soul.

I then went and checked out the names of all the people who had been guillotined. There, on the wall, was a list of de Passys, just as Monique had said. I stood there, imagining her being led to the scaffold and myself as the executioner.

—⁓—

FOR the next few days, I visited the *antiquaires* and fabric houses of Paris, shopping for my one remaining client. I avoided the very expensive dealers, keeping instead to Les Puces, the large flea market on the outskirts of town, and the smaller dealers around the Quai d'Orsay where I was not well known and where I could bargain.

One afternoon, Eugenie invited me up to her atelier. I always loved going there to see what she was up to. That day she said she had something very special to show me. Eugenie designed costume jewelry for a *fantasie* jewelry boutique on the Rue Bonaparte. Her creations were so beguiling that a very rich Indian woman famously bought a slew of the fake pieces and took them back to Jaipur where she had them copied in real gold and precious stones. Eugenie often made replicas of ancient or historical jewelry for special exhibitions. It was one of these pieces that she said she wanted me to see. When I asked her what it was, she said I'd have to wait. She wanted to surprise me.

I took the elevator up to the fourth floor of the commercial building on the Rue la Boétie where she had her workshop. Inside the long narrow room, lit by overhead fluorescent lights, four intent craftsmen sat at wooden tables assembling the one-of-a-kind costume pieces with the same mounting and setting techniques used to make real jewelry. They barely noticed as Eugenie and I walked past them to her small office in the back of the shop.

On her desk lay a large rectangular black leather jewelry case. Flipping up the lid, she turned the box toward me. There, glittering on a black velvet interior, was an exact copy of the famous diamond necklace that Marie Antoinette had refused to buy from Charles Boehmer in the early 1780s. This uncharacteristically frugal act on the Queen's part eventually led to what is arguably the greatest swindle in history and, ironically, to the monarchy's downfall. Goethe dubbed the infamous Necklace Affair, as it was called, "a precursor to the French Revolution."

Knowing of my fascination with the period and with this story in particular, Eugenie couldn't wait to show it to me.

"I made this for the Versailles Foundation," she explained. "It will be in a special exhibition of Marie Antoinette memorabilia—one of the highlights," she said with pride.

"It's fantastic," I said, admiring the fine craftsmanship of the piece.

"Try it on," she urged me, lifting the large, loopy necklace out of the case.

Eugenie fastened it around my neck. The long, drooping ropes ending in thick diamond tassels looked like garish upholstery fringe. I walked over to look at it on myself in the small oval mirror hanging in a far corner of the office.

"Imagine that idiot jeweler thinking Marie Antoinette, of all people, would have liked such a hideous thing,"

Eugenie said. "She, who was the epitome of elegant simplicity."

I fingered one of the heavy diamond tassels. "It reminds me of Monique."

Eugenie cocked her head to one side. "*Why?*"

"We used to talk about the Necklace Affair. We both agreed it was an underrated event in the history of the French Revolution."

"There is no question that historians don't take it as seriously as they ought to because it's about a piece of jewelry," Eugenie agreed.

"And because it has such a wild, theatrical cast of characters."

I'd always loved the story of how a clever conwoman found a prostitute who looked like Marie Antoinette and duped one of the most powerful men in France into handing over a four million dollar necklace. It was the stuff of romantic fiction—only it was all true. As I examined Eugenie's skillful copy, I went back over the story in my mind of how an impoverished noblewoman named Jeanne de la Motte-Valois convinced Cardinal de Rohan, a Prince of the Blood, that Marie Antoinette wanted him to obtain the diamond necklace in secret for her so there would not be a public outcry over another of her wild expenditures. De la Motte dressed up a prostitute named Madame Oliva, who was a dead ringer for the Queen, and arranged for the Cardinal to meet her on a moonlit night in the Parc de Versailles. There, the flighty, sycophantic Cardinal was completely taken in by the ruse. Believing the young prostitute to be Marie Antoinette herself, he threw himself at her feet and swore to do her bidding. He obtained the necklace and handed it over to de la Motte, who he assumed would give it to the Queen. Instead, de la Motte broke the necklace up, sold the diamonds separately, and set herself up in high style until the scam was discovered a year later.

King Louis XVI made the fatal mistake of arresting the Cardinal for fraud. De Rohan's trial exposed the court as a collection of spoiled, arrogant nincompoops. And, despite the evidence, most people believed Marie Antoinette to be guilty rather than the unwitting victim of a sting. De Rohan's acquittal left the Queen's reputation in shreds and the monarchy fatally weakened.

"What happened to the prostitute who impersonated the Queen?" Eugenie asked as she helped me unfasten the unwieldy piece of jewelry.

"Madame Oliva? They let her go. De la Motte was branded on both her shoulders with a V for *voleuse* and went to jail—where I'd like to see Monique."

"Marie Antoinette was the one innocent party in all of it and she wound up losing her head," Eugenie observed.

"Do we wonder why that story has resonance for me?" I took off the necklace and put it back in the case.

"Monique is your Jeanne de la Motte," Eugenie said.

"Not exactly. De la Motte got caught." I snapped the lid shut.

—⁓—

ONE drizzly afternoon, returning home at around two o'clock after an expedition to the Louvre, I found a plain white envelope on my bed. It had no return address on it, nothing except "Mme. Jo Slater" printed in block letters on the front. I opened it, thinking it was a bill from a small shop around the corner where I'd purchased a pair of antique needlepoint pillows for my client that very morning. Inside was the wedding photograph of Monique and Michel wrapped in a single sheet of paper. Unfolding it, I read the following:

> Dear Jo,
>
> Your friend died on August 27, 1989, of a heart attack, aged 68. A drug overdose was suspected but never proved. No charges were filed. The widow waived all her rights to his estate—rather unusual. I hope this helps you.
>
> Je t'embrasse, B.

So Monique had literally gotten away with murder— twice, counting Lucius. And no one could prove a thing.

———《》———

BEFORE I left Paris, I wanted to pay Anne-Marie de Passy one last visit. In order to protect Bernard, I could never tell a soul what I had learned about Monique's second husband, or the way I had obtained that information. But I had decided to take the old woman up on her offer to go through her brother's things. If she would allow me, I intended to sift through every scrap of paper in those old boxes piled up high in her living room until I found the letter Lucius had written to Monique. If, indeed, it still existed, I wanted to examine it with my own eyes, to see exactly what he'd written to her, hoping it would shed more light on how he had been hooked by this lethal adventuress. I was becoming more and more obsessed with Monique in the wake of this new revelation, and oddly more interested in what the letter might reveal about her rather than Lucius.

I took a taxi back to the Rue du Cherche-Midi to see

the old woman. She answered the intercom in a groggy voice and buzzed me in. I ran up the stairs, not wanting to wait for the slow, creaky elevator. I rang the bell twice and waited, then thumped the old bronze knocker in the shape of a shield. De Passy took a very long time to come to the door and, indeed, she looked as if she'd been sleeping. She was wearing a flowered housecoat and slippers. I got the awful feeling I was the only company she ever had except for the cats. I apologized for disturbing her, but she didn't seem to mind. On the contrary.

"I'm delighted to see you," she said, stepping aside for me to enter. "I was going to call you but I lost your friend's telephone number. Do come in." She straightened up her hair, which fell in strings around her haggard face. "After you left, I found the courage to go through my brother's belongings. I cannot say I am happy I did. The effort churned up many memories. The happy ones were the saddest of all," she reflected. "But I believe I have found what you want."

She bade me sit down while she disappeared into her bedroom. I was in a state of anxiety and anticipation, trying to fathom what the letter would say. The slow, deliberate ticking of the clock on the mantelpiece was a heavy reminder of time. I hated the gloom and the dust. The stifling little apartment palpitated with loneliness. The old woman took forever to come back.

She emerged several moments later, smelling of freshly sprayed lavender perfume. She handed me the letter. The neat black ink printing on the envelope read:

Please hold for the Countess de Passy
     Crillon Hotel

I lifted the flap. Inside was a sheet of paper made of heavy crisp white stock with a dark blue border. I knew that stationery well. I'd received many a thank-you note written on it.

I slid out the sheet and unfolded it. My hands were trembling. The monogram at the top, in dark blue to match the border, was "NPN." The signature at the bottom, in neat prep school print, read, "Nate."

Nate Nathaniel was Monique's secret American lover, not Lucius.

———m———

CONTRARY to what one might think, this revelation wasn't some gleaming sword of truth I wanted to pick up and fly into battle with; it was more like a wad of chewing gum stuck to the bottom of my shoe—ugly, sticky, uncomfortable. I couldn't get rid of it. It raised so many terrible questions.

The letter itself was brief, cold, and literary, exactly the sort of love letter I'd have expected of Nate.

My beloved,
  "To conquer without risk is to triumph without glory."
          Nate

I didn't recognize the quote. The letter wasn't dated or postmarked. The Crillon Hotel, where Nate always stayed in Paris, was obviously a drop for them. Anne-Marie de Passy told me her brother showed her the letter in May of 1993, which meant Monique was most likely seeing both Nate and Lucius at the same time. Nate must have known this.

I walked back to Eugenie's apartment with the letter

tucked safely away in my coat pocket, only vaguely aware of the light drizzle permeating the air. When I reached the Rue du Bac, my hair was wet and my clothes damp. Eugenie lit a fire, wrapped me in a blanket, and gave me some of her Russian tea spiked with brandy this time. I showed her the letter the old woman had given me.

"Corneille," Eugenie said, immediately identifying the quote. "*Le Cid.*"

"I should have known you'd know that," I said admiringly. "I was dead certain that letter was going to be from Lucius." She handed it back to me. "I just couldn't believe it when I saw it. I still can't believe it." I folded the letter up and slipped it back into the envelope.

"That awful lawyer," Eugenie said, with a shudder of disgust.

"My daddy always warned me never to trust anyone with two first names." I leaned back on the couch, absently turning the envelope round and round in the fingers of my right hand. "God knows Nate and I had our problems, but in an odd way, I respected him for his loyalty to Lucius. I really believed he was protecting Lucius's interests. Now, though, in light of this," I said, holding up the letter, "I think he had something else entirely in mind."

Eugenie looked at me intensely. "What do you mean?"

I was still formulating my thoughts on the subject and it was helpful to have Eugenie to talk to, to help me think things through.

"Nate set us up, the two of us: me and Lucius."

"It rather looks that way."

"That weekend in the country? He and Monique

should have won Academy Awards the way they pretended to be strangers."

"From the letter they were obviously lovers."

"Still are, I assume. The question is, are they accomplices, too?"

"But how did they meet?"

"That's what I'm wondering. You know what they say: Birds of a feather."

"'God creates them but they find each other,' an old Spanish proverb," Eugenie said.

I was feeling so agitated I couldn't laugh. I couldn't even sit still. I threw the blanket aside, got up, and paced around the room.

"Nate and Lucius go back years, of course. Nate knew everything about him. I mean, it would have been so easy for Nate to set him up."

"But why?"

"The money, of course."

"Yes, but Jo, she got the money, not him."

"I know, but he couldn't have gotten it any other way, could he?" It suddenly hit me. "I bet Nate and Monique are going to get married."

"Really?"

"I bet. And if they do, I'll know it was him. And I'll know he did it for the money."

"And if they don't?"

"Then it was her."

"Have you thought that she might—how do you say it?—double-cross him? I love that expression."

"And refuse to marry him, you mean?"

"Exactly," Eugenie said. "A real adventuress doesn't like to share."

"It'll be interesting to see, won't it? Nate may be in over his head. Wouldn't that be nice for a change?"

"How is it that she can fool so many people, this woman?"

"She fooled me because I grew up with crazy people so she seemed normal. When you grow up in a terrarium and someone says, 'It's hot in here,' you don't notice it. It feels like home to you. Monique was just like one of the family. That's why I was so off my guard."

"You had killers in your family?"

"My uncle actually. He got off, but we all knew he was guilty. He pushed my aunt out the window because he thought she was a social liability. She was. But that's not exactly a rational motive for killing someone."

"No? There's none better in my view," Eugenie joked.

"I guess you never know what matters to people," I said, laughing with her.

"What matters to Monique, do you think? Money?"

"Social life."

Eugenie guffawed. "She's right at home then. There are plenty of killers in society, as you and I know only too well."

"She desperately wants to be accepted by the people she thinks are important. She always has. Even her sister-in-law said so."

"We certainly know the type."

"That whole world is just a collective figment of a few people's imaginations," I said. "It doesn't really exist. And yet there are people who are truly obsessed by it. I was myself now that I look back. I was only comfortable seeing certain people—even people I didn't much like."

Eugenie shrugged. "It's the same here in Paris. We

have a smart set: old families, old money. I don't care for most of them but they certainly care a great deal for themselves. Their main purpose in life, it seems, is to make others feel left out."

"It's sort of like that in New York. But I honestly never thought of it that way. I was in a certain group because of my interests and because of Lucius. He loved hobnobbing with the best and brightest."

Eugenie looked at me askance. "The *best,* the *brightest?* Please! Jo, you and I both know how second-rate and stupid some of these people are. It's *incroyable.* That's why they have to be so chichi and show off. I went to a party in New York last year given by people we both know, and the only reason I wasn't bored to death was because they had a great Van Gogh, which was wonderful to see. And thank God I was facing it in the dining room because the conversation was so deadly dull I can't tell you! All about the stock market and money. I thought I would die of boredom."

"Yes, but it's not always like that. Sometimes it's very interesting. Let's face it, some brilliant people are attracted to that world."

"I suppose. It always amazes me when I see these really accomplished people behaving like utter toadies around the rich," she said.

"I guess."

"Jo, you forget. People danced around you and Lucius like he was Louis the Fifteenth. 'Lucius the Fifteenth' I used to call him, remember? He would laugh and laugh."

"I know, I know. Some people are truly obsessed with social life and it doesn't matter how smart or how talented they are. They just want to be around money and parties."

"We are all like that to some degree. In Paris I can

understand it a bit more because there was once a monarchy here, and there are still old families and ancient snobbism. It's part of the French character in a way. But in New York, it's all about money now. Tell me, Jo, how do you decide who is grand and who is not? It must be difficult with all these new billionaires."

"I think the so-called grand people in New York are the ones who control its great institutions," I said. "There's only one Municipal Museum, for example. Every social climber in the world wants to get on that board because that is instant social power."

"But social power, Jo. What *is* that? It's not real power."

"For some it is. We all have our little spheres, Eugenie, and within them there are ranks and rites and rituals. The design world, your world . . . Tell me that doesn't have a hierarchy."

"I'm spoiled, you know. I like to be around interesting people. People who are doing other things aside from just making deals. I see a lot of social people when I go to New York or when they come to Paris, yes. But most of them are *amis mondains.* I don't feel close to them like I am to you. The nature of that world is against intimacy."

"That's the whole point of social life—the avoidance of intimacy. And it's deceptive because you see everybody all the time so there's an illusion of closeness that really doesn't exist. In fact, social life is less about who people are than about what they represent."

"How do you mean?"

"It's simple: If you're nice and you lose all your money, you're out. But if you're a shit with a private plane, you're in. 'Have plane, will travel.' The social climber's calling card."

Eugenie sighed. "As you know, Jo, I grew up in a certain world. My mother was a princess. My great uncle was a king. But I never saw the point of it."

"That's because you always had it," I said.

"Perhaps. But do you enjoy all those endless parties?"

"It's not just parties, though. It's a philanthropic world. A world of art and culture and beauty. And some of the people in it actually understand and appreciate that. Others don't, I grant you. But if you take the board of the Municipal Museum, for example, I have to say that most of the people on it aren't social climbers. They're philanthropists who love art. They happen to have social power only as a result of what they *do*, not because they seek it out as an end in itself."

Eugenie looked at me skeptically. "I have met a man who is on your board. I forget his name. He has a chic wife. He knew *nothing—nada, rien*—about art." She made a zero sign with her thumb and forefinger.

I knew the man to whom she was referring. He'd donated twenty-five million dollars to the museum and pledged twenty-five more.

"Okay, granted, we do have one or two who are only there because they can afford to be. But in general, people know their stuff."

"Well, anyway, we're off the main subject. You think Monique de Passy is obsessed by this world?" Eugenie said.

"I think she's obsessed, period. Which means social life is the perfect place for her. Money is the tool to open the golden door."

"Exactly. And you stand in her way. It's life at court, my dear. The only way for a newcomer to succeed is to get rid of the old favorite."

18

I arrived back in New York, exhausted from a long flight plagued by delays. I opened the door to my apartment and was shocked to find a bespectacled, harried-looking woman standing in the middle of the living room, surrounded by cardboard boxes and bubble wrap.

"Tinka Marsh," the woman said, extending her hand to me before I'd even had a chance to put down my suitcases.

I recognized the name, of course. She was the woman who owned the apartment, Betty's friend whom I'd never met but only spoken with on the phone.

"Ms. Marsh," I said, nonplussed. "What's happening here? I'm just off a plane from Paris."

"I know. And I apologize from the bottom of my heart, Mrs. Slater. I tried to contact you but the number Betty gave me never answered. I guess it was wrong or something. But anyway, I hate to spring this on you, but I sold the apartment and I have to be out in two days. I'm really sorry about this."

Everything was in disarray, including my files, samples, and invoices for the last job I was working on. It was a mess. I had no lease, no legal rights. She'd loaned me the apartment as a favor. I had no choice but to help her pack.

Since there was only one bedroom, I called Betty and asked her if I could spend the night. She said I could stay as long as I wanted. She also agreed to let me store boxes in her basement until I found another place.

Welcome home.

———

THE next day I went hunting for a rental apartment in a decent location. The only thing I could afford for the moment was a tiny one-bedroom apartment on the third floor of a converted brownstone between Lexington and Third on Seventy-fourth Street. I took it.

I subsequently found out that the purchaser of Tinka Marsh's apartment was none other than Monique. According to Betty, who got it from Tinka, Monique had made her such a large offer, she couldn't afford to turn it down. She told Tinka she was buying it for the new French chef she had hired. She had taken my former apartment off the market and decided to stay in New York.

This was war.

And that wasn't the only startling development awaiting me on my return. According to June, the social barometer, the tide of public opinion had taken a sharp turn in favor of Monique, primarily on account of a long profile of her in *Nous* magazine. June had saved the piece to show me. The thing that caught my eye immediately was the very flattering picture of the Countess, reclining on one of the silk velvet sofas in *my* living room. The article said that Monique was giving small dinners where "one finds a fascinating mix of people, not only titled ladies and tycoons, but politicos, television personalities, actors, artists, and writers of the moment, all of whom are treated to de Passy's extravagant, yet informal style of entertaining, which is reflected in a stack of priceless buffet plates that once belonged to the Empress Josephine. The food is prepared from de Passy's old family recipes by her brilliant French chef."

Oh boy, I thought. I knew that people would now grab any excuse to like her just so they'd be invited to her house.

Furious as I was at Monique, however, the real score I had to settle was with Nate Nathaniel. I had barely moved into my new apartment when I went to see him.

—∿—

NATE'S midtown offices on the seventeenth floor of a fairly old Park Avenue building had the heavy, solid look of a white-shoe firm that catered to Old Money. One stepped off the elevator into a hushed realm of dark mahogany paneling, traditional furniture, wall-to-wall carpeting, and nineteenth-century prints of New York landmarks and maps.

My appointment with Nate was for two o'clock. I was right on time. Nate kept me waiting fifteen minutes. In the old days, he wouldn't have dared. I perused a copy of *Fortune* in the reception area while I waited. At last, an

officious secretary led me down a corridor of enclosed
alcoves to his office.

She showed me into a huge room with bookcase walls,
carpeted in green. Nate was on the phone, his crossed
stocking feet propped up on the leather top of the large
English partners desk. He was wearing a shirt and an
unbuttoned vest, no jacket. He made a cursory motion to
me to take a seat on one of the two chairs opposite him
while he finished up his call.

The decor of this impressive office overlooking Park
Avenue had barely changed in the twenty-odd years I'd
known Nate. He'd spiffed it up, of course, replacing the
carpeting and upholstery at regular intervals. The walls
were still lined with law books and journals interrupted,
at intervals, by the various tennis and golf trophies Nate
had won. The burled walnut humidor that Nate claimed
Fidel Castro had once owned was still prominently displayed on the glass coffee table in front of the leather sofa
under the window.

My favorite object of all—because it was given to
him by Lucius and because it also said so much about its
owner—was the impressive-looking document, framed
in black, that hung directly behind Nate's desk at the center of a symmetrical arrangement of framed law degrees
and professional honors. Written in black ink on parch-
ment, stamped with a red wax seal, it was the official
order, signed by Louis XVI himself, approving Dr.
Guillotine's new invention as an efficient and humane
means of public execution. In effect, the King of France
had signed his own death warrant.

I endured about five minutes of a conversation laced
with legal jargon before Nate hung up the phone, swung

his feet down, and jotted down some notes on a yellow pad. I waited. He finally looked up.

"Sorry, Jo. Hectic day. What can I do for you?"

I focused for a moment on the eighteenth-century document behind his head in order to calm my seething anger.

"Did you know that old Dr. Guillotine changed his name after his invention became synonymous with terror?" I began. "I find that quaint, don't you? Especially considering that in New York, names synonymous with terror are on everyone's A-list."

Nate chuckled. "What's up, Jo? I'm real busy."

"I wanted to tell you about my trip to Paris."

He looked at me incredulously, then started rummaging around in the top drawer of his desk, obviously preoccupied with something else. "Look, Jo, I made time for you this afternoon because you said it was important. But you picked a hellish day. Where is that damn thing?" he muttered under his breath, continuing to search his desk.

"Then I won't beat around the bush," I said, opening my pocketbook and pulling out the letter Anne-Marie de Passy had given me. I slid it across the wide desk so it landed in front of him. He stopped what he was doing and picked up the envelope, giving it a cursory glance. I watched his face closely for any flicker of emotion. He betrayed none. He dropped the letter back on the desk, and slid it back over to me.

"Aren't you going to open it?" I asked him.

He stared at me with cold eyes and did that annoying cathedral thing with his fingers, tapping them together impatiently. He said nothing.

"Liar," I said.

He didn't respond. He just continued to look at me, expressionless.

I held his gaze. We sat there in a sophomoric no-blinking contest for what seemed like an eternity. Finally he said: "What do you want from me, Jo?"

"The truth—for a change?"

"About?"

I heaved a weary sigh. "Do we really have to play this game, Nate?"

Nate rose from his chair, shoving his hands down into the pockets of his gray flannel trousers. He paced the room pensively, looking vaguely ridiculous in his stocking feet.

"Whose idea was it to set him up? Yours or hers?"

Nate turned on his heel and paused in the middle of the room, assuming a kind of at-ease stance with his legs slightly apart and his hands behind his back. The afternoon light flattened his features.

"I have no idea what you're talking about."

"I'm talking about two hundred million dollars."

He made a show of looking at his watch. "Jo, I can't help you."

I rose from my chair. "You know, Nate, sometimes my own naïveté astounds me. I believe what people tell me. That is always such a mistake in New York."

"It's a nice quality, though," Nate said.

"Is it? I'd have thought it would have dimmed the glory of your conquest," I said, paraphrasing his own quote from Corneille.

"Not at all." He proffered a knowing smile.

"Well, if I were you, I'd watch my step. Especially when you two get married. That is one dangerous little lady."

"Thanks for the advice, Jo. Appreciate it."

Leaving that office, I believe I understood more fully than I ever had why handgun laws carry such stiff penalties in New York. Good manners notwithstanding, if I'd had a gun, I'd have shot the bastard.

—⁓—

I literally couldn't afford to dwell on my hatred of Nate or of Monique. I had real financial problems to keep my anxieties occupied. I had no idea how I was going to pay all my debts.

That is not to say I was poor. By any standard—save the rarefied one of the world I'd inhabited for the past two decades where anyone with less than twenty million dollars is considered only "moderately well off"—I was not one of the Hundred Neediest Cases. Far from it. Though none would have called me rich, most people in the world would have thought of me as well off and lucky.

But as we have learned from stock market crashes, everything is relative. I had no fixed income and my decorating business was a bust. Not one new job had come in since the Dent debacle. I sensed there was a whispering campaign against me.

True, I'd been relatively poor as a child, but twenty years of living around people whose idea of economizing was to get rid of their private plane had left me with a skewed sense of values. I wasn't buying nearly as much as I once had, but when I did make a purchase—be it clothes, shoes, bags, cosmetics, food, incidentals—it was always the very best. I was so used to thinking in those terms. It now began to occur to me that I would have to cut down even on what I considered to be the necessities of life. No more gourmet shops. It was the supermarket for me. I was going broke. Fast.

In order to make ends meet, I had no alternative but to discreetly sell off the few remaining possessions of any value I had left—my jewelry, a few drawings, some furniture. I contacted my friend Prince Nicholas Brubetskoi, who worked for Chapel's Auction House as head of their European furniture department. Nicky, as everyone called him, was a great-grand-nephew or cousin or *something* of Tsar Nicholas II of Russia—no one really knew or cared. He was a relative and that was good enough.

Brubetskoi's job was to travel around the world persuading people with pedigreed possessions to allow Chapel's to sell their treasures on the open market. His royal heritage gave him special entrée to the most ancient, secretive families in Europe.

Nicky helped me dispose of some things at auction as "the property of a lady," so no one would find out how tough times were for me. Understanding that important auctions confer luster on lesser goods as surely as important parties confer luster on lesser guests, Nicky had made sure that the items I consigned to Chapel's got into a top sale where they would sell, in some cases, for much more than they were worth.

I did not go to the auction of Important Old Master Drawings where I was getting rid of a set of four eighteenth-century flower drawings from my Southampton house that Lucius had given to me for my forty-first birthday. They were very decorative, but not great quality. After the sale, Nicky called to tell me they had sold well—triple the high estimate. I was pleased. Nicky was gracious, but I knew him well enough to sense a certain hesitancy in his voice, as if he had something more he wanted to tell me. I also knew him well enough to know that though he was usually discreet, there were occasions when he could be persuaded to part with confidential information, particularly if the party asking him was somehow involved. So I pressed him until he said the magic words: "I really shouldn't be telling you this, Jo, *but* you didn't hear it from me, okay?"

"Okay."

"Your drawings were bought by the Countess de Passy."

My gut tightened. "I see."

"And she's instructed a colleague of mine that if anything of yours comes up for sale, she wants to know about it. It's a bit bizarre, no?"

I hung up the phone and sat still for a long moment, remembering how Monique had admired those drawings when they'd hung in the library in the country. I could understand she would want to have them back. They were perfect for the room. But her desire to know whenever anything of mine came up for sale gave me a feeling of being stalked.

A couple of months later I learned that she had hung the drawings in one of her guest rooms in the city. She told everyone they were a gift from me. June told me she was trying to make people think we had made up.

My obsession with Monique was growing, like a cancer. Whereas before there were many days when I went without giving her a thought, now I thought about her all the time. Her image was engraved on my retina. She was my constant companion, my first thought in the morning, my last thought at night. I sat in my bathtub having imaginary conversations with her out loud where I took both our parts. I fantasized running into her in different places and planned what I would do. My plans ranged from attacking her physically to cool indifference, depending on my mood. One thing was sure: we had a score to settle.

Gradually, the obsession took on a life of its own. The more hollow my insides, the more I burst at the seams. I was feeding constantly, but never satisfied. I thought of myself as a master manipulator, but now I know I was only playing solitaire.

19

THE infusion of cash I realized from the sale of the drawings did as much to remedy my financial situation as a Band-Aid on a gaping wound. I had a growing sense of panic. My good friends like June, Betty, and Trish Bromire were supportive. But their lives diverged from mine in one fundamental way: They were rich and I was not. It was as simple as that. I had to watch both my time and my money very carefully. I couldn't donate to my favorite charities—I was still paying off my damn pledge and other business debts. Nor could I go on trips, buy clothes, give parties, or even go out for lunch without calculating the cost. Keeping company with those who lived so effortlessly, even though they were my dear friends, frankly depressed me. Making ends meet was all I ever thought about. I understood too well the priceless comment of another fallen socialite who, years ago, had remarked: "Being poor in New York is hideously expensive."

Ethan Monk was the only one of my friends to sense my distress. He invited me over for dinner one night, just the two of us. Ethan was a marvelous cook. He and I used to joke that if he ever lost his curator's job at the Muni, he could come and cook for me. "God knows, I'd get paid more," Ethan joked, referring not only to his own salary from the museum but to the astronomical wages garnered by private chefs in New York. I used to pay our chef close to one hundred and twenty-five thousand dollars a year, not including benefits or housing.

Ethan lived in a small garden apartment in a converted brownstone in the Eighties, just off Central Park West. Architecturally, it was unimpressive except for a large, well-proportioned living room. Otherwise, the space was cut up and cramped. Nevertheless, it was clearly the dwelling of a cultivated man who had used limited resources and a keen eye to collect wisely. His walls were covered with Old Master drawings he had bought over a lifetime—many for a song—in the early days before drawings became such a major area of interest to collectors. The prize of the collection, which included Jan Fryt, Jacob de Wit, Antoine Dieu, Agostino Carracci, Greuze, Guercino, Tiepolo, and others, was a study of a male nude by Tintoretto I'd given him for his fortieth birthday.

Over a bottle of heady red wine and a delicious dinner of risotto, veal scallopini, and French beans, Ethan and I sat in his library dining room and talked frankly about my situation, particularly regarding the Municipal Museum. Because he was a very good friend and I trusted his judgment, I asked him for his opinion on whether or not I should resign from the board. I confided to him that I might not be able to pay off the entire pledge, particularly not at the rate things were going for me: "To be perfectly honest, Ethan, I'm broke."

"Join the club, Jo. I'm always broke playing the grand acquisitor, as you see," he said sweeping his hand toward the cluttered walls.

"Yes, but I actually *owe* a fortune. It's not just the pledge. I still have to pay the workrooms, the lawyers, taxes. Nothing's coming in. No one will hire me. I have a few things left I can sell, but when they're gone I have no idea what I'm going to do. Do you think I should just resign from the board and have done with it?"

Ethan didn't answer me immediately. He offered me a calvados, which I declined. He poured himself a snifter. I nursed my glass of wine.

"Do you?" I pressed him, hoping he would say no.

"Jo, I don't know what to tell you."

"Oh God. You think I should, don't you?"

Ethan absently swirled the calvados around in his glass, looking down at the honey-colored liquid, obviously avoiding my gaze.

"I'll tell you something that may be difficult for you to hear."

"Trust me, nothing can top what I've heard in the last month."

"This may, actually. Monique had lunch with Roger and Edmond last week."

It was startling and unwelcome news. "Oh, lord, here it comes . . ." I gulped down what was left of my wine. "Her dream is to go on that board."

"They're in a very tough position, Jo. Especially Roger."

I perked up like some sort of trace hound who's just smelled blood.

"He's not thinking of letting her on—the ungrateful rat! He absolutely cannot do that to me!" I leapt up and helped myself to more wine. "You don't have any hemlock I can add to this, do you?" I said, draining my glass and pouring another.

"Calm down, Jo. Roger's very upset."

"So am I!" I turned on my heel. "And what's more you can tell him that I refuse to resign my position so *she* can have it. I refuse, that's it. I absolutely refuse. I'm staying on that fucking board no matter what!"

Ethan crossed his hands over his chest in a gesture of helplessness. "Don't yell at me. I didn't do anything."

"I'm sorry." I was so agitated, I could hardly breathe. I sat back down on the couch. Ethan reached across the sofa and patted my knee.

"Roger discussed this with you?" I asked him.

"Yes," he said in a resigned tone.

"Edmond too?"

"No, just Roger."

"Ethan, *please*. We're such old friends. You've got to tell me what he said."

Ethan exhaled fiercely. "It's pretty simple, really. She's offered him a helluva lot of money, plus all the paintings from Lucius's collection when she dies. A life trust thing for tax reasons."

"*My* collection, thanks very much! I could kill her."

"And this may be the capper: She got your pal Agatha Dent lined up to make a really serious donation."

"Fine. Put Agatha on the board then!"

"Exactly. Only I don't think dear old Agatha has the slightest interest. Her field is politics. She wants to be

Pamela Harriman. Or, barring that, she wants Neil to be Pamela Harriman," he said.

"Great. 'Where does the billion-dollar gorilla sit?'" Ethan joined me in the old retort, "Anywhere she wants!"

We laughed.

"God, it's so typical of this city, isn't it?" I said, shaking my head.

"Money makes the world go 'round."

"What happened to love?"

"You know, I think the saying was always 'love of money makes the world go 'round' and we just got an incomplete translation," Ethan said.

The alcohol was beginning to have a calming effect on me. My insides had warmed up considerably and I drifted into a welcome state of mild inebriation.

"So what's Roger Rabbit going to do?" I inquired.

"He's clearly in a bind," Ethan replied. "I don't think he knows quite what to do. He loves you, Jo. He really does. Not only that, he understands he owes his present position to you. On the other hand, you picked him because he's a great fund-raiser. So here's the quandary: In order for him to do his job well, he's got to betray the person who got him his job. I'd hate to be in his shoes, wouldn't you?"

"Better his than mine."

I reflected for a long moment.

"I don't even know why I'm upset. It's so predictable," I said at last. "There had to come a point when I'd be just too difficult to defend. 'Nice is nice to me,' and all that. But Roger's a real disappointment, I must say."

"It's ain't over yet," Ethan said, trying to be reassuring.

"Let's face it, Ethan. I'm not a player anymore. You

should see the apartment I live in now. It would be a rattrap, only no self-respecting rat would reside there. No, Monique stole all my chips. And now she wants to sit down at the table. They have to let her play, Ethan. That's the game."

"Reminds me of the Metropolitan Opera versus the Academy of Music," Ethan said.

"How so?"

"You know the story."

"Refresh my memory."

"It's a little capsule summary of the way things work in New York. Back in the early 1880s, old Cornelius Vanderbilt was considered too vulgar by the powers that be to own a box at the Academy of Music on Fourteenth Street. So he and a few of the other ostracized nouveau riche got together and built the Metropolitan Opera House. Everyone said it looked liked a brewery. But guess what? They could afford to pay more, so they got the top singers from all over the world. The elegant Academy of Music was soon history."

"I remember the story. But I fail to see how a bunch of rich snobs excluding a bunch of richer vulgarians applies to me, thanks very much."

"The point isn't about the personalities of the individuals, Jo," Ethan explained. "The point is that New York has always been about money in one way or another. Money's the real ticket in this town because it's the *lasting* ticket. Oh, I don't say that power, fame, talent, and beauty don't count in their ways. They do. But in the end, they're all mere diversions at the table money sets. And these days your friend Monique is offering a big, sumptuous buffet."

—◆—

I decided to walk back home to my apartment from Ethan's—right across Central Park, where I was stalked by shadows and a chill wind. I didn't care. I knew as I was doing it what a silly and dangerous thing it was to venture out like that alone in New York at twelve o'clock at night. But I was tipsy and angry and defeated and, frankly, I just didn't give a damn if I got mugged, or worse.

I crossed the park without incident and found myself on Fifth Avenue. And just for the hell of it, I walked downtown toward my old apartment. I stood across the street and stared up at the fifteenth floor. All the windows were lit up. I couldn't see anyone—it was too high up— but I suspected Monique was having a party. And just then, two couples emerged from the front door, laughing and talking as the doorman signaled to a waiting limousine. I didn't recognize the first couple, but the second couple were Neil and Agatha Dent.

This is how crazy I was. I decided to wait around and see who else came out of the building—assuming, rather nuttily, that whoever else did emerge had automatically been to Monique's. I leaned against the gray stone wall that enclosed the park and bided my time. An hour passed. Then two. I looked at my watch. It was close to three in the morning. The lights on the fifteenth floor went out and I decided that was it. Time to go home. Just as I was leaving, however, I saw an all too familiar figure emerge from the building. It was Nate Nathaniel.

He looked around for a taxi. When none came, he buttoned his topcoat and started walking down Fifth. I followed him, keeping a safe distance. I kept wishing I had a gun. It would be so easy just to shoot the son of a bitch, I thought. I figured he was headed home. He lived in a small townhouse in a hidden corner of New York called Sniffen Court. Finally, he grabbed a cab at Fifty-fifth Street and I lost him. I hailed a cab and went home.

I traipsed up the three flights of steps, as usual, ignoring the indefinable stench in the hallway, pushed my key in the lock, leaned on the door, and practically fell into my apartment from fatigue and from a heavy, heavy heart. Stalking exhausted me.

I switched on the lights and looked around the claustrophobic apartment with its brick wall view and thought, this is my life. I'd originally planned to transform the cheerless space into a chic and cozy enclave. But I soured on the idea of decorating, even for myself. I'd settled in with the cheapest furniture, unable to bring myself to unpack the crates and cartons holding the remainder of my possessions.

Why bother?

Putting beautiful objects on display in that place was, well, like wearing couture to a deli. June and Betty had both offered to come over and help me get things "in order," as June put it. I ducked their calls. I had no desire to get things in order. Order for me meant permanence; chaos, at least, held out the possibility of change.

Just before dawn, I got out of bed and located a box of my personal stationery in one of the many cardboard cartons lying around. On the tissue-thin pale blue sheet of paper with "Jo Slater" written in small white capitals across the top, I opted for a short, dignified exit, figuring that good manners were the one thing still within my control.

Dear Roger,
Please accept my resignation from the board of the Municipal
Museum. I have enjoyed working with you and Edmond and the
entire staff over these many years. I wish you all continued success.
The remainder of my pledge will, of course, be honored in due
course.

          Sincerely yours,
            Jo Slater

I purposely didn't sign it "Love, Jo," or "With fondest regards," or anything to imply the slightest warmth. I knew Roger would know exactly how I felt by the formal, businesslike terminology. Mercifully, there were still certain things in social life that didn't need spelling out.

As I slid the letter into the envelope and wrote out Roger's name and address on the front, I thought to myself that if New York City had a great seal, its motto should read: "Out of money, out of mind."

—∾—

ONE week later, I received a long letter from Roger regretfully accepting my resignation. He waxed rhapsodic about the "incalculable" contributions I'd made to the museum. I threw it away.

20

WHEN Dick Bromire heard that I'd resigned from the Muni board, he offered me a "consulting" job—consulting, of course, being a euphemism for unemployment. I turned him down because I was too proud to accept charity—and that's what it was. Still, it was very sweet of Dick, who was still in the midst of his own ongoing legal woes. I think he and Trish felt personally responsible for having gotten me involved with the Dents, although they never said it outright.

On the practical side, I simply couldn't afford to sit home in my apartment, feeling sorry for myself all day, obsessing over the Countess while waiting for my financial troubles to miraculously straighten themselves out. I decided to get a mindless job in pleasant surroundings in order to earn some money as well as to try to put Monique out of my mind. I viewed this as a temporary measure until I could come up with a more definitive career move.

At first I considered tapping some of my pals in the antiques business where I could use some of my expertise. I went to a couple of places where I'd shopped for years and asked them if they wanted to hire me. Everyone's initial reaction was a hearty laugh and then a move to show me the latest stock. They all thought I was kidding. Apparently, not everyone had followed my troubles as closely as I'd rather egotistically imagined. Most of these people, from whom I had bought hundreds of thousands of dollars worth of antiques over the years, couldn't conceive that I was broke and in need of a job. When I pressed them, however, and it became clear I was dead serious, many literally backed away in profound embarrassment, murmuring vague excuses and good-byes as if I had upset something fundamental in their universe.

One day I walked up and down Lexington and Third Avenues, stopping in at the antiques shops where I wasn't known, asking for a job. No dice. I began to realize by the way proprietors looked at me that there was something a little sinister about a middle-aged woman coming in cold off the street looking for work. I decided to try my luck downtown in the Village, where sinister occurrences aren't quite as offputting as they are uptown in the precincts of privilege.

I tried the same tactic, going from door to door. Finally, I was offered a job in a cluttered shop on Tenth Street, filled with third- and fourth-rate antiques and "collectibles" at inflated prices. I was on the verge of accepting when I looked around a little more closely at the fake tole monkeys, Coca-Cola memorabilia, movie posters, and badly restored arts and crafts furniture, and suddenly came to my senses. What was I doing? What was I thinking of? I couldn't sell that junk with a straight face. I left.

After a good night's rest I came to the decision that I needed a proper job in a proper place—somewhere where other middle-aged women, like myself, could associate in easy, familiar surroundings and take home a fairly decent paycheck. I also needed to meet some new people, particularly as I wasn't seeing any of my old friends. New York is a big city. I knew there had to be other women, like myself, who were slightly down on their luck, or in a transition period, or just bored and wanting to get out of the house. I could talk to them and perhaps not feel so alone.

I found a job in a field I knew very well from childhood: selling women's apparel. My mother had been a saleswoman in an upscale department store in Oklahoma City. And now I became a saleswoman at an upscale department store in New York City: Bergdorf Goodman. Designer evening gowns. Fourth floor.

This was a little like an alcoholic getting a job in a liquor store. I adored clothes. In the old days, I'd always made a point of going to the collections in Paris twice a year. I still had most of my old couture clothes locked up in a warehouse somewhere in Queens, along with a few other belongings I refused to part with. I figured that being around clothes, day in, day out, would suppress any residual urges I had to shop for them.

Getting up every morning at a regular hour, walking to work amid the early-morning bustle of the city, punching a time card, mingling with my coworkers was all therapeutic. I felt energized by my new routine. Once in a while, I let slip a detail or two about my glory days to a fellow salesperson. A couple of the older women remembered me. But most were too young or too new to have any clue who I was. One young woman asked me if I was any relation to the Slaters of the Slater Gallery at the Municipal Museum. I said no.

—————⟋⟋⟍—————

I'LL never forget the day I saw June Kahn step off the elevator in one of her ladies' lunch suits, looking neat and prim and perfectly coiffed. I walked up to her and said in a facetiously formal voice, laced with unction, "May I help you, dear madam?"

She looked at me and said flatly, "Yes. I'm going to a wedding and I want something pretty and summery." Then she immediately began searching through the racks paying me no more mind.

I thought she was kidding, so I went on.

"How about a lovely burlap bag?"

She flung me a scornful little glance. "Burlap? In July? I don't think so."

It was only then that I suddenly grasped how badly I had let myself go. June didn't recognize me.

"Junie, aren't you going to say hello?" I finally said, only to be confronted by a blank stare that gradually, comically mutated into a sort of stunned disbelief as it dawned on her who I was.

"Jo?" she said, squinting at me as if she were peering through a pane of dirty glass. "Sweetie, my *God!*"

"Do I look *that* bad?" I said with a self-conscious little laugh.

Apparently I did, because she didn't laugh with me. She just winced.

"No," she replied unconvincingly. "You . . . you've just gained a little weight, what?"

Try thirty fucking pounds, cried my impish inner voice—a voice that was growing crasser and more out of control by the day, I might add. For a second, I wondered if I'd said it out loud, but June carried on blithely so I assumed I hadn't.

"Betty and I have both called you a thousand times, sweetie. You never answer your phone. You've got that damn machine on all the time. We're longing to come visit you, see the new digs and everything. Where on earth have you been keeping yourself? Have you been on a cruise or something?"

"I've been right here," I said trying to be chipper.

"Shopping, I know. Great therapy, isn't it? What are you going to wear to this damn wedding? I can't find a thing."

"What wedding?"

She named a couple we all knew in Southampton whose daughter was getting married. I hadn't been invited.

"Oh, I'm not going," I said.

"Wise woman. It'll be a zoo . . . I've got to find a dress. I hate evening weddings. And I hate this place," she said, looking around at the racks of evening gowns. "There's never a salesgirl around to help you."

"I can help you."

"Thanks, sweetie. You absolutely can. You've got the greatest taste. How do you think I'd look in this?"

She pulled an orange silk organza dress with ruffles off the rack and held it up high, inspecting it from every angle. Exactly June's style, I thought: early Shirley Temple. Glancing at the ticket, she said, "Huge. Size ten. I need a six. Where *are* all the salespeople?"

"You're looking at one," I told her.

June cocked her head to one side for a brief moment. Dismissing the idea as a bad joke, she turned the dress this way and that, saying, "Very funny, Jo."

"June, I work here."

The arm holding the dress dropped to her side. The dress fell to the floor, creating a little orange ruffle campfire at her feet. Her naturally perky expression was flattened by a look of disbelief, then mortification, then pity. She stared at me, slack-jawed.

"Oh, *Jo* . . ." she murmured, unable to complete her thought.

I was determined not to let her reaction get to me. Knowing that something like this was bound to happen sooner or later, I'd prepared myself for my response. I'm the poet of my own life, I told myself. It's not how *they* see it; it's how *I* see it.

"I'm having fun," I said cheerfully, picking up the dress. "It's just temporary, until I decide what I really want to do."

"I know, Jo, but couldn't you have found something, I don't know, something *else*?"

June looked absolutely stricken, as if she were about to burst into tears. I found it amusing that she was the one in need of comfort at this moment when it should have been the other way around. Still, I felt so bad for her that all I wanted to do was to cheer her up.

"You mustn't take it so hard, Junie. It's a very pleasant job. I'm enjoying myself. I really am."

She looked at me skeptically.

"Sweetie, if it's a question of money, I could lend you—"

I cut her off. "You're very sweet, June. I really appreciate the thought, I do. But I wouldn't dream of it. Listen, it beats going down a mine shaft with a canary on my head."

I couldn't even get a chuckle out of her, so I hung the dress back up on the rack and said, "Let's go find you something pretty to wear."

We differed on the kinds of outfits she should try on, but we finally got together a mutually acceptable selection. It was my moment to dress June in clothes that would make her look more elegant. I unlocked the door of our most spacious dressing room, which looked down over the fountain in front of the Plaza Hotel on Fifty-eighth Street. The bright spring day had grown overcast. June took off her suit and started trying on the clothes. I stood by and watched, occasionally helping her with snaps and zippers. The red and white polka-dot dress that she had picked out against my objections made her look so frightful that we both started laughing hysterically. June struck crazy poses in the mirror.

It was during that moment of foolish merriment that I realized how much I missed her and the carefree days of my old life. In a fit of emotion that snuck up on me quicker than a crow's-foot, I burst into tears. Sinking down on the divan, I started to sob. I just couldn't stop crying. June sat down beside me and put her arm around me, trying her best to console me. Oddly enough, it wasn't until that moment in the dressing room that I realized for the first time just exactly how hard it had been, how hard it was, and, indeed, how hard it was always going to be.

"I think I could take it if it weren't for Monique," I said. "Other women survive this kind of thing every day. But it's the thought that she's taken over my life that's so hard for me, June. Can you understand that?"

"I know. It's awful. I don't know what to say."

I clenched my teeth. "I never knew I could hate like this. I recognize it's an obsession, but I can't help it. The harder I try not to think about her, the more I do. Sometimes I'll pick up a copy of *Nous* and turn right to the 'Daisy' column just to see what parties she went to. I'm thumbing through the pages. I don't even want to know and yet I'm desperately searching for her name, dreading I'll find it. How crazy is that?"

"I used to be that way about a boyfriend I had in college," June mused. "I went to all of his hangouts terrified I'd run into him, yet wanting to at the same time. I couldn't keep away. It was so sick."

"Well, I guess love affairs and hate affairs are opposite sides of the same coin. I pray for indifference. But that doesn't seem to be in the cards at the moment."

"It's only natural for you to be upset, sweetie," she said, handing me a tissue from her purse. I wiped my eyes and blew my nose. "Poor Jo," she said. "I hate to say it, sweetie, but maybe you should think about leaving New York for a while."

"Then she will have won completely. I love New York."

June stood up. "Come on, let's go have a cup of tea," she said, getting dressed.

"I can't. My shift's not up until four." Thinking of

Ruth Slater and how Lucius had betrayed her, I said: "Junie, do you believe the dead can wreak revenge on the living?"

June looked at me askance as she was fastening her skirt. "Only at New York dinner parties," she replied without a trace of humor. She put on her jacket. "Jo, dear, if I may say so, you're really not yourself."

I thought for a moment. "I give up. Who am I?" Then I laughed like a fool.

—⁂—

CHASTENED by this encounter with June, I went home and took a good long look at myself in the mirror. It's funny, you know, because there I was, around mirrors all day, helping women try on clothes. And yet I hadn't taken stock of myself in months. It was almost as if I'd become invisible to myself, willfully blotting out the image staring back at me in the looking glass. I was mightily exhausted. The grace with which I'd once moved through life, gliding on a carpet of privilege, was gone. I was scrambling now, like everyone else, tripping over potholes, getting caught in storms, buffeted by worry and regret. I'd fallen back down to earth with a terrible thud.

No wonder June hadn't recognized me. I'd completely let myself go. I barely recognized myself. I looked like a toad—fat, bug-eyed, and bumpy. I recalled something my mother once told me: "Jolie Ann, you have two choices in life: you can be envied or pitied." I was pitiable now. Enviable was better.

21

LATER on that week, I received a call from a woman I'd avoided for years: a third-tier hostess who dealt in tarnished celebrities. She was one of a number around town. Betty called them "scavengers" because they preyed on the carcasses of has-beens with famous or infamous names.

I remember Betty saying about this particular woman, "She likes to portray herself as a concerned individual who reaches out for you in tough times. But actually she's a shameless climber who only gets a shot at people when they're washed up."

Scavenger or not, she had invited me to a dinner with the promise of a curator from the Tate as a dinner partner. If she'd known I worked in a department store now, I doubt she would have invited me. But despite my encounter with June, word had apparently not gotten out yet.

The party was dreary. I didn't know any of the guests. The hostess laughed like an asylum inmate and referred to me, in a not altogether friendly manner, as "a queen bee."

"Jo never invited me to her apartment," she said to the assembled company. "But everyone said it was absolutely divine." I admit I was a bit taken aback by this unsubtle reprimand. If I am a queen bee, I thought, I don't like being surrounded by rude drones.

The young "curator" from the Tate turned out to be a middle-aged art dealer who was interested in peddling some third-rate Old Masters to me, photos of which he just "happened to have" in his tweedy pocket.

The dinner was hippy gourmet. Courses came garnished with flowers that look more appetizing than the food. The conversation was all about money in one form or another: how it related to politics, to art, to science, to culture, who had made it, who had lost it, what stocks to buy, what stocks to sell. Billionaires were discussed with the kind of admiration formerly reserved for Nobel Prize winners. I was bored stiff. Old Economy, New Economy—it was all the same to me, who couldn't make money in any economy.

I felt myself wilting more with each course. Like many ripe women of a certain age, I looked attractive sitting down for the appetizer and embalmed by dessert.

The coup de grâce, however, was delivered after dinner in the living room where coffee was served. The topic of capital punishment somehow segued into a general discussion about forgiveness and how we must all learn the "art of forgiveness" as we get older. At which point, my hostess gestured to me in front of everyone, and said:

"Listen, if she can forgive Countess de Passy, anyone can forgive anybody anything. Right, Jo?"

"I *beg* your pardon?" I said, my demitasse spoon poised in midstir.

She went on, quite oblivious to my consternation.

"The Countess speaks so highly of you. I was at a benefit luncheon the other day and she was going on and on about how wonderful you are and how brave and how the two of you are such great friends."

I removed my spoon from the little cup and placed it primly on the saucer. Setting the cup down on the coffee table, I pulled myself up to my full height on the hideous overstuffed puce brocade couch and announced: "Monique de Passy does not exist for me."

The assembled company fell silent as our hostess launched a nervous flurry of words into the air, complete with hand gestures: "Oh really, because she speaks so highly of you, I mean she really does, she was saying how fond she was of you and how you'd taught her so many things and how you were her mentor in New York and how you and she both loved Louis the Sixteenth and . . ."

It may have been my icy glare, or the not-so-subtle hand signal from her wincing husband across the room, or a combination of the two, that made this insensitive woman stop chattering midsentence. She looked around as if to gather allies.

"Well, I'm so sorry. I had no idea," she said rather huffily. "I was just making a point about forgiveness, that's all. I certainly meant well. I *did*." Her husband was shaking his balding head in dismay.

I now understood perfectly why this woman was a third-tier hostess. She had the tact of a storm trooper and the sensitivity of asbestos. Still, I didn't believe she was lying. It enraged me that Monique was going around making people think we'd patched things up. She may have claimed my life, but I'd be damned if I'd let her claim my friendship as well.

After dinner, the English art dealer—whose accent was getting phonier by the second (I suspected he was an American posing as a Brit)—asked me if he could drop me off at home in a taxi. During the ride, he inquired if I had any "interesting things to sell" in a tone that left me somewhat unsure as to whether he was referring strictly to art. I would have been flattered if he hadn't been so repulsive. When I told him no, he instructed the driver to drop him off at his hotel first. It was downtown, way out of the way. He didn't offer to pay for the cab or say thank you when he got out.

The next morning, I sat down after breakfast and wrote my hostess a thank-you note that was none too effusive, but polite. I had every intention of delivering it myself that day, as was my custom. But I never got around to it that day or in the days that followed. After a couple of weeks, it was just too late. I tore it up and chucked it out.

—◊◊◊—

I spent the summer working at Bergdorf's. I had settled into a routine. Little by little, I was paying down my debts. Twice a week in the evening, I volunteered to work in a women's shelter on First Avenue in the Fifties, hoping that in helping others less fortunate than myself I'd appreciate what I had rather than dwell on what I'd lost. It was not the cathartic experience I had hoped for. These women were complicated individuals whose lives had somehow spiraled out of control. A few were schizo-phrenic and violent. Many were intelligent and highly neurotic. Some talked about their plights with disarming frankness.

"Life just got away from me. Damned if I know how," was how one woman described her situation to me.

In many of these poor souls, I glimpsed the embodi-ment of a future that was far too close for comfort. It may have been cowardly, but it depressed me so much to work there that I quit. I started going up to the Society Library on Seventy-ninth Street instead, where I retreated into the past, reading books about the French Revolution and Marie Antoinette.

In August, I was fired. To this day, I'm not quite sure why. A friendly saleswoman told me it might have been because I was too "intimidating" to the customers. It's true, I did have definite ideas about what looked good on people, and I refused to lie. I told one woman the yellow feathered dress she wanted to buy made her look like Big Bird. It's also possible that my reluctance to be a "team player," as my supervisor said, had something to do with it. On more than one occasion I'd voiced my opinion that many of the clothes we sold were badly made and way overpriced. Still, my growing paranoia about Monique made me suspect that she was somehow behind my dismissal.

Being out of work panicked me. I had to think seri-ously about getting another job, but for the remaining weeks of summer, I decided to give myself a rest.

Monique was out in Southampton in my house, with my friends, swimming in my pool, playing tennis on my court. I was trapped in a steam bath with a weak air conditioner. Both Betty and June had asked me to come and stay with them. Ethan, who had rented a shack in Amagansett instead of going to Patmos, offered to sleep on the couch and give me his bedroom. I probably should have gone, but I just wasn't ready. I begged off, telling everyone airily that I was "off to Paris" so they'd all stop calling me.

—⁂—

AUTUMN is my favorite time in New York, and by mid-September, I was feeling rather social again. I had lunch with Betty and June a couple of times and then, as is often the case, something very silly and inconsequential gave me an unexpected lift. I was going through my mail—mostly bills and circulars—when I came across an invitation to a charity benefit I'd been to many times: the Notable New Yorker dinner, a blue-chip occasion with a loot-heavy guest list held every November.

Among those who subscribe to it year after year, the NNY dinner at the Waldorf is known as a real Bullet-through-the-Head occasion—an interminable evening where, given the choice between shooting oneself or staying put another second, one would happily go for the gun. However, each year an impressive roster of honorees makes attendance mandatory. Everyone bitches but everyone goes. It was the sort of place that Trish Bromire always advised her single girlfriends to go to meet rich men.

"If you want to marry money, never go to a benefit costing less than a thousand dollars a ticket. Birds of a feather, you know," was Trish's sound advice.

And that was the price of the ticket: one thousand dollars. For me, it seemed like a fortune.

Dick Bromire was one of the honorees despite his endless legal troubles. Accompanying the invitation was a very sweet note from Trish.

Dear Jo,
Dick and I would love it if you'd come and be our guest for this very special evening for us. Please say you'll join us! We miss you!
                    Love, Trish

I'd supported Dick in his hour of need. Now it was his turn to support me. So goes the dainty minuet of social life.

Trish's warm words made me think once more of my obligations to my friends, and also of the fact that I might actually have a good time.

I called Trish up. She was delighted to hear from me.

"Oh, Jo!" she cried. "My God, where have you been? We've all missed you so much."

Nobody really wants to hear the story of your life and I certainly didn't want to go into it, so I just said that I'd been away, but that I was back, and I'd found her kind invitation to the Notable New Yorker dinner.

"Please come, Jo. We'd just love it if you could."

"I'd love to, Trish. Sounds like fun."

"I should warn you, though. Monique will be there."

My jaw inadvertently clenched. I said nothing.

"I'm sorry, Jo, but she bought five tables," Trish went on. "Don't worry. I promise you won't be seated together. But I just thought I'd warn you."

"Thanks, Trish. I appreciate that. And thank you for asking me."

"Oh—one other thing. There's this divine billionaire from Chicago who's flying in for the evening. His name is Brad Thompson. He's sixty-three, he's been divorced for five years, and I've told him all about you. He'll be your dinner partner. I can't wait to tell Dick you're coming. He'll be so thrilled!"

I hung up the phone with a tingly feeling of excitement—not, oddly enough, at the prospect of meeting what sounded like an eminently eligible man, but at the prospect of seeing Monique. The thought of her presence lent a horrible thrill to the occasion. I dreaded seeing her and yet I longed to see her at the same time. It was a feeling akin to confronting an old lover whom I wished to impress.

In the days that followed, however, I had time to reflect on the idea of Mr. Brad Thompson. I came to the conclusion that the only way to deal with Monique was to marry someone richer than she was. Fight money with money. Perhaps this billionaire from Chicago would be my knight in a shining Gulf Stream. And even if he didn't turn out to be the one, there might be some diamond-in-the-rough tycoon at that dinner who'd go for me. The NNY dinner was fertile hunting ground for wealthy game.

I couldn't see it then, but my obsession with Monique had infected the way I thought about everything—including my heart. I, who had never cared about money, had developed a severe case of gold rush fever in order to get even with the Countess. I recalled one famous society gold digger who, before she married well, had once said: "I don't care if the man's a zero as long as there are plenty of zeros in his bank account." Passion faded; money kept its color.

—⁂—

THE first thing I had to do was get back into shape. Gone were the days of pampered spas and social boot camps where they march you to Bataan and back on a diet of lettuce leaves for a thousand dollars a day. I couldn't afford it. I joined a local gym and started lifting weights. I jogged every day. I went on a strict diet. After a grueling first three weeks, I was suddenly energized. I dropped fifteen pounds and felt a pilot light of hope flickering inside me. Like a forgotten star making a comeback, I wasn't through yet. The day of the party, I was back to my fighting weight, looking better than I had in years.

As I dressed for the evening, I wondered how people would react to seeing me after all this time. It had been well over a year since the Dent affair, almost three since Lucius's death. By now practically everyone in New York—including the young Filipino manicurist at Hands Up on Lexington—knew my story. I wanted to put all that behind me tonight. I was determined to hold my head high. Also, I knew that rich fish don't snap at droopy bait. If I have one more big catch in me, I thought, I better be perky.

I spent hours getting ready. I couldn't afford to buy a new dress, but I had a closet full of old couture. Old couture was the chicest anyway. It showed I wasn't some upstart who'd just discovered Paris. I managed to squeeze into the strapless burgundy velvet gown made for me years ago to match the rubies of my Marie Antoinette necklace.

The necklace—the one possession of real value I had left. I lifted it out of its red leather case as if it were a holy relic. I held it up to the light, admiring the wine rubies, the twinkling rose-cut diamonds, and the gunmetal black pearls all woven together in a perfect crosshatch design. Monique may have my money, I thought, as I draped it around my neck and fastened the clasp, but she'll never have anything as beautiful as this.

Just before leaving my apartment, I gargled with mouthwash, then sprayed my mouth with eau de cologne to sweeten my breath. (A little trick I learned from Clara, along with never eating shrimp or smoked salmon hors d'oeuvres because they made your mouth reek.) I checked myself out in the mirror from all angles, not just the front. It was important to look equally good from the back and sides. My hair and makeup were neat enough, considering I'd done them both myself. It was a far cry from the old days when a hairdresser and makeup artist came to the house to get me ready for big events.

Still, I felt pretty, relaxed, and confident—ready to face the world. I was actually looking forward to running into Monique to show her that I was doing very well indeed.

22

I stood on a windy corner of Lexington Avenue trying to hail a taxi going downtown. Gone were the days of the waiting limousine. Instead of remembering Caspar as the ill-tempered schnauzer who guarded Lucius, I thought of him wistfully as a jewel of a chauffeur who was on time, rain or shine, and who could hand-deliver forty invitations in an afternoon.

Finally a cab pulled up. I slid into the back, careful to avoid a hand-sized patch of grease on the scuffy black vinyl seat. The stench of some exotic cuisine was overpowering. I gave the driver the address. He didn't know where the Waldorf-Astoria was. He hardly knew where Park Avenue was. It was his first day on the job. I said I'd direct him if he turned down his CB radio. As the meter clicked on, the recorded voice of an ersatz celebrity barked at me to "Buckle up!" The wind from the driver's open window blew apart my hairdo.

With the glittery city whipping by on either side, I recalled the evening at this very dinner when Lucius had been one of the honorees. I remembered how he'd fussed over my outfit that night, wanting me to "look expensive," as he told me, only half joking. Lucius liked showing off his importance in the world through me. Men in his position want wives, like possessions, to reflect their glory. I never dreamed on that long-ago night he would one day discard me like a broken ornament.

Sitting in the taxi I played a little game with myself. I added up how much my whole outfit cost. The couture dress was a cool twelve thousand (it would be much more today, but the *Directrice de la Maison* had given me a deal because I'd purchased so many things that year); the Marie Antoinette necklace was a quarter of a mil; the white gold and diamond minaudière, eight thou; the shoes, seven hundred and fifty dollars; and so on.

And there I was in all that finery, sitting in the back of a smelly, noisy, run-down cab with grease stains on the seat. I felt sorry for myself. I got my comeuppance when the cab stopped for a light and I focused in on a homeless man sleeping in front of a building on Fifty-sixth Street. Next to him was a shopping cart filled with soda cans and a heap of plastic bags, old clothes, newspapers, and other detritus of urban life. The crumpled, colorful cans glinted under the lamplight and I was overcome with sadness. The light changed and we sped off.

"I must remember how lucky I am," I thought, reprimanding myself for any self-pity. "I'm very lucky."

However, each click of the taxi meter reminded me how quickly life ticked away. The image of the homeless man haunted me like the faces of those women at the shelter: apocalyptic visions of my own impending doom. The drawings and the jewelry were all gone. I looked at the minaudière. That was next. I'd be lucky to get half what I paid for it.

In former days I might have given my couture clothes away to the Metropolitan Museum Costume Institute and taken a whopping tax deduction. But now I had no income to deduct a deduction from. I wondered if perhaps a celebrity auction of those beautiful old clothes might tide me over for another few months. But who would buy the dresses of a socialite loser?

I knew that unless a miracle happened I would soon have to sell my most beloved treasure: the necklace. I clutched my throat to reassure myself it was still there.

—◆—

BLOCKING the entrance to the Waldorf was a chain of black limousines and one triple-size white stretch with flashing lights and tinted windows that stood out like a stripper in a line of nuns. I directed the cabbie to drive to the next block, where I could disembark unnoticed. I gave him a nice tip considering his cab smelled like a diner griddle, got out, and walked back to the hotel.

I arrived at the door, chilled to the bone, purposely not having worn a coat. In the days when I had a car and driver, I was dropped off at the front door. If I bothered to take a coat, I always left it in the backseat so I wouldn't have to check it. Standing in line at the cloakroom after a benefit was a degrading, tedious experience, especially for a single woman. It showed she didn't have an escort or a private car. Better to freeze.

I ducked into the ladies' room, ran hot water over my

hands to warm up, recombed my hair, freshened my lipstick, and walked out, head high, prepared for battle.

Just outside the entrance to the Jade Room, on a long cloth-covered table, was a depleted battalion of miniature, hand-calligraphied white envelopes. I perused the group, pretending to search for my own name but really looking to see who else was coming. I spotted the envelope with "Countess de Passy" written on it. I was about to pick it up and peek inside to see which table she was seated at when a scrubbed and shiny young woman in a skimpy black dress handed me an envelope with "Mrs. Lucius Slater" written on the front.

"Good evening, Mrs. Slater. So nice to see you."

Though I hadn't the vaguest idea who she was, I was touched she recognized me. I opened my envelope. The small white card inside read "Table 47." I paused to consider a moment. A two-digit table wasn't necessarily a bad sign. Not *necessarily*. Benefit organizers had learned not to make Table 1 the top table so people wouldn't take one look at their seating assignments and leave if they weren't in the single digits. Still, forty-seven didn't sound promising. I slid the little envelope into my purse, banishing bad thoughts that might mar my confidence, and proceeded into the Jade Room where cocktails were being served.

I'd arrived late because I loathe cocktail hours, even though they are considered opportune times to flit over the pond, sniffing new blood before one gets bogged down at dinner between, as Betty once said, "some crusty old alligator and an Adonis who's more interested in wooing the waiter." Since I already knew who my dinner partner was, I didn't need to go on a scouting mission.

I made my entrance into the room hoping to attract as little attention as possible. I was never one of those socialites who kept packs of hungry lensmen at bay with a smile. One photographer did recognize me and, more for politeness than profit, I think, stepped forward to take my picture. I mustered an obligatory grin, anxious not to betray any sign of desperation. In social life, desperation is as feared as the flu, and as catching.

He took the shot, thanked me, and even asked me for another. As I posed, a youngish, too-casually dressed couple entered the room. A little lightning storm of popping flashes ensued. Splashed with attention, the couple moved on.

"Who's that?" I asked my photographer, who had gallantly stuck with me despite his colleagues' feeding frenzy.

"Mark Whatshisname, that guy who lost four billion dollars in a day. He's one of the honorees."

"Really? He looks so young," I said.

The cocktail hour was in full swing. I strolled through the room looking for Trish and Dick. Some people looked at me as if they'd seen a ghost. Others stopped me and said hello. Everyone I said hi to was very friendly and polite. Yet there was a distance in their manner.

I couldn't help thinking of the legions who used to practically break their necks flinging themselves into my orbit. Where were they now? I had to face it. I was pushing fifty, alone, living in a small apartment with a brick wall view. By society's standards I was all washed up. My case, solved by misfortune, was closed. And still, I felt hopeful. The billionaire from Chicago . . . my chance to get back at Monique.

Scanning the huge, glossy crowd, I spotted Miranda Somers holding court at the far end of the room. Miranda was easy to spot by the flock of people hovering near her, waiting anxiously to bid her hello. Everyone craving a mention in the "Daisy" column paid homage to Miranda. On this particular night, dressed in a cloud of pink tulle, Miranda reminded me of a cotton-candy cardinal with supplicants lining up to kiss her ring. I marveled at the way this canny woman who glorified social life held court year after year after year, growing ever more exalted as society reputedly hobbled off into the twilight of inconsequence.

Who are they kidding, I thought? Society is a form of celebrity, and celebrity is more consequential than ever.

And then I saw it—that marvelous dress—a silver satin sheath, with an elegant sweep of train at the back. I always notice beautiful clothes and I fastened immediately on the flawless cut and the material of this extraordinary gown that shimmered like moonlight. You couldn't get a dress like that off the rack. That dress was haute couture.

The wearer, her back to me, was talking to Miranda Somers. I couldn't see her face, yet there was something disturbingly familiar about her. I drew nearer—moth to flame. The closer I got, the more disconcerting the image became. When I was only footsteps away, the woman suddenly turned and laughed loudly, her long white neck straining upward in a gesture of forced gaiety.

Monique.

I looked at her face, the white complexion, the intense dark eyes, the shiny black hair. I couldn't move. My eyes were anchored to her. I heard nothing except a weird mechanical pounding in my head, like the sound of a cash register drawer repeatedly slamming shut.

A waiter passing a tray of hors d'oeuvres splattered with what looked like pink shaving cream brushed by me. It crossed my mind to grab this tray of disgusting finger food and fling it at Monique *and* her moonlight satin dress, when I felt a distracting tap on my shoulder.

"Hey, sweetie!" said a voice.

It was June Kahn, in that ghastly orange ruffle dress I'd forbidden her to buy at Bergdorf's. This time, she recognized me.

"Oh my God, Jo, you look fabulous! I'm so happy to see you here, sweetie. I was so worried about you." She pointed to my necklace. "Whatever you have to hock, never hock that."

June, who thought she was being funny, had no idea how close to the bone she'd cut. "Jo? Sweetie? You look as if you've seen a ghost."

"I wish," I said, nodding in Monique's direction.

June gave me an empathetic pat on the arm. "I know. Courage."

Nauseated as I felt, I was unable to tear myself away from the spectacle of Monique in all her glory. It is a curious fact of social life that the pain of exclusion often confers a perverse pleasure.

"Look at them all sucking up to her," I said in a purposely languid drawl as if I were amused by the situation. "Remember the days when no one would speak to her?"

"Social life!" June shrugged, as if that were the explanation for all the ills of the world.

I looked at June with sudden apprehension. "*You* wouldn't have anything to do with her, would you?"

"No, sweetie, of course not."

"And Charlie?"

"You know Charlie. He always forgets who he's supposed to hate."

"Well, you make sure and remind him."

"Jo, dear, I know this may sound a bit Pollyanna-ish, but all this is really so unimportant."

"June, dear," I said, trying to contain my irritation, "people always think the things they have are unimportant. By the way, do you know who my mystery man is?"

June looked perplexed. "What?"

"The main reason I'm here is because Trish has some billionaire from Chicago she wants to introduce me to."

June grabbed my arm. "Oh, I bet that's Brad Thompson," she said.

"You know him? What's he like?"

"Paper mills. So rich you can't believe it. And very low-key. Divine. I sat next to him the other night. He's just gone on the board of Chapel's. He loves to sail."

"I'm glad you told me. I guess I won't mention I think boats are prisons on which you can drown," I said, quoting Samuel Johnson.

"No, don't," June said earnestly. "Oh, and his daughter's got something to do with Russia."

"What?"

"Something. I forget."

We were interrupted by waiters with gongs and the flashing on and off of lights.

"Whatever happened to 'Dinner is served'?" I said to June.

—m—

THE Grand Ballroom was studded with dozens of round tables covered in burlap, sprinkled with fresh earth, with a phallic skyscraper made of moss at the center of each one. The bluish green nuclear winter lighting was highly unflattering. People looked like the walking dead.

"A new low in decoration," I whispered to June as we waded in. "What number are you at?"

"Forty-eight," June replied. "You?"

"Forty-seven."

"Goody, goody, we're right next to each other."

A harried young man with a clipboard was directing people to their tables in the vast room. I felt my excitement mounting as we each told him our number and he waved us toward the front. I spotted the number "47" sticking up on a white card on a table directly below the dais.

When I arrived, Charlie Kahn and Dick Bromire both stood up to greet me. Dick seemed particularly pleased to see me.

"Jo, dear. My God, it's been too long," he said, embracing me.

Charlie was, as always, more reserved. But even he gave me a kiss.

Roger Lowry was at the table along with his wife. I nodded politely to both of them, hoping to keep them at bay. But, unfortunately, they both got up from their seats and came over to welcome me with an effusiveness I found slightly off-putting, considering the way Roger had treated me.

Betty was sitting down next to Charlie. She signaled me over to her. I leaned down and gave her a hug.

"All set for a scintillating evening?" she said, squeezing my hand. "Jo-Jo. It's so nice to see you out and about. You look good, kiddo."

"You, too, Betts. I'm just recharging the old batteries."

Betty tugged on my arm and pulled me down closer to her. Her mouth was practically in my ear.

"Listen," she whispered, "your girlfriend switched the fucking place cards. I saw her."

"Who? What are you talking about?"

Betty stuck out her thumb like a hitchhiker, pointing it toward the next table.

"The Cuntess, who else? She stole your eligible. Trish is about to have a cow. Look."

I glanced over at the next table where June was seated. Trish Bromire was standing talking to a tall, rather distinguished-looking, auburn-haired man in a double-breasted tuxedo. They appeared to be having a slight difference of opinion. At one point, Trish took him forcibly by the hand. He demurred with a laugh and sat down in the chair in front of him. Trish pretended to shrug it off, but I could see she was upset and just didn't want to make a scene. She walked back to our table and took me aside.

"Jo, dear, I'm so happy to see you. Thanks so much for coming. Listen, we've had a little glitch. Brad Thompson? The man I wanted to introduce you to? Um, he's going to be over at that table for the first course. He'll join us for dessert, though. It's a mess. I can't go into it."

I, of course, didn't let on I knew what had happened. I could see it was hard enough on Trish. She'd been kind enough to invite me. I sat between Dick and Charlie Kahn.

Dick talked a great deal about the case the government

supposedly had against him. I asked him exactly what was going on. He said they were accusing him of "petty, Leona Helmsley–type stuff."

I didn't feel it my place to remind him that Mrs. Helmsley went to jail.

"I've donated over a hundred and fifty million dollars to charity," he said. "Still, they're out to get me. What have I done wrong except be successful?"

"Sometimes that's enough," I said.

"You know you're right, Jo." He nodded his head. "They resent us. They really do. Trish and I live very well. We make no bones about it. We're visible. And there's this one little prick in the DA's office who wants to make a name for himself through me. He just won't let go." Dick looked pensive for a long moment. "He can't get anything, though, because there's nothing *to* get. I ain't Leona. Plus, I've got a great team of lawyers. Still, it's a bore."

While Dick was talking, I stole glances at Monique— *Miss Moonlight herself*—who was working her wiles on my Chicago billionaire.

The table turned and I now spoke to Charlie Kahn, who was bland as tapioca, talking about golf and Lyford Cay. Sitting next to Charlie was like floating on a raft. I didn't have to do any work at all; I just drifted along on the current of his slow, gentle conversation.

I noticed that the chair on Monique's other side remained curiously vacant. I wondered who was supposed to be there. The unoccupied seat was a godsend for the Countess because it meant that she could devote herself entirely to the handsome Mr. Thompson. I have to admit he looked happy with her company, especially during those frequent times when she tilted her head back and laughed like a demented swan at what I assumed was one of his jokes.

Charlie didn't notice my eyes wandering. Charlie didn't notice much, or if he did, he never let on. I wore a manufactured smile and bobbed my head up and down politely, but inside I was feeling grimmer than Lee at Appomattox.

How could I ever compete with that sexy, seductive killer who was years younger than I?

At one point during the salad course, Betty, who must have sensed my distress, leaned behind Charlie, pinched my arm to get my attention, and whispered to me: "Don't be too upset. I hear his wife left him for another woman."

I didn't really see what that had to do with anything, but I appreciated Betty's effort to cheer me up.

As the night wore on, I felt that familiar fault line of masochism rumbling deep inside my gut. I was catapulted back to my childhood where the delicious torment of exclusion was always more vivid than any positive experience. That was social life in a nutshell: the delicious torment of exclusion.

Suddenly, I caught sight of Nate Nathaniel oozing toward Monique's table, all smiles and smarm, greeting everyone with oily charm. My heart did a cartwheel as I watched him dip down behind Monique and infect her bare shoulder with a little kiss.

"*Bon soir, cheri,* you're late," she said, looking up at him. "Sit down, *mon amour.*"

Nate shook hands with the billionaire and was settling in when Trish, God bless her, saw this as her chance to shift the seating. She signaled to Dick.

"Uh-oh, I have to desert you," Dick said to me. "General's orders."

He grabbed his wine glass and his napkin and walked over to Monique's table. I quickly opened my bag and checked myself out in my compact mirror. I put on some fresh lipstick. By the time Trish escorted my Chicago billionaire to the seat that Dick had occupied, I was ready for battle.

He sat down and shook my hand.

"Brad Thompson," he said in a deep, husky voice.

"Jo Slater."

He was very attractive close up, with solid, masculine Mount Rushmore looks. He smelled good. He had navy blue eyes, like Lucius, and a positive, self-assured manner.

"I hear you're from Chicago. I've never been there but I hear it's a marvelous city," I began, anxious to get the ball rolling in the right direction.

"Chicago's great. But I love New York. This is a really fun town. I like a city with a lot of contrasts."

"What do you mean?"

"There are so many different scenes here, all so interesting. I like going to these little off-Broadway shows. I love experimental stuff. How about you? You a theater fan?"

"Sometimes. I actually love museums. That's my preferred form of entertainment."

"You and my daughter. She's working at the Hermitage Museum over there in Russia, studying to be an art restorer. That's a whole other world, boy. I have no patience for museums. When I see a beautiful thing, I want to own it. Museums are too frustrating for me," he said, only half joking. "They remind me of what I can't have. Hate that."

"I just might be able to change your mind."

"Think so? Okay, I'll make a deal with you. I'll take you to a show and you take me to a museum. Then we'll compare notes. But no faking now. If we're bored, we say so. Deal?"

"Deal." We shook hands. I liked him more and more.

Then he leaned into me with a conspiratorial air and whispered in my ear, "Can you keep a secret?"

"Try me," I said, hoping to sound seductive.

"I need to duck out of here before the speeches begin."

"I don't blame you," I whispered back. "I wouldn't mind myself."

"So if you'll excuse me, lovely lady, I'm going to say good night."

"You mean right now?"

He was halfway out of his seat. I just couldn't believe it. I'd hardly had time to take a good crack at him.

"What's your hurry?" I said, trying not to sound too eager. "Why not stay for a few minutes? I'm thinking of taking a cruise and I hear you're a great sailor. I'd love to get your thoughts on what type of boat I should rent."

"Sailboat . . . I've really gotta run. I want to catch the end of the *Titanic* documentary."

"The *Titanic* documentary?"

"You oughta see that show. It's supposed to be terrific."

"I'm living that show, thanks."

He smiled broadly and pointed his finger at me. "Hey, you're funny. Catch you later, Jeanie."

"Jo."

He was gone. I looked around, vaguely embarrassed.

Trish was staring at me across the table with a perplexed expression on her face. I tried to laugh off his departure.

"Must have been something I said."

Trish shrugged and made a sad face as if to say, "Well, I tried."

I leaned back in my chair and folded my arms across my chest as waiters cleared our salad plates and replaced them with bowls of the most revolting-looking concoction I'd ever seen—some sort of slimy mousse drowning in a curdling raspberry sauce. There were little unidentified black and orange chunks floating around in it as well. God knows what they were. It looked like bloody vomit. I pushed it away.

I glanced over at Monique and Nate, watching them as they flirted with each other, laughing like conspirators. I wondered which one of them had thought up the plan to get Lucius's money?

My loathing of Monique at this moment was so intense I was afraid people could see it. I was electric with hatred. I drank some wine. Even that didn't help. I was in a state. I excused myself to go to the ladies' room, where I splashed cold water on my face and took deep breaths like Swami Shivapremenanda had taught me.

Inhale, one, two, three . . . exhale . . . one, two, three, four, five . . . All those private yoga lessons were finally coming in handy.

Walking back to the table, I retreated into the shadows for a moment.

The room hummed with conversation. The waiters were still passing out that wretched dessert. My eyes were glued to Monique, who looked so stunning, so at ease, and so rich in her magnificent moonlight dress. She was telling a story, using hand gestures and facial grimaces with the timing of a polished actress. Her spellbound audience gazed at her in expectant admiration. The whole table exploded in laughter at her punch line.

Suddenly, a wicked idea occurred to me. Walking to the back of the room, I approached a waiter and explained to him exactly what I wanted him to do. The poor man looked at me as if I were crazy and hurried on about his business. I approached another waiter, and another, and another. They all turned me down once I explained what I had in mind. About to give up, I suddenly spotted a surly-looking busboy idling near an exit, sneaking tokes on a cigarette. Just the ticket, I thought.

"It's not knowing how to do it yourself. It's knowing whom to choose"—one of Clara Wilman's famous dictums.

"Excuse me," I said, approaching him. He folded the cigarette into his palm and looked me up and down—a promising sign. This was definitely my man. "Would you like to make fifty dollars?"

Shifting his weight from one leg to another, he gave me a lascivious little wink. "Whaddya have in mind?"

"I'll give you fifty dollars if you go over there and accidentally spill a bowl of dessert on that woman in the silvery dress," I said, pointing at Monique.

The busboy seemed vaguely disappointed. And disbelieving.

"I'm serious. Here." I handed him the folded fifty-dollar bill.

He gave me the once-over again and shrugged. "Sure."

"Ruin the dress," I said.

Oh, the confidence of wearing couture. No armor

offers better protection. And it's more expensive than medieval chain mail. How well will you behave when your fabulous dress is destroyed? I thought.

I watched keenly as the busboy cleared Monique's table. People had barely touched the disgusting dessert. The young man picked up the full bowl in front of her, hesitated, then tripped on purpose and fell forward. The bowl landed squarely on Monique, dumping a mousse and raspberry car wreck in her lap and splattering the entire dress.

A bomb could hardly have produced a more horrified reaction. Trish Bromire screamed. Nate Nathaniel shot up, grabbed the busboy by the scruff of his collar, and growled, "You clumsy son of a bitch."

Defiant, the busboy cried, "Lay off, dude, it was an accident."

A commotion ensued. People leapt up from their chairs and ran to Monique's aide, offering napkins, sparkling water, sympathy, advice.

Wriggling free of Nate's grasp, the frightened busboy feinted back like a boxer. Nate rushed him. I watched with delight, anticipating the revelation of Nate's true character.

Gil Waterman grabbed Nate's sleeve to halt his charge. The lawyer backed off reluctantly. Monique arose majestically from her chair, revealing the brownish red gelatinous stain fouling her silver gray gown. The dress was ruined. Thirty thousand dollars down the tubes. I savored my triumph from the shadows.

Gallant and stoic, like a battlefield nurse drenched with the blood of wounded soldiers, Monique edged her way out from behind the table and walked slowly toward the insolent busboy so everyone could see. People held their breaths. She stood in front of him for a long, theatrical moment. Then she reached out, patted his cheek, and said: "Never mind, young man. Gray is such a *boring* color."

Monique burst out laughing, sending the tense crowd of onlookers into a round of spontaneous applause. I saw the combination of relief and admiration on their faces. Nate Nathaniel's rage was punctured. He laughed and hugged Monique. Even the busboy hugged her. It was a memorable moment.

I could tell from the approving looks on people's faces that they were all thinking: What class, what elegance, what noblesse oblige. The woman is a queen.

I see now how I had subconsciously engineered the very thing I feared the most. But I couldn't see it then. All I saw then was another social triumph for my archenemy, hand-delivered by me.

—⁓—

I had to take a bus home. I only had two singles left, which wasn't enough for a cab. I took a chance boarding the bus because I didn't have the exact change, but a kindly woman made change for me. I told her I was from out of town. The few passengers on the bus stared at me sitting there in all my finery, wondering, I'm sure, what I was doing on public transportation.

The bus bumped and wheezed up Third Avenue. I sat huddled up in the back, freezing, staring out the window, thinking about the evening, what a disaster it had been, how much I'd been counting on it, and how social life had gone on quite merrily without me. Oh, I knew that people were pleased to see me, but only in the context of a party where one's personal misfortunes are a most untoward topic of conversation. I thought about Monique—how people disliked her but fawned over her because she was rich, how she was bent on destroying me even now that I had no real power left. I thought about Nate, that Draconian worm. He'd orchestrated the whole thing to get his hands on Lucius's money. I was absolutely convinced of that. If it hadn't been for him . . . But that was all water under the bridge now.

I was shivering so hard when I got home that I ran a hot bath to ward off the chill. As I was undressing for a long soak in the tub, undoing the endless hooks and snaps and zippers that are the hallmark of couture, I discovered that my right index finger was bleeding. Apparently, I'd gnawed it harder than I thought sitting on the bus. Staring at the bright smear of red on my skin, I thought: Blood is not a boring color.

23

BRAD Thompson now became something of a fixation for me. Not only was he rich, he was snappy and fun. He had an attractive edge. I liked the fact he was interested in the theater. So many businessmen had little or no time for the arts. Though I viewed him primarily as a pawn in my game with Monique, I felt he had real potential as a suitor. I somehow got it into my head that this billionaire-sportsman-theater buff would have fallen for me if only we'd spent a little more time together. Hadn't he suggested we go to a show? Despite his hurry to get home to watch a television documentary, I was convinced I saw a twinkle in his eye when he looked at me.

I called Trish the next morning to thank her for "a lovely evening," as I put it. I was too shy to come right out and ask her if Mr. Thompson had said anything about me so I brought up the egregious switching of the place cards as a way to ease into the topic without appearing too obvious. Monique's rude behavior had apparently been forgiven in light of the dessert incident.

"I'm not crazy about her—although it was sweet of her to take five tables. But I have to admit she behaved like a queen," Trish said, barely drawing breath. "Did you see her? No, that's right. You were in the powder room. But she got up and she said to this poor little innocent busboy, who'd just spilled this raspberry guck all over her by accident and who was obviously terrified out of his wits, she said, 'Gray is such a boring color.' I happen to know that dress cost thirty thousand dollars because I almost ordered it from Balmain couture. You really do have to hand it to her."

I wasn't interested in handing another thing to Monique de Passy, thanks very much, or in hearing Trish's character assessment of the "poor little innocent busboy." I pressed on with Topic A.

"Well, I'm sorry I didn't get much of a chance to sit next to Mr. Thompson. He seems quite charming," I said.

"Did you like him? He thought you were neat."

"Did he indeed?"

"Yes, I spoke to him this morning and he told me how funny you were. He said he was sorry he had to leave."

"Tell him to call me then."

"Now, Jo, you know how spoiled men are. You'll have to call him. He's a bit of a rough diamond, I have to say. But he loves New York. He says he's thinking of moving here. He wants to get to know the right people. He's quite conscious of who's who and what's what, if you know what I mean."

"He and Monique seemed to be hitting it off quite successfully," I said, fishing.

"No, no, no. She's with that awful lawyer."

"Nate."

"Your old pal. That's why I thought it was so ratty of her to switch the place cards. But I guess she'd trade up for a billionaire in a second. Anyway, Jo, it was so good to see you again. Everyone was saying how wonderful you looked and how much we all miss you. You know, Jo, you really ought to give yourself a coming-out party."

I laughed. "What do you mean?"

"I'm serious. Give one of your elegant little dinners to announce you're back in circulation. It'd be such fun. Invite Brad. He adores parties. Did I tell you he thought you were cute?"

—⁂—

OLD Swahili proverb: "It's better to live a short life as a lion than a long life as a chicken."

I decided to take Trish's advice and go down in a blaze of glory. I *would* give a party. This was a daring and desperate act, requiring the last of my funds, but I didn't care. The planning of it would concentrate my mind, yoke it to a semicreative harness, and stop it from running wild through the fields of obsession. Plus, there was now a real reason: Mr. Brad Thompson. Hook him and I was back in action.

I saw parties as theater: Anyone with money could put on a show, but it took real talent to create a hit. For me, parties were ends in themselves, oases of good cheer in a careworn world. Was it so frivolous to want to give one's friends a perfect evening? What is life in the end but a collection of memories? Can't some of them just be charming for charming's sake?

I found, through years of experience, that it was preferable to give a party *for* someone. That way, one didn't have to include everyone, just those with a particular connection to the guest of honor. Feelings were less likely to be hurt.

I decided on my auction prince, Nicky Brubetskoi. Nicky was a personable man whose Romanov ancestry was reflected in his suave good looks and regal bearing. People liked him. He was easygoing, well mannered, and impeccably dressed. He had connections everywhere and a colorful history. Family lore had it that the Red Army invaded Nicky's grandparents' dacha during a dinner party in 1917 and they escaped with only the clothes on their backs. Fleeing to Paris, they set themselves up in style by selling the jewels sewn onto his grandmother's evening gown and slippers and the sapphire studs and cufflinks belonging to his grandfather.

I was grateful to Nicky for all his help in unloading my possessions, and, in any case, he was a perfect guest of honor for an elegant occasion requiring some clout. But, I confess, my real reason for choosing Prince Nicky had to do more with Brad Thompson. June had mentioned to me that Brad was on the board of Chapel's and Brad had told me his daughter was studying at the Hermitage. Was there a more perfect guest of honor than a Russian royal who worked for Chapel's, I ask you?

—⁓—

I made up a guest list of fifty people, including my pals, select *amis mondains,* and Mr. Brad Thompson. Before I settled on the date, I called Brad Thompson's office in Chicago, pretending to be my own secretary—thus breaking my rule of always calling to issue an invitation myself. I told his secretary that I was calling for Mrs. Jo Slater to invite Mr. Thompson to a party in New York in honor of Prince Nicholas Brubetskoi on such-and-such a date. I wanted to make sure that Brad Thompson could come to this party before I arranged it. Thompson's secretary said she would get back to me. She called back that afternoon. This time I answered as myself. When she said that Mr. Thompson was out of town all that week, I told her that my secretary had made a mistake and said the party was actually the *following* week. She got back to me again the next day. Brad Thompson accepted the invitation with pleasure.

NATURALLY, I would have liked to have given the party at home, but rat holes are not condusive to conviviality. I settled instead on the private dining room upstairs at Le Poisson, which was large enough for the occasion. The hand-calligraphied invitations read:

> *Jo Slater*
> *requests the pleasure of the company of*
> *[the invitee]*
> *at a small dinner in honor of*
> *Prince Nicholas Brubetskoi*
> *on Saturday, December 20th*
> *at eight o'clock*
> *at Le Poisson*
>
> *Black Tie*

(Nicky preferred "Prince" to the more formal "His Royal Highness.")

I hand-delivered all the invitations myself, hoping nobody would spot me as I went door to door. I didn't bother to attach them to a Baccarat bud vase with a single white rose in it, as I often did in the old days. That was an extravagance way beyond my means now.

All my pals accepted immediately: the Kahns, the Watermans, the Bromires, Ethan. The *amis mondains* were not far behind because Miranda Somers was coming. The word was out. The only couple to refuse were the Lowrys. In the back of my mind, there lurked a tiny suspicion that Roger's refusal was a harbinger of things to come. But I dismissed this as a slight case of hostess jitters.

———

SINCE all of my friends knew the upstairs space at Le Poisson so well—everyone gave lunches and dinners there when they didn't want to be bothered entertaining at home—I hired Trebor Bellini to transform it into an eighteenth-century *salon*. If Brad Thompson liked theater, I'd give him a beautiful set.

Bellini, a former set designer and landscape gardener whose dark brooding looks and impish charm accelerated his rise to become New York's best-known party designer, was a particular favorite of mine. Our collaborations were famous. Bellini concretized the atmospheres that merely shimmered like mirages in my mind. I would describe the mood I wanted in detail and Bellini, the alchemist of the visual, would transform my wishes into pure entertaining gold. We both shared a passion for La Quintinie, Louis the Fourteenth's landscape artist of

genius. Trebor and I sometimes spent long lazy after-
noons at the Morgan Library and the Frick Collection
researching historical interiors and gardens. We had once
journeyed together to Paris to see seventeenth- and eighteenth-century Old Master drawings of French chateaus
in the archives of the Louvre—a special showing just for
us because I had given them a coveted Watteau painting I
bought at auction in New York and returned to its native
land.

For this party, as I explained to Trebor, I wanted my
guests to feel as if they were walking into one of Marie
Antoinette's private apartments in Versailles for an intimate supper. He suggested we hide the walls with trompe
l'oeil paintings of old boiserie, slipcover the dining chairs
in a pretty hand-painted silk damask I'd bought in Lyons
years ago and was saving for the right occasion, and
import those luscious pastel-colored roses I loved from
France, the ones that smelled so fragrant because they
were from gardens, not hothouses. He told me to use
some of my Marie Antoinette memorabilia for the occasion—fans, gloves, hatboxes, letters, keys, and porcelain.

"We'll place things randomly on side tables and chairs
as if they were just dropped there. A fan here, a hatbox
there. A letter, a teacup . . . priceless little throwaways.
We won't draw attention to them in any way. We want to
make it look like the Queen just passed through the room
in a hurry on her way to an assignation," said Trebor.

I loved the idea. There was only one drawback. I'd
sold all my Marie Antoinette memorabilia to a private
collector through Nicky; the silk from Lyons was packed
up in a crate that was in storage; and I barely had funds
enough for American roses, no less French ones.

Trebor, God bless him, understood perfectly.

"Anyone can create a great atmosphere on an unlimited budget," he told me. "It takes genius to do it on a shoestring."

And we both agreed he was a genius.

My next duty was to plan the meal with the restaurant's talented twenty-four-year-old chef, Jean-Paul. Recently plucked from the obscurity of a Bordeaux bistro, Jean-Paul was the latest gastronomic sensation in New York. Together, we collaborated on a menu of eighteenth-century delicacies: truffled foie gras, Belon oysters with buttered bread, veal roast in pastry, meringues, fruit compotes, and, of course, Krug champagne—only I couldn't afford Krug, so he suggested an acceptable substitute at a fourth of the price.

I hired a string quartet from Juilliard to play selections from Gluck, the Austrian composer Marie Antoinette championed against the Italian Piccinni.

Naturally, I planned to wear my famous necklace, this time with a different dress, in honor of Mr. Brad Thompson. I splurged and bought a bright red silk sheath for the occasion. Men love red.

I wanted this to be a truly memorable evening, an evening everyone would talk about. Most of all, I wanted Monique to hear about it. I wanted her to hear that Mr. Brad Thompson had fallen madly in love with me over the Belon oysters at my fabulous soiree.

This dinner was for the Countess, and she wasn't even invited.

24

ONE week before the dinner, I smelled trouble. Ethan Monk called me and said: "Jo, dear, just checking. What time exactly will we be sitting down for dinner?" Translation: "Can I be out of there by ten so I can get to another party?"

"Okay, Ethan, what's up?"

"Nothing, darling."

"Come on, Ethan. I know you. Who else is giving a party?"

"Jo, don't be so paranoid."

"Paranoids are the only ones who notice anything these days," I said.

"It's just that I'm thinking of driving out to the country afterward, that's all."

"You're a rotten liar, Ethan."

The Monk sighed. "I don't know why I even try. You're going to hear about it anyway."

My heart beat faster. "What?"

"Your friend the Countess is giving a dinner dance for the Dents on Saturday night."

I drew a breath. "I don't believe it."

"It's true."

"The Dents. Those ridiculous people."

"What is it June always says? Social life."

"And Saturday? *This Saturday?* Everyone's coming to *my* dinner on Saturday. Are you sure?"

"I just got the invitation. Hand-delivered, tied to a Baccarat bud vase with a single rose in it. Sound familiar?"

"You're *kidding.*"

"Imitation—sincerest form of flattery and all that? Except the rose isn't white. It's red. It's sitting right here in front of me, a nice, plump, and juicy red rose."

"Bought with blood money. How appropriate. Wait a minute. You just got it? Today?"

"Chauffeur-delivered an hour ago."

"Well, our standards have certainly lowered. I take it we no longer care about being invited to things at the last minute," I said, wanting to tweak him a little.

"They were all delivered today. I checked."

"I see. You mean she's organized a dinner dance in a week?" My brain started clicking. I thought out loud. "That's why the Lowrys declined. You want to know what I bet happened? Monique invited the Dents and the Lowrys for dinner and when she found out about my dinner, she decided to give a dance. She waited until the last moment to invite everybody just to spite me."

"That sounds about right."

"Trust me, Ethan, that's what happened. The woman has a thing about me."

The truth is that I was obsessed with Monique. But as Clara Wilman always said: "Tell me what you criticize and I'll tell you who you are."

"If you go to her dance," I told Ethan, "you can plan on never speaking to me again."

There was a long pause at the other end of the line. I knew better than anyone that Ethan was a shameless party hound, often wedging six or seven events into a single evening. I once invented a torture for him where he would be invited to three really glamorous parties on the same night. It's understood he can accept only one. The party he accepts is canceled at the last moment and there's no room for him at either of the two other parties he's turned down. Ethan spends a night of torment, all alone, knowing that two fabulous festivities are going on without him. Even he thought this was amusing.

"Jo, seriously, I won't go if you tell me not to."

"You want to go, don't you?"

"Not to see *her,* you know that. To see the apartment and the whole scene. You know me, Jo. I love social theater and I have no scruples."

"Do what you want," I said, knowing how useless it was to try to legislate the feelings of others.

"I'll be your spy," he said. "Give you a full report. You know you can rely on me to notice all the tacky details."

"I can't stop you." I was hurt he wanted to go, but curious at the same time.

"I'm not going unless I have your permission."

I thought for a moment.

"You can't leave my dinner early."

"I won't."

"Okay. You can go."

"You're sure?"

"Yes. And wear a video cam and tape recorder. I want all the poop."

"Know thy enemy, Jo. New York's version of Plato."

—m—

A queasy feeling came over me as I hung up the phone. Monique was clever. The Dents were perfect guests of honor. Neil Dent had power—not the superfluous social power of some washed-up royal like Brubetskoi whose family saw its heyday shot to hell in a basement eighty years ago—but real power, modern power: the Ability to Make People Money.

I knew I could call Betty or June and find out exactly what was going on. Or I could ignore it and go on with my own party as if nothing were amiss, clearly the most elegant thing to do.

The hell with it. I called Betty.

"Did you get her invitation?" I said.

"At first, I thought it was from you with the fucking bud vase," Betty said. "Can you believe it? I was about to call you."

"Are you going?"

"Hell, no. But Neil Dent just bought a Matisse collage and a Monet 'Haystack' from Gil, so he may have to go."

"You understand it's the same night as my dinner?" I said.

"Business, sweetie. Obviously, if Gil goes, he'll go afterward."

"I wish he wouldn't go at all."

"Don't sweat it, Jo, it's just a party."

"Betty, you know as well as I do: Nothing is *just* a party in New York."

———✠———

THE morning of my dinner, I received two cancellations from people who said they were down with the flu. Apparently, it was an epidemic because throughout the day I received numerous calls from other guests who bowed out of the evening. Twenty-nine out of my fifty guests pleaded illness. I figured it was either the plague or Monique, which in my view were pretty much the same thing.

Every time the phone rang, I prayed it wouldn't be a call from Brad Thompson. He had become the focal point of the whole exercise. If he came, at least the evening wouldn't be a total loss.

I rushed to the restaurant early to redo the seating. I had little time to dress properly. Standing in front of the mirror on the inside of my bedroom closet door, I put on my Marie Antoinette necklace with sober ceremony.

"Protect me from the slings and arrows of social life," I whispered aloud to the necklace as if it were a magic charm.

More cancellations greeted me when I arrived at Le Poisson.

Harried waiters busily reset the tables. My original fifty guests had dwindled down to seventeen. Three of the five round tables set for ten had to be dismantled and carted away. Only two tables remained, dwarfed by a roomful of overblown period decorations.

I surveyed the wreckage. What the hell was I going to do with seventeen people?

I tried putting ten people at one table and seven at another. But that made the table of seven look sparse. Then I tried putting eight at one table and nine at another, but that made both tables look sparse. I consulted the maître d', whose practical suggestion was to scrap the remaining two round tables and bring in one long table where everyone could sit together. That meant giving up the delicate ropes of rosebuds mingling with the hand-painted flowers of the silk tablecloths for plain white restaurant nappery and some restaurant lamps with pink shades.

"It's an interesting idea, Charles, but let's try and make do with what we have," is what I said. What I thought ran more along the lines of: If you think I paid six thousand dollars for these goddamn table decorations so no one will see them, you're even dumber than you look, Chuck. *Donnez-moi un break.*

After endless tinkering with the place cards, I finished the seating. The numerous cancellations had screwed up my carefully planned even numbers of men and women. The women now outnumbered the men, and women were seated next to one another at both tables, which was too bad. Well, it couldn't be helped. I seated myself next to Brad at the table of eight. I put Nicky, my guest of honor, at the table of nine. I figured that way none of my guests would feel slighted.

I drew back to survey the fruits of my labors.

Good-bye, Versailles. Hello, funeral home.

The two remaining silk-draped, flower-laden tables reminded me of shrouded biers. Some coming-out party. This was a wake.

As I waited for the guests to arrive, I kept telling

myself that, after all, it was only a party, instead of the *only* party I could ever again afford to give. I hoovered down two flutes of champagne to steady my nerves. Nicky arrived a little before eight—nice, polite, punctual guest of honor that he was. We stood together near the room's entrance waiting for the other guests to arrive. I pasted on my hostess smile and said to Nicky: "You can't believe the last-minute cancellations. Apparently, everyone has the flu. I hope the party won't be ruined."

Nicky, ever gallant, kissed my hand and said: "My dear Jo, the party is wherever you are."

—⁂—

THE Kahns and the Watermans were among the first guests to arrive. Betty Waterman took one look around the room and said in a voice laced with sarcasm, "My, isn't this festive?" I nudged her to shut up.

Gradually, others arrived. Miranda Somers popped in for a drink then left. She'd already told me she couldn't stay, so I didn't mind. Miranda often attended five functions in one night. Social life was a real job for her, unlike the unpaid labor it was for the rest of us. The Bromires, Ethan, and others dribbled in, but no Brad Thompson. People milled around, admiring the flowers, talking in hushed tones. The overdecorated room dwarfed the small crowd. Everyone seemed to know about the cancellations, which contributed to the general air of oppression.

I took Ethan aside and said: "Look what she's done to my party. I had six more cancellations at seven o'clock. *Seven P.M.* the night of an eight o'clock dinner. What would your pal Ward McAllister say about *that*?"

"Poor old Ward's been dervishing away in his grave

since the eighties," he said, moving on to chat with Nicky.

Brad Thompson was the last to arrive. Seeing him walk through the door, I felt relieved. He looked as dashing as I'd remembered him. Things were looking up. I strolled over to greet him, slipping my arm into his and walking him into the room.

"Hello, Brad. How nice to see you again. I'm so pleased you could come."

He beamed down at me. "Trish says you're the hostess with the mostest in New York. That's praise from Caesar as far as I'm concerned."

It wasn't as far as I was concerned, but I was grateful to Trish for the buildup.

"Let me introduce you to my guest of honor, Nicky Brubetskoi," I said, guiding him in Nicky's direction.

"Sure, I met Nick the other day. I just went on the board of Chapel's."

"Oh, really? Congratulations," I said, feigning ignorance. "Then it's doubly nice you're here for a party in Nicky's honor."

The two men seemed pleased to see each other again. Brad immediately started talking about his daughter who was working at the Hermitage. As I stood by, listening to the conversation, I studied Brad. He was confident, polished, very personable. I couldn't imagine what Trish had meant when she referred to him as a "rough diamond." Dressed in an immaculate tuxedo, his auburn hair slicked back neatly over his handsome head, conversing with an animated, interested expression on his face, he looked like a D-flawless to me.

As I stood there admiring him, out of the corner of my

eye I happened to catch sight of a voluptuous blond woman entering the room. I heard the maître d' telling her this was a private party. I figured she must have been heading for the ladies' room and gotten lost. But she wasn't going away. She and the maître d' seemed to be having a bit of a tiff. Nicky and Brad were deep in conversation so I excused myself to go see what was happening.

"Charles," I said to the maître d', "is there a problem?"

"This lady says she is dining here, but all your guests are present, Mrs. Slater."

Her blondness broke into a beauty-queen smile. "Are you Jo Slater?"

"Yes," I said warily.

She stuck out her hand to me. "My name is Taffy Fischer. Brad Thompson told me to meet him here? I just hope he remembered to tell you," she said with disarming candor and a hint of a southern accent.

I blanched and took a closer look at her, trying not to betray any sign of annoyance. She looked to be in her late thirties, early forties. She had a pretty, round face and a creamy complexion. Her deep cleavage was shown to maximum advantage in a low-cut, tight-fitting, black chiffon dress. Her diamond jewelry was real and expensive. Though she seemed friendly and on the ball, there was a slight toughness about her.

"He didn't tell you, did he?" she went on. "That boy is so naughty. Listen, if there's no room for me, I certainly understand. I'm a hostess myself, so trust me, I know what it means when someone shows up uninvited to a seated dinner, and I apologize. I really do."

"Don't be ridiculous. I'm delighted to have you.

Actually, we had a few cancellations today so space isn't a problem." My jaw was tight and my voice sounded to me like I was speaking under water.

"You're a doll," she said. "We have to go to this big dance later on and I really didn't feel like going back to the hotel and waiting on Brad, so I thank you so very, very much."

By this point, I was too exhausted to react, but I guessed what dance she was referring to. I escorted Ms. Taffy Fischer over to Mr. Brad Thompson, thinking, oh, the hell with it. He immediately put his arm around her waist, ostentatiously snuggling her close.

"Brad, honey, you forgot to tell our hostess I was coming, you bad boy," she said, scolding him in a singsong voice.

He mumbled some excuse about his secretary calling. I nodded politely because at that point I really didn't give a shit. One more plan down the drain. June danced up to me as I was getting another drink. She made her usual effort to be upbeat.

"Jo, dear, the room looks absolutely divine."

"Fuck the room, June."

I had an extra place set for Ms. Fischer beside Brad because he asked if it was okay if they sat together. They held hands most of the evening.

At dinner, I got the kind of headache basketball players must sometimes get when they try to keep the ball in play against formidable foes. Even my earlobes ached. Our table had somehow veered off into a detailed discussion of great maritime disasters—conversational hell. Brad seemed enthralled, but as I listened to one particularly calamitous account, I knew that ancient ship wasn't the only thing going down in flames. The party had beat it to the bottom.

I drank one glass of wine after another, hoping to obliterate as much of the evening as possible. I felt like one of those puppets with fixed macabre smiles whose heads endlessly bob up and down.

Brad and Taffy were the first ones to leave. In fact, they left during dessert. Brad said he had a business engagement. I, of course, knew better. Miss Gator Bowl had inadvertently spilled the beans.

Betty informed me that Brad Thompson rarely made it all the way through a dinner party in any case.

"Listen, sweetie, he's been known to have his plane standing by to take him to a party in another city," Betty said, trying to cheer me up. "These big tycoons have the attention span of a gnat. They're only interested in business and sex."

All the guests left early. I sat down at one of the tables and polished off the dregs of three separate wine glasses. "All's hell that ends like hell," I thought, looking around the room, the ambience of which felt to me like the last act of *Götterdämmerung*. I got up to leave, shook hands with all the waiters, thanked the maître d', signed the bill, leaving an overly generous tip, polished off two more glasses of wine, and left. I remember hailing a taxi on the corner of Madison Avenue, getting in, and giving the driver an address. But I must have been very drunk because I gave him my *old* address.

I found myself in front of my former apartment building where literally dozens of limousines were parked outside. Before I really noticed where I was, I was being helped out of the cab by good old Pat, the doorman, who knew me from the time I'd lived there and who acted pleased to see me. He held open the lobby door for me, obviously assuming I'd been invited to Monique's party. I walked to the elevator in the back, and before I knew it, I was floating up to the fifteenth floor.

When I stepped into the apartment, I had no idea where I was. My precious eighteenth-century enclave had been swept away by modernity. In its place was a sleek mausoleum with no warmth, no charm.

Après moi, le déluge.

All my beautiful crown moldings had been stripped away along with the seventeenth-century boiserie. The furniture was massive and angular and looked like it was covered in wrinkled bedsheets.

My stippled pomegranate-colored dining room with its hand-painted chinoiserie figures and animals was now gray. Flat, dull, depressing gray. Didn't this woman know that dining rooms must always be painted a *warm* color, flattering to a woman's complexion, because when women feel beautiful they make better conversation? Didn't she *know* that? Bedrooms and dining rooms must never be gray. If they are, say adieu to good conversation or good sex.

My beloved Fragonard oil paintings, those exquisite views of aristocratic eighteenth-century French country life that I'd purchased from Fautre, the most famous antiques dealer in Paris, in their original carved and gilded wood frames, were hanging side by side on the gray walls in thin black metal frames, like they were posters. I was appalled.

All the furniture had been cleared out of the living room. People were dancing to the music of a smooth Latin band playing "La Vie en Rose" with a salsa beat.

I grabbed a glass of champagne from the tray of a passing waiter and wandered through the buzzing crowd. A few people seemed perplexed by my presence. "What's *she* doing here?" they said with their eyes.

The Lowrys were there, plus the Dents and all the people who had accepted my dinner then canceled at the last minute, miraculously cured of their sudden illnesses. Everyone who had *come* to my dinner was there, too, except Betty Waterman and June Kahn. Gil was there, though. Charlie was there. Even my erstwhile guest of honor, Prince Brubetskoi. Miranda Somers was chatting with Ethan Monk. When Ethan saw me, he looked a little shocked and ran to my side.

"Jo, my God, what are you doing here?"

"Isn't it amazing, Ethan? Look who's here. Everyone. She's done in two years what it took me twenty to achieve. And she's done it on my nickel."

Monique learned quickly. She was one of those women who transform the art of social climbing into a contact sport, hurling herself on top of the heap without any pretense of an ascent. One day she was *there,* proud and glistening, like a snow-capped peak on Everest. It was too much for me to bear.

The moment when I spotted Nate Nathaniel and Monique welded together on the dance floor something in me snapped. Watching them slithering around to the Latin rhythm, gazing deep into each other's eyes, I thought: I am like Marie Antoinette coming back after my execution and seeing Robespierre and Charlotte Corday playing kissy-face in my parlor at Versailles.

Monique and I locked eyes as she was dancing. A flash of triumph flickered on her face. Flinging me a saucy little smile, she broke away from Nate and cut through the crowd to greet me. I stared, transfixed, as this vision of evil incarnate, this chattel of Satan in red satin and diamonds, slithered toward me with her arms outstretched like some sort of gorgeous gorgon.

"Jo, dear," she said, taking my free hand in hers. "I'm delighted to see you. It's wonderful that you could come. Look, everyone," she announced to the room. "It's our darling Jo."

I just stood there, vaguely aware that the music had stopped playing and people were standing, staring at the two ladies in red. Their ogling faces hung like big white moons all around me. I had an urge to denounce Monique in front of this crowd as a lying, scheming murderess. But the words wouldn't come. Her vile graciousness had disarmed me. Instead, I threw the glass of champagne in her face and walked out.

I don't remember anything after that except waking up the next morning with a nuclear headache. I noticed a blossoming bruise on my right arm. I had no idea how it had gotten there.

Throughout the morning, fragments of the evening's events bombarded me like shrapnel, each piece sinking in deeper than the last. By the afternoon, I'd recalled the entire debacle. My phone was ominously silent. That evening, June called to see how I was. She'd heard at least ten differing accounts of the story, the worst one being that I had pummeled Monique on the dance floor and it took three men to restrain me. She told me not to worry.

"People in New York have short memories," she assured me. "It's all just Social Life." This mantra from a woman who once described the fall of the Soviet Union as "that scandal in Russia."

Betty also called to commiserate that evening. A romantic at heart, she told me Gil reported to her that Brad Thompson left Monique's with another woman— *not* Ms. Fischer, if that was any consolation.

It wasn't.

Ethan called, too. I was anxious to know what he thought because he was the only one of my friends who had been there to see what actually happened.

"What on earth possessed you?" he asked.

"I made a spectacle of myself, didn't I?"

"Worse. You made a martyr of her."

I hung up the phone with the most sickening feeling. Nothing is more mortifying than one's own bad behavior. And, justified or not, I had acted abominably toward Monique. My own party had cost me a fortune, in more ways than one.

—⁓—

Two days later, I received a warm letter from Nicky accompanied by an expensive coffee-table book on Imperial Russia to which he had written the foreword. That afternoon a huge flower arrangement was delivered to my apartment as well. I recognized the diaphanous bluish white tissue covering the blooms. It was from Celeste, a "floral designer," as she liked to call herself, who catered only to private clients and whom I, actually, had discovered many years ago. After I started sending Celeste's original flower arrangements to people, others took her up. She became all the rage in New York for a time, but eventually derailed by gossiping about her clients. Many people dropped her. Those who still used her were willing to overlook her indiscretion because she was so very talented.

Tearing away the paper, I found a profusion of all-white flowers, including peonies, which were out of season, set like an enormous globe in an antique blue and white cachepot—an exquisite arrangement that could easily have cost twice my current monthly rent. I fully expected to find another note from Nicky thanking me for that spectacularly costly evening in his honor. Instead, there was a small calling card. The embossed name on the card had been crossed out with a line of black ink. The message in neat handwriting read: "Dear Jo, a memorable evening." It was signed "Monique de Passy."

25

I spent a bleak Christmas and a joyless New Year all by myself. At one point I picked up the phone and heard the words "Hello, Deadbeat." With creditors circling, the time had come for me to think the unthinkable: I would have to part with the possession I loved most in the world—my necklace. The thought of selling it was anathema to me. It was like selling a beloved pet. Not only was the piece my trademark, it was the last link to my former existence. Even in my worst nightmares, I never thought it would come to this. Giving up the necklace was like giving up all hope of ever returning to the world I had known and loved. I'd much rather have donated it to the Municipal Museum to put on display in the Slater Gallery. But I desperately needed the money. I could no longer afford to be Lady Bountiful.

I called Nicky at Chapel's. He arranged for a courier to come and pick it up. At the door of my apartment, I said good-bye to the necklace like I would have said good-bye to a cherished old friend, hugging the box one more time before handing it over to the messenger.

—⁓—

THE "Marie Antoinette Necklace" was featured alone on the front cover of Chapel's "Important Jewelry" catalogue for April 1999. Shown to advantage against a white velvet background, it was the talk of the sale. The piece was listed as "the Property of Mrs. Lucius Slater" and accompanied by a picture of myself in happier times wearing the necklace to the opening of the opera. There was no point hiding the seller's identity. Everyone knew it was mine. Inset into the middle of Nicky's brief essay on the necklace's historic provenance was a small oval portrait of Marie Antoinette. The estimate was $200,000 to $250,000.

None of my friends could believe I was selling my most beloved possession. Through Ethan, I soon got wind of the fact that Monique was planning to bid whatever it took to get the necklace.

"She's going around town telling everyone she's absolutely got to have it. She told Roger she was willing to pay a million dollars."

I subsequently heard the same thing from June, Betty, and Trish. The million-dollar figure kept cropping up, which gave me an idea. I started hatching a plan. But I needed to do a little research first.

I went to see Jerry Medina, the proprietor of Nolan Pearce, Ltd., one of New York's most elegant, most expensive jewelry stores. I'd once been a good client, though it had now been a few years since I could afford to shop there. When I entered the glittery boutique, the bald, heavy-set Medina was behind the counter showing an Art Nouveau cobra bracelet to a mousy, crop-haired woman in black. They were both admiring the way the enamel serpent coiled down her forearm, its jeweled head resting on the back of her slender wrist.

"Lalique designed it for Sarah Bernhardt," Medina was saying.

"*Who?*" the young woman asked.

"Sarah Bernhardt . . . The famous old actress? You never heard of her? A real character. She slept in a coffin."

"Before or after the reviews?" the young woman said with a straight face, as she examined the bracelet. "Gee, I'm not sure, Jer. It's pretty cool, but I think the diamonds are more her."

Medina waved a discreet hello to me without walking over to greet me. I confess I felt a bit slighted, thinking how in the old days he would not have kept me waiting.

I wandered around the shop looking at the jewelry gleaming under the bright lights. Exquisite as some of the pieces were, not one of them compared to my Marie Antoinette necklace. My feelings of deprivation at having to part with it suddenly exhausted me. I sank down on the beige suede couch and lit a cigarette, eavesdropping in on Medina's conversation. Apparently, the woman he was waiting on was a stylist for a rock star who was borrowing jewelry for her client to wear on an upcoming MTV special. When the woman finally left, Medina sauntered over to me, carrying a copy of the Chapel's catalogue featuring my necklace on the front cover.

"Mrs. Slater, you should've come to me first," he said

in a mock scolding voice, tapping the glossy cover. "By the time you pay that *gonif* auction house's commission and get the money, you'd've been better off with me."

"That's actually why I'm here, Jerry. I need to talk to you about the necklace."

"Yeah?" He sat down next to me on the sofa. "So what can I do for you, Jo, honey?"

I flinched a little, taken aback by his unexpected familiarity. "Jo, honey" sounded jarring, even coming from the amusing, irreverent Medina, who cultivated the air of a jovial cocktail party host to disguise the consummate salesman and jewelry aficionado he was. In the past he had always addressed me as Mrs. Slater.

"There's a woman who wants that necklace very badly," I told him.

"There are several I can think of," Medina said, flipping through the catalogue. "It's gorgeous." He admired the inside photograph of the necklace, in which it was set against a darker background and looked even more dramatic. "Estimate is two to two-fifty. Sounds about right. They always lowball the good stuff. You'll get four. Four-fifty. Maybe five."

"I believe this woman will go to a million."

Medina guffawed. "A *million*? What is she—nuts? I could've gotten you five. Five-fifty maybe. But a million? Forget it."

"It belonged to Marie Antoinette," I said.

"Coulda belonged to the Virgin Mary. It still ain't worth a million bucks."

"It's worth it to her. Believe me."

"Fine. And what idiot's gonna bid against her?"

"Well, I thought maybe . . . me."

"You?" Medina looked at me suspiciously.

"That's what I came to ask you about. In strictest confidence, of course. Is it legal for me to bid up the price?"

"In strictest confidence? No."

"Why not? The only risk is that I buy back my own necklace and I have to pay a big commission to the auction house."

"It still ain't legal. It's called being a shill, Mrs. Slater."

At least we were back to Mrs. Slater. I thought for a moment.

"Okay, well then, what if someone else—not me—bids the price up?"

"The law's pretty clear on this. Neither you, nor any member of your family, nor any *agent* of yours can bid up the price of an object on your behalf."

"But what if they don't know I asked this person to bid it up?"

"Let's put it this way. Some thieves don't get caught."

A long silence ensued. Medina stared at me. I knew he knew what I was thinking.

"Take my advice," he said. "If you're up to what I think you're up to, you better be damn sure this person is a really good friend—discreet, you know? Who won't blab."

―⁓―

I left the shop feeling disconsolate. Ethan was discreet, but he wasn't rich. Betty and June and Trish were rich but God knows they weren't discreet. Wait . . . what about Dick Bromire? Dick was rich and he was always helping people. Why not me? He'd helped me before. But no. He was already under investigation. What if he told Trish? She was bound to talk. Who did I know who was rich *and* discreet?

Gil Waterman was a possibility, but I didn't dare keep another secret from Betty.

And then it came to me: Charlie Kahn.

Charlie was better than discreet. He was practically lobotomized. He never opened his mouth if he could help it. I'd lived with Charlie. I'd been through entire meals with him where he'd said only three words: "Pass the salt." June always complained he never talked to her about much except golf and the stock market and forgot any gossip he heard. I knew he could keep a secret, mainly because he would probably forget it. But it was absolutely essential he not tell June. He'd have to swear on his life he'd keep his mouth shut.

I asked Charlie to meet me for a drink, telling him I had a "private matter" I wanted to discuss with him. He suggested the Knickerbocker, where he was a member. As a boy, Charlie Kahn, a native New Yorker, had been in the Knickerbocker Greys, whose membership was then restricted to prominent old New York families. We sat upstairs in one of the reception rooms of the venerable club, overlooking Fifth Avenue. Staid portraits of past members dotted the walls. Social chitchat wasn't Charlie's forte, to say the least, and with the auction just days away, I was far too distracted to be charming. I got straight to the point.

"Charlie, I need to ask you a big favor."

I explained the situation as he sipped his Dubonnet. He looked like a mummy, dry, desiccated, bound up tight in a three-piece suit and bow tie. I tried to cast my request in the most innocent possible light. He listened expression-less until I stopped talking. I seriously wondered whether he had taken in what I had said. You could never tell with Charlie.

"So you want me to bid up the price so you can soak her, eh? That's illegal."

Not as dumb as he looked, old Charlie.

"Strictly speaking, I guess you could say it is," I said. "But, say you were bidding on the necklace as a present for June, who would know?"

"I would know."

"That's true." I was a little ashamed at having asked him.

"What if your friend stops bidding and I get stuck with it?"

"I'd buy it back from you."

"Forgive me, Jo, dear, but with *what*?"

"Well, I get the proceeds when you buy it. It's *my* necklace, after all. The only thing I'd have to come up with is the auction house commission and the tax. You'd have to trust me for that. I'd pay you back, I promise."

"But you don't get your money until I pay the house. So I'd have to come up with the full amount."

"Right." Now I felt even more sheepish at having to persevere with the idea. But I was desperate. "Look, Charlie, I can almost guarantee you that won't happen. Monique really covets that necklace. She's been going all around town telling everyone she has to have it."

"It's been my observation that what people say and what they do are often two different things," Charlie said.

"That's true, too. But I can tell you this, Charlie. She definitely has this thing about me. She's obsessed by me.

Look how she's stepped into my life. That necklace is my trademark. When she gets her hands on that, her conquest will be complete in her eyes."

"And in yours?" he said, probing my face.

It was a fair question. Charlie, perhaps without meaning to, had picked up on my obsession with the Countess. The two of us sat in silence for a long moment.

"Okay," I said at last. "I understand you don't want to do it. I'm sorry I put you on the spot, Charlie, dear. I just didn't know who else to turn to whom I could trust. Please don't say anything."

Charlie had a faraway look as he sipped his drink. I was about to get up from my chair when he flicked his eyes onto mine.

"Who said I don't want to do it? Did you know I got suspended from St. Paul's for making book on the Kentucky Derby?"

"Did you?" I said, not having the vaguest idea what that had to do with the price of eggs.

He cleared his throat and said proudly, "I once put a dead shark in our neighbor's swimming pool in Manhasset. Bastard dived in for his morning swim and nearly had heart failure," he said with a snort.

I was beginning to view old Charlie with new eyes.

"I know no one thinks I have a sense of humor," he went on. "But I enjoy a good prank now and then. I really do. Haven't had one in ages."

"Well, this is a good prank."

"Sure is." He paused. "I'll do it," he said, slapping the table with his palm.

I knew he'd die if I hugged him so I blew him a big kiss. "Thank you, thank you, Charlie. But listen, one thing? You absolutely cannot breathe one word of this to June. Not one word, I beg you."

"I never tell my wife a thing. But I warn you: What she doesn't find out she makes up."

"She won't find out if you don't tell her, Charlie. And you have to swear to me never to tell her. Do you swear?"

He put his hand on his heart. "We who are about to bid, salute you."

I took that for a yes.

—m—

THERE was no way of knowing whether or not Monique planned to attend the sale in person or not, but Charlie had to bid over the phone in order to preserve his anonymity. I was anxious to watch the proceedings so I sneaked into Chapel's the day of the Important Jewelry auction in disguise, wearing a black wig, no makeup, and an ill-fitting mauve coat. This disguise was just in case Monique showed up. I pretended to be viewing the upcoming sale of Americana Furniture currently on display in one of the adjoining galleries. The battered weathervanes and grim, thin-lipped early American portraits were depressing.

Each auction always attracts its own brand of bidders. The Americana collectors were as drab as colonial paint compared to the jewelry crowd, who, with the exception of some black-clad dealers, were mostly shiny, well-heeled individuals in designer clothes. I parked myself behind a life-size carved wooden Indian, keeping an eye on the incoming crowd, in case my nemesis showed up.

A full hour into the jewelry auction I spotted Monique and Nate Nathaniel walking up the stairs. I followed them inside, careful to keep my distance. They seated themselves off the center aisle near the front of the room. I found myself a place on the sidelines near the back where I could observe the unholy pair without being seen.

The room was packed. The sale was up and down, as sales go, with some lots going for triple and quadruple their estimates and others being bought in. I watched Monique and Nate closely, peeved by their smug intimacy.

As soon as Lot 333 was announced, Monique sat up attentively, her paddle poised for action. This is it, I thought, praying Charlie was standing by on the telephone.

The auctioneer gave a brief description of the necklace, mentioning it had belonged to Marie Antoinette and to "that great patron of the arts, Jo Slater." I heard what he said. But it was as if Jo Slater were another person entirely. In disguise as a bag lady, about to witness the sale of my most precious possession, I felt no kin whatever to the Jo Slater whose name was supposedly an inducement to buyers.

Bidding got off to a brisk start. The necklace reached the three-hundred-thousand mark in seconds. Paddles and hands popped up all around the gallery. I spotted several women I knew vying for the necklace, women whose idea of a blunt force trauma was being outbid at auction. At four-twenty-five, several people dropped out. The bidding slowed. There was a lull. Monique raised her paddle for the first time for a four-hundred-and-fifty-thousand dollar bid. Silence. She put down her paddle and flashed Snake Nathaniel a victorious little grin.

I watched the grin fade as the bidding resumed. A phone bidder made it four hundred and seventy-five.

Charlie. Yes. Monique upped it to an even five hundred thousand.

The suave auctioneer crooned: "I have five hundred thousand dollars . . . Do I hear five hundred and twenty-five?"

Monique sighed and raised her paddle again . . .

It was between Monique and the invisible bidder, whose agent was a blond, businesslike woman standing, along with other Chapel's representatives, behind a bank of phones, whispering into a black receiver.

Back to the phone bidder.

Back to Monique.

Back to the phone bidder.

Back to Monique.

Phone bidder.

Monique.

Phone.

Monique.

Back and forth like a tennis match. The price went up and up and up. The live Theater of Greed was in progress. An excited hush gripped the room.

I knew Nate Nathaniel was getting anxious by the way he tugged occasionally on his starched white collar. I saw him whisper to Monique as Charlie's efficient agent raised her charm-braceleted hand yet another time.

The bidding soared to eight, eight-fifty, nine, nine-fifty . . .

"I have nine-fifty . . . On the phone . . . I have nine hundred and fifty thousand dollars . . . Nine-fifty . . ."

Monique lowered her paddle. Poised on a blade of anxiety, I craned my neck to try to make out what was going on. Why was she hesitating all of a sudden?

The auctioneer stared directly down at Monique.

"Make it a nice round million, Countess?" he said playfully, bringing home to me yet another unpleasant realization, namely, that this auctioneer knew my nemesis on sight. Which meant she was a bidding regular. Which meant she was spending lots of money. My money.

Monique smiled and coyly shook her head no.

My heart was thumping so hard it hurt.

In the ensuing pause, I suddenly wondered if I'd been had. Had Monique gotten wind of my plan? Did Jerry Medina spill the beans? Or Charlie? Had Charlie told June? June was one of the ones who told me Monique would pay a million dollars for the damn thing. Had I been set up? No, wait, that didn't make any sense. My head was swimming. Then the dreaded words bled through my panic: "Going once, at nine hundred and fifty thousand dollars . . ."

A hush in the room.

"Going twice, at nine hundred and fifty thousand dollars on the phone. Fair warning. At nine hundred and fifty thousand dollars on the telephone then . . ."

I squeezed my eyes shut, held my breath, and stuck my fingers in my ears, like I was about to hear an explosion.

"*Sold* to the telephone bidder for nine hundred and fifty thousand dollars."

The room burst into spontaneous applause.

I'd just bought my own necklace back for close to one million dollars, roughly one million two hundred thousand, if you added in the sales tax and commission.

Monique must have known. Somehow she must have gotten wind of my scheme. My very first thought was that Jerry Medina must have tipped her off. He was the only one besides Charlie who knew what I was up to.

I flew out of the sale room over to Pearce's. The guard buzzed me in through the two security doors one at a time. I was so agitated, I pushed the second door before the catch had released and hurt my hand when the goddamn thing didn't open. There were no customers in the shop. I demanded to see Medina. The young saleswoman called him out of the back office.

At first the portly jeweler didn't recognize me. "You wanted to see me?"

I pulled the wig off my head. I caught a glimpse of myself in one of the mirrors. My hair was matted down like a thatched roof. I looked godawful.

"Mrs. Slater?" Medina said with a guffaw. "What's with the getup?"

"You didn't mention anything about our conversation to anyone, did you?" I asked, trying to remain as calm as possible.

The jeweler shook his head. "What happened?"

"The bidding stopped at nine-fifty. I still own the necklace."

Medina hit his forehead with his palm. "*Jeez*. Told you so. You realize that just the tax and commission are gonna come to more than the thing's worth."

"You're *sure* you didn't mention this to anyone?"

"Hell, no. I told you I thought it was a cockamamie idea."

I steadied myself against the display case. "May I have a glass of water, please?"

Medina led me into the back office to keep me out of sight of any customers who happened in. Distraught women in expensive jewelry shops aren't an advertising bonanza. He sat me down in the wooden chair in front of his desk next to a huge black safe and fetched me a cup of water from the cooler.

"Who'd you get to bid on it for you?"

"A friend. You can't tell anyone."

"No, no. Do you have to reimburse this friend?"

"Of course."

"Well, you could tell your friend to renege on their bid. Then the auction house would contact the next highest bidder."

"Renege on a bid? No. This person would never do that."

"Can this person afford to pay them?"

"Yes. But obviously I have to pay this person back. And just at the moment, I don't have an extra two hundred thousand dollars—or an extra two cents, for that matter. I'm in debt."

"Okay, well then, here's what I suggest. You get this person to call Chapel's and ask to get an extension on the payment. They'll charge interest, of course, but in the meantime you can sell whatever you have to get the money."

"Jerry, I don't think you quite understand. I owe hundreds of thousands of dollars. I have nothing left to sell."

"You can't raise a couple of hundred thousand?" He looked at me incredulously.

There was a time when "a couple of hundred thousand" didn't sound like a fortune to me—merely the minimum ante for a round of social life. Now it was the national debt.

"Jerry, I can hardly pay my Con Ed bill, for God's sakes."

The young saleswoman poked her head into Medina's office to inform him he had two customers up front who were asking for him. Medina excused himself for a moment while I sat in the back room of Pearce contemplating my fate.

I tried calling Charlie Kahn but his secretary said he was out.

Medina's stifling little office closed in on me. I got up, tossed the black wig into the wastebasket, and walked out, craving some fresh air. Entering the boutique, I stopped short when I saw Monique and Nate Nathaniel. Jerry Medina was waiting on them.

I wanted to do an about-face and go back into the office, climb into the safe, and close the door behind me. But Nate spotted me.

"Jo? Is that *you?*" he cried, making no effort to disguise his amusement at my ghastly appearance.

Head high, shoulders back, like Marie Antoinette on her way to the guillotine, I walked toward the front of the shop, refusing to acknowledge either one of them. Monique regarded me with a gloating little sneer. Not that I entirely blamed her. The last time we'd seen each other, I'd thrown a glass of champagne in her face.

"Well, congratulations," Nate barked. "Nearly a million dollars for your necklace. Well done."

"We were there. It was thrilling," Monique said. *Three-leeng.* "I was just telling Jerry that I'm looking for a consolation prize." She seemed completely unfazed by our last meeting, talking to me in a friendly way as if the incident had never occurred. I, on the other hand, refused to utter a word to either of them.

"You will be amused to know that I was the underbidder," Monique said as I walked past her. "I was going to go to a million. I told everyone I would. Isn't that right, Nate? Then, as I was bidding, I suddenly thought there must be someone who wants this necklace even more than I do. So I decided to let them have it, if they wanted it so much. I wonder who bought it," she said as if she knew exactly.

God knows how she found out what I was up to. Maybe she guessed. Maybe Charlie blabbed. Maybe Jerry. Who knows? That was New York, though: If you want to keep a secret, you can't breathe a word of it—not even to yourself. It will get out.

I reached the front door and stood with my back to the showroom, waiting for the guard to buzz me out. He released the catch on the first security door. I walked into the little glass cocoon, hearing Nate Nathaniel call after me: "Have a nice day."

Another buzzer sounded, releasing the catch on the second security door. I was out on the street. Literally.

Ask not for whom the buzzer sounds, I thought. It sounds for thee.

———✳———

I went home and tried Charlie a few more times. When I finally reached him he seemed more perplexed than irate our little plan had backfired.

"Guess we got hoisted on our own petard," he said, quickly adding: "Know what a petard is? A fart."

"What do you want to do, Charlie?"

"What do I have to do?"

"Well, you could renege on your bid, which means that they'd offer the necklace to Monique because she was the underbidder."

"Can't do that. Never reneged on a deal in my life."

"Then I'm afraid you have to pay for it," I said, mortified. "Which means you own it until I can pay you back."

"I can't keep it. You have to keep it. Otherwise June'll find out, and then . . ." For the first time I detected a hint of panic in his voice.

"I'm happy to do that. When you pay them, and they pay me, I'll pay you back—which would be everything except the tax and commission. I'll just have to owe you that, I'm afraid. I haven't figured it all out yet, but it could come to, um, well, over two hundred thousand dollars."

"Fine. Let's do that."

He seemed so unconcerned, I wondered if he really understood.

"Charlie, you do realize that even after I pay you, I will still owe you nearly a quarter of a million dollars?" I said in a clear, measured voice. "You're sure you realize that?"

"I've been owed more. Pay me when your ship comes in."

I thought for a moment.

"Remember the *Andrea Doria,* Charlie? That was my ship."

26

I was grateful to Charlie, I really was. He was cool under fire and a generous friend. With the necklace back in my possession, I now thought of myself as "jewel poor."

Naturally, people found out that Charlie had bought the necklace and that he'd sold it back to me. This is New York, after all. Nothing is a secret for long. No sooner was that information on the wire than it was also being whispered that I had roped my old friend Charlie Kahn into bidding up the price of the Marie Antoinette necklace in order to get even with Monique. This time the gossip had the added advantage of being true. June naturally got wind of it and called me up demanding to know point-blank whether I had conspired with Charlie to bid up the piece. I couldn't tell her the truth because what we'd done was, in fact, illegal. What I said was that Charlie had bought the necklace for her on my advice, but then he decided to get her something else.

"He said that once he saw it again, he didn't think it would look all that good on you so he called me up and asked me if I wanted to buy it from him," I told her, lying through my teeth. "Naturally, I said I did. So I bought it back for roughly what he paid."

June didn't believe me, but even she knew that if this all got out Charlie could be in serious trouble. Of course, Charlie and I maintained the fiction that he'd bought the necklace for June, then changed his mind and sold it back to me. Not that anyone believed us. But what could they prove? Once again, I was being accused of behavior that was at best illegal and at worst unladylike. And once again, instead of blaming myself for what had occurred, I blamed Monique.

—⁂—

THE Dent debacle and the champagne catastrophe had set the stage. The "Necklace Affair Part Two," as it was referred to by those aware of my fascination with the original incident, rang down the curtain on what was left of my credibility. I had given people another convenient peg on which to hang their "concerns" about me. I was finished. I wasn't even invited to events I had to pay for, which in New York is the definition of being washed up.

I'd always enjoyed observing the bloody theater of New York social life, never once imagining that I, myself, would one day be among the casualties.

—⁂—

I owed money to Charlie Kahn, the IRS, two workrooms, three fabric houses, lawyers, and let's not forget the Municipal Museum for the remainder of my pledge. I still had the necklace, but I couldn't sell it for even a fraction of what it was worth. To use auction house parlance, it had been "burned." Nobody would touch it for any price. My talisman, my trademark, was considered very bad luck.

The great white shark of poverty that had been circling around me moved in for the kill. I felt isolated and afraid. Dunned by creditors and shunned by former friends, my future was now behind me.

I read what Lord Gower wrote about Marie Antoinette in 1886:

> *The pure ore of her nature was but hidden under the dross of worldliness: and the scorching fire of suffering revealed one of the tenderest hearts and one of the bravest natures that history records.*

Well, I thought, at last I'm being forced to confront the pure ore of my nature. The result was I got pushy.

I called Trebor Bellini and asked him flat out if he would hire me as his assistant. He thanked me but turned me down, saying: "I think it would be just too confusing for my clients, Jo. I'm sorry."

I then set up a little party-planning business, hoping to trade on what was left of my reputation as a great hostess. In my mind's eye shimmered a vision of that burgeoning class of young billionaires who had limitless money and no clue how to spend it. I placed a small ad in a few glossy magazines. Listing my name and telephone number at the top, the copy read:

> *Elegance for All Occasions*
> *A Renowned Socialite and Hostess Shares Her Secrets*

I loathed the idea of promoting myself in this way, but these were desperate times requiring vulgar methods. I had several inquiries, but no real commitments. That idea quickly fizzled.

In order to eat, I landed a steady job (salary plus commissions) selling wholesale carpets and hotel furnishings on Lexington and Twenty-sixth Street, figuring I'd never, ever, *ever* run into a soul I knew in that cavernous, ground-floor, fluorescent hellhole they called a showroom. I took the subway to and from work. I ate at Soup Burgs and greasy lunch counters in the neighborhood. I was on my feet eight hours a day, five days a week. Most of the people I dealt with had a lot of taste—all of it bad. I sometimes found myself staring at the mammoth chandelier with the nine thousand gold quills sticking out of it like a porcupine, wondering how a sane person could actually look up and say, as many did, "I'll take that."

My feet swelled up so much, I had to walk home a couple of times without my shoes on, in stocking feet. I finally broke down and bought myself a pair of Hush Puppies for twenty-five bucks on sale. They were cushioned on the inside and bulbous on the outside, shoes with shoulder pads, like the kind nurses wear. But they were heaven compared to my sleek, expensive, designer boots. Symbolizing my ugly new life of drudgery and hopelessness, those Hush Puppies were just about the most depressing purchase I had ever, *ever* made.

Though I still harbored dreams of a rich protector, I could no longer afford to go to expensive benefits or take trips to posh vacation spots. It was impossible to hunt where there was no game. Brad Thompson was out of the picture, of course. I had no desire to date. The two experiences I'd had in that area were desultory: One man asked me if I wouldn't mind paying the check; the other was a sixty-year-old who confessed after three glasses of wine that he was physically attracted only to women in their twenties.

"You think that's weird?" he asked me.

"I think it's male," I replied.

Wading deeper into middle age, my life was grim and getting grimmer. I couldn't afford to keep up my beauty maintenance: the monthly haircut and color, the collagen injections, the manicures, skin treatments, exercise classes. No wonder rich women look better than poor women; they can afford it. Feeling like an old car that needed parts replaced, I tried to keep the engine running smoothly. But it was hard with no tune-ups.

Fallen socialites became the hobgoblins of my imagination. Over the years, I'd seen a number of prominent women drift off into the fatal currents of alcoholism and drug addiction. In my dreams, these women reached out and grabbed me. Looking like a mob of grubby old toothless bag ladies, they crowed: "*High and mighty, were you, Jo? Now you're one of usssss.*"

Always exhausted, always yearning, always plotting, I felt the days and nights crash down on me, drenching me in bitterness and regret. To be honest, I have to say that many of my friends tried to rally around me during this troubled period and it was I who withdrew from them. Betty and June called me every day, checking to see how I was.

Much as I appreciated everyone's efforts, there was something about the well-meaning kindness of my friends that irked me more than the straightforward snubs of the *amis mondains*. I couldn't stand the soulful look in my friends' eyes whenever they saw me. I hated being an object of pity. But everyone assumed I was going nowhere, no matter where I went.

Once again, I came to the conclusion it was better not to see anyone I knew for a while. At first I felt strengthened by this resolution. Quite quickly, however, the lack of company produced the most undesired effect imaginable: I thought of Monique more than ever. She was now firmly planted in the center of my brain. She was the first thing I thought about when I got up in the morning and the last thing I thought about when I closed my eyes at night. She took up the better part of my waking moments as well.

It had taken over four years for my misfortunes to sink fully into my consciousness. The turmoil of each setback had blinded me to the lasting effects. Now that I awoke day after day all alone to a landscape of uncertainty, I saw the true emptiness of what lay ahead. I had drifted away from my friends despite their efforts to support me. I couldn't bear not being on an equal footing with them. It was my nature to be generous, to always give more than I took. Unable to reciprocate, I felt a deepening shame coupled with a sense of inferiority. I withdrew further and further into my own little world.

I tried giving myself a pep talk, telling myself that I was strong, healthy, not *that* old. People start over and over and over again, I thought. This is not the end of the world. But it was the end of my world and I knew it. I sometimes fantasized another life for myself, independent of money and society. If only I had never married Lucius. Perhaps I could have become a teacher, I thought, or a curator. A curator, yes. I would have liked that. I could have been that. But then I thought, *no:* You *are* what you could have been.

Being in debt was hell, like a Sword of Damocles hanging over my head. I hadn't the slightest idea how I was going to pay back everyone I owed, or, indeed, how I was going to keep my own head above water in the coming years. Plus the fact I sorely missed my old life—not just the money and the society, but the sense of being a part of a world I genuinely enjoyed. I had to face it: I was all alone—no kids, no husband, no family. The friends I had were loyal, but I knew I was drifting away from them forever.

For the first time in my life, I felt truly afraid—not the amorphous fear of the unknown that you get when you're young, but the concrete fear of the known you experience in middle age. I was old enough to understand the fragility of life and the horrors that could await me. This knowledge made everything seem more dreadful.

All these feelings were coupled with a seething sense of indignity that I had been robbed of my life. I was serving a life sentence for a crime I didn't commit. *And* I had to watch a murderer living high off the hog while I was behind bars. It really was an awful lot to bear.

Depression dogged me until I no longer functioned. On weekends, I lay in bed with the shades drawn, and lost all track of time. I stuffed myself with comfort foods, drank straight vodka, and watched television programs about serial killers, deriving a perverse cheer in wading through the dark marshes of the human soul.

Just for the hell of it, one night I washed down one of Monique's Rotinal tablets, which Anne-Marie de Passy had given me, with a shot of vodka. I crawled back into bed and pulled the covers over my head figuring with any luck I would die. I was out for nineteen hours straight.

When I came to, my eyes took a frightening amount of time to focus. For a moment, I thought I'd impaired my vision. My mouth tasted chalky. I was so weak I could barely stand up. I found, to my utter horror, that I'd relieved myself in the bed—just like Marie Antoinette relieved herself on the way to the guillotine. There wasn't a single message on my answering machine. It occurred to me that I could have died in that little hole alone, without anybody knowing or caring.

I pulled up the shades and looked out the window at the crack of blue sky that was visible high above me. It was a sunny winter day. I made myself a cup of hot tea and sat down on the sofa in my living room, bundled up in a sweater with a throw blanket around my feet. The book I'd been reading on Marie Antoinette was on the coffee table where I'd left it. As I picked it up to find my place, it fell open, and I caught a glimpse of two lines:

> *Harlot, you dare to take my role*
> *And flaunt yourself as a queen . . .*

It was the start of one of the seditious little poems written and distributed by the anti-Monarchist press during the trial of the Necklace Affair.

I closed the book and repeated the lines to myself, applying them, of course, to my own situation. Why should I take this lying down, I thought? Was I going to be one of those pathetic statistics so common in big cities, one of those forgotten people who die alone in their apartments and lie undiscovered for days until the stench of their rotting corpse alerts the neighbors? *No.* Such an end is not for Jo Slater.

New York is court life, I thought. And in court life,

coups and revolutions are always possible. There was no reason for me to accept this dreary fate. I hadn't gotten where I was in life by mere acceptance. I'd made things happen for myself, hung in there, fought some hard battles in my day, and won. And it was once again time to gird my loins, strap on the armor, and regain my territory. I will get even with Monique, I thought, send her packing back to Paris. I will do anything in my power to trounce her.

Sitting there, bundled up on my couch that cold, clear February morning, I vowed that no matter what it took, or what I had to do, or how long I had to wait: I would get my revenge.

27

In the months following my new resolve, I was once more united with a true sense of purpose. I had two goals: to dethrone Monique and recoup my fortune. The means to accomplish these ends would have to be daring and drastic. I felt like an artist who has a burning idea for a picture in her mind but cannot quite see the details as yet. I was constantly casting around for the perfect plan. Everything that I saw or read or experienced had the potential to be a plot against Monique.

I bided my time, waiting for the Great Idea to fall on me like Newton's apple. But it didn't. I began to think that only one of my goals was indeed possible—getting rid of her. But what use was that if I had nothing to gain except satisfaction? Perhaps that was enough.

In the meantime, I had no choice but to go on about my business, showing up at my job every day, keeping to myself at night, and plotting, always plotting. A year went by during which I filed for bankruptcy. The next winter, in January, the following item appeared on Page Six of the *Post*:

> *Monique de Passy, the very gregarious, very social Countess, and Nathaniel P. Nathaniel, Esquire, the very sporty, very sought-after extra man-about-town, announced their engagement at a splashy party thrown for the couple by Agatha and Neil Dent. Le Tout New York was on hand to raise their Cristal champagne glasses to the happy pair. A June wedding in Southampton is planned . . .*

It was surprising how little the news affected me, even though I was reading it in that fluorescent hellhole of a showroom I still worked in. My only question after seeing it was what had taken them so long? I wondered if Monique had tried to back out of the deal. Had passion fueled evil or had evil fueled passion? Not that it really mattered anymore which one of them had thought up the scheme. If they weren't in it together from the beginning, they were certainly in it together now.

—⁓—

ONE unseasonably warm evening in early March, I walked home from work, choosing Fifth Avenue as my route because I still liked looking in the shop windows despite the fact I could no longer afford to buy anything. Finding myself in front of the St. Regis Hotel, I decided, just for the hell of it, to go inside and have a drink at the King Cole Bar, an old haunt in happier days. It was a splurge, but I didn't care.

Walking into the grand little bar, I saw the captain from Lespinasse, the restaurant just outside, give me a haughty once-over, like I didn't belong there. I didn't give a good goddamn. So I was carrying a plastic fake Chanel bag. "When you *are* the real thing, you don't have to carry it, Buster," is what I wanted to say to him. Not that it would have done any good. Who was it who said, "Being a lady is like being famous. If you have to say you are, you ain't."

I traipsed up to the long bar, picked out a stool in the far corner, away from the other patrons, ordered a double vodka on the rocks, and sat staring up at the big, colorful Art Nouveau Maxfield Parrish mural stretching the length of the wall. It depicted Old King Cole with his pipe and his bowl and his three fiddlers. The fat, merry old soul reminded me of Lucius—*that son of a bitch.* Once again, I reflected on the cruel fate that had reduced me to drinking alone in a hotel bar at the unpromising age of fifty wearing Hush Puppies.

I nursed my vodka for a long time, not wanting to shell out another ten dollars for a drink, thank you very much. I glanced around the room a couple of times to see what sort of patrons were there. The crowd had changed since my day. I remembered the King Cole Bar as being a trysting place for young people. Now there were a lot of older corporate types sitting around doing business, men mostly—but a few women, too.

And then, all at once, I saw Monique coming into the bar. I spun around and lowered my head over my drink. No, wait, it can't be, I thought. I waited a few seconds before stealing a second look out of the corner of my eye.

There she was, standing at the entrance, talking to the captain from the restaurant, who had followed her. It was definitely Monique. My low moment turned electric as I stared surreptitiously at the cause of all my hatred and suffering. I covered my face with my hand, fearful the slut would spot me. It was humiliating enough to look as bad as I did without having my archenemy gloating over me once again after all this time.

I eyed Monique through my fingers, wondering what she was doing there, whom she was meeting, what she was up to. Was Nate Nathaniel coming, too? Maybe she was having an illicit tryst. Wouldn't that be interesting? She'd streaked her hair and gained a little weight, which was becoming. God, how I hated her.

Monique was having words with the captain. They looked like they were doing a minuet as she tried to edge past him and he artfully blocked her way into the cozy little bar. Their discussion grew more animated. Monique finally withdrew. I ordered another vodka, wondering what the hell was going on. Just when I thought the coast was clear, Monique returned and shook the captain's hand in that special, unmistakable way. He glanced down, then up again at her, slid his hand into his jacket pocket, and let her pass.

That's odd, I thought. She just gave him some money so he'd let her in.

I watched her heading toward the bar, expressionless, her hips moving in a cold, seductive, runway-model type of walk. I hunched down over the bar to avoid being seen, still eyeing her as she perched on a stool at the far end of the bar. She ordered a martini from the bartender, crossing her legs so the slit on the side of her demure black dress split open to the middle of her thigh. The bartender served her the drink and before she could take the toothpick out of the olive, she had company. A man sitting at a nearby table got up, sauntered over to her, and said, "Hi, there. Can I buy you a drink?" I thought this scene only happened in B-movies.

Looking him over, she wetted her lips, and gave him the nod. He sat down. They started talking.

The minute she opened her mouth and I overheard her voice, I realized she wasn't Monique. To my utter amazement, I was staring at Monique's double, her lost twin. The resemblance she bore to the Countess was truly uncanny.

I'll be damned, I thought. She's a hooker. She's paid off the captain to let her in to solicit trade.

I continued to watch her, more fascinated than ever. She and the man were talking and laughing with that fake intimacy common to total strangers on the make. I was transfixed by the sight of her, this double of my nemesis, wondering if there were any way I could use her to my advantage. Maybe set her up in some compromising way and send photographs to the press identifying her as Monique. Or engineer it so Nate would see her with another man, or a woman even. Not that that would deter him. But something like that.

Pretty soon, she got up and left with the guy who had picked her up. On their way out, she hung back and gave the maître d' another discreet handshake. He saluted her as if they were friends. I finished my drink and left. Walking home in the twilight, I felt there was a reason this woman had been thrown in my path. I had the odd feeling Fate was beckoning to me in some strange way. If only I could figure it out.

When I got home, I sat on my couch and lit a cigarette, thinking about another famous lookalike—Madame Oliva—the prostitute who impersonated Marie Antoinette in the infamous "Necklace Affair." I recalled that day in Eugenie's workshop in Paris where I'd tried on the diamond necklace she had copied for the Versailles Foundation—the necklace that was at the heart of that grand historical swindle.

I mulled the story over in my mind: Jeanne de la Motte hired a prostitute, Madame Oliva, who was a dead ringer for Marie Antoinette. Madame Oliva impersonated the Queen one night in the park at Versailles, and duped Cardinal de Rohan into getting the necklace from the jeweler and handing it over to de la Motte, who he believed would deliver it to the Queen. De la Motte did no such thing, of course. She broke up the necklace, sold the diamonds, and got rich. No one was any the wiser until the jeweler came to the Queen and demanded payment for the necklace that he believed she had received.

It was a complicated, improbable scam, the essence of which, however, was fairly simple: A prostitute impersonated the Queen and fooled a powerful man. The deception resulted in financial gain for an adventuress, whose only mistake, as far as I could see, was in sticking around Paris when she should have skipped the country.

I'd always loved that episode in French history. I saw different things in it every time I read it. At first, it had been fascinating to me because it was one of the least appreciated causes of the French Revolution. Afterward, it became much more personal when I, too, was duped by a clever adventuress. And now, thinking of it in light of having seen Monique's double, I saw something new in the story: a plan for revenge.

28

WHERE there's a will, there's a way, I said to myself, contemplating how to use this piece of fortune to maximum advantage.

Ping.

The tap of silver on crystal.

I paced around the room, cigarette in hand, talking to myself out loud.

What if I hired that woman to impersonate Monique? And what if she signed a new will in a lawyer's office? And what if that new will left everything to *me*?

Far-fetched? Perhaps . . . but certainly no more so than the true and successful historical sting on which it was loosely based. And just look how far that went. *Good-bye Bourbons, hello Revolution.*

I had always thought of Monique's departure in rather vague terms. It was more a question of how to get her out of New York. I wanted her to quit my sphere and go back

to Paris or wherever, just so she was no longer in my
vicinity. However, in contemplating this new plan, I was
aware of a budding ruthlessness deep inside myself.
Wills, I thought, are essentially meaningless documents
until the testator dies.

For the first time, the thought of getting rid of
Monique was framed in a much darker light.

—◊—

UNFORTUNATELY—or fortunately, as I was now beginning to look at it—I already knew a little something
about wills thanks to my devastating experience with
Lucius's estate. One of my earliest concerns at the time
of his death was, naturally, whether his will could conceivably have been a forgery. No such luck. It was legal,
duly signed and witnessed in the office of a reputable
lawyer.

The interesting thing was that Lucius's will had been a
relatively short document considering how much money
and assets were at stake. It was typed by Lucius on the
old Smith Corona he used to write his letters. And it was
an unlucky thing for me that he typed it because, as Mr.
Sullivan, the lawyer who supervised the signing,
explained to me in great detail, handwritten wills are not
admissible in New York State, except if you're a service-
man in wartime or a mariner at sea.

Sullivan told me he believed Lucius himself honestly
thought of that two-page document as an interim measure. "I just want to make sure a certain person is taken
care of," is what Lucius had apparently told him. Sullivan
had offered to draw up a more comprehensive will for
him to sign at a later date and Lucius, again according to

Sullivan, had told him Nate Nathaniel was his principal attorney. Later that week, of course, Lucius died.

I envisioned myself typing up a short will that left everything to me, then sending this Monique look-alike, posing as Monique, to a lawyer's office where she would sign it under an attorney's supervision and have it properly witnessed.

Simple. Except for one little glitch. The signature.

I had a nice, fairly recent example of Monique's signature: the note she sent me with the flowers. That wasn't the problem. The problem was that Nate Nathaniel was a very clever man. He would immediately smell a rat and probably figure out what had happened. He'd have the signature examined and the jig would be up. A forged signature was easily detectable, particularly under circumstances where the forger is being closely watched.

This got me wondering what happened in cases where people were physically unable to sign a will themselves. Let's say you'd broken both your arms or were incapacitated by a stroke or something equally ghastly. What did you do then?

The next morning, I did some legal research on this point. For obvious reasons, I couldn't consult with any lawyers I knew, but I did need a thoroughly reputable opinion on the matter. I called the New York State Bar Association in Albany, which referred me to the Legal Referral Service in Manhattan, which in turn referred me to one Jeffrey Banks, Esq., a trusts and estates lawyer practicing in midtown Manhattan. To be on the safe side, I called him from a pay phone in a luncheonette.

Speaking to Banks on the phone, I told him I'd gotten

his name through the Legal Referral Service (as I, in fact, had), and I claimed I was a nurse with a private patient who had two broken arms and who wanted to sign a new will.

"Can your patient come into my office?"

"Mr. Schwartz can walk, but he can't write."

"Strictly speaking, he doesn't have to sign the will himself," Banks informed me.

"He doesn't? But how can there be a valid will without a valid signature?"

"We would have someone here in the office sign it for him. Obviously, in his presence, of course, and in the presence of witnesses."

"Is that legal?"

"Perfectly legal. There are unfortunate people like your patient who are physically incapacitated for the moment or even permanently injured, who simply can't sign their own wills."

"Sound mind is more important than sound body, eh?" A little attempt at humor that obviously failed, judging from his silence. "So tell me, Mr. Banks," I went on, "how exactly would that work?"

"Well, in Mr. Schwartz's case, he would come here to our offices, and I would be present at the signing, but not as an attesting witness. Mr. Schwartz would say something to me like: 'Jeffrey Banks, I instruct you to sign my will in my name and by my direction.' Then I would sign the will in Mr. Schwartz's name and write my own name and address directly beneath that signature. That way, if there was ever any dispute, I could swear that Mr. Schwartz had been present in the room when I signed his will and, indeed, that he had verbally directed me to do so. The witnesses would be able to swear to that as well."

"That's interesting. Even as a nurse, I never knew that. So, what do they call it—a probate court —?"

"Actually, in New York, it's called the Surrogate's Court."

"The Surrogate's Court wouldn't have any problem with that?"

"Not as long as the execution of the will has been properly carried out, which, of course, it certainly will be if Mr. Schwartz signs it here," Banks said with a confident vocal flourish. "I assure you we've done this for at least three clients I can think of. One fella quite recently, in fact. He'd just had an operation on his right hand . . . Does Mr. Schwartz have a current will or would he like me to prepare one for him? If he'd like any assistance, I'd be glad to speak with him."

"Could he get back to you? He's napping now. Thank you for your time."

Before Banks could ask me where he could get back to Mr. Schwartz, I hung up.

—∿∿—

THAT evening, I stopped off at the King Cole Bar again in search of my Madame Oliva, the nickname I had given Monique's double in honor of the prostitute who had impersonated Marie Antoinette.

This time, I made sure I was better dressed. No Hush Puppies. I waited at the bar for over an hour. When she didn't show, I approached the captain, a sour-faced individual with an air that managed to be both officious and obsequious at the same time.

"There was a woman who came in around this time last night," I said. "About my height. Streaked hair. Black dress with a slit up the side? I'd like to get in touch with her. I have a proposition for her."

Glancing at me with eyes that had seen it all twice, he merely shrugged. So I shook his hand and palmed him a twenty-dollar bill to perk up his enthusiasm. It worked. He pocketed the money.

"Tell her to meet me here tomorrow night at six o'clock if she's interested."

"Yes, madam. Tomorrow night. Six o'clock," he said, pretending to make a note in his reservations book. "I'll see what I can do."

—————

THE next night I arrived at the bar a little after six because I got held up at work. She wasn't there. Had I missed her? I looked inquiringly at the captain.

"Don't I have a reservation?" I said.

"I believe you do. But your party seems to be late. Perhaps you'd care to be seated in the bar?"

I waited at one of the small round tables off to the side of the room, away from the long bar. The little room was crowded. Music played softly in the background.

When the captain showed my Madame Oliva in, I couldn't believe it wasn't Monique. I did a double take again as he pointed her toward my table. The resemblance was astounding. She was wearing a different outfit: a tailored black pants suit and a white shirt with a string tie. She looked sexy in a mannish way, like Marlene Dietrich in tails. She sat down and ordered a dry martini with an olive. I ordered another spritzer.

"Nice outfit," I remarked as a way to break the ice.

"Well, I wasn't sure what kind of a gig this was." There was a suggestive lilt in her voice.

"Oh, it's nothing like that," I said quickly—perhaps a little too quickly because she gave a knowing little laugh and looked at me like I was a prude.

"So what's the deal?" she asked.

"Well, first of all, what's your name?"

Cocking her head to one side, she glided her tongue across her upper lower lip and said, "What would you like it to be?"

Oh boy, this babe was *something*.

"How about Oliva?"

"Oliva? That's a new one. But hey, whatever turns you on."

Our drinks arrived. I was contemplating how best to approach this wondrous being with my scheme.

"I'm just assuming you're a professional?"

"A professional what?"

"Uh, working girl. You know . . ."

"I'm a businesswoman," she said, pulling a cigarette from her purse, which she lit in one smooth, continuous motion with the flame of a gold lighter.

"May I ask where you're from?" I said.

"Look, sugar," she said, exhaling a steady plume of smoke. "I didn't come here to play twenty questions. Whaddya want?"

"Actually, what I want is an actress."

"What happened to central casting?"

"Can you do a French accent?"

She preened. "I can do anything—*ena-sing*—your

heart desires, *chérie*. French—*Frawnch*—*Churman, Espanyol, Eetalyano*."

I just marveled. Each of her accents was flawless.

"Okay, look," I said, "the deal is this: I'm playing a little joke on a friend of mine, and what I need you to do is to impersonate her for an hour or so in front of some lawyers."

"No group sex," she said.

"It's nothing like that. This doesn't involve sex. I just need you to dress up as this friend of mine and go to a lawyer's office and sign a will."

"Whose will?"

"Hers."

Our eyes locked for a split second. I looked away and took a sip of my drink to calm my nerves.

"She's this Oliva person?"

"No. That's just a little private joke."

"You're full of jokes, aren't you?"

I laughed uncomfortably. "One more thing. You're not actually going to sign the will yourself."

"I'm not?"

"No. You're going to fake an injury so that one of the lawyers in the office will have to sign the will for you."

She leaned back in her chair, absently rotating the olive in her glass with her finger. I noticed her long red nails.

"Tell me something," she said, after a time. "Do the lawyers know this is a joke?"

"What do you mean?"

"I mean it sounds like you're asking me to commit a crime."

"No. Not at all—well, maybe a minor one. But it's just a little joke. Really."

I knew she didn't believe me so I was relieved when she asked the next question.

"And what sort of compensation are we talking about here?"

"Oh, I thought somewhere in the neighborhood of around, oh, five thousand dollars?"

"I'm not wild about that neighborhood, sugar."

"Okay. What neighborhood do you like?"

She hesitated for what seemed like an interminable moment.

"I'll do it for ten."

I gave an inward sigh of relief.

"That sounds reasonable," I said, trying to be cool. "We'll need a couple of practice sessions first. I mean, you understand you really have to *be* this person."

"That's my specialty, sugar—being whoever you want." She popped the olive into her mouth and grinned.

—⁓—

MUCH AS I loathed doing it, I had to borrow the money from Betty. She'd always told me that if I needed money, all I had to do was tell her. She was true to her word. She lent me ten thousand dollars, no questions asked. I said that if certain things worked out, I'd pay her back with interest. She said she never loaned money expecting to get paid back and she considered this our secret. She gave me the full amount of cash.

One week later, Oliva came to my apartment where I gave her a five-thousand-dollar down payment and showed her pictures of Monique from some recent newspaper and magazine clippings. Oliva acted as if she had never heard of Monique or anyone else in New York Society, for that mat-

ter—including me. I found this immensely refreshing, if
she was telling the truth, which I doubted.

I dressed her up in one of my old couture suits,
because presentable as Oliva's own clothes were, they
weren't custom-made. Not that those lackluster lawyers
would ever be able to tell the difference. But I was a per-
fectionist, in art, in clothes, and now, hopefully, in crime.

Oliva and I agreed she would have to darken the color
of her hair and cut it like Monique's. She practiced her
French accent and copied Monique's makeup. She was a
quick study. She never talked about herself, nor did she
ask me any personal questions. I appreciated her profes-
sionalism but I soon began to grasp the fact that I was
dealing with a very strange person.

—⁓—

AFTER we'd worked together for a time, Oliva informed
me she had to go away on a business trip for a few days. I
believed *that* like I believed most billionaires' second
wives aren't in it for the money.

"Where can I get in touch with you?" I asked, nervous
I'd never see her again.

She gave me her pager number, but told me not to use
it unless it was an emergency. She promised to call me
the minute she returned.

By now, I'd seen enough crime shows to know that the
first thing the police did when they suspected someone of
something was to check their LUDS (Local Usage
Details), a list of all the calls made to and from that person's home phone number.

"Let's not ever communicate by phone," I told her,
thinking of the future. "Where do you live?"

"I have no fixed address," she said.

I was vaguely aware that people like Oliva existed—people who lived on the fringes of society, attaching themselves to big sharks in big cities like remora fish, cleaning them out, then moving on. Coming face to face with one was chilling. Cold, self-contained, and focused on the job at hand, Oliva was a sexy sociopath. She reminded me of Monique in more ways than one. I was intrigued by her, and wary at the same time.

I fixed a date and time for Oliva to come back to my apartment. I was worried about the star of my show leaving even for a short interval. Plus, I'd given her a lot of money. For the moment, however, I had no choice but to trust her. My work was cut out for me. The hour had come for me to write Monique's will.

29

I bought a secondhand typewriter from a thrift shop on Third Avenue. I worked on the will every night, polishing it to make the tone just right. This was the moment to use the information I had uncovered in Paris—information that only I, Monique, and presumably Nate Nathaniel knew about Monique. As an extra precaution, I used gloves when I handled the paper so I wouldn't leave any fingerprints. The final version read thus:

> *I, Monique de Passy, currently residing at 815 Fifth Avenue in New York City, do hereby revoke all other Wills and codicils and declare this to be my last Will and testament . . . First I must make this confession: I obtained my fortune under false pretenses. I coerced Lucius Slater into leaving me over half his estate to the detriment of his loyal wife by persuading him that I was pregnant, when, in fact, I cannot have children. I now wish to make amends for the wrong I have done her.*

I, therefore, bequeath my entire estate to my dear, long-suffering friend, Josephine Slater, who resides at 212 East 74th Street in New York City.

Jo, if you are present at the reading of this will, I wish you to know how profoundly sorry I am for all the terrible things I have done to you. The world sees a different Monique de Passy from the one you have seen. Only you know how much I am suffering, what torment I am in. But what else can a person do but smile for the cameras?

I appoint Nathaniel P. Nathaniel, Esq., the executor of my Will. Though I suspect that Mr. Nathaniel will not approve of the course I have taken regarding the disposition of my property, I trust him to see that my wishes are carried out in full. However, should he fail to qualify or act as executor, Jo Slater shall serve as executor in his place.

I particularly liked the phrase "long-suffering friend," which referred so very accurately to me. But the stroke of genius, in my view, was in making noxious Nate Nathaniel the executor and therefore the beneficiary of a lucrative executor's fee. That way Nathaniel would have a lot to gain if he kept his mouth shut. And a lot to lose if he didn't.

—m—

THE next obstacle was Monique herself. Reestablishing communication with the now popular Countess was repellent to me, but necessary for two reasons: The first was that if Monique and I were seen acting friendly toward each other in public before her untimely demise, the will might not come as a complete shock to people.

The second, far more important reason had to do with

logistics. There was bound to be an inquiry regarding the will, and therefore it was vital that Monique not be seen by anyone during the time her impersonator was in the lawyer's office signing the fake will. To make absolutely certain of Monique's whereabouts during that critical couple of hours, I needed to be alone with her myself.

—m—

I sat in my living room, staring at the telephone, thinking how best to approach Monique. I wanted to rehearse what I was going to say out loud, but the words wouldn't come. The idea of being civil to the bitch turned my throat to sandpaper. A couple of straight vodkas loosened me up. I dialed Monique's number.

"Countess de Passy's residence," said a dour English voice on the other end of the line. I assumed it was the butler.

"May I speak with Countess de Passy, please?"

"I'll pass you through to her secretary, madam," the butler said.

I sipped my vodka and composed myself, waiting for the secretary to pick up.

Another English person came on the line, a woman with a nauseatingly chirpy accent: "Hello, Anthea Hayes speaking. May I be of assistance?"

I wondered if staffing her house with Brits was Monique's small revenge for Waterloo.

"I'd like to speak with Countess de Passy, please."

"May I ask—*ausque*—who's calling?"

"Jo Slater."

"One moment please, Mrs. Slater."

She put me on hold. A long minute passed. I grew nervous thinking Monique might refuse to speak to me. At last, I heard the familiar voice.

"Hello, Jo, how are you?" Monique said in a somber tone. "It's been a long time."

"All right. How are you?"

"Very well, thank you."

We were as tentative as two old lovers who had had a bad breakup.

"I was wondering if we could have a drink. There's something I'd like to discuss with you."

"What?"

"Do you still want the necklace?" I had no time to beat around the bush.

"Yes. Do you have it?"

"I do. And I need the money. So if you're interested . . . ?"

"I'm not going to pay you a million dollars," she said.

"I understand. I'm asking two hundred and fifty thousand, which was the high end of the auction estimate, as you no doubt recall. I think that's fair, don't you?"

"More than fair. In fact, a bit foolish. You could get a higher price."

"Look, Monique, I'll level with you. I feel terrible about everything and, frankly, it's all water under the bridge now. It doesn't much matter what happens anymore."

"Please don't say that, Jo. It's too sad."

"I didn't want to tell you this on the phone, but . . . I'm dying."

Was it shock or concern that made her gasp?

"My God, Jo, no."

"Yes . . . I don't want to go into it, but the doctors say

I'll be lucky to last out the year. All this hatred and stress have corroded my insides, you see."

There was a brief silence.

"I'm sorry, Jo. Truly, I am."

I thought I detected a note of genuine concern in her voice. Well, why not? After all, if I died, who would she have to torment? We'd fallen into a kind of socialite Stockholm syndrome where torturer and victim lived in symbiosis. She would miss me. Just as I would miss her.

"I'll level with you, Monique. Jerry Medina wants the necklace. But we both know he'll just turn around and sell it for double. Probably to you. And anyway, it's my last grand gesture. If I didn't have all these medical bills, I'd give it to you as a present."

"Where can I get in touch with you?"

"I work during the day and they don't like me taking personal calls. But you can always reach me at home in the evening."

I gave her my home telephone number.

"I'll call you tonight. We'll make arrangements," she said.

"Oh, and Monique," I added as a pretended afterthought, "please don't tell anyone about my being ill. I don't want people to know. I can't face another shred of pity."

"Don't worry, Jo. *All* your secrets are safe with me," Monique said pointedly, then hung up.

That night, she called back. I purposely didn't answer the phone. I let the machine pick up.

"Allo, Jo. It's Monique. Are you there? Have you gone out? Please call me so we can arrange the details. *A bientôt.*"

I didn't call back. I let her call again, and again, and again. I think she regretted not paying the million dollars for it at auction because she seemed to be salivating for my signature piece. And why not? It was the final spoil in the complete conquest of my life.

I saved all her messages on my answering machine. I wanted a record of her voice.

—⁓—

I finally called her back, suggesting we meet for lunch at Pug's, where we were bound to run into several people from the old crowd. I set a tentative date that I hoped would give me enough time to make all the arrangements.

"I'll bring the necklace. You bring the check," I told her.

"Shall I send my driver for you?" Monique asked.

I realized I'd neglected to factor in this crucial detail. I'd been out of the fast lane too long. Of course, Monique had a driver. She was rich. And the driver would be the one person who would know where she was at all times.

"How sweet of you," I said, betraying no sign of concern. "Why don't you send him to pick me up at work at around twelve. Then we can swing by and pick you up at home or wherever you're going to be. That way you won't have to drive all the way downtown."

Monique agreed this was a good idea. I gave her the address of the showroom.

"Very good. I will send Caspar for you at noon two weeks from tomorrow," Monique reiterated.

I felt a swift pang. "Caspar is working for you?"

"He said he missed his old job."

I silently cursed that traitor schnauzer, but said smoothly, "It'll be nice to see him again. Just like old times."

I hung up, wondering how to get around this little glitch.

When I began to think it through, however, I realized having her send Caspar, as opposed to some chauffeur I didn't know, was probably a good thing. Caspar had once worked for me. I knew just how to deal with him.

—⁓—

THE next hurdle was to make an appointment with a lawyer. I'd given a great deal of thought to this. I had to be very careful whom I chose to oversee the execution of this will. I first thought of Jeffrey Banks, the lawyer I'd contacted on the telephone about the signature. He sounded competent enough, but if ever there were a question about the will, Banks was an unknown quantity. I had to be sure that whoever supervised the signing of this document was thorough, a worthy adversary for Nate Nathaniel, who was bound to smell a rat.

I decided to go for broke and use Patricia McCluskey, the lawyer Nate himself had recommended to me. And indeed, when I'd met her, in what seemed like a lifetime ago, she had lived up to her reputation. I remembered there was something rather sympathetic about her. She liked and defended women. I harked back to that comment she'd made the day I went to see her in Sagaponack about Lucius's will. When I remarked she was playing *Don Giovanni*, she'd said, "I play it to remind myself what shits men are," or words to that effect. I don't think she much cared for Nate Nathaniel either—Nate the Enforcer, as she called him. But then, who did?

The tricky part was in getting McCluskey to meet with Oliva disguised as Monique without suspecting the real purpose of the visit. The only way to do this was to make a very favorable impression over the telephone. I knew exactly what tone to take, exactly what had to be said. I could imitate a rather good French accent myself, so I made the call.

I went to the Carlyle Hotel to use the phone there. I didn't want a record of this call coming from my apartment. I sat in the little booth and called Patricia McCluskey's law office, posing as the Countess de Passy. McCluskey took the call right away.

"Patricia McCluskey," she said in that gruff, husky voice I remembered so well.

"Ah, Miss McCluskey," I said. "Thank—*zank*—you so much for taking my call. I am a friend of Nate Nathaniel and Nate has always spoken so highly of you that—*zat*—I thought I could call you for some advice."

"Did Nate refer you to me?" she asked.

"No, *non* . . . On the—*zuh*—contrary . . . I wonder, I must ask you . . . Is it—*eet*—possible that we could keep our conversation completely private? Especially from Nate. You will understand."

"It is."

"Nate and I have just—*jus*—become engaged and I would like to come in and speak with—*wiz*—you about prenuptial agreements in this country."

"I'd be delighted, Countess. When would you like to come in?"

"I think I am going away soon . . . Shall we say two weeks from today?"

"Morning? Afternoon?"

"Afternoon is a bit better for me."

"Three o'clock?"

"Perhaps two-thirty?" I offered.

"Two-thirty on the afternoon of the fifth. You have the address?"

"350 Madison Avenue?"

"Fourteenth floor."

"*Merci bien . . . Oh, pardon.* Thank you so much. I look forward to meeting you."

"Likewise."

I hung up that phone with a real feeling of accomplishment.

———ᴍ———

OLIVA called me at work two days later to inform me she was back in town, ready for "the show," as she referred to it. I took a long lunch hour so we could meet in my apartment. I stood on the landing and watched her trudge up the stairs holding on to the banister, with a stylish black nylon duffel bag slung across her shoulder. Her eyes were bloodshot. She looked like she'd had a rough few days.

"How can you stand not having an elevator?" she panted, reaching the top.

In fact, I was extremely grateful I had no doorman or elevator man and a handful of neighbors I rarely saw. That way Oliva and I could meet unobserved. I showed her in.

"How was your trip?" I asked.

"Necessary."

She dropped the duffel bag on the floor and collapsed theatrically on the couch.

"I need a drink," she said.

I fixed her a vodka on the rocks, then played her the saved messages from Monique on the answering machine. She listened carefully two or three times, then did a credible imitation of Monique's voice. I was impressed.

"Do you actually speak French?" I asked her.

"Restaurant French and bedroom French. That's all you need of any language in this town . . . Allo, Jo. It's—*eats*—Monique—*Meun-eek* . . . What are you trying—*try-ang*—to do to me?" she laughed.

"You should have been an actress."

"Sugar, all women are actresses, whether they know it or not."

I told her that I'd already set up an appointment with the lawyer.

"This is how it's going to work," I said, explaining the scenario. "You are Monique de Passy, a French countess. You've just gotten engaged to a very tough lawyer by the name of Nate Nathaniel. Got that?"

She nodded, sipping her drink. "Got it."

"Nate Nathaniel has a lot of respect for this lawyer you're going to see. The apparent reason you've made an appointment with her is—"

"Wait," she said interrupting me. "This lawyer I'm gonna see is a woman?"

"Right. Her name is Patricia McCluskey. She's tough and she's smart. So you're going to have to watch your step."

"I always watch my step, sugar, believe me."

"Okay, McCluskey thinks you're seeing her to talk about prenuptial agreements in this country. You're French, remember, so you want to understand how the law in New York works. And when you get there, you want to be very charming and let her do most of the talking. Get her to give you a basic rundown of everything. Got that?"

"Got it."

"But the real purpose of your visit is to get your will signed. But she can't know this. It has to look like an afterthought. Something like, oh, I didn't realize the time . . . I'm going away . . . I need to get this will signed as an interim thing, just to put my mind at ease. Is there any way I could do this now? That kind of thing. And all in a French accent. Think you can do it?"

"Sugar, this is a piece of cake compared to some of the things I get asked to do."

"Well, there's just one more little glitch," I said. "You can't sign that will yourself."

"Come again?"

"No, listen, you're going to pretend to have something wrong with your hand so you can't sign it."

"You lost me."

"In New York State, you can direct someone to sign your will as long as it's in front of witnesses. And that's what you're going to do. This lady's a crack lawyer. She's going know about this, okay? And if it doesn't work out with her, we'll try it with another lawyer, okay?"

"Okay . . . But what if she starts asking me questions about this guy Nate?"

"That's true. Since you're consulting her about a prenup, she may ask you some questions about his character," I said, thinking out loud. "Just imagine Nate Nathaniel as a cross between, oh, Robert Redford and Ted Bundy, okay? He's all preppy charm on the outside and a serial killer underneath. You don't have to be explicit about him, though. Just be very vague and steer the conversation back to how you could be protected by a prenup. And remember, you're going there completely confidentially. Stress the fact that you don't want anyone to know about the visit. Especially not Nate. Got that? She won't be able to tell him she saw you so she won't be able to pick his brain. Plus, they loathe each other."

Oliva narrowed her eyes. A sinister smile crept over her face.

"That's your story and you're stickin' to it, right?"

I tried not to register any expression, but I was growing leerier by the second of this woman who was set to play such a crucial role in my life. I saw no point in denying anything to her since she knew I was up to no good anyway. She was too smart a cookie. I sat there frozen, waiting for her to up the ante and demand more money. But she was curiously contained, which made me even more nervous.

"I know this is a ridiculous question," I said. "But how do I know I can trust you?"

"Trust me how?"

"Well, for example—not to go to the police."

Oliva let out a whoop of laughter. "Sugar, now that is one thing you can definitely trust me on. I'm so allergic to cops I break out in a rash just watchin' 'em on TV. What if she asks me for some I.D.?"

"I don't think she will. After all, she's seen your picture in the paper. And by that time you two will have presumably gotten to know each other a little. You understand I want the will to look like an afterthought—something that just occurred to you on the spur of the moment. It's not supposed to be the focus of your visit."

"I got that, sugar. But I could also get some fake I.D. if you want. Just to make sure."

"You could?"

"I know a guy who'd do it for me this afternoon. Nothing easier, trust me."

I thought for a moment, then decided against it. Using Oliva was risky enough. I certainly didn't want a third person involved if I could help it.

"No," I said firmly. "If she asks you for identification at that point, you just say you're running late and scrub the whole thing. Got that?"

"Suit yourself," she said, preoccupied with examining the polish on her nails.

"Listen, Oliva, I'm counting on you not to tell anyone about all this."

She looked up at me. "Don't worry, sugar, my business is strictly my business. You're a little nervous 'cause you're just getting your feet wet."

I didn't know whether to be frightened or reassured. A murky figure operating outside the law was hardly the best person to trust. But what else could I do? When you ain't got nothin' you got nothin' to lose, as the poet said. At least I wasn't hiring her to kill Monique. That honor I had reserved all for myself.

30

MURDER concentrates the mind.

Was I capable of taking a life? Could I do it even if I knew I wouldn't get caught? I kept thinking about the moral consequences of homicide, wondering if I could live with myself after committing such a heinous act.

It was inventory week. I was counting lamps in the stockroom, thinking of Uncle Laddie, who had pushed Aunt Tillie out the window. I always liked my Uncle Laddie. He was a funeral director but he had the looks of a mad scientist—large wild eyes and a high, wide forehead topped by a halo of frizzy brown hair. He loved physics. His hero was Albert Einstein. I remember one evening when I was sitting next to him at the dinner table, he was talking to me about space travel, one of his favorite topics. He explained to me that every act in life could be described by a mathematical equation. Then he purposely tipped over his glass of grape juice (he was temperance) onto the white tablecloth. It looked like a spurt of purple blood.

"Reflect on this, Jolie Ann. When we can mathematically describe something as simple as a spill, from the second the glass tips over to the time when the stain has all dried up, we'll be sophisticated enough to travel to other solar systems . . . What do you think about that?"

"It's interesting," I said. I always told Uncle Laddie the things he said were interesting, even when I didn't really understand them.

"There's a good lesson for you, Jolie Ann. Shows you the power of thinking a simple thing through. That little stain," he said, pointing to it with his fork, "can lead to the discovery of new worlds." He had a far-off look in his eye.

"Yeah, Mama's gonna brain you for ruining her best tablecloth," I told him jokingly.

He didn't seem to hear me. Then he said in a monotone, "A crime is like a stain."

Two months later, my Aunt Tillie was dead. And they could never prove a thing against Uncle Laddie. I never told a soul about our conversation. But I always remembered it, and I was thinking hard about it now.

I marked down the number of four-light, brass "Athena" floor lamps we had left in stock on the master tally sheet, wondering how could I "describe" Monique's murder from beginning to end. There, in the dim stockroom surrounded by all shapes and sizes of brand new unlit lamps, I realized for the first time that I was far more concerned about getting away with murder than I was with committing it. My mind had turned that corner in the human psyche where dark wishes become firm plans. I had jumped off morality's fence and landed smack on the devil's trampoline.

The only question now was how to do it?

Coming out of the stockroom I caught sight of myself in one of the smoky showroom mirrors. I hardly recognized the person staring back at me. I had bloomed into a poisonous flower.

—⁓—

How to commit the perfect crime? I considered my options one by one, dancing around each method like a bather around a cold pond, dipping in a little at a time before getting up the courage to take the plunge. A gun was the first thing that occurred to me. Shooting people on television always looked so easy. But you needed a good aim and a clear shot. I knew how to handle a shotgun from my days in Oklahoma. I was one of the rare women who actually shot with the men on the quail and pheasant shoots Lucius and I went on. The big headache in shooting someone, of course, was the gun itself. Obtaining and disposing of a weapon was too difficult. Guns were as noisy, obvious, and risky as singles bars in New York. Guns were out—along with knives, blunt instruments, and bare hands. All these methods were too chancy what with sophisticated forensics and pesky DNA. A pinch of hair, a morsel of skin, a soupçon of saliva—and before I knew it I'd be the one who was cooked.

Poison, the woman's weapon, was a possibility. I read up on poisons and watched crime shows dealing with poisoners and their methods. A nice, heavy metal poison like arsenic might suit me well. Arsenic, readily available in weed killer, was called "the great impostor" because it mimicked other symptoms and was often mistaken for a bad case of flu or food poisoning. But the thing with poisons was that you had to administer them correctly, assuming you had the opportunity. Even then, they weren't guaranteed. They didn't always kill the victim and they could usually be traced.

All the TV documentaries on homicide I watched agreed that crimes involving hit men were the toughest ones to solve because there was nothing to tie the victim to the murderer. Hit men were the Julius Caesars of homicide: They came; they saw; they murdered. And if they were professionals, they left no trace. The drawback was in finding such an individual. Hit men didn't advertise. There were no Hit Men Boutiques where I could stroll in and pick one out, like a coat.

I figured finding a good hit man was like finding a good plastic surgeon: You discreetly extracted his name from a friend who had used him with successful results— which means you didn't look like you'd been to one; you just looked better. However, to the best of my knowledge, none of my friends had ever used a hit man. And it wasn't safe to hire someone off the street. He could turn out to be an undercover cop, or a blackmailer, or some bungler who wouldn't get the job done properly.

One evening, while pondering these options, I tuned in to one of my favorite crime shows, *American Justice*. That night, the program was about Andre Castor, the celebrated performance artist, accused of pushing his wife out a window. Castor swore he was innocent and that his wife, a depressive, had jumped.

Yes, Castor had been in the apartment. *Yes,* Castor and

his wife had been fighting about getting a divorce. *Yes,* Castor would have had to pay her a bundle if they split up. *Yes,* Castor had a history of violence toward women. But *no,* Andre Castor swore he had not pushed her.

Who was this man kidding?

Castor claimed his wife jumped out the window *because* they had been fighting about getting a divorce and because she was depressed. He insisted her death was suicide.

The district attorney had a difficult time building a case against the artist, despite all the circumstantial evidence. Finally, after two years, Castor was brought to trial. It looked like he was going to be convicted for his wife's murder when the defense suddenly scored an enormous coup. They introduced into evidence a rambling letter written to Castor by his wife a week before she died. The letter stated, among other things, "No one in the world but you suspects that my insides are being eaten away by worms and I long for death every single hour of every single day."

Here was a view of the deceased radically different from the image of the happy-go-lucky housewife the prosecutors had presented.

According to Bill Kurtis, the authoritative host of the show, that letter had a profound effect on the jury, persuading them that Mrs. Castor was hiding her true nature from the outside world. That, and the fact that no one actually *saw* Castor push his wife, led to his acquittal.

However I killed Monique, I was bound to be a suspect the minute they discovered the will in my favor. However, if Andre Castor—who had achieved his artistic reputation by stunts like drenching his naked body in cow's blood while singing "The Star-Spangled Banner"—could get away with murder like that, so could I.

—⁓—

PUSHING Monique off a great height was undoubtedly the most expeditious way to get rid of her. The question was where to do it? Luring her up to a roof was a long shot. Positioning her in front of a window at just the right moment and just the right angle was tricky as well. She was younger and stronger than I was. I'd have to catch her off guard. A terrace was a possible place. It had certainly worked for Uncle Laddie.

Or better yet, a secluded balcony—just like the one off the bedroom in my old apartment. The low stone balustrade and narrow ledge were ideal for the swift maneuver of a nimble murderer. It was the perfect spot for the perfect crime.

I envisioned my former bedroom and the French doors leading to the tiny balcony overlooking the service alley fifteen floors below—a completely private place. No one lived across the way. The balcony itself was a precarious spot. One had to be careful. I recalled the last time I'd walked outside onto that half-moon of stone and nearly fallen over the side myself. If I could get her out there, I'd hardly have to push her, just get her off balance so she'd fall.

There were logistical problems, to be sure: getting myself invited up to the apartment; being alone in the master bedroom with Monique; luring her out onto the balcony; shoving her off without being seen. Last, and most critical, of course, I had to get away before the body was discovered so I could claim I'd left the apartment before the fall occurred.

The more I thought about it, the more I saw the dangers inherent in the plan. Finally, I decided this approach was just too risky for me.

I went back to the idea of poison. A drug overdose, perhaps. That would at least give me some time to get away.

I suddenly remembered the Rotinal tablets Anne-Marie de Passy had given me. I still had the vial with Monique's name on the prescription. I knew how powerful they were. One had knocked me out for almost an entire day. Four or five of them ground up in some beverage and Monique was history. The advantage of using the Rotinal was that the prescription was in her name. How could anyone prove she hadn't taken them herself? I just had to figure out a way to administer the dose.

The more I thought about this method, the more I warmed to the idea. Anne-Marie de Passy had suspected Monique of killing her brother with an overdose of Rotinal. It would be poetic justice if Monique died the same way.

The hurdle in front of me now, however, was the will itself. If the signing didn't go smoothly there was no point in killing Monique, for I'd have nothing to gain.

—⁂—

TUESDAY morning I called the showroom to inform my odious supervisor, Mr. Armand, I'd be late for work. He pointed out that this was the fourth time I'd been late in a month. I didn't care. I knew I wasn't long for that dead-end job no matter what happened.

Oliva arrived at my apartment a little past nine. She had darkened her hair and cut it the way we discussed. She walked up the stairs with a heavy step. I let her in. She was puffy-eyed and cranky.

"I don't do mornings," she said, plopping down on the sofa.

I gave her a strong cup of coffee to wake her up. I offered to help her get dressed but she turned me away at the bedroom door, saying, "Back off, sugar. This ain't the prom."

I waited anxiously in the living room, smoking to calm my nerves. Forty-five minutes later, Oliva emerged from the bedroom wearing the black couture suit and hat I was lending her for the occasion. I couldn't believe my eyes. She looked exactly like Monique. She *was* the Countess de Passy, right down to the deceptively gentle demeanor. It was remarkable.

As I wrapped an ace bandage around her right hand, we talked through all the important points one last time.

"What do you do when you first get there?"

"Be charming," she said with a smirk.

"That's right. Be charming, relaxed . . . but businesslike. Say how much Nate admires her as a lawyer. You can even make a little joke about how if he knew she was going to be representing you on the prenup, he might be upset . . . Chitchat. Know what I mean?"

"Gotcha."

"Then what do you do?"

"How many the hell times do we have to go over this?" she said.

"Just go on."

"Okay, okay, . . . So after she's talked to me about the

prenup for a while, I tell her I have this one other thing that's on my mind. I mention the will. I say I'm anxious about it because I've got this trip coming up. I say I just happen to have a copy of it with me and I'd love to get it signed right away just for some peace of mind. I know she probably can't help me because I've hurt my hand."

"And if she asks you how you hurt it?"

"I'm vague. I say it was a stupid little accident."

"Right. Now, if I read her correctly, she's going to offer to supervise the signing for you right there. She wants your business so she'll want to show you how efficient she is."

"You're sure I don't have to sign the damn thing myself?"

"Positive. Trust me. Under no circumstances do you sign that will yourself. Understand? And if they ask you for I.D., forget about it. Got that?"

"Got it."

"Charming but distant. That's how you want to be. Now if all goes well and you get the will signed, after you sign it, ask her to keep the original copy. Tell her you're pressed for time now but you want her to represent you in the prenup. Make sure she understands the meeting is confidential."

"You really think she's gonna go for this?" Oliva asked.

"If you play the part right, she'll go for it. Look, I'm sure she's seen your picture in the paper. You're engaged to her friend. You're worth a couple of hundred million. Remember, she wants you as a client. She'll go for it."

Oliva bridled. "*How* much am I worth?"

"A lot," I said uneasily.

She leaned back, appraising me with a cool eye.

"Know what you are, sugar?"

"No, what am I?"

"A whale."

"I beg your pardon?"

"In Vegas, we call the high, high rollers 'whales.' And you're rollin' mighty high, sugar."

"If it all turns out, I'll make it worth your while. I promise."

"Oh, you can bet on that." She laughed.

What have I gotten myself into? I thought. It wasn't too late to back out, but it was a measure of how much I hated Monique that I was ready to get into bed with this shark.

I took one last precaution. I put clear plastic tape over the tips of Oliva's fingers, so when she handled the will she wouldn't leave any prints.

"Can they get prints from paper?" she asked me.

"I don't know, but I'm not taking any chances. I wore gloves when I typed it."

I could tell she was impressed with the amount of planning I'd done. There was no point in pretending this was merely a joke anymore. She and I both knew the score. I was taking a huge gamble in trusting her, but I figured it was better than spending the rest of my life obsessed with what might have been.

As the time drew near for her to leave, I watched Oliva get into character. I reminded her not to lay on the French accent too thick, and I played Monique's voice back to her on the answering machine once more just to make sure she understood.

She practiced a few phrases as she walked around the

living room in a languid way. Finally, she turned and faced me, resting her hand on her hip and striking one of those insouciant poses I'd shown her that were so reminiscent of Monique. In the black suit I had loaned her, Oliva embodied the careless elegance and underlying evil of her double.

"Is this—*zis*—what you have in mind, *chérie*?" she said.

It was uncanny. She really *was* Monique.

At the door, I handed Oliva the envelope containing the two-page, typewritten will.

"Make sure you don't touch it. And whatever you do, *do not sign that will yourself.* Got that?" I said.

"I got it the first five hundred times you told me," Oliva said.

She put the envelope in her purse and held her palm up, showing off the invisible plastic tape protecting her fingertips.

"This is a damn good idea . . . *Au revoir,* sugar." She winked at me as she went out the door.

31

I carefully dressed for my lunch with Monique. I wore my work suit, which was dark and drab and cheaply made, but not badly cut. I grabbed my fake Chanel bag and put on clunky, comfortable shoes—not Hush Puppies, but not far short. Monique was sure to notice such details. Hard luck had taken its toll on my figure and my skin. I was slightly overweight again and my complexion was blotchy. My nails were short, unmanicured. My hair, which I dyed myself to cover the gray, looked flat, like a wig. I was perfectly presentable if you hadn't known me before, but I knew my old friends would be moved by the changes in my appearance. All this would work in my favor. Part of Monique's pathology was the need to outshine others.

Paranoid about being robbed, I kept the Marie Antoinette necklace in the freezer in an empty Stouffer's TV dinner box. I opened the box, took out the red leather case sealed in tinfoil and a plastic bag, unwrapped it, and took one last loving look at my beloved talisman, gleaming in its little nest of gray velvet. I hated to part with it, even for a short time. Instead of putting it in my purse, I wrapped it up again and stuck it back in the freezer.

I fluffed up the pillows in the living room, turned out all the lights, and started to leave the apartment when I suddenly remembered something crucial: the ice pick. It was lying on the hall table. I'd put it out there on purpose, so as not to forget it. I wrapped it in some newspaper and shoved it down deep into my purse and zipped it closed. Now I had everything. I just needed a little luck.

———— ❦ ————

I took the subway downtown as usual and arrived at the showroom at ten-thirty. Thank God it was a busy morning. I was nervous. I took several phone orders, including a very large one: five complete bedroom suites of cherry wood colonial furniture that was going to an inn in New Hampshire.

On my way out for lunch, I dropped off a self-addressed envelope at the front desk. The envelope contained nothing but a few sheets of blank paper.

"A man will be by to pick this up," I told the receptionist, a bottle blonde with an IQ below the national speed limit who was busy pasting tiny flower decals on her nails. "Please give it to him when he comes."

The young woman looked up at me and snapped a wad of purple chewing gum in my face. "A man?"

"Yes, dear, a man. He'll probably be in a chauffeur's cap and uniform. He'll come and ask you for an envelope addressed to me. This is the envelope right here. See my name written right on the front: Mrs. Jo Slater? Just be sure to give it to him when he comes, okay?"

"Yeah, whatever."

"By the way, don't ever go to Singapore."

"Huh?"

"Chewing gum is a crime in Singapore. I plan to retire there."

I was outside on the street at exactly 11:55. And there, right on time, was good old Caspar in a spiffy black uniform, standing in front of a black Mercedes sedan. He looked the same, blunt and brick-wallish. I shook hands with him and gave him a warm smile.

"Hello, Caspar, it's so good to see you again."

"Hello, Mrs. Slater," he said, opening the rear door of the car for me.

I climbed into the coffee-colored interior, which smelled like new leather. Caspar slid into the driver's seat. I opened my purse, making sure the ice pick was still there. My timing had to be just right.

"How have you been, Caspar?" I asked, as we pulled away from the curb.

"Fine, thank you, Mrs. Slater."

Was it my imagination or did I sense a trace of nostalgia in his voice? Did he have some guilt about going to work for Monique? I wondered.

"It's been a long time, hasn't it?"

"Yes, ma'am . . ."

"And you've been well?"

"Well enough."

We were almost at the corner.

"Stop the car, Caspar! I forgot something. Make a left here and pull over, please."

Caspar did as he was told. He was used to taking orders from me. I made a show of rummaging through my bag.

"Oh dear, I feel so stupid. I left a very important envelope with the receptionist. Would you mind just running back in and getting it for me?"

"Sure, Mrs. Slater. But—uh—what about the car? Maybe I oughta go around the block."

"That'll take so much time. I'll be right here. They won't bother us on a side street. Just tell the girl at the reception desk you've come to pick up the envelope for Mrs. Slater. Mrs. Jo Slater. It won't take you a minute. Don't worry. I'll hold off the police if they come."

"Yes, ma'am. Back in a jiffy, ma'am." Caspar hadn't changed. He could so easily be persuaded. He did seem rather happy to be doing me a favor, however, as if it made up for his disloyalty in going to work for Monique.

The minute Caspar walked around the corner out of sight, I took the ice pick out of my purse and partially unwrapped it, carefully leaving the newspaper around the handle to prevent any fingerprints. I got out of the car, looked around to make sure that no one was watching, then knelt down and stealthily punctured a deep hole in each of the rear tires. The whole operation took less than twenty seconds. I tossed the ice pick into the trash can on the corner, feeling it was important to get rid of the evidence. Then I climbed back into the car and composed myself, waiting for Caspar to come back.

He showed up in less than five minutes, carrying the envelope.

"Thank you, Caspar. You're a lifesaver." I stuffed the

envelope filled with blank paper in my purse, acting as though it were important.

As we pulled away from the curb, the car felt different.

"Uh-oh," Caspar said. "I think we got a flat."

"Oh, no," I said, glancing at my watch for effect. "Dear me. We're late."

Caspar pulled over to the curb again, stopped the car, and got out. He walked around to the back of the automobile. I rolled down my window and watched him as he stooped over to examine the rear tires.

"What's the problem?" I said.

He straightened up, took off his cap, and scratched his head—a veritable cartoon of puzzlement.

"We got *two* flat tires," he said glumly.

"Oh dear."

"Now how in the heck did that happen?"

"Maybe we rolled over some broken glass?" I said.

He searched the distance in several directions. "You see anyone hanging around the car?"

"I wasn't really paying attention. I'm sorry."

"One I could fix. But two—forget it. I gotta call a tow truck. This is gonna take all day."

Exactly.

"Oh, dear. Well, I guess I better take a taxi."

Caspar opened the door for me and I got out of the car.

"Sorry about this, Mrs. S."

Mrs. S. . . . I hadn't heard that in ages.

"Never mind, Caspar. That's life, isn't it? So unpredictable." I paused for a moment. "You remember that time we got a flat on the Long Island Expressway going out to Southampton and I helped you change the tire?"

"Sure I do, ma'am."

"Those were the good old days, weren't they?"

Caspar lowered his eyes. "Yes, ma'am."

"It was nice to see you again, Caspar, however briefly." I touched the sleeve of his uniform.

"You, too, Mrs. Slater. I'm real sorry about, you know . . . everything."

From his morose tone of voice, I sensed he meant the cosmic Everything, not just the flat tires.

"Thank you, Caspar . . . Oh—would you please call the Countess and tell her I'm on my way to pick her up in a cab?"

"Sure thing, ma'am," Caspar said.

I hailed a taxi on Third Avenue knowing that Caspar wouldn't be showing up for the rest of the afternoon. Which meant he wouldn't be able to swear that Monique hadn't gone to a lawyer's office to make a new will. He'd have to say he didn't know where she was.

First equation done. Second equation coming up.

—◦—

I waited in the lobby of my old apartment building for Monique to come downstairs. I chatted with dear Pat, the burly, white-haired Irish doorman who had lent an Old World air to the surroundings for years. I hadn't seen him since the night I'd gone to Monique's party and thrown champagne in her face. His white gloves and gold-braided uniform seemed as anachronistic as his attitude: Pat was genuinely proud of being a doorman.

"It's good to see you, Pat. How have you been?" I asked.

"Can't complain. And *yourself*?" He asked this question so soulfully I figured I looked like hell.

"Well, thank you," I said.

"God works in mysterious ways, don't you know?" I knew that Pat was a diligent Catholic. "We miss you here, Mrs. Slater. Things aren't what they used to be. Nobody bothers to know our names anymore. Sure, the stories I could tell you . . ." he said in a lilting Irish brogue.

"Lots of changes in the building, eh?"

"We got a whole raft of new tenants I can live without, don't you know? Mutton dressed as lamb, they are . . . Uh-oh," he said suddenly, "that'll be her high and mightiness the Countess comin' down now."

"How do you know?"

He pointed behind me to a small room. I peered inside. It was filled with electronic equipment. There was a bank of six security cameras on the left wall showing grainy black and white images of the service entrance and the long back halls of the building. In front of the door was a panel with rows of switches and lights. One light was blinking.

"We had a robbery in 9F a year ago and they put in this whole system," Pat said. "It's a pain in the you-know-what. You can't just take the elevator up anymore. You got to be programmed. I can tell what floor's comin' down by the lights . . . But, sure, you can't blame them with all the muckety-mucks who live here."

This was most unwelcome news to me, for it meant there was no sneaking in or out of the building.

In the distance, I saw the elevator door open and Monique step out wearing a black suit. I was glad I'd chosen a black suit for Oliva to wear that day. The Countess had a glittery look about her, like a dark sequin glinting in the dim lobby light. As she walked purposefully toward me, her high heels clicking on the marble floor, I wondered if I could really kill this woman.

Pat and I were standing in the bright front entrance hall. When Monique reached me, she kissed me once on each cheek, European style. I returned her greeting cordially, strictly for Pat's benefit. My mind had leapt ahead to the day when he might have to testify at my trial.

"Such a bore about the car, no?" Monique said. She turned to Pat and said, "Get us a taxi, please."

Pat flung me a beleaguered look that told me exactly what he thought of Monique.

As we settled into the backseat of a cab, Monique turned to me and said, "Well, here we are, Jo. Just like old times."

"Not quite," I said with a wan smile. "Life must be agreeing with you, though. You look very well."

"Do I?" she said as if she knew she did. "I'm a bit tired. I went to a rather boring dinner last night."

"Oh? Whose?" I couldn't restrain my curiosity.

"The Lowrys."

"Ah, yes. Are you enjoying being on the board?"

"Yes, it's fabulous. Boring but fabulous."

"Boring? Really? You find the meetings boring, do you? I'm surprised."

She patted my knee and changed the subject. "I'm very sorry to hear about your troubles, Jo," she said in a cloying voice. "I feel awful for you. I really do. Have the doctors told you anything more?"

"No. And if you don't mind, I'd rather not talk about it." I'd nearly forgotten all about my imaginary illness.

We rode the rest of the way in silence.

32

A little before one, Monique and I walked into Pug's. I loved the cozy atmosphere of the place with its dog pictures, waiters in long white aprons, and brown leather banquettes. The maître d' hadn't forgotten me. He seated us at the round table in front of the window, the best table in the house, if one cared about such things. Not only was it gratifying to be treated well in one of my old haunts, I knew that in that highly visible location we were bound to be spotted by at least one person with a big mouth.

I ordered a glass of white wine. Monique ordered a Perrier—a sure sign she was on a heavy social schedule. Women with a full social calendar who know they're going to be photographed a lot stop drinking altogether. Alcohol, even in moderate amounts, takes its toll. I didn't drink for years when Lucius and I were constantly going to parties. Now I drank all the time.

"I'm making up for lost wine," I joked when our drinks arrived.

Monique didn't laugh. I'd forgotten that humor was not her strong suit. We both ordered the "Designer meatloaf," a specialty of the house. Monique took a little time to settle down. As she sipped her Perrier water, her eyes darted around the restaurant to see who was there and who was coming in.

That lunch was interesting for me on a number of levels. In the early days of our friendship, Monique had a secret she was keeping from me. Her charm was all calculated, tainted by cunning and manipulation I never suspected at the time. Now the tables had turned: I had a secret I was keeping from her. This knowledge allowed me to be compliant and malleable in a way that would have been repugnant to me otherwise. Just as she had learned style from me, I had learned guile from her. I made a big effort to be convivial. I was on a mission.

Anyone listening in on the conversation would have thought we were two women who didn't know each other very well. We picked our way through the meatloaf, talking mainly about Monique's social life—whom she was seeing, where she was going, what she was up to. We talked about mutual acquaintances in the broadest terms—Monique having apparently learned the wisdom of not repeating gossip to anyone who knew less than she did. I was so out of the loop, I knew very little about what was going on—only that Dick Bromire had supposedly settled his problems with the government and was apparently out of danger.

Later in the lunch, I steered the conversation around to the problems of running two households, a topic

Monique seemed only too happy to discuss. Not only did this give her an opportunity to tell me all about her staff problems (her chef had quit and so had my old caretaker in Southampton), it was an irresistible opportunity for her to show off while pretending to complain—the "good help is impossible to find" syndrome.

In telling me exactly how many people she employed and what their duties were, I ascertained the size and schedule of her staff in the New York apartment—valuable information I stored away for future use. I learned, for example, that Monique didn't like people "living in." She had two maids, sisters from El Salvador, who occupied small rooms in the bowels of the building where a rabbit warren of such quarters existed mainly for building and tenants' staff. One of the sisters came in every morning at eight-thirty sharp to fix Monique breakfast.

"As you remember, Jo, I cannot function without café au lait in the morning. And this idiot girl makes the coffee exactly the way I like it, just like mud. She's stupid but very dependable. And she cleans like a dream."

"You're lucky . . . Who was that very grand-sounding Englishman who answered the phone when I called?"

"That's Trevor, my butler. He used to work for a member of the British royal family. He never talks about it. He signed a contract saying he wouldn't. I made him sign one with me. He's very good. Very correct."

Trevor, I learned, didn't arrive at the apartment before ten.

Anthea, the English secretary, came in at one in the afternoon. The new chef never arrived until the evening, unless there were "people for lunch," as Monique put it.

Under the circumstances, one would have imagined

Monique would have been on top of the world, above the petty peeves and jealousies affecting has-beens and wanna-bes. But as our lunch progressed, a curious thing happened. Little barbs crept into her conversation. They were innocuous enough at first, so I let them pass. But by the time we reached dessert, Monique had become quite aggressive. We were talking about Southampton when she said: "That first summer was horrible. Everyone was so nasty to me, including you, Jo."

"Me?"

She looked at me incredulously. "My God, yes. You were dreadful."

"In what way?" I was truly mystified. I thought I'd been so kind to her, taking her in and all.

"You treated me like a servant . . . Making me answer the phone, giving me your cast-off clothes . . ."

"You offered to help me to pay me back for my hospitality. That's what I understood anyway."

"I certainly did *not* offer to run your errands," she said with indignation.

Was she purposely lying? Or did she really not remember? And which was worse?

"You took advantage of me because I was poor and I had nowhere to go," she went on. "You never would have treated Betty or June or any of your grand friends like that if they had come to visit you. You used me, Jo. You know you did."

I simply could not believe it. If there were a definition of chutzpah, this was it. A woman who was fucking my husband behind my back in order to get all his money now had the nerve to accuse *me* of using *her*. Still, I kept cool. I decided not to remind her of Lucius's plan to bring her in as my new social secretary once he had gotten rid of my old one. I just let her complain.

"I remember all the people who treated me badly," she went on. "What was it you always used to say? 'I may not remember, but I never forget.' I will never forget those people who ignored me as if I did not exist . . . But I don't hold a grudge against anyone. Not even you. And when they die, I will go to their funerals and cry as if I had cared about them."

As I listened to this bizarre tirade, I wondered exactly whom she was addressing. She was definitely talking to somebody, but it wasn't me. It was as if she were replaying some ancient childhood drama. I suddenly had the oddest feeling that perhaps this whole nightmare I'd been through had been some sort of macabre revenge—not on me, but on an unresolved past. She still had an ax to grind. And clearly, her victory over me did not appear to be complete in her mind.

"You know, Jo, I really did love you," she said. "You betrayed my love by treating me so badly. You know that, don't you?"

"I don't see it that way. I'm sorry you do."

Her conversation was striking in its narcissism and insularity. The world was a mirror in which she saw only different reflections of herself. The rest of lunch was spent on more of her petty grievances. When the coffee finally arrived, I was exhausted. At that point, she asked to see the necklace.

"It's back home," I said, adding three lumps of sugar to the espresso to give me energy.

"*What?*" she cried out.

Other diners glanced at us.

"Naturally, I didn't dare take it to work," I said. "I thought we agreed you'd stop by after lunch."

"I never said that."

"I'm sorry. I misunderstood."

"I have the check right here in my purse. You were supposed to bring the necklace." She was indignant.

"I apologize. I've had a lot on my mind. So if you want the necklace, you'll have to come back to my apartment."

"I can't. I have an appointment."

My heart froze.

"Oh? What time?"

"Two-thirty."

Shit. That was precisely the time Oliva would be walking into McCluskey's office to sign the will.

"Do you mind being a little late?" I sipped my sweet espresso, trying not to look doomed.

Monique reached inside her purse and pulled out a tiny white phone that looked like a compact. She punched one button and waited. Whoever she was calling was on her speed dial. I signaled the waiter for another coffee. Monique whispered into the phone.

"Nate, darling, I'm going to be a bit late . . . I don't know . . . Around three or three-thirty, probably . . . Yes . . . Yes . . . No, I will meet you there . . . Fine, I'll tell you everything . . . Me too . . . *A bientôt, chéri* . . ." Monique put the phone back in her purse. "I'm meeting Nate," she said.

"So I gathered. When's the wedding?"

"We haven't set a date yet. We're going to Pearce this afternoon to pick out a ring."

"No ring yet? The papers said you two were engaged a while ago."

"I want to pick it out myself. I don't want a diamond. I want an emerald this time."

I noted her use of the words "this time."

"Emeralds are supposed to be bad luck in an engagement ring."

"Only for those who can't afford them," she said.

While she talked, my brain was clicking. I figured this unforeseen scheduling conflict might work very well in my favor one day. If trouble ever did arise regarding the will, Nate Nathaniel would have to swear in court that Monique called him to say she'd be late for their appointment that afternoon. And even if Monique later told him she had gone to my apartment after lunch, he couldn't prove it. I'd swear in court that Monique and I had had lunch, yes, but that afterward, Monique left me to go to an appointment.

I could see myself on the witness stand saying, "I think she mentioned something about going to a lawyer's office . . ."

I insisted on picking up the check to save time. I paid cash. My credit cards were long gone. We had to leave the restaurant by two o'clock to be on the safe side. As we were walking out the door, we ran into Betty and June, who were just coming in. June gave me a tepid greeting. I couldn't blame her under the circumstances. I'd gone behind her back to Charlie and I still owed him a lot of money as well. I owed Betty money, too—the ten thousand dollars I'd borrowed from her to pay Oliva. But knowing Betty, I figured she'd forgotten all about it.

Betty blurted out: "Talk about the odd couple."

"Hello, Betty, hello, June," I said in a somber voice.

Monique, who was always uncomfortable around June and Betty, hurried past them, murmuring a brief hello.

I knew June was still angry at me, so I whispered something to her calculated to whet her interest. "I've got something amazing to tell you. I'll call you."

June and Betty went on chatting. They were having one of those Wasn't-That-Dinner-Divine-Last-Night? conversations, where all compliments are calculated to end in criticism of the hostess.

I followed Monique out the door, pleased we'd been spotted by the Town Criers. I had purposely chosen Pug's because it wasn't too far from my apartment. We walked home. I looked around to make sure no one was watching us before we went inside.

"I cannot believe you live here," Monique panted, following me up the steep flights of stairs leading to my apartment.

"Hold on to the banister," I cautioned her. "The stairs are rickety."

Once again, I was grateful not to have a doorman because it was so important that no one see us for the next hour. I glanced behind me to check if Monique was using the banister for support, like I told her. She was.

Just before I reached the second landing, I feigned a swoon. Monique was directly behind me. I teetered back and forth and then, in a great lurching movement, I pretended to fall backward. In an effort to save myself, I grabbed her hand which was on the banister, "accidentally" grinding the sharpened silver key ring I was holding into her skin.

"*Aieee*," she cried, clutching her hand in pain.

I steadied myself. The infliction of such suffering was a queer and terrible sensation for me. Monique moaned. I saw blood where the key ring had bit into her flesh.

"*Oh my God, I'm so sorry, I'm so sorry.*" I steadied myself with some effort—not just for effect, but because I really did feel dizzy as a result of this intentional act of violence.

"*Merde alors*," Monique cried. "*Tu es vraiment folle, toi.* What have you got there? A razor?"

"Monique, please, I didn't mean it. It's my key ring. The drugs make me woozy."

"I need a bandage," she said testily. She wasn't hurt too badly, just badly enough.

I unbolted the police lock, opened the door of my apartment, and showed her in.

"Come this way," I said, leading her toward the kitchenette.

She stood for a moment, seeming to forget about her wounded hand as she took stock of the bleak surroundings. Most of the crates were gone and I'd neatened things up a bit, but there was still a striking impermanence to the place. It was more like a pit stop than a home.

"Jo, I had no *idea.*"

"Oh, it's not so bad. You get used to it." I turned on the cold water in the kitchen sink.

"How could anyone get used to *this*?" She said it under her breath, but I heard her.

"Most people in the world would find this apartment more than adequate."

Her attack made me oddly defensive about my little

lair. She walked into the kitchenette. "Put your hand under here," I told her.

I ran cold water on the top of her hand. She smarted from the pain. She had a nasty scrape and some swelling.

"I'm so sorry," I said again.

And I actually was. I couldn't believe I'd done it. I wrapped an ace bandage around her hand—one I just "happened" to have—identical to the one Oliva had worn to the lawyer's office. It was bulky, but it did the trick.

Monique sank down on the couch in the living room in slow motion. She seemed kind of stoned, looking around with a vacant expression and her mouth half open, cradling her wounded hand close to her chest. I could see she was suffering less from the accident than from an overdose of reality.

"Monique, I really am so sorry, I—"

"Stop apologizing," she interrupted me. "It's a bore."

"Can I get you anything? Some water?"

"The necklace. You can get me the necklace . . . I hope my hand is not going to scar . . . Imagine having to try on rings today. Thank God it's my right hand . . . Here's the check," she said, pulling out an envelope from her purse with her left hand. She threw it onto the coffee table.

"I'll get the necklace."

I went back into the tiny kitchenette and opened the refrigerator door.

"Don't tell me you put it in *there*?" Monique said.

"The freezer's a wonderful place to hide things. Come see."

She got up reluctantly. I took out the Stouffer's TV dinner box and showed her how I'd carefully hidden the necklace case inside it in tinfoil and a plastic bag. I handed her the red leather case. She opened it, remarking how cold the case was. Her eyes flashed when she saw the necklace. She forgot all about her hand.

"*Fantastique,*" she whispered.

"You're still happy you bought it? It's not too late to change your mind."

"I adore it. I have always adored it."

"Try it on."

"I'm so late."

"Nate won't mind. Don't you want to see yourself in it?"

Monique hesitated, looking at her watch again. "Quickly *alors.*"

She took off her jacket. I helped her put on the necklace. She had trouble fastening the clasp with the bandage on her hand. I showed her into the bedroom where she could admire herself in the full-length mirror inside the closet door. She unbuttoned her blouse to gauge the full impact of the necklace against her décolleté. Striking a pose, she said: "*C'est vraiment magnifique.* The necklace of a queen."

I stood beside her and we both admired her reflection together for a long moment. Then I helped her take it off, pretending to have some trouble with the clasp in order to buy more time. "Hurry," she said. "I'm so late."

She wedged the red leather case with the necklace inside it into her large pocketbook. I could tell her hand was smarting from the way she kept rubbing the bandage.

"Will you get a cab?" I asked her.

"Yes, if I can find one in this neighborhood," she said testily.

"I'd walk up to Lexington, if I were you."

I didn't want some cab driver to remember picking up Monique in front of my door. I let her out of the apartment, waited a couple of minutes, then followed her. My luck seemed to be holding. There were no taxis. She walked as far as Park, paused, then proceeded towards Madison. Pearce was only a few blocks down. She'd obviously decided to walk the rest of the way.

As I watched her, I wondered if Oliva's part of the plan had gone as smoothly as mine.

33

ON my way back to work that afternoon, I stopped briefly at Bloomingdale's for alibi purposes. Then I dropped off Monique's check in an ATM at my bank. I knew she would meet Nate and tell him everything about our time together. But if he ever asked me, I would simply deny it all, saying something like: "I gave her the necklace at lunch, Nate. She mentioned she was meeting you but that she had another appointment first. I think she said something about a lawyer. I forget. I went shopping."

I would swear on a stack of Bibles that I had no idea how she had hurt her hand or, indeed, that she had hurt her hand at all. "When we had lunch, her hand seemed fine. She must have done it later."

I stayed at work late to appease my supervisor and also because the thought of being by myself frightened me a little. I couldn't believe what I had done. So far I'd pulled off my end of the scheme successfully. But I couldn't shake the moment when I had purposefully pummeled Monique's hand, grinding my key ring into her skin. If that bothered me, how in hell was I possibly going to *kill* her? At least with the Rotinal, I could dispose of her in a way where there would be no contact.

———ɯɯ———

I figured it was about time I used New York's rumor mill to my own advantage for a change, so I called June, who was genetically incapable of keeping a confidence. The coolness in her attitude didn't last long when I told her I had a big juicy secret to tell her. I made her promise, swear on her life, that she would not breathe a word of what I was about to say—knowing full well that this was like telling a bird not to chirp.

"The grave?" I said.

"The grave," June swore. That was our little code for top secret.

"Well," I began solemnly, "when I had lunch with Monique today? She told me she thinks she might be—"

"Pregnant?" June jumped in.

"No. Terminally ill."

June gasped. "No! You're kidding. With what?"

"She wouldn't tell me exactly, but I think it might be—"

"Cancer," June immediately said. "Everyone has cancer. It's an epidemic. Has she seen a doctor?"

"She won't go. She's too afraid."

"Tell her she has to go immediately. Early detection. That's what I tell women all the time. Remember my scare?" June said, referring to her lumpectomy eight years earlier. "Tell her to come to my Cancer Survivors benefit next month. She'll see."

"I gave her the name of a doctor. But who knows if she'll go?"

"Well, let's face it, she's French. French doctors are the worst. They nearly killed Charlie when we were in Provence. Gave him cortisone for a sore throat. He blew up just like a balloon. Interesting she told you, of all people, though, isn't it, Jo? Betty and I couldn't get over the fact you two were having lunch together. Betty said it was like Hitler and Churchill having a friendly bite."

"Honestly, June, I think she feels really guilty about everything that's happened. She was so sweet at lunch, I can't tell you. She kept apologizing to me, telling me one day she'd make it all up to me. I have no idea what she meant, but I have to say I felt sorry for her."

"Jo, that is so big of you."

"She said to me, 'Jo, if I am sick, I know it's because of some sort of divine retribution.'"

"She said that? She actually *said* that?"

"She did."

"Who knows?" June sighed. "Maybe it is."

I hung up knowing that in a matter of moments, the rumor that Monique was terminally ill would be on the wire, along with the fact that she and I were friends again.

— m —

OLIVA showed up at my apartment a little after eight that night. I had a nice, cold martini ready for her when she arrived. I hardly recognized her. She was wearing a blond wig and a tight skirt and sweater. I figured it was better not to ask. She handed me a shopping bag with the suit and hat I'd loaned her folded up inside it.

"So how did it go?"

"Fine."

She sat down on the couch. I perched on the edge of my chair in anticipation.

"*Tell* me."

Oliva sipped her drink at her own leisurely pace. She lit a cigarette.

"That little McCluskey gal's a real pistol," she said. "I like her."

"*So?*"

"So I did exactly what we said. You ever been to her office?"

"No."

"She's got bonsai trees all over. You know, those freaky little trees that look exactly like big ones? They all look just like her. And she's got this cool collection of southwest Indian art. She goes to Taos every winter. And on her desk, there's this huge scorpion in lucite. She caught him in her house. Calls him 'Fred.' Says he's her alter ego. And she's got one autographed photo. Know who it's of?"

I shook my head. I really didn't care.

"That opera singer guy. What's his name? She told me. The cute one. I forget."

"What *happened*?"

"Hold your horses, sugar. I'm supposed to be an actress. So I'm settin' the scene. Know how you said you wanted me to be charming? I was so fuckin' charming I thought she was gonna ask me out on a date. She's a dyke, by the way."

I sighed in exasperation. Oliva got to the point.

"Okay, okay," she said. "First thing she asked me is what happened to my hand."

"And you said?"

"I was vague, like you said. 'A little—*leetle*—accident,' I told her. "Nothing—*nussing*—to worry about.' So then we sat down and talked about everything under the sun. She asked me all these questions about Nate."

"What did you tell her?"

"I was cool. I said he was very cute but that he had this really mean side and I just wanted to be protected. I was real general, like a horoscope. She offered me coffee. I said no. I didn't smoke. Didn't want to leave any DNA in the office, particularly since I was wearing those little patches on my fingers."

"Did she mention me at all?"

"Nope."

"That's good."

"Then she gave me a rundown on prenups. That gal really knows her stuff. She doesn't believe in tying the knot. She believes in tying the *noose*. Anyway, so then I looked at my watch. I said, 'Oh, dear, I'm rather—*rahzere*—late.' Then, kinda like an afterthought, as I was getting up to leave, I said I had this will I wanted to get signed, and that I didn't know where to go. And she said why didn't I bring it in and have her look at it. And I said, 'Oh, but I have *eet* right *heeere.*' You know, purring. I said obviously I couldn't sign it today on account of my hand, but just like you said, she said that I could direct one of her associates to sign it for me in front of witnesses. So that wasn't a problem if I really wanted to do it. I told her I'd really like to get it over with if she didn't mind. Bingo. She obliged."

"She didn't ask you for any I.D.?"

"Nope."

"Did she read it?"

"She glanced at it. I pointed out the part about the lawyer, her friend, being the executor. And I also told her that he definitely wouldn't approve of the will, which was another reason I didn't want him to know I'd seen her. Anyway, then she asked three of her associates to come into the office. We all sat down at a little conference table. She asked me if I was Monique de Passy, residing at 815 Fifth Avenue. I said, '*Oui, oui, Madame.*'"

"Please don't joke," I said.

"Lighten up, sugar. It was all a formality at that point. I had snowed her, trust me. She asked me if I'd read the will. I said yes, I wrote it. Then she asked me to direct her paralegal to sign it for me. I did. He signed it. The two associates witnessed it. They left. She asked me if I wanted her to keep the signed will in her vault for safe-keeping. I said yes. She made me a copy. She asked me if I wanted to have her draw up a more comprehensive document. I said yes. We talked a little more about prenups. She asked if I wanted her to prepare something. I said I had to go but I'd be in touch. Then I left."

"What time?"

"About three-forty."

"Good . . . *Perfect.*"

"I aim to please . . . Oh, and you're gonna love this. As I was leaving, she said she'd seen me at a cocktail party a few months ago. I was apparently with your buddy, Mr. Nathaniel."

"You're kidding."

"Nope. She said it was a great pleasure to meet me at last . . . So, sugar, where's my money?"

"Where's the copy of the will?"

"Money first."

I handed her a manila envelope with five thousand dollars inside it in hundred-dollar bills. Oliva extracted the money, wet her right index finger, and counted it quickly, expertly, like she was used to handling large sums.

"Did you ever work in a bank?" I asked, impressed with her dexterity.

"Casino," she said flatly.

She finished counting. She made two fat packets of bills, securing each with a rubber band. She wedged the packets under the waistband of her skirt in the front, side by side.

"Worried about your bag getting snatched?" I said.

"No, sugar. I just like the feel of money next to my skin." She drew back a step and planted her weight on one of her long legs. "So that's ten thousand total you've given me . . . And one million you still owe me."

"I *beg* your pardon?"

"Oh, I'm not saying you have to pay it right away, sugar. I'm assuming your friend the Countess is gonna make one or two more stopovers on the way to her final destination. But when she finally does get there, I will come back for my money. You can count on it, sugar."

I swallowed hard. "Look, you mustn't contact me again. I mean, we can never let on we know each other. I just assumed you understood that."

Oliva smiled and patted my cheek. "Sugar, I understand *everything*." She walked to the door and opened it to let herself out. "I'm keeping the copy of that will— just in case you go getting any ideas."

"It's mine."

"I know. And you can have it. It'll cost you one million dollars . . . Boyfriend of mine once told me I was like that old show *Candid Camera?* You know, 'when you least expect it . . . it's your lucky day'?"

I really didn't know what to say. She had me over a barrel and we both knew it.

"Oh, one more little thing?" she said.

"What's that?"

"McCluskey said she'd send me a bill for her time. So you might want to think about that."

I watched from the window as Oliva walked out onto the street in the fading light. Whoever she was and wherever she came from was irrelevant now. When she showed up again, I would deal with her.

Later that night, I cut up the suit and hat Oliva had worn and threw the pieces into three separate garbage cans many blocks away. I hated to ruin a beautiful suit, but I figured getting rid of evidence was, in this one case, more important than style.

—⁂—

BASICALLY, I looked at the situation this way: The minute Monique got that bill from Patricia McCluskey, the jig was up. I had to act fast now if I was going to act at all.

I had already decided that the drug overdose was the best way to dispose of her. My brush with even slight physical violence left me in no doubt I would be unable to push her off the balcony. I got out the Rotinal tablets Anne-Marie de Passy had given me in the vial with Monique's name on it. I ground up five tablets into a fine powder with a mortar and pestle. I put the powder into an envelope.

The next day, I called Monique up again.

"Hello, Jo," she said curtly.

I could tell from Monique's put-upon voice that she was loath to take my call. And why not? She had what she wanted: the necklace.

There was no point in my trying to act on her sympathy. The key, as always, was to act on her greed.

"How's your hand?" I said, a polite way of easing into the conversation.

"It will be fine. What do you want, Jo?"

"I have something I'd like to give you."

"Jo, whatever it is, it's not necessary."

"They're the earrings that match the necklace? The original ones."

There was a slight pause. "Really?"

"They were part of the parure. I never wore them because they're too big."

"Why didn't you sell them along with the necklace? It would have made a better set."

"I wanted to keep something from my old life. The necklace is grand enough without them. But with them, it's quite dazzling."

"How much do you want for them?"

"Nothing. Accept them as a present from me."

"Really?"

"Please. I have no use for them. Let me make this one last grand gesture. I don't get to make grand gestures anymore."

"I'm touched."

I figured now was the time to embellish my argument a little.

"I've been thinking about what you said to me at

lunch, how I lorded my position over you that summer. Perhaps I did without realizing it. There was a time when I thought having great wealth and great possessions made me better than other people. It was basically a form of insecurity. Anyway, they don't much matter to me anymore. There isn't a diamond in the world that can cure me."

"I applaud your spirit," Monique said unconvincingly. There was a long pause.

"I can't come to you again," she said. "You must come to me."

"Fine. When?"

"You're the working woman."

"I'll come tomorrow."

"What time?"

"Morning. I'll stop by your apartment on my way to work. We can have a coffee together, like old times."

"Come at nine."

"I'll be there. Oh, and would you mind calling me in the morning just to confirm?"

I wanted a telephone record of Monique having called me so that if there were an investigation, I could tell the police that she was the one who had wanted to see me.

34

MONIQUE telephoned me at eight the next morning to confirm our appointment. I dressed with the calm of a hit man. I arrived at Monique's at eight forty-five with both the Rotinal vial and the ground-up powder in an envelope in my purse. I had rubbed the label on the prescription vial to make it look as if wear and tear had taken off the date and part of the doctor's name. Monique's name was still legible.

Another doorman was on duty, one I didn't recognize.

"Countess de Passy is expecting me," I said, hurrying past him.

"Mrs. Slater?" he called after me. She had obviously left my name.

"Yes." I waved without looking back.

I got into the self-service elevator. The button for fifteen was already lit. The doors closed. The elevator whooshed upward. I took long deep breaths to steady my nerves.

A thin young woman with dark almond-shaped eyes and jet black hair was waiting for me at the door when I stepped out of the car. She was wearing a starched gray and white uniform that was slightly too big for her diminutive frame. She greeted me with a shy smile, immediately averting her eyes. She partially hid behind the door as she opened it further to let me in. Closing the door behind me, she said, "*Por favor, Señora,*" in a timid voice. She led the way through the apartment I knew so well, yet which seemed so different now with its new decor.

We reached the master bedroom. The maid inclined her head toward the door, knocking softly with her small fist.

"*Condesa? Condesa . . . ?*"

"*Pase,*" replied the voice from within.

Stepping aside for me to enter, the maid followed me into the bedroom. The pearly light of a cloudy April morning suffused the room, which, unlike the rest of the house, seemed at first glance exactly the way I had left it. The yellow silk taffeta curtains, the canopied bed, the bergère chairs, the Jacob commode, the Aubusson carpet, the dressing table, the porcelain bric-a-brac—everything was the same, which was strange considering that throughout the rest of the house Monique had gone to great lengths to replace my Old World luxury with a cold, minimalist decor, devoid (in my opinion) of charm and joy. Yet she had left my bedroom completely intact.

The morning newspapers were on the bed, along with a copy of *Nous,* open to the "Daisy" column where there was a big color picture of Monique at some party or another. I pretended not to notice. Monique was sitting at the skirted dressing table wearing a bright pink silk peignoir, brushing her hair. The Marie Antoinette necklace lay on the glass tabletop. Even in the opaque light of an overcast day, the deep gray pearls seemed lit from within.

"Good morning, Jo," she said brightly, looking at me in the mirror without turning around. "Would you like some breakfast?"

"Have you already had yours?" I asked her, slightly panicked.

"No, no. It's just coming."

"Then I'd love some coffee, thanks."

"Carmela, café para la Señora, por favor."

"Sí, Condesa," the young maid said. She left the room, carefully closing the door behind her.

"You didn't change the bedroom? How come?" I asked her.

She smiled at me in the mirror. "I will one day. But it's comfortable, this room. I like it. It reminds me of you. And no one sees it."

"You changed the rest of the apartment."

"Well, of course. I can't be Jo Slater," she said with a derogatory little laugh.

I ambled over to one of the front windows and stared down at Central Park.

"I'd forgotten how nice it is to have a view," I said.

"Have you thought of leaving New York, Jo?" Monique said, getting up from the dressing table.

I turned around and stared at this impudent interloper who was fluffing up the pillows preparing to get into *my* bed.

"Where do you suggest I go?"

She slid into the embroidered linen sheets.

"I don't know. But I believe one can live much better for less money in other cities, no?"

"I guess. But just at the moment, I can't leave my doctor," I said in a pointed play for sympathy.

"Is that going a bit better?"

"Not really." I sat down on one of the bergère chairs near the window. "So where are you and Nate planning on living after you get married?"

"Certainly not his house. Have you ever seen it? It's so dark. Like the black hole of Calcutta. I don't know how people live without sunlight."

"You get used to it. Remember the last time you and I were together in this room?"

"I saved you from committing suicide," she said, rather astonishingly.

I let the remark pass.

"Do you ever use that balcony?" I asked. "I used to sun myself there sometimes."

"I hate air-conditioning so I keep the doors open when it's hot. It gives a nice circulation . . . Where are the earrings? I'm longing to see them."

"I see you brought out the necklace," I said, avoiding her question.

"No, no, I wore it last night. It's divine. I got so many compliments. I know why you loved it. It does makes one feel like a queen."

I wasn't really listening to her. I was thinking how to get my timing just right. The maid had been gone nearly ten minutes. She'd be back soon.

"May I use your bathroom?" I asked.

"Of course."

When I closed the door, I waited a minute or so, then flushed the toilet. I opened my bag and got out the packet of powdered Rotinal and put it in my pocket where I could easily get at it. I ran some water and washed my hands. I came out just as the maid was laying a white wicker tray on the bed beside Monique.

Her breakfast consisted of a plate of strawberries surrounded by a circle of sliced oranges, four pieces of white toast slotted into a silver toast rack, a large pot of coffee, and a pitcher of hot milk. There were two Limoges cups on the tray with yellow and gold rims and bright blue cornflowers dancing on the white porcelain. My old china.

The maid left, closing the door behind her. All I could think of was how I was going to get the drug into the milk.

"Do you have any aspirin?" I asked Monique as she was pouring the coffee.

"There's a bottle of Tylenol in the medicine cabinet. Just take it."

"I already looked. I didn't see any."

"Look again. It's there."

"I promise you, I looked. I don't think you have any."

With an air of great imposition, she flung back the bedcovers and marched into the bathroom. I dashed to the bed and quickly emptied the contents of the envelope into the hot milk, then ran back to my chair and sat down. Monique emerged seconds later holding up a bottle of Tylenol in her hand.

"It was right there on the second shelf," she said, handing it to me.

"Sorry. I honestly didn't see it."

"Do you need some water?"

"No, thanks. I'll take them with my coffee."

She got back into bed and finished pouring out the coffee.

"Do you take milk? I forget," she said, holding the milk pitcher poised above the cup.

"No, thanks."

"Sugar?"

"Just black, please."

She handed me the cup of coffee. I pretended to take the pills, but palmed them instead. Later, I slipped them into my pocket. I put the cup and saucer on the dressing table, watching Monique intently as she poured nearly half the pitcher of milk into her own coffee, then added two lumps of sugar.

"This coffee is very strong without milk," she said, stirring the cup.

"It's very good. I like it." In truth I found the taste bitter, but I pretended to take another sip.

My attention was focused on the moment when she was going to drink her coffee. She picked up a slice of orange with a silver fork and slipped it into her mouth as though it were a delicacy. Then she ate two strawberries. Dotting her mouth with her napkin, she said: "The strawberries are getting better. They were quite tasteless for a time . . . So where are these famous matching earrings you want me to have?"

"Monique, I did the stupidest thing. I was in a hurry this morning and I left them at home."

She paused with the fork in midair. "*Again?*"

"I'm sorry . . . But you know, now that I'm here, I would really like to talk to you about something that's been on my mind for a long time."

"You know, Jo, you really didn't have to invent a pair

of earrings for me to see you. I'm always happy to see you. You know that."

I wasn't surprised she'd seen through my ruse.

"Okay, well, you've won now. You have everything you want. You seem to know everything about me and the way I work. So I wonder if you'd do me the courtesy of telling me the truth."

"About what?" she said innocently.

"About you . . . Who you really are? How you and Nate got together? Did he contact you, or did you contact him? Who dreamed up the whole scheme?"

She looked at me with a defiant sort of hauteur. "What scheme are you talking about, Jo?"

She dropped her fork to the plate in mild exasperation. She picked up her coffee cup and took two small sips. I was watching a woman poison herself. I heard myself say, "I went to see Anne-Marie de Passy when I was in Paris . . . I know about Michel and I know about your second husband, who died just like Lucius."

Not even a flicker of concern crossed her face as she picked up her fork once again and stabbed a strawberry. She ate it, then put the fork down and picked up the coffee cup again, taking another sip. She put the cup down and looked at me.

"To quote one of my countrymen: 'The secret of being a bore is to tell everything,' " she said.

I opened my purse and took out the vial of Rotinal. I handed it to her. She examined it with some amusement.

"That crafty old bitch . . . This proves nothing," Monique said, putting the vial on her night table. "She was in love with her brother. That's the real reason she hated me."

She took another sip of coffee. There was a faraway look on her face as she played absently with one of the pink satin ribbons on her peignoir. I can't say exactly what it was that made me feel quite desolate all of a sudden—whether it was her pensive expression, or the drift of her fingers as they intertwined with the ribbon, or whether it was just the sight of her sitting in the bed, propped up against a little mountain of pillows, looking rather fragile and, well, very human, really. But whatever triggered it, the wave of remorse, horror, terror, guilt—you name it—that swept over me in that instant was dizzying.

I shot up from the chair.

"Excuse me," I said, running over to her and reaching across her for the coffeepot before she could stop me.

"Jo, what are you doing?"

I picked the pot up and knocked over both the little milk pitcher and her cup of coffee. Monique screamed as the liquids exploded over the tray and onto the sheets.

"Tu es folle, toi. My sheets. My beautiful sheets."

As I set the coffeepot down on the night table, muttering my excuses, Monique reached up and slapped me hard across the face.

I was stunned for a second. I looked down at her. Her features were all twisted. She started screaming at me in French: *"Mes drapeaux, mes drapeaux, mes beaux drapeaux . . ."* she cried over and over.

She pushed me aside and leapt up from the bed, running into the bathroom. Moments later, she returned with a towel soaked in cold water. She leaned over the bed, rubbing furiously at the muddy stain. She was in a real frenzy. The light brown spot faded quickly into the white sheet.

"It's coming out," I said.

Finally, when the stain was nearly all gone, she calmed down. She stood staring at it, still holding the towel dripping wet in her hand. When she finally turned around, her face was swollen with anger and neurosis. She looked ugly.

"You did that on purpose," she said. "I saw you." She glared at me across the room.

I had opened the French doors and was standing out on the balcony, facing her.

"What are you doing? It's cold," she said.

"You wore my necklace last night. I have so many happy memories of that necklace. It's like an old friend. I wore it at a dinner I gave for the president of France years ago. When I told him who it had once belonged to, he said: 'I trust you will escape her fate, Madame.' Looks like I didn't," I said.

Monique instinctively glanced over at the dressing table. The necklace, of course, was gone.

"Give me back my necklace, Jo."

I ignored her. I had the necklace in my hand and I pulled it out from behind my back. I stuck my arm out over the balustrade and dangled it in the air high above the alley.

Monique let out a horrified gasp.

"Que fais-tu? What are you doing?"

"You can have my life, Monique, *but* . . . you can't have my necklace."

"I bought it. It's mine. Give it to me, Jo. Give it to me this instant."

I arced my arm back, getting set to throw my beautiful talisman, my trademark, my link with my own past and with French history over the balustrade. The next thing I knew Monique was hurtling at me with fire in her eyes, her arms flailing like a madwoman.

"*No. No. No!*" she screamed, lunging for the necklace. Too late.

Just as she reached the balcony, I threw it high into the air. This was my real revenge. The baby out with the bathwater. I loved seeing her face contorted with the agony of greed.

She was still running, though—chasing it into the wind—and the next thing I knew, her waist had doubled over the railing as she attempted to catch it as it fell. I grabbed her peignoir to keep her from falling, but it was too late. She issued a startled cry as she tumbled over the edge.

I couldn't believe it. I watched her fall with her arms flapping as if she were trying to fly. Then she hit the ground. All I could see of her was what looked like a scrap of pink ribbon lying in the alley below.

I stood there, frozen with disbelief. Finally, I walked back into the bedroom. I was breathing very hard. It had all happened faster than a dream.

In my mind I replayed the event in slow motion.

I was out on the balcony with the necklace, dangling it in the air, taunting her, about to pitch it down fifteen stories. She ran out, thinking she could grab it. Just as she got there, I threw it up into the air. She followed it with her eyes as it arced and fell, reaching out for it with an anguished cry. She lost her balance. I saw her teetering against the thick stone railing that came to just below her waist. Her legs were pressed up against the bulbous columns supporting the balustrade. I saw what was about to happen so I grabbed hold of her peignoir. The fabric bunched in my hand. She was still teetering. I grabbed her waist with both hands thinking I would steady her . . . But instead, I pushed her, propelling her over the edge.

I had no time to contemplate what I had done. I was in a state of pure panic. Objects in the room looked grainy and indistinct, like I was viewing them through a sandstorm. I didn't know where to put myself in the wake of this terrible act. I couldn't believe it had happened.

"Calm down, Jo, calm down," I said to myself out loud over and over, willing the incantation to bring me back to myself, as it were. I had to force myself to think straight.

Mercifully, my instinct for survival kicked in. Just like that, I stopped pacing, shaking, and fretting. I was possessed by a miraculous calm. I glanced at my watch. Nine-forty. Trevor, the English butler, was due to arrive at ten. I had to get out of there fast, but I couldn't leave in a hurry.

I looked around the room, surveying the situation with a cooler eye. The Rotinal tablets were on the night table. Should I leave them there? Yes, why not? They would find the drug in her system and her fingerprints on the vial.

One fact I'd learned from watching so many crime shows on television is that very often people see and hear what they expect to see and hear, rather than what is actually occurring. If I could make the young maid think that she had heard Monique and me talking just as I was leaving, no one would be able to accuse me of murder. I also gambled on the possibility she might be self-conscious since she didn't speak much English.

I stood outside the bedroom door and said in a loud voice, "Good-bye, Monique . . . I love you. Don't worry about anything . . ."

I closed the door and waited for a moment. I started to walk down the corridor when I saw the young maid coming toward me. I smiled at her. She smiled at me. She was about to escort me to the door when I let out a little gasp.

"Oh. I forgot something," I said, running back to the bedroom.

I knocked on the door and entered.

"I forgot my glasses," I said loudly.

"Here they are, Jo," I said in a French accent, pretending to be Monique. "Thank you again for coming over. Close the door, please."

I left the bedroom. The maid was standing near enough for her to have overheard everything. I poked my head back inside the door one last time, and said: "Take care of yourself, Monique. I love you."

I closed the door and looked sadly at the maid, shaking my head with a rueful smile, hoping to convey that I was worried about Monique. The shy young woman nodded as if she understood and escorted me to the front door. She waited with me until the elevator arrived.

"*Muchas gracias,*" I said in a fractured Spanish accent as I got into the car.

"*Señora,*" she said with a slight nod.

On the way down in the elevator all I could hear was the sound of my own heart. I stayed in control by counting slowly as if I were doing an exercise. On my way out the front door, I said a glum good-bye to the doorman.

I left the building feeling numb. Part of me wanted to

go around the side to the back alley to see if I could see
Monique lying there, maybe even to retrieve my necklace. But I kept walking, one foot in front of the other in a
steady stride, down Fifth Avenue, just like any other
passerby.

35

"DOWN FOR THE COUNTESS" was the banner headline in
the next morning's *New York Post. The New York Times*
featured the story on the front page of the metro section:
"SOCIALITE IN FATAL FALL." "SOCIAL SUICIDE?" asked the
Daily News, reporting:

> *The broken and battered body of the notorious French socialite,
> Countess Monique de Passy, 40, clad only in a pink nightgown, was
> found by a deliveryman in a back alley adjacent to her Fifth Avenue
> apartment earlier today.*
>
> *It is believed that the Countess either jumped or fell from a
> small, sheltered balcony off her master bedroom that overlooks the
> alley fifteen floors below. Also recovered in the alley was the
> valuable necklace once belonging to Marie Antoinette, which was
> recently sold at auction for nearly one million dollars . . .*

All the news stories rehashed the old scandal about
Lucius's death and the will, then chronicled Monique's

rise in New York Society, starting with her windfall inheritance. Every account said that Monique was engaged to "prominent New York attorney Nathaniel P. Nathaniel," and that police were "continuing to investigate the accident."

———m———

IT was bad enough being hounded by the media once more without fearing I was going to be arrested for murder. Having all the events of the past few years regurgitated in front of the public was humiliating, not to mention nerve-racking. One minute I was up, thinking I was in the clear. The next minute I was serving a life sentence with no possibility of parole at the Women's Correctional Facility in Bedford. There was no in between.

Everyone was calling: June, Betty, Ethan, Trish, all my pals—all the *amis mondains*. I couldn't speak to any of them before I had my story absolutely straight in my head.

I expected a visit from the police. They would quickly learn that I was the last person to have seen Monique alive. And sure enough, three days later, in came Detective Ted Shreve to the showroom. At first glance this mild-mannered cop looked to me about as threatening as beige. I led him to the carpet section where we could talk. We sat across from each other on separate stacks of fake Persian rugs.

This weary-faced detective had pasty skin, brown hair, brown eyes, a brown suit, brown shoes, a brown note-book, and, to my way of thinking, an entirely brown manner—until we started talking. Unfortunately or fortunately for me—I could hardly tell which at this point—

he was no drab, dull fellow with plodding sensibilities and the understandably grim view of the world I imagined was quite common to those in his profession. He was interested and lively. I knew I'd have to watch my step.

Flipping the cover back on his little notebook, he said: "First of all, Mrs. Slater, I want to say how great it is to meet you. My wife and I admire the Slater Gallery at the Municipal Museum very much." He had sort of a Boston accent.

"Thank you, Detective. That's so kind of you to say."

"I assume you know why I'm here—*heah.*"

"About Countess de Passy," I nodded.

"So I understand from the doorman on duty that day," he said, referring to his notebook, "that you visited Countess de Passy the morning of her death?"

"Yes, that's right," I replied in a somber voice.

"Why?"

Show time. I was ready to give him the speech I had practiced for long hours while soaking in my tub, playing both myself and the detective. I sat up a little straighter on the pile of carpets, making a show of composing myself. I wanted to create the impression I was a thoughtful, coherent, but ultimately grief-stricken person with a deeper story to tell.

"Well, I was on my way out the door that morning when Monique rang me up. I told her I was due at work, but she pleaded with me to come over and see her right away. I really didn't want to go. But she sounded upset."

"What about?"

I looked down for a moment, taking a deep breath. I was nervous. I understood the impression I made on this man at this moment would count for a lot. I drew on my considerable social skills to point the conversation in the direction I wished to take it. I figured, I've gotten blood from stones at dinner parties, there's no reason I can't charm a member of the police force.

"She didn't exactly say, but I had a feeling I knew what it was."

"What was it?"

"Look, Detective, you must know my history with Monique. It's not exactly a state secret that my husband died and left her all his money," I said with a little laugh. He smiled. "Needless to say, we had this very difficult relationship for a while and both of us behaved in ways we ultimately came to regret. But we had lunch together a few days ago because she told me she wanted to buy this necklace that I own which belonged to Marie Antoinette and which she always loved. And, of course, that's a long story because she tried to buy it at auction but a friend of mine wanted it for his wife and then his wife ultimately didn't want it, so he sold it back to me . . . But I won't go into that . . . The point is that we had lunch so I could give her the necklace."

"And did you?"

"Yes. She gave me a check for two hundred and fifty thousand dollars."

He made a note.

"But at that lunch, she confided to me that she believed she was seriously ill."

"With what?"

I sighed deeply. "She was vague, but I think it was probably cancer. She made me swear I wouldn't tell a soul."

"Had she been to a doctor?"

"No . . . She said she was afraid to go to the doctor's. I told her she had to go. I even offered to take her. You know, I said to her, you just can't afford to wait with something like this—particularly because there's so much they can do nowadays if they catch it early . . . Anyway, that's what I figured she wanted to see me about because she'd been so upset at lunch."

"So you went over to her apartment?"

"Yes."

"And was that the reason she wanted to see you?"

"Well, it was certainly part of the reason. But she definitely had something else she wanted to tell me."

"What?"

"It was sort of amazing. She begged my forgiveness. She told me she thought God was punishing her for what she had done to me and she swore she was going to make it up to me somehow. She seemed very distressed."

"Walk me through the morning you went up to her apartment, will you?" Shreve said.

"Um, this young—I guess she's Hispanic—maid let me in and showed me to Monique's bedroom. Let's see . . . Monique was at her dressing table. She hadn't had her breakfast yet. She asked me if I wanted some coffee. I said yes. She told the maid. The second the maid left the room, Monique got up from the dressing table and put her arms around me and burst into tears. I was quite taken aback. She kept saying, 'Forgive me, forgive me' over and over."

"Forgive her for what?"

"Obviously, I thought it was for what she'd done to me and to Lucius and everything. Sort of a replay of our lunch. I don't know. Anyway, I remember I used the bathroom. And when I came out, the maid was putting the breakfast tray on the bed. I had some coffee. I asked Monique if she'd been to a doctor yet, and she said she hadn't. I threatened to call Nate if she didn't go soon. And then she said she had something very important she wanted to tell me . . . She seemed a little, sort of, out of it, you know?"

"Out of it, how?"

"I don't know. Spacey, sort of. She showed me some medication she'd been taking. Then she spilled her coffee and got really upset about that, I remember. She was scrubbing out the stain with a wet towel like she was Lady Macbeth with the blood. 'Out, out, damn coffee spot.'"

"What kind of medication was it? Do you remember?" Shreve asked.

"Not really. She handed me the vial and I just handed it back to her. She said it relaxed her and helped her sleep. Could have been valium. I don't recall."

"So what was it she told you that was so important?"

"Oh, well . . . The most amazing things. She said that she'd been married three times before. Can you imagine? She told me that she'd lied flat out to my husband. She told him she was pregnant when, in fact, she couldn't have any children. She had a botched abortion when she was young. She and Mr. Nathaniel started having an affair in Paris and concocted this whole scheme to get my husband's money. Detective, I was absolutely shocked. I was."

Shreve had been jotting down notes the whole time I was talking. He looked up and pinned me with a probing gaze.

"And why do you think she told you all this now?"

I heaved a great sigh and pretended to reflect for a long moment. "I honestly have no idea. It's so bizarre."

"Take a guess."

"Well, the only thing I can think of is that Monique seriously believed she was dying. I don't know. Maybe she felt guilty about everything that had happened. You know, though, looking back, she really was acting quite odd . . . Like she was *on* something—"

"What do you mean?"

"She seemed, well, stoned."

"On drugs?"

"On the medication. Who knows? . . . Look, she and I had a long, complicated history, Detective. As I said, we both regretted many of the things we'd done to one another. I certainly regretted some of the things I did to try and get even with her. Apart from everything else, they weren't polite."

"So then what happened?"

"I made her swear to go to a doctor. She promised she would but I didn't believe her. I told her I'd call her the next day to check up on her. Then I didn't want to be late for work, so I left."

"Did the maid show you out or did you let yourself out?"

"The maid showed me out. But I was very worried about Monique, I really was . . . Oh," I said, pretending to remember something. "As I was leaving . . . ? I suddenly realized I'd forgotten my glasses in the room, so I went back in to get them."

"Where was the maid?"

"What do you mean?"

"When you went back in to get your glasses? Did the maid see you and the Countess together?"

"Uh . . . I really don't know. She could have, yes, definitely. Why? Is that important?"

He put down his pen and notebook and readjusted his position on the stack of rugs.

"Some people might think that you were so upset with the Countess for what she'd done to you that you pushed her off that little balcony."

I lowered my eyes and said with the piety of a nun: "I seriously doubt anyone would think that, Detective Shreve. Do I look capable of murder?"

"I've been in this job twenty-three years, Mrs. Slater. I still don't know what a murderer looks like. Ted Bundy looked like a choirboy."

"Ted Bundy never served homemade foie gras to three presidents of the United States," I said. Shreve laughed. "And besides, I'm not that strong. Even if I'd wanted to push her, how would I have done it? I hate to say it, but Monique was much younger than I am and in far better shape."

He paused for a moment, searching my face with his shrewd eyes.

"I've spoken to Mr. Nathaniel. He tells me the Countess told him that *you* were the one who was terminally ill. That's why you sold her the necklace. You said you needed money for your medical bills."

I feigned astonishment. "*Me?* I'm as healthy as a horse . . . Knock wood." I made a fist and tapped my skull lightly.

"Why would she make something like that up?"

"I have no idea. Maybe it was her way of deflecting

her own fears. You know how people do that sometimes? They talk about something that's on their mind, only pretend it's about another person."

Shreve folded his notebook shut and hopped down off the carpets.

"Mrs. Slater," he said. "Are you aware that you are the sole beneficiary of Countess de Passy's will?"

This was the moment I had rehearsed ad nauseam, replaying it countless times in front of my mirror so I would get it just right.

"You're joking," I said with a little gasp.

I slid down from the pile.

"No. She left you everything."

"That's . . . That's truly . . . I . . . I'm dumbfounded. Are you *sure*?"

"The Countess didn't tell you?"

I shook my head over and over. "No . . . Are you *sure*? I mean, are you *positive*?"

"Absolutely positive. She named Mr. Nathaniel the executor of her will and you the sole beneficiary."

"That's wonderful. I mean . . . Oh, I mean, don't get me wrong, I'm sorry she's dead . . . But what a wonderful, decent, marvelous, kind, generous, *magnificent* thing of her to do. I can't believe it. *I just can't believe it.*"

"You realize that this gives you a powerful motive for murder?"

I dismissed him with a wave of my hand. "Don't be ridiculous. Oh, I just can't believe it," I went on. "Oh, this is too amazing. Oh, thank you, Detective. Thank you, thank you, thank you." I ran over and gave dear Detective Shreve a spontaneous hug, from which he quickly extricated himself.

"Don't thank me yet," Shreve said.

"Why not? This is wonderful. Amazing."

"There are a few more little details we need to clear up."

I held my breath. "Like what?"

"Like the fact that the Countess de Passy didn't sign the will herself."

I gasped theatrically. "Does that mean it's *invalid*?"

"No, it's valid all right. In New York State, if you're incapacitated you can direct another person to sign your will."

"Really? How interesting. Was she incapacitated?"

"Her hand was injured. But that's not the problem. Now I understand from Mr. Nathaniel that you two had lunch together the day the will was signed. Her chauffeured car had two mysterious flat tires and you picked her up in a taxi to go to the restaurant where you gave her the necklace."

"Was *that* the day she signed her will?" I asked innocently.

"Yes."

"Really? Well, she was very emotional at lunch, I must say. But I had no idea she was planning anything like that."

"What about the car? Any ideas about those two flat tires?"

"No."

"Each one was punctured very neatly with a sharp object. You have no clue how that might have happened?"

"None whatsoever. Caspar and I were both quite mystified. He went back to the showroom to get an envelope

I'd forgotten. I waited for him in the car. When he figured out we had the flats he asked me if I'd seen anyone lurking around. Frankly, I wasn't paying attention. I suppose I should have been since one always hears about how these expensive cars are so often the target of malicious pranks. There was a similar one last week, I believe."

"Do you own an ice pick, Mrs. Slater?"

"You know, I don't believe I do."

I was growing nervous answering all these questions, so I tried to edge him toward the door. But he was planted in front of the stack of carpets like a stump.

"Was her hand injured?" Shreve asked.

I pretended to think back. "No. Not that I knew of."

"Mr. Nathaniel doesn't believe that the Countess wrote that will."

"Then why did she sign it?"

"She didn't sign it, as I said."

"I'm sorry, Detective. I don't understand what you're getting at." I gave a little sigh. "I mean you can't blame Mr. Nathaniel for being hurt. If what you say is true and she really did leave everything to me, then he has every right to be upset. After all, he was her fiancé."

"Tell me what happened after lunch."

"Let's see now. We ran into Betty and June on our way out the door. I think Monique said she had an appointment. I had some shopping to do and then I had to get back to work."

"Did she say who her appointment was with?"

"No . . . Well, wait a second. Now that you mention it, maybe she did say something about a lawyer. But I couldn't swear to it. We walked a little bit, then said good-bye, and that was that."

"Where did you go?"

"I walked over to Bloomingdale's because I wanted to buy a sweater. But I couldn't find one I liked. I deposited the check in an ATM. Then I went back to my office downtown."

"How did you get there?"

"The bus."

"And what time did you get back to work?"

"I guess about four."

He looked at me skeptically. "That's kind of a long lunch hour, isn't it?"

"I wasn't planning to go back at all. I told them I was going to take the afternoon off, actually."

"Why did you change your mind?"

"Frankly, because I had nothing better to do. I'm not a lady of leisure anymore, Detective."

"So you don't know where the Countess went after lunch?"

"The only thing I know for sure about that is that she called Nate from the restaurant to say she was going to be late meeting him at Pearce's. She told me they were shopping for an engagement ring."

"But she didn't tell you why she was going to be late?"

I shook my head. "No."

"Mr. Nathaniel says that when she met him at the jewelry store she told him she'd been with you."

"Well, obviously. We'd just had lunch."

"*After* lunch. He claims she told him that you didn't give her the necklace at the restaurant. He says the two of you went back to your apartment to get it. On the way upstairs, you stabbed her with a key ring. That's how she hurt her hand."

"That is the most insane story I've ever heard. I know he dislikes me, but this is really too much."

"Are you saying you did give her the necklace in the restaurant?"

"I certainly did. And she gave me a check, which I deposited."

"Was the necklace loose, in a bag, what?"

"It was in a red leather case hand tooled with gold."

"Did anyone see you give it to her?"

"I doubt it."

He narrowed his eyes. "Why? You were in a restaurant."

"You're a detective. How smart is it to hand a big jewelry case to someone in a public place? We were very discreet—at her insistence, by the way. She put it in her bag."

Shreve shook his head in mild amusement.

"What's so funny?" I asked.

"You have an answer for everything, Mrs. Slater."

"I'm just telling you what happened."

"You know, if I find anyone who saw the two of you going into your apartment after lunch, you're gonna have some serious explaining to do. You realize that."

"Excuse me," I said, growing testy. "But if Monique was in a lawyer's office signing or not signing her will, as the case may be, how could she have been with me, pray tell?"

"They say we all have a double roaming the earth. Maybe you found the Countess's twin."

"That's just absurd. You give me far too much credit. Have you talked to the lawyer? What does he say?" I was careful to say 'he' not 'she.'

Shreve fixed me in his sights, his probing brown eyes alert to my slightest move or expression.

"I'll be getting back to you, Mrs. Slater," he said, finally moving toward the entance. I followed him out.

"Monique said she wanted to make things up to me, Detective. I guess this is what she meant. If I were you, I'd look a little more closely at Mr. Nathaniel's motives here. 'Hell hath no fury like a lawyer scorned.'"

Shreve shook my hand. I believe he was dead serious when he said, on parting, "Mrs. Slater, you're quite a lady."

36

NATE Nathaniel, the named executor of Monique's will, was holding everything up pending an investigation. I can't say exactly where my mind was at this point. Naturally, I felt extremely apprehensive. Uncertainty perched on me like a big black spider I couldn't shake. All I could do was wait.

Several days after Shreve had paid a call on me, I walked home from work in the twilight of a balmy April evening. I stopped off at the Silver Spoon, a little gourmet shop around the corner from my apartment, where I bought myself a roast chicken and some precooked vegetables for dinner.

Rounding the corner of my block, I noticed a shiny black BMW sedan double-parked in front of my brownstone. I didn't think anything of it until I reached my front door and heard that hoarse preppy voice I knew so well yelling out, "Jo. Hold it."

I turned around and saw a face like a fist barreling toward me. It was Nate Nathaniel. He grabbed my right arm tight and jerked me around. I dropped my purse and the bag of gourmet food.

"Listen to me, bitch. I don't know how the hell you did it. But I swear to you, on my mother's grave, that I'm going to find out."

"I didn't know you had a mother, Nate," I said, wincing.

"You're crazy, you know that? And you're gonna fry. You hear me? Fry. I have friends downtown."

I managed to wriggle my arm out of the grasp of his tentacle.

"I have no idea what you're talking about."

"You killed her. You pushed her off that balcony as sure as my name is Nathaniel Prescott Nathaniel."

"Prescott? I always thought that P stood for Prick."

He grabbed the collar of my coat with both hands and jammed me up against the side of the building so hard the back of my head bounced against the stone. I cried out in pain trying to push him away. No use. He tightened his grip to choke me then planted his big round face right up against mine so we were practically touching noses. The smell of his breath was sickening.

"Look, you psychopath," he whispered in a voice packed with fury, "I know you wrote that fucking will yourself. And I know you had someone impersonate her at the signing. And if it's the last thing I do, I'm going to find out who that person was . . . You're guilty as fucking sin, Jo."

"I'll scream . . ."

"Understand me?"

He let me go, reluctantly. I gasped for air and rubbed

my hurting throat. Nate stood in front of me without budging, still shaking with incendiary rage.

"You think you were so clever using Pat McCluskey and that thing with her hand."

"What thing with her hand?" I played innocent, just as I had with Detective Shreve.

"So she couldn't sign the will herself. Monique told me how you stabbed her with the key ring on the way up to your apartment when you two went to get the necklace."

"Oh, then her hand *was* injured?" I said with wide, incredulous eyes.

"You *know* it was, bitch. You injured it."

"I don't know what you're talking about. So she went to Patricia McCluskey, did she?"

"You slammed her hand on purpose. At the same time she was supposedly having that fucking will signed she was right here in your apartment."

"You're mistaken . . . And besides, Patricia McCluskey's a very good lawyer. You said so yourself. I doubt she'd be fooled."

"Pat McCluskey's a lesbian bitch who hates men. She hates *me,* okay? She'd do anything to fuck me over, okay? And I got news for you: She's not that good a lawyer, if you want to know the truth."

"Really?"

"Yeah, I'm a hundred times better lawyer than *Mister* McCluskey, lemme tell you."

"I see. You recommended her to me because you thought she wasn't any good. Thank you."

I could see Nate's jaw grinding hard as he paused to think.

"I don't know who you got to go to her office that day, but it sure as hell wasn't Monique," he said.

"Does Ms. McCluskey think it was Monique?"

"Obviously, but how the fuck would she *know*? She never met Monique."

"I have no idea, Nate. You'll have to ask her, I guess."

Nate stepped back, raking his hands through his hair in exasperation.

"Look, Jo, you've been very clever. Diabolically clever, I'll give you that. But it ain't gonna work. I told the police," he said, his head bobbing up and down. "Oh, yeah, I told 'em—told 'em everything."

"Everything?" I interrupted. "About the whole plan you and Monique concocted to get Lucius's money? That must have been interesting."

He ignored my comment. "The DA's a friend of mine," he went on. "All that crap about how Monique was stoned and how she thought she had cancer and you're the only one she confided in? Ever heard of an *autopsy*, Jo? When they do that autopsy and find out you're lying, *you're gonna fry*."

"Nate, what did the will say *exactly*?"

His cheeks churned in anger. "Look, I don't know how the hell you found out some of the things you did . . . but you just wait. Most murder cases are tried on circumstantial evidence, Jo. You had the motive. You had the means. And you had the fucking opportunity. And just because some dumb little spic maid thinks she *may* have heard Monique's voice when you were leaving isn't gonna get you the hell off the hook. The autopsy's gonna show that you are a lying cunt. I'll get you, Jo. I'll get you."

"'You get me, I'll get you.' It's on my family crest," I said.

Nate started to say something, then stopped. He turned on his heel and headed for his car. I watched him slink down into the black driver's seat like some batrachian creature disappearing in an inky tarn. He drove off into the night.

The chicken was in the gutter. My appetite was ruined anyway, so I skipped dinner.

37

I barely slept a wink for nights wondering if Nate could possibly be right about the autopsy and the circumstantial evidence. My nerves were shot. And if Shreve could find someone who had seen me with Monique going into my apartment that day after lunch, I was done for. I thought of Uncle Laddie and the anguish he had endured while under a dark cloud of suspicion over my aunt's death. I kept reminding myself that he got off in the end, as did Andre Castor. I wondered if I would have to endure the ordeal of a trial.

I was upset about what I'd done, but the truth is that my guilty conscience paled in comparison to my survival instinct. I was no Raskolnikov. I saw no reason to compound my wretchedness by going to jail. I knew that if I really put my mind to it I could feel as culpable in the lap of luxury as in a prison cell.

A week later, I spotted Detective Shreve out of the corner of my eye as I was sitting at my desk taking a phone order for twenty Laz-Z-Girl recliners for a nursing home in Rochester. I gave Shreve a tentative little wave as he strolled over to my desk and perched himself on the corner. Completing the paperwork, I hung up the phone and forced a smile.

"Hello, Detective Shreve. Should I be worried that you're here?"

"I came by because I have some news for you and I wanted to tell you in person."

"Oh, I hope it's something good." Here it comes, I thought, expecting him to get out the handcuffs.

"We got the results of the autopsy."

I held my breath.

"Countess de Passy had traces of a Flunitrazepam in her system."

"What's that?"

"A powerful relaxant used in the short-term treatment of insomnia. It's known here as the date-rape drug. She had an old prescription of it around from France under the name Rotinal. It makes people woozy. Remember? Just like you said she was. That must have been the medicine she showed you. Your fingerprints were on the vial."

"Oh my . . ."

"And something else," he said, pausing. "Apparently you weren't the only one she confided in about being ill."

"I wasn't?"

"No. It seems that a lot of people knew it. A lot of her friends anyway. Everyone except Mr. Nathaniel."

"No kidding. She made me swear on my life I wouldn't tell a soul." I shook my head in amazement.

"Mrs. Kahn knew it. Mrs. Waterman. Mrs. Bromire. That gossip column lady—what's her name?"

"Miranda Somers?"

"No, Mindy something."

"Eve Mindy?"

"Yeah, her. It's in her column tomorrow."

Clearly, June had done her work.

"Well, I just don't know what to say, Detective. Does this mean she could have killed herself?"

"It's interesting you should ask that because she was right."

"Who was right?"

"Your pal, the Countess. She was afraid she had cancer? Well, she did."

"What?"

"Have cancer. Just like she thought."

I could hardly believe my ears. "*What?*"

"She definitely should have gone to a doctor sooner. She had breast cancer."

I blinked twice in utter disbelief.

"She did?"

"A large lump. Could've been treated maybe. Pity. Never said a word to Mr. Nathaniel."

"She didn't?"

"Nope. Poor guy's in shock. What's that they say about the husband always being the last to know? The fiancé in this case. Anyway, this explains her behavior."

"Yes . . . Yes, it does."

Nate Nathaniel wasn't the only one in shock.

"We'll probably never know whether she took her own life or whether she accidentally fell because the drug took effect. But I think it's fairly safe to say that you're no longer a suspect, Mrs. Slater."

"I'm not?"

"Nope."

"And the will? Has that been resolved?" I asked tentatively.

"The lawyer who supervised the signing, Ms. McCluskey, swears that the woman who came to her office that day was Countess de Passy. She says she knows this for certain because she was introduced to the Countess at a cocktail party once."

I remembered Oliva telling me how McCluskey had told her she had seen her across the room at a cocktail party. I imagined that in order to protect her reputation McCluskey was now claiming she had actually met Monique so she could not be blamed for unwittingly abetting the signing of a fraudulent will.

"We have the bill she sent the Countess at her home," Shreve went on. "She's a confident woman, Ms. McCluskey. A good choice of a lawyer . . . And I couldn't find anyone who'd seen the two of you together after lunch. In short, they'd have a hard time making a case against you, Mrs. Slater. You're exonerated."

"I am?" I was still hearing the word "exonerated." "I mean, I *am.* Yes. Well, I should be. Good. Yes. It's what I've been saying all along."

"I gotta tell you something, Mrs. Slater."

"What?"

"I thought you were guilty."

"You did?"

He looked at me closely with a vaguely amused expression on his face. "Now I'm not so sure."

"Well . . . Thank you for bringing me that lovely news, Detective. I hope we meet again under pleasanter circumstances."

He shook my hand and held it for a longer moment than necessary. "I have no doubt we'll meet again, Mrs. Slater. No doubt at all. And in a professional capacity." He turned to go, then stopped and turned back for a moment.

"Oh, by the way, congratulations," he said.

I thought he was congratulating me on having gotten away with murder. But then he added: "I understand you're about to become a very rich woman. Again."

38

MONIQUE'S memorial service two weeks later was held at St. Thomas More, a small Catholic Church tucked away on an Upper East Side side street. The pretty little church, so conveniently located, had a long history of illustrious social funerals to its credit. Nate Nathaniel, the grieving fiancé, organized the event himself. At considerable expense, he'd hired Trebor Bellini to decorate the church, which was uncharacteristic of Nate because he was such a skinflint. I thought he'd only done it for appearances, but when I saw him that day, he seemed genuinely broken up over Monique's death, or perhaps over my exoneration, or both. I didn't really care.

Instead of the traditional flowers, Bellini filled the church with bunches of brilliantly colored autumn leaves. He even scattered them on the stone floor. As he told June Kahn: "I made it fall in honor of a fall . . . I want people to feel like they're walking into an autumn wood that just happens to have pews."

Le tout New York showed up, including many people who didn't like Monique but for whom funerals, like weddings, were social occasions not to be missed. The Kahns, the Watermans, the Dents, the Lowrys, Miranda Somers, Ethan Monk, Nicky Brubetskoi, Eve Mindy, and many, many others all paid their last respects to this faded comet—and to one another, while they were at it. Their grief, if not heartfelt, was at least polite.

Nate gave an endless eulogy. At one point, an irate Betty leaned in and whispered to me: "He's talked longer than she lived, for Christ sakes."

After the service, Nate and I walked out of the church together. It was a cold spring day. An unseasonable wind whipped our clothes as we stood on the curb. I held my hat to keep it from blowing off.

"Funny how you can live with a person and never really know them," Nate said, rubbing his rat-red eyes with a soggy white linen handkerchief.

"Tell me about it," I said.

"She never said a thing to me, Jo, not a thing. Nothing about the drugs, nothing about the will, nothing about being sick. I guess that explains why she refused to marry me for so long. She had so many secrets. Everyone but me knew. I know now exactly how you must have felt about Lucius."

"Thank you, Nate. It's very big of you to admit that."

"Friends?" he said, extending his hand.

"*Amis mondains,*" I said, shaking it.

He stared hard at me with an air of weary resignation, then scuttled away toward a waiting limousine.

Eventually, I received all monies and property from Monique's estate. I paid off my creditors and the rest of my pledge to the Municipal Museum. I gave Charlie what I owed him for the necklace. I paid Betty back her ten thousand and bought her a sapphire clip from Pearce as interest. I paid the workrooms and the lawyers. In short, I settled all my debts. I sold the New York apartment. I never wanted to set foot in it again. I bought another one, even bigger, in a building up the block. I moved back into my house in Southampton and rehired Caspar and other members of the staff—except dear Mrs. Mathilde, who said she preferred to remain in Jamaica with her grandchildren.

Miranda Somers did a profile of me for the January 2001 issue of *Nous* magazine, with the amusingly macabre title, "Jo Slater Looks at Life." The long piece was accompanied by a flattering photograph of me wearing a creamy white linen suit, holding a single pink rose, a conscious echo of the Vigée-Lebrun portrait of Marie Antoinette in her muslin dress, which had so outraged the silk manufacturers of Lyons. At first glance, there appears to be a glint of triumph in my expression. People remarked to me how well I appeared in that picture. If only they'd looked at it a little closer, they would have seen not triumph but a hardened sadness set deep into my eyes. I wanted to say to them: You're not looking at glory. You're looking at someone who knows she is a murderess and wishes it were otherwise.

Dare I confess it? I missed Monique. I missed the object of my obsession. In killing the Countess, I had killed a part of myself.

Freedom from my obsession was disorienting. It was hard to stop looking in the mirror for my definition, to stop using Monique's direction for my compass, to stop plotting my life around her death. The worst thing she took away from me turned out to be herself. It was the one thing I had trouble replacing.

When anyone tried to curry favor with me by saying something nasty about Monique, I always told them: "Tell me what you criticize and I'll tell you who you are."

Try as I did to resume my old life, something inside me had changed. My innocence had gone. I no longer viewed the world with the same rapt enthusiasm. The New York I knew and loved seemed to me now to be nothing but a conjuror's trick, the figment of a collective imagination, an exquisite card castle constructed to ward off demons. But illusory or not, it was still the most exciting place in the world.

39

NEW York is a great place to hide and be seen at the same time. In that spirit, I organized a masked ball at the Municipal Museum, calling it Le Bal de la Reine, in honor of Marie Antoinette.

The four hundred hand-calligraphied invitations were accompanied by my signature white rose in a Baccarat bud vase. It was the first big event of the season. Trebor Bellini outdid himself with the decorations on an unlimited budget.

I surveyed my courtiers from behind my mask. "Jo's Four Hundred"—like old Mrs. Astor's Four Hundred—was what the press had dubbed us.

I wore a dress of red and silver, the Queen's colors. The hoop skirt, with its flounces of silver lamé, was so enormous, I had to turn sideways to edge through ordinary doors. The museum's magnificent halls and generous archways afforded me the chance to stride along straight ahead like a galleon in full sail, making a grand entrance wherever I went. I sported a high white wig with a replica of the Statue of Liberty nestled into the hair— an homage to my own freedom and to the fashionable women of the eighteenth century who celebrated famous events and victories through their coiffures.

Everyone was there. Everyone had made an effort. It wasn't every day the Municipal Museum opened up the Slater Gallery *and* the Great Hall for a private party. No last-minute cancellations this time. People were desperate to be invited, calling up at the last minute: Could I please fit them in? And I did. Perhaps it was a narcissistic wish for my old enemies to see me prosper. But whatever the reason, I excluded no one, not even the Dents.

It was what Betty Waterman referred to as "a vault occasion," where women opened up their safe-deposit boxes and got out the really great jewels—the ones that were too expensive to insure all year round, the ones reserved for spectacular parties where all the women tried to outdo one another. I, of course, was wearing the Marie Antoinette necklace—not the real one, which had been broken to bits in the alley, but a replica my darling Eugenie Pourtant had made for me with the salvageable stones. It shone even more brightly because it was new and mostly fake. The original had glowed from within. The copy sparkled under the lights. Only an expert could have told the difference.

It's always best to be kind and forgiving when fortune lifts you up. If your time comes, you must be magnanimous in victory—a good queen. I invited Nate Nathaniel. He came as Talleyrand, telling everyone that treason was a "matter of dates." Miranda Somers was there, playfully dressed as a shepherdess, which her devoted social flock found very amusing. Dick Bromire came as Ben Franklin, Trish as Madame du Barry. Roger Lowry came as Lafayette. My dear friend Eugenie Pourtant flew in from Paris and came as Madame Vigée Lebrun, Marie Antoinette's official portrait painter. The Dents came as Napoléon and Josephine. They both looked too tall and out of period. June came as Madame de Pompadour—wrong king, June, but who cares? Charlie came as Necker, the finance minister. Ethan Monk came as Axel Fersen, Marie Antoinette's great love. Gil Waterman came as David, the painter. Betty came as the fictional Madame Defarge and kept poking people in the behind with her knitting needles. She asked me point-blank: "How the hell could you have invited all these people who shit on you when you were down?"

"Social life," I shrugged.

I was on the lookout for one guest in particular: Mr. Brad Thompson. Brad called me shortly after Monique's memorial service. He said he'd like us to get together. I was feeling so depressed at the time that I actually put him off. But now I was ready. It was gratifying to know that I still had some oomph left in me. What a formidable team we would make. I figured I could polish up that rough diamond given half a chance. He was late for the party but he finally showed up wearing a tuxedo and no mask—so reminiscent of Lucius. I liked his attitude. I seated him on my right.

At dinner, the winter scene of spun sugar adorning the two U-shaped tables in the Great Hall each seating two hundred guests slowly melted into a spring scene—just as in the eighteenth century. Only then men with blowers sat under the huge tables to melt the sugar. Trebor Bellini had designed something much more cost-effective and efficient: heaters on timers. There was applause as each course arrived, brought in on silver trays by liveried footmen.

During dessert, Nicky Brubetskoi, who came as Peter the Great, dressed in a glorious blue velvet doublet festooned with ribbons and medals and orders given to his family by various real tsars, toasted me as "New York's Queen."

Everyone stood up to salute me.

The talk of the evening was how Dick Bromire had suddenly been indicted. No one could believe it. We all thought Dick was home free. The news had been splashed over the front page of the *Wall Street Journal* and *The New York Times* that very morning. And, of course, the party was livelier on account of that. Society had another scandal to move on to. I was history now.

I was sad for Dick and Trish, but they were both there at the party, laughing and talking, as if nothing at all were amiss. I knew they'd get through it. We all managed to get through these things somehow.

After dinner, I danced with Brad. He adored the party. We talked about all the places we wanted to visit in the world. He told me he'd take me wherever I liked on his private plane, starting with London, where we would go to all the plays. It couldn't have been a more perfect evening, except for one little thing . . .

As Brad and I were dancing, a slender man in a full-face white mask walked toward us. He was dressed like a French Revolutionary, wearing a simple gray waistcoat, matching breeches, white stockings, black buckled shoes, hair pulled back in a ponytail, and a black tricorn hat. He carried an ebony cane, the top of which was a gold eagle with ruby eyes. He tapped Brad with the cane, cutting in on him for a dance with me.

"Citizen Robespierre, I presume?" I said to the lithe young man, wondering who this striking figure was.

The man lifted his mask for an instant.

It wasn't a man.

It was Oliva.

"We have some business to discuss," she said.

She bowed slightly to me, backed away, and drifted off into the crowd. It took me several seconds to compose myself. Of course, somewhere in the recesses of my mind I'd always known she'd show up again. But now that she was here, I felt . . . How did I feel? Not exactly afraid . . . More apprehensive.

How much did she want? A million dollars? More, perhaps. What form would this blackmail take? Would it be a one-shot thing? Or would it go on and on forever? God knows I was grateful to her. I couldn't have done it without her. Still, I hoped for both our sakes that she wouldn't make any unreasonable demands.

I scanned the crowd, but she was gone. At first I refused to let dark thoughts mar my triumph. I wanted this night to be a memorable one for all my guests and for me. As I ate and drank and danced throughout the evening, flirting with Brad, gossiping with everyone just like old times, I knew that I was in my element.

I enjoyed myself but I confess I grew more worried as the night wore on. Oliva was lurking around somewhere like a threatening cloud on my clear horizon and I knew I was going to have to deal with her one day. I'd just have to try to reason with her, that's all. Maybe even befriend her, like I'd befriended Monique. Looking on the bright side, I had a new focus in my life.

———∽∽∽———

THE party broke up around two. Brad offered to take me home. We walked outside together. The façade of the museum was all lit up. Brad went in search of his car. As I waited for him in front of the entrance, I wondered if Oliva was out there in the night waiting for me. A dark thought flitted like a bat across my mind, but I repressed it. Oh well . . . I spotted Brad signaling to me from the back of his big black limousine.

I took a deep breath and walked down the wide stone steps, inhaling the sweet air of the city that is my home. I felt like a queen. I'm Jo Slater again, I thought. And I belong here. I do.

ACKNOWLEDGMENTS

I am grateful for the support of all my friends, several of whom read this book in its various drafts and offered perceptive comments. I particularly want to thank: John Novogrod, a gifted lawyer with a literary sensibility, who was instrumental in guiding me through the legal aspects of the story; Linda Fairstein, a generous friend who is always willing to share the vast knowledge she has acquired as Chief of Manhattan's Sex Crimes Unit with a fellow novelist; and finally, Jonathan Burnham, a steadfast and brilliant editor, with a perfect sense of humor and proportion, who just kept believing.

ABOUT THE AUTHOR

JANE STANTON HITCHCOCK is the author of *The Witches' Hammer*; *Trick of the Eye,* which was nominated for both the Edgar Award and the Hammett Prize as the Best First Novel of the Year; and *One Dangerous Lady*. She is married to syndicated foreign affairs columnist Jim Hoagland. They live in New York and Washington, D.C.

More
Jane Stanton Hitchcock!

—✳—

Please turn
this page
for a preview of

One Dangerous Lady

—✳—

Available in hardcover
from Miramax Books.

One

It is a truth universally acknowledged that a widow in possession of a good fortune must be in want of a husband. Or so all my friends constantly tell me. Being such a widow, however, I'm a little more skeptical. Just as I'm skeptical of those who say that doing something once makes it easier to do a second time. That may be true of such things as skydiving or buying a couture dress. It is not true of murder. Believe me, I know. But let me begin where it all began again for me.

My name is Jo Slater and I am happy to be back on top of the tiny, privileged world known as New York society—a hallowed, some say hollow place—from which I had been cast out for several years because of the treachery of my late husband (may he rot in hell). I doubt I will ever remarry, despite my friends' constant hopes and meddling. How could I ever trust a man again? But just because I don't want to tie a legal knot doesn't mean I've entered a convent. I'm open to trying my luck on the romance market once again, paltry though the pickings are in Manhattan. That is especially true for women like myself, who are what my friend Betty Waterman calls "of an uncertain age."

Romance was not the main reason I accepted Betty and Gil Watterman's kind invitation to stay with them in Barbados for the wedding of their only daughter, Missy. Betty was, after all, one of my very closest friends, and I had known Missy her entire life. Still, the possibility of romance was definitely alluring, and Betty had made a point of letting me know that among those she had invited to join the wedding party was Lord Max Vermilion, who she termed an "international catch." Known as "the Lord of the Rings" because he had been married so many times, Max was available once more, having just been divorced from his sixth or seventh wife—no one ever could keep track, not even Max. Betty thought he would be perfect for me, if not as a husband, then at least as "a juicy walker," which was how she put it.

At a little past ten in the morning of the day before the wedding, Betty and I were having breakfast out on the terrace of the lovely, old coralstone villa on the beach the Watermans had rented for the weeklong festivities. We barely said a word to each other because the two of us were so miserably hungover from the night before. Wearing a bathing suit and one of the fluffy white terry cloth robes Betty had thoughtfully provided for me in my guest room, I poured myself a cup of strong, black coffee and gazed out over the pale aquamarine sea. Though fun, the trip so far had not turned out as I'd expected. Id' been to Barbados years ago with my late husband, Lucius Slater, and I was sure that the soft, tropical air and the leisurely pace of island life would provide a welcome change of pace from the hectic New York social life. How wrong I was. We hadn't stopped since I'd arrived. The constant round of lunches and dinners and excursions thus far made Manhattan seem monastic by comparison. Last night's dinner in a local restaurant had ended somewhere around two in the morning.

"I may not survive this wedding," Betty said at last. Taking a sip of her vodka-laced papaya juice, she lapsed into silence once more.

"So what's on the schedule for today?" I asked her.

"Well, there's a tour of Cockleshell. I suppose you'll want to go on that," she said with a dismal air.

Cockleshell was the sprawling seaside villa owned by Freddy and Mina Brill, the parents of Woody Brill, Missy Waterman's fiancé. Missy was getting married there. Mina Brill, an American married to a Brit, was an expert on gardens, and the gardens of Cockleshell were featured in a classic book entitled *Paradise Found, Splendors of the Tropical Garden*. Betty couldn't be bothered with gardens, but she knew of my passion for horticulture.

"I'd love to see them," I said.

"Fine. I'll take you. Call it an errand of mercy. But I warn you, if you and Mina start schmoozing about herbaceous borders, I'm going to deadhead the pair of you."

"Don't worry, I'm too hungover to have any kind of conversation, even about flowers."

"Max just arrived. He'll probably be there. Then tonight's the bridal dinner on the Cole yacht," she said with a glimmer of brightness. "And tomorrow, of course, is the wedding. Frankly, I can't wait for it to be over. Why Missy couldn't get married in New York and have a party at the Plaza or the St. Regis roof like everyone else is beyond me!"

With that, Betty got up from her chair and staggered over to one of the blue-and-white-striped chaises facing the ocean, where she lay down and dozed off. Alone, I sat at the table thinking about Max and about romance in general. I wasn't exactly past my prime; and it would be nice to have a steady companion, someone with whom I could travel and share common interests. In truth, though, I have to say I had less hope for myself and Max than Betty did.

Max, the eighth Earl Vermilion, was reputedly one of the richest, brightest, and most elegant men in England. The sun had never set on his personal British Empire— nor was it ever going to, if Max had anything to say about it. Taunton Hall, his ancestral home, was famous not only for its priceless Old Master paintings, including two Titians and a disputed Vermeer, but for having the largest collection of Chinese bronzes in the world. Scholars and collectors came from all over to sit under the vaulted arches of its sixteenth-century wing and pore over the famous collection assembled by Max's great-grandfather when he lived in China in the nineteenth century, replenishing the family fortune in the very unaristocratic way of earning money by trade. Having made a fortune importing tea and silk, the Vermilion family had gone on to distinguish itself as a major social and philanthropic force in England.

I had actually met Max in London years ago when I was married to Lucius, but I doubted if he would remember me. We'd all been guests at a large party. I remembered Max as a tall, handsome man with a long, thin face, bright blue eyes, thinning gray hair, and the lanky physique of an athlete. He spoke in a deep, drawly voice, which ladies found sexy. Everyone agreed that when Max turned his charm on you, he was very difficult to resist. He was polite to a fault, and brilliant, but he had a streak of mischief in him that made those who knew him wary of his charm. All his wives and mistresses said his naughtiness was both what seduced them at first and alienated them eventually. No, in so many ways he wasn't my type, and his marital record didn't bode well, either.

It was common knowledge that he was a great philanderer. In fact, the speculation was that his second-to-last wife, Henrietta, was actually driven to her grave by Max's infidelities. Still, in a world where rich, single, heterosexual men are scarcer than ninety-carat diamonds, I knew that there were literally hundreds of women, both married and single and on both sides of the Atlantic, who were now atwitter with the idea that they might become the next Lady Vermilion—especially those with whom Max already had had affairs. Unrealistic though some of those middle-aged hopes undoubtedly were, the contest had begun, and it would be interesting to see who would nab him. Betty was sure that if I stuck my foot in the ring I would get the glass slipper, because Max always married rich, socially prominent women—with one grand exception. It was always rumored that Max once had a very brief marriage to a much younger woman no one knew. She was known as "the shady Lady Vermilion."

Despite all my misgivings, I had to admit that Max held a certain allure. Most of the men my age were interested in women half my age, as my last walk out with a Chicago billionaire had ultimately proved. After he suggested a threesome with our twenty-year-old female ski instructor in Aspen, I packed my bags, thinking how chivalry was not only dead but dismembered. And since I'd always preferred older men, my horizons were narrowing. My friends were constantly trying to fix me up with that tattered crew of "eligibles" around town. I resisted their efforts because, frankly, I hated wasting even a single evening making polite conversation with some careless Casanova who was only interested in me for my social access or a free ticket to some coveted event. Better to stay home and read or watch a movie. Drawbacks aside, therefore, Max was indeed a possibility. And I confess, I was rather excited about seeing him again.

Betty finally awoke from her hungover stupor and glanced at her watch.

"If you want to see those gardens, we'd better get going," she said. "I've just been dreaming that you would marry Max and become the mistress of Taunton Hall."

"'The Mistress of Taunton Hall' sounds like a gothic novel in which a New York socialite garners the title only to be attacked and torn to pieces on the property by a wild pack of English debutantes," I said.

"Or by Max," Betty said, as she loped into the house.

—᠊᠊ᨦ᠊᠊—

WE arrived at Cockleshell at around noon. The Brills' sprawling pink stucco villa with two tennis courts, a huge swimming pool, and separate staff quarters was dramatically set under towering palm trees on six acres of prime oceanfront property. It was so big, it looked more like a hotel than a private residence. As we walked through the luscious grounds rife with exotic flowers, plants, and fragrant trees, a high-pitched, stylized laugh rang out over the air, trumping the chirping birds and rustling palms.

"That's Mina!" Betty said with irritation. "She's from Hagerstown, Maryland, but now she even laughs like the Queen of England." Betty was none too fond of her only daughter's future mother-in-law.

We changed direction to follow the rippling sound. Betty led the way through an alley of towering banana palms into a little forest surrounding a man-made pond nestled among large, mossy rocks. Low-slung tree trunks curled out over this miniature lagoon like thick, black snakes. Murky rays of sunlight filtered through the thick foliage gliding patches of the dark water. Mina Brill, a tall, wild-haired woman who was dressed in a pair of khaki safari shorts, which accentuated her skinny legs, and a white T-shirt, which accentuated her large bosom, stood at the edge of the pond. Surrounded by the familiar crowd of well-heeled wedding guests we had seen throughout the week's events, she was pointing up at the trees. Everyone's gaze was intently focused on something high above in the tangle of branches.

"Uh-oh, not that fucking monkey again," Betty moaned as we approached. She apparently knew the drill.

When Mina spotted Betty and me out of the corner of her eye, she waved us over to join the group, signaling us with forefinger to lips to be very quiet. The air of expectancy was palpable. Betty and I trod cautiously across the lawn. No one dared move.

"The green monkey," Mina said softly as we drew close. "Be very quiet or you'll scare him away."

"With any luck," Betty muttered under her breath.

The vigil resumed. Betty scanned the group.

"I don't see Max," she whispered. "Oh, wait! There he is! Right over there!"

She pointed discreetly—or discreetly for Betty, at any rate—at a tall, attractive man standing off to one side with his arms crossed in front of him, peering up at the trees with a slightly bemused expression on his face. Max had the kind of looks that appear mature in youth, and young in maturity. At sixty, he was even more attractive than I remembered him. There was a grand air of detachment about him that I suspect rather appealed to sophisticated women possessed with a slight streak of masochism. I'm not sure why, but in observing him I sensed immediately that he was one of those men who are emotionally unattainable. His aloofness had a soft sheen to it, rather like a well-worn suit of armor.

"He looks pretty good for an old codger, doesn't he?" Betty said, nudging me.

"Betts, if he's an old codger, what does that make us?" I asked.

"Old bats," she replied, and walked on.

I have to say that the prolonged and earnest viewing of monkeys, however rare and exotic, is not my thing, and it certainly isn't Betty's. For the sake of politeness, however, I stared up at the trees like everyone else, although after a while my attention wandered, as I was more interested in looking over the crowd. I saw mainly the same faces I'd seen all week, including Missy, the bride-to-be, who resembled an Afghan hound with her long face and long hair; Woody Brill, her fiancé, a clean-cut stockbroker in his late twenties; and my old pals, Ethan Monk, now the curator of Old Master paintings at the Municipal Museum, and Miranda Somers, the beautiful and ageless chronicler of New York society. Miranda writes the "Daisy" column for *Nous* magazine, and her presence at any event signals that it is the right place to be. Miranda, Ethan, and I had all sat at the same table the night before, and like myself, they both seemed a little the worse for wear. In fact, seeing their haggard faces made me wish I was meeting Max in light slightly more forgiving than bright, tropical sunshine.

There were also some new additions to the crowd today, a few more pals, some people I didn't recognize at all, and one couple whom I hadn't seen in ages, Russell and Carla Cole. Russell Cole was Missy Waterman's billionaire godfather, and he and his wife were giving Missy her bridal dinner that night aboard their spectacular two-hundred-and-twenty-five-foot yacht called *The Lady C*. Carla Cole was Russell's controversial second wife. I didn't know her well, but I had always liked her. Theirs had been a famously celebrated and stormy union.

Anyone familiar with the history of costly breakups in New York knows that Russell Cole paid almost as dearly to get out of his first marriage as did Henry the Eighth. In a road-company version of that historic split, the Cole divorce some years ago caused a major rift in our social circle. Lulu—the first Mrs. Cole—did not only not go gently into the divorcée night, she went raging into it with the fury of a thousand women scorned. I remember Betty joking at the time, "If Russell had known Lulu was capable of that much passion, he might not have left her."

I watched the Coles as they stood next to each other, attired in color-coordinated outfits. With their fixed smiles and slightly vacant demeanors, they subtly proclaimed a pampered and privileged existence, a life lived far above the fray. They were both uncannily well groomed, neat and immaculate in chic, razor-pressed linen with shiny, unwilted hair. Their manicured appearance was miraculously immune to the humidity. It was as if their presentation was in some inexplicable way a great measure of their life together. The accoutrements of wealth—the custom-made resort clothes, the most expensive watches, the latest sunglasses, etc.—were on view, but they were understated, not flashy or obvious, meant only for those who understood them.

Russell Cole, in his late fifties, was not a prepossessing man. He had slim confirmation and was only slightly taller than his much younger wife. His boyish face harbored a pair of melancholy gray eyes. He had sand-colored hair, perfectly parted to one side, and the rigid stance of someone who either had once been to military school or had served in the armed forces. He was wearing a pale blue voile shirt, and in a chic, offbeat touch, he had threaded a blue necktie through the loops of the waistband of his cream linen trousers and tied it in a loose knot off to one side. Very Fred Astaire.

Carla, a slim, striking woman in her late thirties, had asymmetrical features, and an exotic aura. She was truly what the French call a *jolie laide*—a "beautiful ugly." Her nose was slightly too long, her eyes were set too close together, and her lips were thin, like two slashes. Yet all together, they formed a fascinating face, enhanced by her inner vivacity and the allure of a throaty foreign accent. She had luminous skin, which, despite the fact that she spent most of her time on a boat, was creamy white, as if she never saw the sun.

"Oh, look! There's Russell and Carla," Betty said. "I've gotta talk to Carla about tonight. Come with me."

As we quietly edged our way closer to the Coles, there was a sudden, faint swishing noise in the branches above. Mina went on high alert.

"*There*!" she said, pointing up. "*He's there*!"

Betty and I paused to look. I saw the glint of what could conceivably have been a simian face—or, more likely, the knot of a tree exposed when a gust of wind parted the surrounding leaves. I couldn't tell which, and I seriously doubted if anyone else could, either. Nor, I might add, did we care.

"*See him there! There!*" Mina cried out.

Betty and I kept our eyes peeled, straining to see what some of the others apparently saw, until finally young Woody Brill threw his hands up in exasperation and stormed off, saying, "Forget it, Mother! That bloody monkey's a figment of your imagination!"

The spell effectively broken, everyone began chattering away, obviously filled with relief. Betty and I continued heading over to the Coles and to Max, who was standing nearby.

"Carla, darling!" Betty shrieked. "You're here!"

"Well, of course, we are, darling," she said in her husky Italian accent. "We could not let you have the bridal dinner in the water, after all."

Forced laughter all around.

"And, of course, you both know Jo Slater," Betty said.

"Jo!" Carla cried. "So nice to see you again! We were very excited when Betty told us you were coming."

Carla and I air kissed on both cheeks. I had always preferred the younger woman to Russell's first wife, Lulu, who had dropped me the second I lost all my money and, indeed, had befriended my late husband's mistress. But that's another story.

"Hello, Carla, it's so nice to see you again. And Russell. How are you?"

"Hi, Jo," Russell said with his usual reserve.

"We never see you guys around New York," Betty said. "You're both so busy gallivanting around the world in that big, beautiful tub of yours."

Russell gave her a thin smile. It was well known that Russell adored his yacht *The Lady C*.

Betty leaned in and whispered conspiratorially to Carla, "Do you know Max Vermilion?"

"Well, we have met, of course," Carla said. "But I cannot say we *know* him, no."

I noticed how Carla referred to herself as "we," as though she and Russell were one person. Then Betty said something that made me want to kill her.

"I want to fix Jo up with Max. He's such a fabulous eligible, and we all know how much he loves attractive, rich, and cultivated women!"

My teeth clenched as I cringed with embarrassment. "*Betteeee* . . ." I said softly.

Betty was someone who thought that the love life of all single women was fair game for general conversation—even among relative strangers. It was one of her most annoying traits.

"Oh, come on, Jo, now don't be shy," she went on, irritatingly oblivious to my discomfort. "I'm going to take you over and introduce you to Max this minute."

She grabbed my arm, but I demurred.

"Not just now," I said, shrugging her off. I couldn't think of anything worse than having Betty drag me over to Max like some sort of prom wallflower who had asked to meet the most popular boy in senior class.

It was not long, however, before Max approached us with a mischievous twinkle in his eye. He tapped Betty on the shoulder and said in his very laid-back, upper-crust English accent, "I say, is that the bride or the mother?"

Betty whirled around.

"*Max*!" she exclaimed, throwing her arms around him. "How're ya, kiddo?"

"It's the mother! I could hardly tell the difference. Betty, dear, how lovely to see you. Don't you look marvelous!"

"You look pretty swell yourself. Divorce obviously agrees with you."

"No, but settlements do," he said dryly.

"Do you know everyone here? Russell and Carla Cole? My best friend, Jo Slater?"

Max bowed slightly to the Coles. "We have already greeted one another," he said. "But I haven't seen this charming lady in a very long time." He mock kissed my hand. "I wonder if you remember me, Jo. We met years ago on a private tour of the Tate."

"I remember it well, Max. You love Louis the Sixteenth furniture as much as I do, as I recall."

"Indeed. How lovely to see you again after all this time." His bright blue eyes met mine. Even in a crowd, he made me feel as if I were the only one he was really interested in talking to.

Max was still an able flirt. What would have seemed rather oily in another man, merely added to Max's veneer of charm. I think that's because he had a slightly mocking air about him, as if he didn't take anything seriously, least of all himself. It was obvious why he was catnip to women.

"And where is my good friend Gil? Scouring the island for hidden treasure?" Max said, referring to Betty's art dealer husband.

"On the golf course, where else? Christ, if you think I could get Gil over to look at gardens and invisible monkeys, you're crazy."

Max smiled somewhat tolerantly at Betty's brashness. He looked like he was going to say something dismissive like, "You Americans . . ." but he resisted.

Mina then stalked over and looped her arm through Max's arm and dragged him off to the next point of interest, her orchids. He looked back at me rather soulfully, I thought, as if he'd rather have stayed behind. Betty and Carla followed suit, walking away together, deep in conversation about the upcoming bridal dinner that night. I lagged behind with Russell Cole. I didn't want to look as if I were chasing after Max. Also, Russell hung back from the crowd, and I sensed he wanted to talk to me.

"It's so nice to see you again, Jo," he said. "A friendly face from the old days."

By "the old days," he meant premillennium New York when Russell was married to Lulu and I was married to my first and only husband, that rat, the late Lucius Slater—a time that now seemed to me as distant and uncomplicated as the Stone Age. We chitchatted about this and that, how time flies, how people change—or don't, as the case may be. I asked Russell if he was enjoying the peripetetic existence of the perennial yachtsman. He said he "rather liked" traveling the world, "deciding where to go, as we go." He then described a life of endless options.

Picking up anchor whenever one felt like it and sailing anywhere in the world on a moment's notice may have sounded idyllic, but I knew from observation that that sort of eternal aimlessness could easily wear thin, and eventually lead to only one real destination, boredom. And, indeed, as Russell and I strolled together and he aimlessly brushed some leaves with his hand, I sensed that the old, deep-seated weariness had returned. He had lost his exuberance and seemed a bit the way he was during his final years with Lulu—polite but distant, slightly distracted, a touch melancholy, and shy of crowds.

"That was an awful thing that Lucius did to you," he suddenly said to me.

"Yes, it was," I said softly, as we continued to stroll.

"And you had absolutely no idea? No sense that he was betraying you?"

"Not a clue. I can tell you, it was quite a shock. But all's well that ends well, as they say. And here I am."

That episode of my life now seemed like a bad dream. Russell was, of course, referring to the fact that my late husband, who had been carrying on an affair for a year behind my back, compounded the outrage of his infidelity by leaving all his money to his mistress when he died. I figured that was the reason Russell had hung back to talk to me, to let me know he empathized with what I'd gone through. But it was over now and I saw no point in dwelling on it.

"Do you think it's possible to ever really know another human being?" Russell asked me.

"Well, based on experience, I'd have to say no," I replied, half joking, thinking of how profoundly my husband had deceived me.

"No, I don't think so, either. Because so few of us really know ourselves, you see. And if we don't know ourselves, how can we possibly expect someone else to know us?"

"That's very true," I responded, although when I looked at Russell I realized that he was talking more to himself than to me.

Then he said, "How well do you know yourself, Jo?"

Rather a heavy question for a casual afternoon stroll, I thought.

Flashing back on all I'd gone through, I replied, "Well, I believe I'm better acquainted with myself than I once was. How about you?"

"Me?" He seemed surprised by the question. He thought for a long moment, a pensive look on his face, and finally said, "I'm kind of like that monkey in the tree."

His intriguing answer made me smile. "How so?"

"Well, sometimes I think I get a glimpse of myself. But I can't be sure if it's really me or not. And then . . ." He stopped suddenly, as if deep in thought.

"And then . . . ?"

"Then I disappear," he said with a little shrug.

VISIT US ONLINE @
WWW.TWBOOKMARK.COM

AT THE TIME WARNER BOOKMARK WEB SITE YOU'LL FIND:

- CHAPTER EXCERPTS FROM SELECTED NEW RELEASES

- ORIGINAL AUTHOR AND EDITOR ARTICLES

- AUDIO EXCERPTS

- BESTSELLER NEWS

- ELECTRONIC NEWSLETTERS

- AUTHOR TOUR INFORMATION

- CONTESTS, QUIZZES, AND POLLS

- FUN, QUIRKY RECOMMENDATION CENTER

- PLUS MUCH MORE!

Bookmark Time Warner Book Group @ www.twbookmark.com